Shepherd, Potter, Spy

and the

Star Namer

Peggy Miracle Consolver

Carpenter's Son Publishing

Shepherd, Potter, Spy—and the Star Namer

Scripture taken from THE HOLY BIBLE, NEW INTERNATIONAL VERSION®, NIV® Copyright © 1973, 1978, 1984, 2011 by Biblica, Inc.™ Used by permission. All rights reserved worldwide.

Published by Carpenter's Son Publishing, Franklin, Tennessee.

Published in association with Larry Carpenter of Christian Book Services, LLC. www.christianbookservices.com

Cover and Interior Design by Suzanne Lawing

Printed in the United States of America

978-1-942587-09-5

Dedication

To my loving husband:
Patient beyond understanding,
Constant encourager,
Steadfast supporter,
A bulldog of a research assistant,
Uncommon wisdom.

Acknowledgments

First of all, I want to thank Dr. Charles Ryrie for his Study Bible with a chronological reading plan. Repeated annual forays into the Old Testament using his plan made the whole story come alive for me as I found elements of the story in far-flung passages.

I must also thank:

My critique group of Anne, Lana and Kathy who taught me new writing techniques and challenged me to write from the deeper point of view.

My daddy, a wheat farmer of southwest Oklahoma—so similar to the seasons and latitude of Israel.

My brothers, I wonder if they might see or hear themselves in some of the action and dialogue. I do.

Dr. James B. Pritchard who led four digs at Gibeon in mid-twentieth century.

The U.S. Cavalry officer who wrote of exploring the West with mule trains.

Dr. Bryant Wood and Associates for Biblical Research for such a memorable tour of Israel and the dig at Khirbet el-Maqatir in 2010.

The Palestinian guide and cab driver who took us to Gibeon, El Jib, in the West Bank.

Dr. Eugene H. Merrill, Distinguished Professor Emeritus of Old Testament Studies, Dallas Theological Seminary, who gave invaluable insights and encouragement in the historical elements of the story.

My friend, DeNora Dial, for a delightful day of puttering with clay.

Jackson Allen White, grandson model for book cover, and our daughter Dana Consolver White, photographer.

And to the One who named the stars, I give You all the praise. After all, it is Your story of grace to the Gibeonites I have tried to tell.

Contents

Characters and Relationships

CANAANITES

AGH-TAAN, local farmer, nearest the main spring, leader in the community

AIJALON VALLEY, central valley of Canaan

BEEROTH, sister city of Gibeon in Aijalon Valley

BILDAD, Agh-taan's son spies with Eschol

BIN-ZEDEK, son of Adoni-Zedek, king of Jerusalem, becomes "Plain Zed"

DA-GAN', the village bully and son of Ra-gar'

DEYAB, old Bedouin man at Jericho

DO'NI, youngest son of Adoni-Zedek

DU'BO, Beerothite spy

EIN EL-BELED, Gibeon's spring, one of the most reliable in Canaan

EL GAYAH, wadi leading to Ai, tributary of Wadi Qelt

ENDO, old trader in Jerusalem

ESCHOL, third son of Ishtaba, also called "Eskie"

EZAK, second son of Ishtaba

GHALEB, Sir, crippled Hittite soldier, military trainer for Gibeon, name means "victor"

GRAN-BABA RA-EEF', deceased

GRAN-MAMAA AMARA, wife of Ra-eef', blind widow

HAYDAK BIN-KHANJAR, favorite caravanner, "khanjar" means small sword

ILI and ILAI: twin brothers of Lehab, two years old

ISA'NA, Ezak's twin sister

ISHTABA, eldest son of Ra-eef', master craftsman of Ra-eef' pottery

JABAL, refugee from Heshbon, name means "mountain"

JHO-EE, Keshub's favorite lamb, and name of nephew of Rahab of Jericho

KARISHMA, Balaam's donkey, Persian word for "miracle"

KEPHIRA, sister village of Gibeon in Aijalon Valley

KESHUB, fifth son of Ishtaba

KHALI, name of Haydak's favorite camel, named for desert in Arabia--*Rub al Khali*, means "empty".

KHALIL, farmer and tanner, lives near Yaakoub

KIRIATH-JEARIM, sister village of Gibeon in Aijalon Valley

LA'NA, Keshub's younger sister

LEAH, elder daughter of Uncle Samir, younger sister to Lehab

LEHAB, Uncle Samir's eldest son, a little younger than Keshub

LELA, escapee from Adoni-Zedek's harem, mother of Do'ni

MAMAA DANYA, wife of Ishtaba, older sister to Raga (Yaakoub's wife)

MATTAH, Lehab's younger brother

MAYDAN, refugee from Moab

MICAH, Uncle Yaakoub's second son, same age as Keshub

NABI, oldest resident of Gibeon, teller of legends and old stories

RACHEL, daughter to Uncle Yaakoub

RA-EEF' the Hivite, deceased family patriarch, name means "mercy"

RA-GAR', Amorite in Gibeon

RAJA, Keshub's favorite donkey

RAMATH, man from Moab

RA-MI', fourth son of Ishtaba

RA-HEEB', means "welcome," eldest son to Uncle Yaakoub, apprentice to farmer Khalil

RANINE, eldest son of Ishtaba, first grandson of Ra'eef, name means "sound"

SABAH', wife of Uncle Samir, name means "the morning", sister to Agh-taan

SAMIR, third son of Ra-eef'

SHIBAM, cranky camel belonging to Haydak

SHIRAZ JIROFT, Sheik, Persian caravanner

TA-JHE, grandson of Deyab

WADI QELT, flows to the Jordan River near Jericho

YAH-YA, nephew of Haydak, means "live", "survive"

YAAKOUB, second son of Ra-eef'

HEBREWS

AHIRA, Hosiah's uncle, mother's brother

CALEB, Joshua's contemporary from tribe of Judah

CO-ZI, Midianite captive

ELAH, Hosiah's father, deceased, Joshua's brother

ELISHAMA, leader of Ephraimites in the wilderness

ELKANAH, Hosiah's older brother

ENAN, Elishama's son

HOSIAH, Hebrew boy in tribe of Ephraim, about Keshub's age

JOSHUA, appointed leader to succeed Moses and lead Hebrews into Canaan

KENAN, younger leader of Ephraimites when Hebrews cross Jordan

MOSES, leader of the Hebrews for forty years in the wilderness

MOTHER BORAH, Elishama's wife, Enan's mother

MAGDALYN, or MRS. ELAH, Hosiah and Elkanah's mother, Joshua's widowed sister-in-marriage

ZU-ZU, toddler Midianite captive, neice to Co-zi

Prologue

The Gezer Almanac, Israel, ca. 1000 B.C.

... *"His month is harvest of barley...*

...His month is harvest and feasting...

...His two months are vine-tending...

...His month is summer fruit...

...His two months are olive harvest...

... His two months are planting grain...

...His two months are late planting...

...His month is hoeing up of flax"...

This young boy's writing exercise is a calendar describing the farmer's seasonal work. Etched in limestone in the Iron Age, the *Gezer Almanac*, as it is known among archaeologists, was discovered in early twentieth century not far from Gibeon, the setting of this Late Bronze Age tale.

Chapter 1:
A Shepherd Boy

"His sword flashes in the sunlight .... Hatred is a burning fire in his eyes .... Staff up. I block his deadly blow .... Now! An upward thrust slashes his exposed wrists .... The fire goes out .... The enemy invader ... whimpers for mercy."

Keshub gazed at the horizon—the dividing line between the lush green of spring and the bluest of blues. In his mind's eye he could see himself, someday, as a victorious hero. Today, he would settle for not always being thought of as the baby brother.

With the back of his hand he wiped sweat from his brow and took the stance of a sword fighter one more time.

"Slash to the left."

"Feint to the right."

"Back-hand upper cut to the right."

"And lunge!"

A wooly mama-ewe munched tender grass and glanced his way from pink-rimmed eyes. Glaring back at her, he jabbed his wooden sword between the layers of the acorn-dyed woolen sash around his waist. "The footwork is not as easy as it looks."

Keshub breathed deeply of the cool spring air and surveyed the wide green valley in the heart of Canaan. Caravanners, in colorful robes and with exotic cargoes, criss-crossed Aijalon Valley on their way to exciting places beyond his horizon. He ached to see the amazing sights they told about. The sun's first golden rays cast his shadow in giant proportions against the hillside. The only sounds were the soft na-ah-ah-ah's of mother ewes who cautioned their lambs to stay close.

Alone, he practiced with sword and slingshot and dreamed of praise from Sir Ghaleb, the old Hittite soldier who taught Gibeon's military training school. Their teacher always chose Keshub's third oldest brother, his top student, to demonstrate techniques. As the fifth oldest son of Ishtaba the potter, Keshub dreamed of praise from four older brothers and his father more.

How could he compete with Number One who was already becoming a master potter like his father? Or Number Two whom Uncle Yaakoub said was a natural born trader at market? Or Eschol, Number Three, whom everyone called Eskie? He excelled in archery and all things related to Sir Ghaleb's school. And Number Four? Ra-mi' the quiet one could hardly wait to work the clay like his father.

Keshub's longings lay beyond the horizon since he first ventured out of the family courtyard to play among the grape arbors on the ledges above his home. Maybe he, Number Five son of Ishtaba, would be a soldier like Sir Ghaleb, or a caravanner.

He clenched his fists. His younger cousin Lehab, the youngest shepherd in the family, presented a more immediate challenge. Why did the pest taunt him so?

Keshub whined to Ram-ram, the curled-horn leader of the flock, who walked at his side. "Lehab always makes trouble for me. This morning he grabbed my victuals pouch. Does he purposely try to provoke me? Does he purposely try to get me in trouble with Baba? I had to chase him across the courtyard to get my pouch.

And who was rebuked for playing instead of going to the sheepfold to call our flocks? Me. Not Lehab. Me!"

Gritting his teeth, he turned to check the flock behind him. A spindly-legged lamb dawdled behind the rest, heading off on his own.

"Whe-e-et. Whe-e-et."

At his whistle, the lamb bobbled his head and scampered back to his mother's side. In the next moment, a throaty roar rumbled over the rocky hillside. The rams and ewes jerked up their heads. Ewes gathered their offspring, and Ram-ram tightened the flock. Over the hill, high-pitched cries clashed with deep growls and the bleating of sheep. Another shepherd needed help.

His staff and slingshot in hand, Keshub crested the hill running. At the base of the hill, he recognized cousin Micah's narrow backside. Keshub's heart rose to his throat. Micah wielded his staff with both hands. His glancing blows landed on a snarling gray-brown bear, twice his size. Keshub flung his staff to the ground. He singled out a small round stone from the pouch slung over his right shoulder and lodged the stone in place to set it whirring overhead.

The bear's raised forepaw showed long deadly white claws as he slashed toward Micah. A young spring lamb lay helpless and bleeding with its side heaving between the combatants. Cousin Micah sidestepped to his left with every leftward swing and back to his right with the next swing.

Keshub's stomach clenched. His sling stone's release would be a life or death matter—for Micah. He scanned the scene for a better position. Slowing his stone, he grasped it before it fell to ground and veered to the right. Firm determination hardened Micah's face as he put everything he had into each blow. With the beast's fierce glare locked on his cousin, Keshub reset the stone and circled it overhead. He focused on the bear's backside while the stone picked up speed. The first stone launched, and he reached into his pouch for another.

Thump. The stone whacked the enemy on the rump while the next gained speed.

The blow distracted the beast from Micah and the lamb. He turned his fiery eyes toward Keshub before they disappeared behind his cavernous mouth gaping with great yellow fangs. He roared, and strings of slobber caught the morning light.

The second stone whacked his shaggy back, and the bear turned all his wild contempt toward Keshub.

Micah grabbed the helpless lamb and backed away.

A yellow stare bore into Keshub and seared his courage. Fear welled up inside him like a summer dust devil. He let the third stone fly before it gained full speed, and it merely whapped the beast's shoulder. Unblinking, the shaggy brown enemy lowered his head and took a menacing step toward the scrawny source of his irritation.

With his heart pounding, Keshub released the fourth stone too soon. The missile curved in a downward lob. He had only one smooth round stone left in his bag. Expecting the hulking enemy to charge, he stepped backward. Now he had only his wooden sword. He grabbed it from the girdle around his waist and darted his eyes left and right for a place to run.

The fourth stone hit the charging bear's left front paw, and he stopped. He lifted the white-clawed paw to his massive chest and howled in anguished pain.

As the enemy turned away, Keshub gaped at his stubby tail bobbing while he lumbered on three legs toward the forested hills. Keshub sucked in a deep breath with his heart still pounding and wiped his brow with a trembling hand. His brother Eskie's recent one-legged dance with his foot in hand came to mind. Eskie had stubbed his toe in their courtyard. Keshub laughed.

Micah gasped. "What are you laughing about?"

Keshub turned back to his cousin.

Micah frowned and leaned on his knees with both hands. His black hair hung in sweaty tendrils. He nodded toward the bear. "I thought I might be his breakfast at any moment."

"Sorry, cousin. I was thinking how weak my strongest blows were and how my weakest stone happened to hit old man bear on his sore foot. Are you all right?"

"Yeah. Scared to death, but all right. Where is your flock?"

"My flock? Oh, my flock is over the hill. Alone. Wait here. I will be right back."

On the other side of the hill, the sheep grazed with heads down. He counted to be sure none was missing and whistled to gather them at his feet. Ram-ram and the others followed him over the hill to join Micah who held the injured lamb against his chest.

"Keshub, I can feel the lamb's heart beating, but he is not moving. Let's take the flocks to the stream. Maybe water will help."

Keshub agreed and led them to a nearby stream gurgling with spring rains. At the edge of the rushing waters, he moved stones the size of a camel's footprint to divert the water. He made a quiet pool where the timid sheep could drink. In the dry season the stream would retreat, and sheep and shepherd could step over it. While Keshub oversaw the sheep at water, Micah hiked up his colorless homespun tunic stained red by the lamb's blood. He knelt at the stream below the pool. By handfuls, he dipped water and poured it on the lamb's back.

Keshub helped his cousin unwind his gray woolen girdle and wrapped it around the pink-skinned lamb shivering in his arms. He added Micah's slingshot and breakfast pouch to his own girdle.

When the last sheep finished drinking, Keshub replaced the rocks and heard shouting in the distance. He rose and dried his hands on his tunic. In the distance a lone shepherd, with flock grazing around him, took a menacing crouch as if to spring into action. "Who is that?"

Micah looked and turned back with a shrug. "Is he raising his fists to tell us he wants a fight?"

"He must be an Amorite. They claim the land from that hill to Jerusalem."

Micah looked again. "We are not on their land."

"So let's ignore him."

Keshub helped his cousin place the swaddled lamb across his narrow shoulders and handed him his staff. Micah's flax-cloth tunic hung shapeless as he held the ends of his girdle in his other hand to keep the lamb in place. They whistled to their flocks, and Keshub took the lead up the gradual circular path worn by many shepherds and many flocks before them.

At the top of the rocky hill, they stole another glance at the belligerent Amorite shepherd who raised his fists and pantomimed hand-to-hand combat.

Micah mumbled. "What did he have for breakfast that makes him so disagreeable?"

Back to back with his favorite cousin on a rock near the center of the meadow, Keshub could see all his sheep at once. While he removed the leather victuals pouches from his golden-brown girdle, Micah gentled the injured lamb onto his lap.

Keshub fingered the stitching done by their Gran-mamaa Amara's gnarled fingers almost two years ago when they began shepherding. He handed Micah's to him and opened his own— flatbread, raisins, and a few almonds. Looking at Micah's meal, he smiled. Their mothers were sisters. The cousins' meals were almost the same.

Keshub took a drink of water from the pottery flask he carried and replaced the grapevine stopper. "Our favorite caravanner stayed in the guest quarters last night."

"Haydak bin-Khanjar? Did he tell you stories of giants?"

"He always does."

"Tell me, Kesh. I miss the good old days when our family lived in the Ra-eef' family homestead, too. Did Haydak move on this morning already? Or will he be at the fireside tonight? If he is, I do hope Baba will allow me to come."

"Hold on, cousin. You are like a runaway sheep tumbling down a steep hill. Who can answer your questions if you ask three more before listening for an answer?"

He popped a raisin in his mouth and chewed slowly to tease his favorite cousin and prolong the suspense. "It is no to the first question. Our friend is still with us. He is at a nearby market today.

"It is no to the second question. He will talk to our fathers and

Uncle Samir tonight about pottery lamps he wants us to make for him to sell in Egypt. And there was something else he and Baba talked about. Something about a people called the Hebrews. Haydak said they are coming up out of the Desert of Sinai. Maybe coming here."

He flicked a green bug that lit on his homespun tunic. "It took forever to get through our meal so the caravanner could tell his stories. Cousin Lehab forgets we do not talk while we eat. He could not be as patient or as quiet as I.

"During supper Uncle Samir shook his head and frowned at Lehab for speaking. After his rebuke, he pouted and poured his flint rock collection onto the dinner mat. Uncle Samir had to send him to bed before the stories began."

"Kesh, our younger cousin has much to learn about holding his tongue. It is usually wagging at both ends." He took a bite of flatbread and chewed slowly.

"But let me guess. Was Haydak's story a fable about the giant bird that buries its eggs in the sand west of here?"

"No."

"Or was it about the giant lizards that lie in wait looking like logs floating on the Jordan River?

"Unh-uh."

"Or was it a story of the giant four-footed beast that eats huge mouthfuls of papyrus in the swamp north of the Jordan?"

"No. No. Our friend has told us stories of those giants before, but this one is about a king. Friend Haydak has traded in the marketplace near the palace of this giant king on the other side of the Jordan River. He is Og, king of Bashan."

"That is a strange name for a king. It sounds more like a grunt than a name."

"I agree, but our friend Haydak said Og is a powerful king who rules over sixty cities."

"Sixty?" Micah held up six stubby fingers. "Six. Ten times? We have only four in Aijalon Valley. How far away is Bashan? Did Haydak say?"

"Not very far ... a two day march."

He finished his meal and turned his victuals pouch inside out to air it. "Haydak said Og has a great army led by giant sons, and the cities have high walls with gates and bars. But listen to this. Og's bed is made of iron and is more than nine forearms long and four forearms wide."

"Whoa. That is nearly as long as our house is wide."

Keshub tucked the pouch away in his girdle. "Cousin, it seems everything in this valley is small when compared to the world outside. Someday I want to see a bigger world for myself."

Keshub gauged his shadow. The sun had climbed high enough to shrink his shadow to his own size. "Time to return my sheep to the sheepfold at Gibeon, cousin. We do not want to be the last to arrive at Sir Ghaleb's school on the summit."

He helped his cousin shoulder the injured lamb to return to his home nearby. "You look funny, cousin, with your tunic un-girdled. It hangs too long, and you look like a little old man."

"After meeting the bear this morning, I am hoping to be a little old man some day."

Chapter 2:
Military Training School

At mid-day when their shadows lay at their feet, Keshub and Micah, with his tunic girded again, faced off on the mount called Gibeon. At the olive grove budding with new leaves, homemade wooden swords clattered and clashed around them in the warm spring air. Guttural grunts and groans of would-be soldiers locked in battle, mixed with commands from their teacher.

Keshub licked his lips and grinned as he leaned into their crossed swords. With lowered brow, he sent a silent challenge to blink and paused. He sprang to his right like lightning and thrust his sword to his cousin's vulnerable left side. Yes! He had Micah on the defensive.

Micah pivoted and blocked him with the flat of his blade to bind and deflect. Keshub whipped his sword lower for a mid-section jab. He felt the sting of contact burn from the hilt to his hand when Micah's sword blocked him again. Back and forth Keshub thrust his sword, staying on the offensive with attempts to touch for a kill. A few days older and slightly taller, he surely had the advantage.

He considered the move his brother Eskie demonstrated recently to the whole school. Keshub feinted to send a false signal, and then cross-stepped in the opposite direction for a thrust and kill. His feet tangled. His arms flailed the air, trying to regain his balance. Gravel bit into his elbows and hind side as he fell to ground with a helpless "A-agh."

Micah seized the advantage, lunged with a touch to Keshub's mid-section, and cried, "You die!"

Sir Ghaleb, with his always erect soldier's bearing and commanding voice, happened to be nearby and saw it all.

"A good, gentle kill, Micah. I heard you boys fought off a bear this morning."

Micah nodded.

"Well done. That is why we train here. We never know when our skills will be needed." Sir Ghaleb extended his rough hand to help Keshub up. He spoke with clipped words that hinted of his Hittite background.

"Keshub, feint to your left so you will be balanced to side-step and lunge with your right. Good try, though. That is a difficult move. Carry on." The only person in Gibeon with a real bronze sword, moved down the line of sparring boys with a slight limp.

Ashamed to be so clumsy in front of the very person he wanted to impress, Keshub hung his head. Tears stung his eyelids demanding release to embarrass him more. He fought for control.

His double cousin who understood him better than anyone, challenged him with hands on hips. "Kesh, you were winning before you tripped yourself. Shake it off, and let's go for another round."

Before long, Sir Ghaleb's two shrill whistles split the air and signaled time to assemble. Keshub tucked his wooden sword through his girdle and retrieved his slingshot and gear. As they trotted past a pomegranate bush full of brilliant red-orange blooms, his eyes met Da-gan's who sat with jutting jaw and sullen eyes. Sir Ghaleb had taken his sword from him earlier for reckless swordplay.

The bully taunted so only Keshub and Micah would hear. "Clum-sy-wood-en sword, wood-en feet."

Sudden fury welled up. Keshub stopped in his tracks. His muscles hardened for a fight. His cousin and best friend grabbed his arm. Keshub glared at the village bully and allowed Micah to pull him away. With the scraggly bunch of tousle-heads at the top of the trail to the village, Keshub leaned on his knees. He stared at the ground; his face still hot, sweat dripping from his brow. *Who else witnessed my most embarrassing moment?*

"Atten-tion!"

He straightened with shoulders back, cringing to hear Lehab's voice among the high-pitched voices who did not obey. Finally, Sir Ghaleb's piercing stare achieved the silence he demanded from the younger class. Straight as a rod, eyes ahead, a few tense moments passed.

The old soldier barked. "Dis-missed!"

Shoulders relaxed as chatter burst upon the olive grove. Some played catch-me-if-you-can while they waited their turn at the top of the narrow trail. The clatter faded as the village boys scrambled down to their homes on the east slope. In the quiet that followed, Keshub waited with the other grandsons of Ra-eef' the potter while Eskie finish helping Sir Ghaleb.

The old soldier clapped a hand on Eskie's shoulder. "Tell your father I look forward to hearing from our friend the caravanner at your fireside tonight."

"Yes, sir. I will." Eskie's voice croaked from low to high pitch. He ducked his head and swallowed to hide his embarrassment.

Keshub dreaded when he would begin sounding that way.

After Sir Ghaleb's broad shoulders disappeared down the trail, Da-gan' called out from where he had sulked all afternoon. "Teacher's pets. The pottery boys are teacher's pe-ets."

Keshub clenched his teeth and put up his fists. His eyes connected with Eskie's, waiting for a cue. The bully was a hand's breadth taller than himself, but together...

Eskie instructed the rest under his breath. "Ignore him. His words are not worth our time."

Keshub glared at the bully again, but turned away with a threatening scowl. He let go of his anger and resentment to wave goodbye to Micah. He and his brothers watched cousin Micah's back disappear among the gray-green overhanging branches of gnarled old olive trees. Micah's family managed the Ra-eef' pack animals and lived in the valley south of Gibeon.

Without looking toward Da-gan' or acknowledging his taunting words, Keshub turned north toward home with the remaining grandsons of Ra-eef'. He walked beside Eskie whose broad shoulders beneath his homespun tunic bulged with muscles hardened by chopping wood.

The champion marksman of the Ra-eef' family, and the village, picked up a rock and called his shot. "See that oak tree? Head high."

Eskie wound up and hurled the rock to whack the tree—head high, precisely in the center. "You had a good day today, Keshub. You chased a bear away from the sheep, and you were the best with your slingshot in your class. Not too bad for a green sprout like yourself."

"That is until you tripped yourself and fell in a heap, you big show-off." Lehab, the pest, doubled over laughing like Keshub's embarrassment was the funniest thing he had ever seen.

Keshub drew back his fist, but Lehab ran several paces away.

Eskie reached out to grab Keshub's forearm and prevented his pursuit. "Like it was with Da-gan', your best answer to Lehab is to ignore him. "And besides, little brother, you do not wish to feel the wrath of our mother or of Aunt Sabah'. If Lehab the faker arrives home crying because you hit him, you will be in big trouble."

Lehab, with curly dark locks wagging, continued to taunt from a safe distance.

Ra-mi', the quiet brother between Eskie and Keshub in age, cautioned. "That is enough, Lehab."

Lehab obeyed his shepherd-teacher who worked with him every morning. Working together, they had a special bond, just like Keshub's with Eskie who trained him two years ago.

Eskie followed his own advice and ignored Lehab's childishness. "Keshub, the footwork for sword fighting is difficult, but you will get it soon."

"What can I do to improve, Eskie?"

"Have patience, little brother. Gran-baba Ra-eef's favorite advice was 'Have patience.' So, keep trying, and you will get it soon."

"Eskie, why can I not carry a sword?"

"Lehab, Sir Ghaleb has little patience with bellyachers or whiners. You are too often one of the whiners when you should be listening. Or you are watching the flight of a butterfly like you did today."

Eskie continued in his most grown-up voice. "You will train with a wooden sword when Sir Ghaleb thinks you are ready for one. You will show him you are ready for it when you listen for his commands and obey at once."

"But Eskie..."

"Lehab, stop now the whining. Such childishness does you no good."

Lehab sighed and shrugged. "I will try ... Eskie?"

"Wha-ut?"

The irritation in Eskie's voice brought a surge of satisfaction. *He is tired of Lehab the pest, too.*

"Why does our teacher limp?"

Lehab is a pest, but he is persistent—and brave enough to ask the question I have been wondering.

Eskie picked up another rock and pointed to a vine-covered tree branch making a looped opening the size of a circle of flatbread. "Through that loop I will hit the branch behind it."

Keshub watched with mouth open as his brother's rock sailed where he said it would and thunked the branch.

Eskie shrugged. "Lehab, no one knows Sir Ghaleb's story. At least the students do not. We do know he was a captain in the Hittite army. Perhaps our father knows, or perhaps Gran-baba

Ra-eef' knew. Our teacher walks with a slight limp, but the limp does not detract from his skill. Sir Ghaleb does not speak of it, and neither should you."

Keshub pushed his forelock of hair aside. "Eskie, Micah and I saw an Amorite shepherd this morning. He was on the next hilltop, but he made threatening gestures to us. We were not on Amorite land, but perhaps he thought we were. Should I tell this to Baba?"

"Yes, Father will know what to do, if anything. It is probably nothing more than the usual Amorite way of acting tough. But you should report such encounters to Baba. Tell him before the evening meal, if you can, since friend Haydak will be with us.

"But for now, let's hurry along to finish our chores so we will be ready in time for Mamaa's cooking. You know she always cooks something special when our Bedu friend is with us. And I am *hungry.*"

"You are always hungry, Eskie." Lehab ran several paces ahead with the end of his yellow and gray-striped girdle flapping behind him. He tossed a challenge over his shoulder. "Let's race to the top of the stairs."

Elbows pumping, Keshub vowed to show his pest of a cousin who of them was faster.

Chapter 3:
A Guest at Dinner

Skidding to a stop at the base of the hill, Keshub looked over the Ra-eef' livestock pen and punched the warm spring air. With nobody but the caravanner's camels to hear, he mumbled through clenched lips. "It is not fair. I have to do Lehab's chores. He was faking a headache. I know it."

He wagged his head from side to side. "I had graduated from this job. But Aunt Sabah' believed her darling boy, and now I have to do his chores."

He threw another punch. What would the satisfaction feel like if he connected with Lehab's stomach?

One of Haydak's camels shifted his awkward looking body with sloping neck topped by a flat head and bulging lips and eyes. He directed a condemning eye.

Keshub gulped down his anger. The placid-looking animal could deliver a powerful kick with its two-toed hind feet. With a heavy sigh he palmed the handle of the three-pronged pitch fork

Uncle Samir had made. He slid his left hand down the smooth surface of the oak branch. Still fuming, he speared the hay and jammed it into the manger. Lehab's smirk of victory from behind Aunt Sabah's back had to go unchallenged.

He consoled himself that he had no choice to talk back or to disobey her. She was Uncle Samir's wife and Keshub's elder. Baba did not allow disrespecting an elder. Of all the things that could get him in disfavor with his father, back talking was the quickest way to go to bed without supper.

Forking the sweet-smelling hay into the manger for the camels was actually all right. The animals brought daydreams of riding the trail to far places with strange names, strange languages, and strange customs. But scooping up the fresh dung? That was disagreeable work. He filled the round-bottomed reed gufa basket, squinched his nose, and carried the smelly stuff at arm's length. At the dung heap, across the caravan trail from his home, the camels' waste dried at a fly-infested heap.

Returning, he paused in the middle of the trail to gaze at the clouds painted orange and gold by the setting sun. He imagined seeing the orange sun sink into the water of the Great Sea beyond his horizon. His chest expanded to breathe in the fresh breeze. The trail he stood on marked the steps of too many camels to count. He could almost hear the clamor of a market with crowds of people selling and trading their goods.

Back in the livestock pen he checked once more for droppings. Everything in order, he put away the homemade tools, latched the gate behind him, and took the gray stone steps along the wall of the guest quarter two at a time. The smell of wood smoke and baking bread drew him. From the entrance gate at the top of the steps Keshub surveyed the familiar surroundings. At the far end of the Ra-eef' courtyard his mother and sister tended supper over an open fire. Flatbread baked on a thin stone suspended over glowing coals in a shallow pit.

His mouth watered.

A half wall of stacked stones partially shielded the cooking area from view. He smiled at Gran-mamaa stooping to tend her little flower garden at the wall. She took great delight in smelling the pink-tipped white flowers that danced in the breeze.

He crossed the courtyard and offered his arm. "Gran-mamaa? Do you need help?"

"Thank you, Keshub."

He waited while she bowed low to inhale their fresh fragrance. Gran-mamaa's weight on his arm felt as light as a bird.

"I was afraid if I got down I could not get up. I do love to smell these little darlings you dug for me in the olive grove, Keshub. I used to take my work to the grove when they bloomed."

"Gran-mamaa, I remember playing in the grove with Micah and Lehab while you worked. At the time, I thought you wanted us out of the courtyard and out of trouble."

Gran-mamaa cackled. "Yes, Keshub, you are right. But it was for me, too. Go wash up, now. You do not want to be tardy to supper."

Keshub and Eskie arrived at the same time at the wash basin on a stand beside the steps to the pottery yard. If not for Lehab's pretend headache, Keshub would have helped Eskie chop wood for the pottery yard and Mamaa's cook fire.

Lehab arrived behind them looking quite healthy. With chores done, apparently the pest's headache was much better. Keshub twiddled his fingers, determined not to make a fist again at sight of his cousin.

In silent agreement, Keshub and Eskie spread their feet and elbows wide to block Lehab from the wash basin. Eskie dipped his fingers and flicked water in Lehab's face. Keshub followed his older brother's lead. He glanced over his shoulder at Lehab's red face and pressed lips while he kept a wary eye on Baba to avoid rebuke. He tried to keep a straight face when he and Eskie turned away and allowed their younger cousin to be the last to reach the murky water.

Lehab was tardy already when he emptied the water from the basin onto Gran-mamaa's small garden in the last orange light of twilight.

Rocking back and forth from heel to toe, Keshub gloated until Lehab elbowed in next to him to join the line of Ra-eef' grandsons. Keshub had to lean into Eskie to give the pest space.

The faker smiled and feigned innocence, but gave Keshub a hard pinch near his elbow.

Keshub grimaced and jerked his arm to rub away the sting of pain while standing at attention until Baba and Uncle Samir formally welcomed their guests. He had learned the consequences of impatience with the rites of hospitality. Baba would not allow a hungry offender to continue in the company of guests. He would be sent to his sleeping mat without supper.

A silent sigh eased past his lips when, finally, Baba and his guests took the seats of honor on a mat of woven grasses on the courtyard floor. In the middle of the mat, a round leather covering defined their eating area.

The caravanner with gray hair and beard streaked with brown sat cross-legged at Baba's right hand. The caravanner's bashful nephew, Yah-ya, sat on Baba's left. Uncle Samir sat across from Baba, his elder brother.

When Baba nodded for his sons and nephew to sit, there was no elbowing to gain advantage since birth-order seating was a time-honored tradition. When cousin Lehab joined the Ra-eef' men a few moons past, he took the right-hand position of eldest son to his father Samir. Keshub was glad Ra-mi' sat between him and the pest.

When everyone settled, Mother Danya came from behind the kitchen wall with her head draped in modesty. She delivered the best Ra-eef' pottery bowl, etched with graceful lines and used only for special occasions.

Baba placed it in the middle of the leather covering. The bowl held Keshub's favorite stew of lentils, herbs, and bits of dried mutton with vegetables. His sister Isa'na carried fresh brown flatbread on a woven reed carrier. She handed it to Baba who served their guests and himself before passing the fragrant bread to his eldest son Ranine. Each one tore a piece of bread for himself before passing the tray.

Keshub and Ra-mi' still had no bread when the woven platter reached Lehab. The pest pretended innocence when he took more than his fair share, but Keshub saw his cousin's glance from under his bush of curly locks that told the real truth. Keshub wanted to protest but could not.

Ra-mi', always the peacemaker, took slightly less than half of what was left. When he held the wide tray to serve Keshub, only a small piece remained. Being the last to receive bread meant Keshub was also the last to dip his bread in the stew. With mouth watering, he tore a smaller piece and made a scoop to dip a bite of stew from the ornate favorite dish. Being the last, he chewed fast and gulped to catch up.

Talking was not allowed. "Mealtime is time to eat," their Granbaba Ra-eef' would say. "We will talk later." Indeed, if Keshub talked, he would miss his turn to dip his bread in the bowl and would end up hungry. Finally, Baba offered the last morsel of stew to the honored guest. Keshub watched its disappearance with open mouth.

As head of the household, Baba delivered an appreciative belch followed by another from the honored guest. Immediately after the belches, Mamaa began serving a tea made from dried rosemary and warm milk.

With the meal finished, Baba rose to his feet and extended a hand to assist the caravanner. They crossed the Ra-eef' courtyard and sat where the wood for the evening fire lay ready to be lit.

"Friend, this is an important day. My fifth son was initiated into the ranks of defenders of Ra-eef' today. He scared away a bear attacking our sheep. Is that right, Keshub?"

"Yes, sir."

While his father lit the fire with a glowing stick from Mamaa's kitchen fire, friend Haydak looked at Keshub with new admiration. "How big was he, Keshub? And how were you able to run him off?"

"He was bigger than Micah and I together, sir. My best sling stones only made him angry. My weakest lob hit him on a foot, and he took off running on three legs."

Eskie chuckled. "Kesh, next time you could save sling stones by just stomping on the bear's foot."

Keshub heard the note of pride in his father's voice and received the playful jabs and nudges from his brothers as congratulations. Warmth crept up his neck to his face at the attention and laughter.

When the fire first crackled, Uncle Yaakoub's "Hall-oo!" preceded him from the top of the stairs. He had come by way of the shortcut over the hill to his home. Micah was not with him.

Keshub whispered to Ra-mi'. "I wonder if Micah got into trouble at home or Uncle Yaakoub expects to be out too late. He really wanted to come."

Ra-mi' hugged his knees to his chest in defense against the cool evening breeze. "Or at the end of the day, the bear had taken away all strength for long walks and climbing hills. Micah is probably on his mat already."

When men from the village knocked at the Ra-eef' gate, Keshub's brother Ranine, as eldest son of Ishtaba, opened the gate and welcomed them. The men entered, clad in flowing caftans, with little but gnarled toes and rough hands sticking out of their homespun garb. The Hittite teacher, Sir Ghaleb, stood out from the group, for he wore the short leather-laced tunic of a soldier over his caftan.

Ra-mi' leaned into Keshub and pointed out that the men settling onto the limestone floor had unusually serious faces. "I heard old Nabi at the sheepfold saying we might be invaded."

"Invaded? Who? Here?"

Baba cleared his throat and began with his deep rumbling voice. "Gentlemen, we have news from afar from the lips of my trusted friend and guest, Haydak bin-Khanjar. We would do well to listen to what he has to say."

Chapter 4:
An Evening with a Caravanner

Keshub pressed his back against the still-warm rock wall of the pottery yard. He shivered with excitement and dread. Would his favorite caravanner warn them of an impending invasion? Over the years, Haydak had told the most vivid tales of all their guests and had cast full-blown, colorful pictures of faraway places on the backdrop of Keshub's imagination.

"Good men of Gibeon." Haydak bin-Khanjar's accent and precise diction revealed the influence of trading in far off places.

"For a long time I have traveled the high mountain passes, fair valleys, unpredictable rivers, and predictably dry deserts along the routes of commerce. I was hardly more than a boy when I left my Bedu family in the Sands they call 'Empty.'" The caravanner extended both hands palm up.

"You think this region has a salt sea that has no equal, but where I come from is a salt sea that is named Umm-as-Samim, 'the mother of all poisons'. Hah! Ha, ha!" The old caravanner laughed with his head back and his mustache and beard framing his large lips and mouth.

"Life on the trade route can be both exciting and monotonous in the same day. The greatest pleasure of my life as a caravanner is the times I sit at community fireside gatherings such as yours. I am honored to be with you."

"Sir, you came from Egypt this time, right? Do you have news of the old pharaoh there?" This from a Gibeonite neighbor sitting to Keshub's right in the deepening shadows of evening. Maybe he had not heard the rumors of invasion.

"Yes, brother, I did. I prefer to trade in that region when the 'sweet breath of the north wind' cools the brow. The Egyptians themselves describe it so. The heat of their dry season makes traders, myself included, much less willing to bargain."

Keshub drew up his knees and rested his chin on them while the old caravanner, whose mid-section preceded him wherever he went, rambled on.

"Egypt's capital is an amazing city. Always the pharaoh is building something. He needs a house for a new wife, or he needs a tomb for an old one. Always it is something."

Haydak chuckled. "It makes for lively trading, I can say that."

"How many wives does the pharaoh have, sir?" This came from a young voice to Keshub's right.

Haydak angled his jaw and scratched his neatly trimmed beard. "No one knows exactly, my boy. The old pharaoh has been on the throne for many years. In truth he is probably building his own tomb. People in the streets seldom see the pharaoh or the people of his court.

"To a traveler like myself who is used to open country, the pharaoh's life sounds like a prisoner's life. Give me the view of the distant horizon and an interesting destination before me. Too many nights between walls and my feet itch to move on."

Keshub stared at the crackling, dancing fire while Haydak's words held his ears captive.

"Friend Haydak, this land has had peace for many years now.

But there is a rumor that an enemy lurks. Is there any talk of Egyptian ambition for conquest?" Always the soldier, Sir Ghaleb kept on guard against forces far from their peaceful valley.

"Friend, I believe ambition is the very nature of any Egyptian pharaoh. The talk I hear on the streets is they are rebuilding their army after some mysterious loss of a whole chariot brigade some time ago."

"Yes, I heard about that from my baba." Baba Nabi, the oldest man in Gibeon, began with a scratchy voice.

When he shifted his position on the hard limestone floor, Keshub did, too. "My baba worked in the copper mines down around Beersheba—about forty dry seasons ago when I was just a young one. Baba said there were a great number of plagues in Egypt about that time. Have you heard reports of a people called Hebrews?"

"Aye, sir. I was getting to that." Haydak nodded with a suddenly serious and downcast look. His voice lost the storyteller lilt Keshub loved. "They are a curious bunch, and curious stories have circulated about them for years."

With eyebrows raised the old trader looked up again and continued. "In fact, there was much anxious talk about them when I came through Kadesh Barnea ten days ago. Rumors and speculation abounded on why the Hebrews recently moved to a place near there."

Keshub turned to the caravanner. Earlier, Ra-mi' said there was a threat of invasion. Was the news of the Hebrews cause for alarm?

With every eye on him, Haydak continued. "Some caravanners have tried to trade with them, but they seem to have need of nothing. They discourage anyone from approaching their camp.

"The locals around Kadesh always know where those folks are. There is a strange cloud over them by day and a glowing column of light by night. In Kadesh I myself witnessed the unnatural brightness among the hills where they are known to be."

Savoring Haydak's words, Keshub turned again to the dying embers of the fire. What would invasion mean for Gibeon? For the

Ra-eef' family? For him?

A squawk from Nabi, the old-timer, broke the silence. "I have heard they are the families of twelve brothers and direct descendants of a legendary hero from these very hills."

Haydak turned to the slight man beside him. "Is that so? Tell me more, sir."

Old Nabi made a great effort to clear his croaky voice. "It was a very long time ago, but it was told to me as absolute truth. There was an old man who lived down by Mamre whose name was Ibrahim or maybe Abraham. He was a very rich man with many servants and much livestock.

"When four kings from the North came and captured some of Ibrahim's kin, he got three other heads of their clans together. They went after those buzzards. He got his kin back and all the loot the marauding kings had ransacked, too. But that man Ibrahim would not take any reward for his trouble. He only wanted his kin back safe."

The old-timer grinned and wiped his mouth with a gnarled hand. "Well, as I said, Ibrahim was old at the time, and his wife was also old, way past childbearing. But the story goes they later had their first child in their old age and named the boy 'Laughter.' Gran-baba said the whole land of Canaan laughed at that." The old man cackled with one hand over his mouth to hide his gap-toothed mirth.

Laughter echoed off the courtyard walls around him as Keshub gazed into the embers bravely fighting a losing battle against the increasing darkness. Over his head, stars twinkled down on him and the comfortable gathering of friends and neighbors. Too soon, a nod from Baba and a nudge from Ra-mi' told Keshub it was bedtime. He sidled around the circle of men to head to the sleeping quarters on the roof of their house. Behind him, the old trader's voice took on an even more serious note.

"Reports about the Hebrews are increasing. Besides all the rumors and speculation, I have been hearing reports that suggest we should all be watchful."

Keshub stopped in his tracks to hear more.

"Why is that, Haydak?" Baba asked and loudly cleared his throat.

Even with his back to his father, Keshub knew the tone of rebuke. How he would have loved to stay and hear more, but Baba's look and nod in the direction of the sleeping quarters was an unmistakable command not to be ignored, even if unspoken.

On the rooftop, he unrolled his straw mat and the woolen blanket his mother had woven. He settled into his place next to Ra-mi' on the rolled clay rooftop. Soon he heard light snores coming from his older brothers.

Softly, he rasped. "Ra-mi'?"

Softly came the answer. "What?"

"Why does Lehab make fun of me?"

Ra-mi' yawned. "Do you never make fun of him?"

"Well, maybe. Sometimes I do. But I do not get him in trouble like he does me. And I do not take more bread than I should."

"Kesh, he is young. He will learn. But right now he is jealous of you."

"Jealous of me?"

"Yes, the things you do well and easily are harder for him. But he is very clever. Sometimes you have made fun of him watching a spider building a web or a lizard clinging to our wall. Instead of making fun of him for the things he likes to do, ask him what he is learning from those creatures."

Ra-mi's last words were barely above a whisper. A soft snore followed. Keshub looked up at the stars, puzzled by what Ra-mi' had said. He forgot about the pest that Lehab was in his life. The stars fascinated him, just as they fascinated Baba. The lights in the heaven seemed to stand still, and yet they seemed to dance. Slowly sleep descended.

Haydak had said, "We should be watchful of the Hebrews." *Watchful? What should we be watching for?*

ॐ

IN THE HEBREW CAMP NEAR KADESH BARNEA

On a rocky hillside dotted with patches of sparse grass, Hosiah surveyed his sheep grazing around him. He had found these patches of sparse grass shortly after dawn when the dew sparkled and manna lay abundant. Every day, he and his brother took the family's flocks out. In that dry, dusty land the morning dew might be the only water the sheep got. And every morning, he gathered manna.

"Hosiah. Hey, dreamer boy. Lost in your thoughts again, brother?" Hosiah's older brother Elkanah called from a distance as he jogged up the hill.

Elkanah teased him about his quiet moments and called it day-dreaming. If repeating the scene of his father's death over and over again was a dream, Hosiah wanted to wake up. Hosiah could not get rid of the scene two months ago when his father Elah died. As the twelve tribes of Israel's descendants broke camp to trek northward to Kadesh Barnea, a hammer head had flown loose and hit his father in the head. Hosiah had seen his father fall to the ground. He died in an instant.

His father had told them his death was near. Because he was a man of great strength, Hosiah did not believe his father's prediction. And yet, suddenly an accident took his life.

Besides daydreams, Hosiah sometimes had nightmares and always a great sadness.

Uncle Joshua had tried to explain. His uncle told him about the twelve spies Moses sent into Canaan thirty-eight years ago. He said he and Caleb believed God would help them take the promised land of Canaan. For the disbelief of the people and the other ten spies, God pronounced a curse of forty years of wandering in the wilderness—forty years that were almost over. God had said no man who was older than twenty years at that time, thirty-eight years ago, would enter Canaan—except Joshua and Caleb.

But in his grief, Hosiah wrestled with the sense of losing his father.

He continually asked himself, *How can the God of Israel do this to His people? If in fact we are His people?*

Breaking away from his thoughts and questions, Hosiah answered his brother. "You called, Elkanah? What do you want?"

"Get ready to move out. Moses has made water come from a rock! Plenty of water. All we can drink or carry. Be ready to bring your flock up to water when we get the signal."

"Water? In this place? How?"

"He just hit the rock with his staff and out poured a stream. See in the distance that reddish solid rock at the foot of that mountain? That is where water is gushing out. I am sure Uncle Joshua has his hands full trying to keep order with this thirsty mob."

Elkanah turned to rejoin his flock and tossed these words over his shoulder. "Keep alert and watch for my signal to move up to the water."

"Water? From a rock?"

Chapter 5:
How to Treat a Lady

"Pssst. Keshub."

Half awake the next morning, Keshub struggled to understand his pre-dawn reality. I am on my mat on the rooftop. *I am not wielding a sword like Sir Ghaleb's against a shadowy enemy.*

"Wha-ut?"

"Mamaa says it is your turn to help in the stable with our lodger's animals." His younger sister La'na peeked over the parapet of the rooftop from the outside stairs.

"Coming." He groaned and rubbed his eyes before he shed his cocoon of a woolen blanket. Gathering his still-warm bedding, he brushed past his sleeping brothers on their rooftop. When he inserted his bedding in its place on the rack Uncle Samir had made, this daily task brought the memory of Gran-baba and words he had spoken. "Put it where it should be, and you can find it when you need it." Baba repeated them often.

His bare feet whispered on the limestone steps as he descended from the roof and crossed the Ra-eef' courtyard by the light from Mamaa's small kitchen fire. He did not see her, but he heard her humming as she worked. At the courtyard gate, he fastened his sandals on and hurried past the guest house to the stable on the other side.

The caravanner's young handlers had their camels at the trough trying to slurp the last bit of water. The camels swung their heads away from the trough to follow his every move. He grabbed his yoke and water pots and headed to the spring. After he splashed more water in their trough, they drank deeply.

The old caravanner and his nephew entered the stable settling their over-the-shoulder leather bags. The scent of Mamaa's fresh flatbread revealed their contents and made his empty stomach growl.

"Good morning, sirs."

"Good morning, Keshub."

Haydak and Yah-ya pulled at the bulky packs stacked against the guest house wall. Covered and tied with rough cloth or leather the day before, odd bulges hinted at the mysterious goods they had traded for in Egypt and every stop along the way.

Among the packs, Keshub recognized sturdy reed baskets stuffed with wheat straw and Ra-eef' pottery. No doubt, Mother had a new supply of sea salt and Egyptian linen. The old caravanner directed the two handlers to lift a pack onto a camel from either side. They stood by until Yah-ya cinched and tied the burden. As Keshub forked new barley straw, he watched Haydak feel the tightness of each cinch and tie-down on each camel.

Haydak took special notice of a particular camel and spoke to her softly. "Shibam, my dear, I see in your eyes this morning a desire to assert yourself as queen of your realm. What is the matter? Did one of the others keep you shut off from the manger? Do you want to take your anger out on poor Haydak?"

If Keshub were not in the stable with camels, he would have thought his favorite caravanner talked to a person.

In soft tones the caravanner said to his handlers, "Remove this pack, please. Shibam is not happy."

With one handler holding the reins, Haydak patted and rubbed the wary animal from neck to hindquarters crooning words of comfort. Keshub edged closer to see what Haydak was looking for. At last the caravanner straightened and pointed. The handler's shoulders drooped at what he saw—a small wound on Shibam's right shoulder.

"Nephew, bring me the salve for wounds. We must take care that dear Shibam is not suffering from this little encounter with her trough mate. Keshub, my boy, will you hold this small measure of grain for Shibam's dining pleasure?"

Keshub grasped the opening of the rough flax cloth bag and resisted the pull from half the camel's head buried in it to munch her treat. While Haydak attended her wound, Keshub gazed into Shibam's liquid amber eyes swept by eyelashes half as long as his finger. When she raised her head to Keshub's level, the deep pool of amber reflected the colorful swag of rein on the camel next to her. After the salve treatment, Shibam chewed her cud slowly while she received her pack again.

Keshub had to ask. "Sir, how did you know about the wound?"

"A camel is much like a man, son, or a woman, for that matter. You can tell much about him or her from the eyes. Shibam suffered injury, and she chose to respond with a rebellious eye and flared nostrils. She tensed her muscles so her cinch would loosen later on the trail and cause us much delay and possible injury as well.

"Such a small injury to the camel lady you may say, but tending to her needs now will no doubt save much time and trouble later. Remember to look into the eyes, Keshub. With people, too, watch the eyes. They give a look into the heart."

Friend Haydak turned to the next camel and patted her neck. "Look into the eyes of my favorite, Khali. She is named for the desert where I grew up, and her name means 'empty', but see in her eyes how full of contentment she is. I do everything in my power to make her so. I see to her needs before my own. On the trail, my life depends on her."

Keshub nodded. "Sir, do you think someday I might travel with you? The life of a caravanner sounds much more exciting than making pottery."

Haydak's eyes focused on something behind Keshub.

Baba cleared his throat.

Keshub knew his father had heard his restless words. He picked up the pitchfork and concentrated on camel dung.

Baba gave Yah-ya a friendly slap on the back and spoke to the old caravanner. "Friend, we have known each other many years now. Ever since your nephew Yah-ya here was injured by a kick from a camel."

Haydak laughed. "Yes, that was when my newest camel-handler found out the hard way how many toes a camel has. How old were you, nephew?"

Yah-ya grinned. "About the age of Keshub, I guess. It was my first trip with you, and I remember Keshub was just out of loin cloths at the time."

"Yes, you stayed behind, and Gran-mamaa Amara pampered you for nearly six moons, as I remember. I have been indebted to these folks for their kindness to you about ten dry seasons now."

Baba cleared his throat and swallowed. "Haydak, my friend, it is because we have known you for so long that we agree to enter into a partnership with you. We have decided to make lamps to sell in Egypt like the one you brought us."

The old trader's smile spread across his leathered face, and he nodded a slight bow. "I am pleased to hear this, friend."

Baba returned the bow. "Ra-eef' potters will be investing a great deal of time and materials in making these lamps. We have never before made them, for we have not felt a need. But we will test them ourselves and take a few to market in Jericho and Jerusalem to see if folks of Canaan will use them."

Baba clasped his rough hands together. "So, my friend, I wish for you an uneventful trek and successful trading. We will be ready for your return during olive harvest."

The caravanner made a deeper bow. "Friend, I believe the prospects for this venture are very good for us both."

Baba scratched the back of his neck and lowered his voice. "Never have we relied on anyone outside our family for something this important. I am sure you can understand our concern."

A broad smile spread across Haydak's face. "It is interesting, my friend, that you should say this. My nephew has recently asked if your lovely Isa'na has been promised in marriage."

Haydak bowed at the waist before going on. "Think about this, and when we return we will talk more."

Keshub stood with pitchfork in mid-air, shocked and stunned by what he had heard. To the sound of scrunching leather and a low moan from his kneeling camel, the hefty caravanner climbed onto his saddle. Keshub looked for Baba's reaction. Would Baba say yes to Haydak's proposal? Baba, too, seemed stunned. He had not moved, and his weathered face was unreadable. Keshub watched the caravan receding on the trail north to Damascus in the rosy dawn's light and ached to go too.

"Keshub!" Baba's tone held rebuke.

"Yes, sir?"

"Think no more of caravanning. It is not for you. Your place is here."

"Yes, sir." Keshub agreed on the outside, but Baba could not make him stop thinking about an exciting life in exciting places.

Baba turned toward the back entrance to the pottery yard, his stooped shoulders told of uncounted hours spent at the pottery wheel—never seeing the horizon.

Keshub's mind whirled. The Ra-eef' family would risk a new partnership. Perhaps Isa'na would risk marrying a caravanner. He secured the stable gate and turned away. *Things cannot stay the same.*

Occupied with his thoughts, he climbed the steps beside the guesthouse to the courtyard. One of Gran-mamaa's roses brushed his cheek before he saw it. A thorn snagged his sleeve.

Getting a bee's eye view of the dawn-colored flower, he dislodged his sleeve. What adventures would come his way as a potter?

Chapter 6:
The Son of a King

A FEW DAYS LATER

"Whe-e-eet. Whe-e-eet."

Leading the flock, Keshub whistled to a straying lamb and placed a hand on Ram-ram's ridged horns beside him. "Stay." He left the ram in charge and loped up the hill to intercept the wooly wanderer.

"Jho-ee, little lamb, what will I do with you? You cannot be satisfied with following your mamaa-ewe, can you? You think you must see what is on the other side of the hill? You do not understand the danger you will find there."

Keshub extended his shepherd's staff to redirect the errant lamb to his mamaa's side and rejoined Ram-ram. A short time later, he checked again and threw up both hands. "What? Jho-ee is gone again, Ram-ram."

He shaded his eyes to survey the area in every direction before he confirmed the passive members of the flock had ample grass and grazed with heads down. They seemed safe. He turned back to look for Jho-ee. Over a small hillock a less worn path led around an outcropping of boulders. Could this be where Jho-ee left the flock? Looking left and right, he followed the faint path until a shower of pebbles pelted his head and shoulders.

"Who goes there? You dare to trespass on Amorite land with your rag-tag flock of sheep?" the threatening voice came from above.

Keshub looked up to identify his assailant, but the early morning sun partially blinded him. At eye level a rugged X, chiseled in the rock and emphasized by a slash of black tar, doubled the warning. A clench of fear tightened his chest.

"Turn back and take your mangy sheep with you, if you know what is good for you," the voice threatened. "Or you will learn what the fury," the deep voice broke and squeaked, "of the Amorites will bring."

Keshub realized the threat came from a boy not much older than he. His brothers, Eskie and Ra-mi' experienced the same croaking embarrassment. Keshub pushed down his fear and kept his voice light. "In truth, sir, you have misjudged me. I have come in peace and mean no offense. I am seeking only one wandering lamb. May your humble servant climb to the top of your boulder to look for him? The rest of my flock is on Gibeonite land, and I need to return to them as soon as possible."

"All right, peasant boy. Look, and be gone with you."

With a knot in his stomach, Keshub clambered to the top of the outcropping. Glaring eyes and an angry face met him, coming from a boy about his own height. The Amorite held his shepherd's rod high, ready to attack. Not wanting to stare, Keshub nodded acknowledgement of the boy/man's demands and turned to survey the area from their lofty vantage point.

Still searching for his lost lamb, Keshub sucked in courage. Perhaps he could make a friend. "My name is Keshub son of Ishtaba who is head of the house of Ra-eef', the potters of Gibeon."

He met the Amorite's eyes and asked in a more calm tone than he felt. "What is your name, friend?"

The Amorite grounded his staff, raised his chin, squared his shoulders, and growled. "I am bin-Zedek, son of the king of the Amorites. My father is called Adoni-Zedek. He is a mighty warrior. My father fights the sons of Anak to keep the hills of Canaan safe. That is why he is king of Jerusalem."

Looking down from the boulder, Keshub spied his flock grazing peacefully. He scanned the area until his eyes lit on a familiar wooly form grazing not far away.

"I am very glad to have made the acquaintance of bin-Zedek, the Amorite. Please excuse my trespass on your land. As I said, I meant no offense. In fact, look there."

He pointed. "There is my wooly wanderer now. Whe-e-et. See how he recognizes my whistle? Do you have sheep nearby as well?"

"My flock at the end of this ridge is twice as big as yours. I must return to them, and you must leave Amorite land with your lamb—now."

Keshub nodded. "Aye, I too am anxious to get back to my flock with the lost one, but these hills are usually quiet, and the sheep offer little companionship. I wonder if you would agree to watch our flocks from that boulder near the small spring? I would like to hear more about the giants who live in Canaan."

The Amorite raised his chest and chin before he answered with head back. "I have nothing better to do while I watch the flock of the famous Adoni-Zedek. Perhaps I could tell you a few stories of the Amorites that will let you know just who you are dealing with."

Keshub retrieved Jho-ee and called his flock. He could not help admiring bin-Zedek's swagger and obvious confidence. Like himself, the Amorite was a shepherd. But this shepherd was also the son of the king of one of the most powerful city-states in Canaan. That must be where he got his great confidence and courage.

With their legs dangling, Keshub sat on a rock next to the king's son. He breathed in to ask a question, but the Amorite launched into what must have been his favorite subject.

"For three generations before me, my family has protected

Amorite land. My gran-baba fought against the wilderness tribes all the way to Hormah with the Amalekites in his youth. My father fought the sons of Anak. Not many moons from now, I, too, will join my father's army to challenge intruders to this land."

Keshub hitched his shoulders and looked sidewise. "Have you *seen* any of the sons of Anak?"

"No, but my brother has. He said the giant stood taller than a shepherd's crook. He had palms as big as a circle of flatbread. And his voice sounded like the rumble of thunder."

"Was your brother afraid of him?"

"Of course not. Amorites fear nothing and nobody. We have the god of Molech who makes us brave. We fight in the name of our god." The scrawny Amorite ranted and tapped his rod on the ground for emphasis.

"Molech?"

"You have not heard of our god? In Molech's power we Amorites control the choice land around Gihon Spring, the best spring in the highlands of Canaan."

Bin-Zedek's voice rose and squeaked. He cleared his throat to keep it deep and commanding and rose to his feet on the boulder. He gestured to an unseen multitude. "It is in the power of Molech the Amorites subdued the sons of Anak on mount Hebron and make them pay tribute."

Keshub narrowed his eyes and furrowed his brow. Did giants pay tribute to the Amorites? Was this truth from the mouth of the son of a king or a made-up boast from the mouth of an undersized shepherd boy? Whichever, Keshub did not challenge the king's son.

The Amorite raised his chin and threw back his shoulders like a speckled rooster about to crow. "The god Molech is a consuming fire. Smoke continually rises from his temple. But only a few of the chosen may enter. My older brothers are guards to the sanctuary. My father like his father before him has entered and says Molech is awesome indeed. Molech is so powerful that no one dares disobey his decrees."

"What kinds of decrees?"

Bin-Zedek lowered himself next to Keshub and answered in a hushed voice. "Oh, like give your sons to be soldiers, deliver a cart of wood or ten baskets of wheat to the temple. Once in a while, someone refuses a decree."

Keshub detected a shudder passing through the shoulders of the boy beside him.

"When that happens, the unbeliever is summoned to the sanctuary. No one ever sees him again."

Eyes wide, Keshub checked his shadow to gauge the time, and slapped his knees. "I must go now. Please excuse my intrusion earlier, but I hope to meet you again soon. I would like very much to learn more about the sons of Anak."

Keshub slid down and headed to his sheep, calling over his shoulder. "I will watch for you the next time I bring my flock to this area."

He whistled and beckoned his flock to follow while he pondered his meeting with bin-Zedek. The boastful son of a king had told him one story after another to prove how brave his father and brothers were. Stories of men of action stirred his imagination and added to his desire to travel outside Aijalon Valley. If bin-Zedek's stories were true, his father the king was a hero.

Keshub could not avoid comparing his own father with the stories he had heard. In his home, Baba ruled with a firm hand and a stern look. Keshub would have said his family respected and loved his father. His father never raised his voice to anyone. He dealt with neighbors and caravanners with quiet words, thoughtful words. Keshub had never seen one pebble's weight of bravado in his father.

Baba's hands were strong and rough from working the clay, but Keshub had never seen his father use a weapon. If giants threatened their home, what would his father do?

Chapter 7:
No Meat

Keshub chewed a dried fig as he returned his flock to the Gibeonite community sheepfold. The gritty morsel was the last of the morning meal he had forgotten to eat when he met the son of the king of Jerusalem. At the sheepfold Da-gan', son of the night watchman, chewed a wheat straw and leaned against the wall of uncut stones.

Keshub clamped down on the crunchy seeds and scowled.

"What are you looking at, dirt face?" The bully snarled.

Keshub stopped at the narrow entrance and eyed the bully. "What is your problem, Da-gan'?"

Da-gan' glared back.

Ram-ram nudged Keshub's leg and bleated. Finally, Keshub averted his eyes. "I have to settle my sheep inside for the afternoon. Do ... you ... mind?"

"Go right ahead. Did you know you have a bug on your lip? Hey, a new name. Bug Lip!"

Keshub clamped his jaw and turned away, but he could not help running his finger over the mole on his upper lip. He stomped through the opening with his sheep following and found a place. "Ram-ram, watch our flock, old man. Chew your cud, but keep an eye on that bully and his baba. I will return at first light tomorrow."

When he exited, Nabi the old-timer had taken the afternoon watch.

Keshub's shoulders relaxed. "Good day, Baba Nabi."

"Afternoon, lad. Anything exciting happen while you were out this morning? Did you meet the bear with the sore foot again?"

"No, sir. But I met an Amorite shepherd. He said he was the son of the king of Jerusalem."

"Was everything peaceable? Those Amorites can be a sour bunch of grapes."

"I was not sure at first. I met him when searching for a lost lamb, but we parted becoming friends, I think."

Keshub tossed a thank-you over his shoulder to the old-timer and jogged to join the stream of boys scampering up the central stairway of the village to the summit. Half way up the rough-hewn stone steps, Da-gan' stepped in front of Keshub to join the herd of mountain goats. Keshub slowed to avoid a collision but kept in close step behind his nemesis. Huffing and puffing, he neared the top step when Da-gan' stopped in front of him without warning. Keshub bumped into Da-gan's hind side. Da-gan' whirled and threw a punch at Keshub's head quick as lightning. Lip bleeding, Keshub drew back to return the blow when Sir Ghaleb grabbed Da-gan's arm.

"You will sit out all of archery today, young man."

Da-gan' kicked at stones as he stomped to the worn spot under the pomegranate bush.

After class, Keshub turned all directions looking for Da-gan' to see if there would be trouble again. Where did he go?

***

In the Ra-eef' courtyard, Keshub and his brothers pressed close to the wash basin. He rubbed his grimy hands together. "Eskie. Look. No guests."

Eskie rolled his eyes and inhaled the cooking smells. "Oh, yes. There will be more lentil stew for all of us tonight even if there is no meat."

The stew disappeared and every crumb of bread vanished, leaving the second-best wide pottery bowl wiped clean. Baba's familiar belch complimented the cook. Since there were no guests, Keshub dipped his chin and bubbled up his best burp joining a chorus of belches from the other men of Ra-eef'. Laughter echoed off the courtyard walls. Keshub rocked to his feet with the rest when Baba rose and led them to the evening fire circle across the courtyard. He wrapped his arms around his shins and propped his chin on his knees to force himself to wait patiently to share his news.

Baba called on Number Two son. "Ezak, tell us about market day in Jerusalem. The woodcutting crew will be glad for the new bronze ax."

Keshub listened with both ears hoping one day he would sell Ra-eef' pottery in Jerusalem.

Across the fire circle from Keshub, Ezak leaned in. "Baba, a great number of people new to Jerusalem crowded into the market place. For fear of the Hebrews, they had left their homes in the Negev and Edom for the safety of a walled city. They brought only what they could carry, so we sold every cook pot we had. The bronze ax came from a man from Beersheba."

At the mention of the Hebrews, Baba's eyes clouded with concern.

"Did any of the new arrivals have first-hand knowledge of the Hebrews?"

Ezak sat cross-legged and placed his hands on either knee. "Well, no. Not the ones Uncle Yaakoub and I met. None knew why the Hebrews came out of the Desert of Sinai recently. Everyone agreed, however, they surely will not stay long near Kadesh Barnea. They say it is not possible there is enough water for so many people in that place."

Ezak scratched his stubbled jaw. "One customer made a wild prediction that the Hebrews are coming here to conquer Canaan. That is when I overheard our friend Endo muttering."

"Endo?" Baba questioned.

Ezak chuckled and rolled his eyes. "Have I not told you about our friend Endo? He is an old homeless character who on market day always sets up his odd assortment of goods in the same place. Between market days, he scours the forest for kindling, acorns, or mushrooms or such from the forest. And he goes house to house to trade for anything he can get."

Keshub shifted his position to place his elbows on his knees. *What would it be like to have no family, no home, and no pottery to sell?*

Ezak nodded to Baba. "Now Endo saves the place next to him for us because he says he does more business when we are there. Today he had brisk trading with the new folks for used garments and mushrooms from the forest. Some had only what they wore, and they all needed food. After the customer declared the Hebrews intend to conquer Canaan, Endo muttered, 'There's more to worry about from Molech and the strutters-about than from the Hebrews.'"

Ezak grinned broadly. "'Strutters-about' is what he calls Adoni-Zedek and his soldiers."

Keshub sat up straight with knees down. "Baba, I met the king of Jerusalem's son this morning. I was searching for a lost lamb when I saw the Amorite boundary mark on a big boulder. I did not see him standing there on top. Before I saw him, he threatened me and tried to scare me away, like he was used to ordering people about."

Keshub shrugged. "But when we talked a while, he told me his name was bin-Zedek. He is a shepherd, too, not much older than Ra-mi'. His father has fought the giants of Anak at Hebron. His father must be very brave."

Ezak leaned in with a frown. "Baba, I have seen the king and the leaders of Jerusalem parade by our booth. They may be brave, but they look down their noses at common folks. Certainly, they do not buy pottery. People clear a path for them when they appear. Yet the looks on the faces do not reflect respect—mostly fear, it seems to me."

Ezak met Keshub's eyes. "Endo says their soldiers strut around every day as if they were giants themselves and take advantage of others. They look like ordinary men, but they claim the god Molech has special plans for them."

Keshub leaned in to peer into Baba's eyes beside him. "Who is Molech, Baba?"

"Keshub, Molech is the name the Amorites of Canaan use for what they say is their god." Baba directed his gaze to his brother. "Before your gran-baba led our family here from the Lebanon mountains near Mt. Hermon, people who sought power over others came to our family. They demanded the Ra-eef' potters make hand-held pottery icons of their god Baal for them to sell."

"Those men were very angry when your gran-baba refused." Uncle Samir nodded with eyes wide.

Baba lowered his chin and raised his left eyebrow. "I believe greedy men encourage poor desperate people to ask favors of a god of carved wood or stone. They become rich at the expense of others. I have seen the poor so desperate, they believed a hand-held figure could help them. They bowed before a god of wood or stone and never considered the so-called god was made by someone's hands."

Baba turned his palms up and extended his hands. "I have crafted many things with these hands. Nothing I have created has ever moved or spoken to me, and I have never seen their gods do anything for them. Your gran-baba believed, and I do too, those gods are no gods at all."

"Do we have a god, Baba?"

Baba dipped his chin for a moment and glanced sidewise at Keshub beside him. "Fifth Son, that is a very hard question. All I can tell you is what your gran-baba Ra-eef' taught me. When he was a young boy, he sat at the feet of an ancient wise man for several days while the man stayed in their home. He told stories about the invisible Creator God."

"Invisible?" Lehab pushed his curly locks out of his eyes.

"Yes, invisible. The wise man knew the names of all the brightest stars in the sky. He described a struggle written in the stars—a war between the invisible Creator God and the forces of evil."

Keshub leaned back and found the Bear constellation over head and the North Star it pointed to. "Like the Bear, Baba? Is it on the side of the Creator God?"

Baba placed a hand on Keshub's knee. "Perhaps so, son, since the North Star helps us find our way. The old man said invisible forces of good and evil wage war here among us—in the hearts of men. He said we choose in our hearts every day which one will win—whether we do good or whether we do evil."

Ezak nodded. "Baba, Uncle Yaakoub and I see a lot of people choosing evil when we go to market in Jerusalem or Jericho."

"I am sure you do, son. But the wise man assured your granbaba of the outcome of the battle in the heavens. He said the Creator God and the forces of good truly, in the end, will win the struggle."

Baba's gaze roved over the men of their family and came to Keshub beside him. "So back to your question, Fifth Son, 'Do we have a god?'"

He pointed beyond the crest of the hill toward the south of Gibeon. "My father often pointed to one of the brightest stars in the southern sky and spoke of the One who named it. The star is called Toliman which means *the Heretofore and Hereafter.*"

Baba paused. "That star and its name gave your gran-baba hope the Star Namer watches over us and knows both our past and our future."

"Your gran-baba would say, 'We can learn from our elders who have lived *heretofore.* But no one knows the future or *hereafter,* except the Creator God, the Star Namer.'"

Baba arched a dark bushy eyebrow with a few gray hairs mingled in. "We do not bow down to anything made by a man. We trust the Star Namer is watching over us and that good will triumph over evil. We choose to live our lives on the side of good, not evil. That is our integrity, our North Star.

"Your gran-baba chose not to waste time worrying about the future. He would say, 'We prepare for the future as much as possible. We endure with integrity what we cannot prepare for.'"

Keshub gazed at the stars above the crest of the hill.

Cousin Lehab's snore broke the silence. "Zhe-zhe-zhe-zhug-zhe-zhe."

Baba gave his brother Samir, Lehab's father, a crooked grin and slapped both knees with his hands. "Tonight, we prepare to sleep, for we must work tomorrow. What we know about the future is that we must eat every day, and every household will need pottery."

Keshub stood and stamped his feet to quell the tingling from sitting so long. *Did I choose good or evil today?*

Chapter 8:
New Assignments

A FEW DAYS LATER

With the sun high in the sky, Keshub led his flock back to the sheep fold down rock-walled lanes between ripening fields of grain. The dry season had arrived. He neared the runoff stream from ein-el-Beled, Gibeon's only reliable year-round spring. Choosing a place a stone's throw down stream from another shepherd and flock, he rolled rough stones to pool the water. Ram-ram inspected his work and took the first drink.

Done with that task, Keshub turned to the neighbor shepherd, ready to call out a greeting. "Hall-oo, th—." He swallowed his greeting.

A sneer and glowering eyes cut him off. "Hall-oo yourself, dirt digger. Have you eaten any dirt lately?"

Keshub sucked in his breath, but had no clever retort. What was Da-gan's problem?

"Did a cat get your tongue, pottery boy? Let's see how you like this." Da-gan' kicked away a few stones in the stream below his own flock. He jabbed his shepherd's staff at the exposed soil. The fresh, clear water turned a murky gray and flowed Keshub's way.

"Why did you do that, Da-gan'?" He sprang into action and dammed his small pool by grabbing more stones to divert most of the murky water away from where his sheep drank.

"Later, dirt face." Da-gan' saluted and led his flock to the sheep-fold.

Keshub seethed. When he arrived at the sheepfold, he greeted old Nabi the day watchman. "Good day, sir."

"Good day to you, Ra-eef' grandson. Now, which one are you? Not Eskie, not Ra-mi.'"

"I am—"

"Dirt-Digger, Nabi. His name is Dirt-Digger, did you not know? Or Bug Lip." Da-gan' jeered and sauntered toward the village.

Keshub gaped at the bully's back.

The old man raised his croaky voice in rebuke. "Da-gan', name-calling does you no good. Get your head on straight, boy."

Keshub tried to swallow the anger he felt.

"Aw, forget it, Ra-eef'. Oh, yeah, Keshub, right?"

"Yes, sir."

"Da-gan' is a sad case, my boy. With Ra-gar' for his father, you have to feel sorry for him."

"I do not feel sorry for him. He is mean."

"Mean? Hmmm. Yeah, but maybe he just needs a friend."

"Well, I do not want him as a friend. He is bad enough as an enemy."

***

Keshub rose before the sun and began work by first light at his new assignment in the pottery yard. Making storage jars for the harvested wheat made this the busiest time of the potters' year. When the sun made a tentative peek over the gray hills to the east, he and Ra-mi' fetched water for the pottery yard in the grayness.

He skipped down dew-covered stone steps to the small spring closest to his home. Clay jars hung by leather cords from a strong cedar yoke across his shoulders. Under the weight of full jars of water, he concentrated on climbing each step to deliver the water with not a drop spilled.

Before the cool morning turned to a hot afternoon, he and Ra-mi' worked at two settling basins chipped into the solid limestone ledge. Baba filled the depressions with sticky mud from the wadi. To the mud he poured water from a gourd dipper.

Over and over Keshub squished mud through his toes with Ra-mi' doing the same nearby. At first his feet felt cool going left, right, left, right in the sloppy mix. As the excess water trickled away through a narrow groove, the mixture warmed. He made silly faces and turned about, challenging Ra-mi' with a game of "do like I do".

Baba cautioned in an even tone. "Keshub, keep your eyes on the clay at your feet. You must pick out every tiny bit of straw and every pebble larger than a mustard seed. If we use clay that has not been well prepared, our pottery will not be strong."

"Yes, sir." Watching his feet, he made a game of identifying the bits and keeping score. A bit of straw, a gray pebble from the wadi—out they came. The more elastic the clay became, the more obvious the foreign material. Gradually, the sticky mud became firm, pliable clay beneath his feet.

Baba nodded to Ranine, son Number One, when the clay was ready. Ranine swept the limestone floor beside Baba's workspace while Baba gathered the clay from both basins and threw it onto the freshly swept floor.

Keshub and Ra-mi' took turns drinking from the gourd dipper while Baba and Ranine, on hands and knees, kneaded the clay by hand.

"Boys, we do this to remove air bubbles."

After a time, the pottery masters rolled the clay back and forth under their flattened palms. Little by little, a clay snake appeared, longer than Baba's body and as big around as Keshub's little sister's wrist.

Baba removed his tunic, revealing graying chest hairs. He dipped his hands in the water pot next to his wheel and moistened his muscular upper body and shoulders. Ranine draped an end of the clay snake over Baba's shoulder so one end hung down his back. The other end extended onto two large flat stones stacked between Baba's feet. The top stone balanced on the raised center of the bottom stone.

As he squished a new batch of sticky mud through his toes, Keshub wondered at the quickness of Baba's hands.

His father formed a flat bottom. Round by round Baba coiled the snake to form the sides and left a wide opening for the mouth of the emerging container. With wet hands, one working inside and one working outside, he smoothed and flattened the ridges of wet coiled clay while he rotated the wheel with his right foot.

Baba set the new container aside to dry in the hot sun until firing day and cautioned. "No one is allowed in the back corner of the yard where we set the greenware. At this stage, it is fragile. In the kiln it will become durable and useful."

At mid-day Keshub trod a new batch of sloppy mud. What was he missing at Sir Ghaleb's school today? Baba said no one would go until after firing day when they would have plenty of storage jars for harvested grain.

Baba raised his deep voice. "No good."

Keshub cringed and slowed his footwork.

Baba pinched out a pebble the size of a grain of wheat and smashed the partially coiled container. He held up the tiny pebble. Keshub bit his lip and squinched up his face to apologize, knowing it was probably his mistake.

"Watch more carefully, boys. Keshub, bring me a drink of water, please."

Baba drank the gourd full of water and let some dribble down his chest while Ranine readied the snake again. When Baba coiled clay on the wheel, Ranine needed more well-trod clay from Keshub and Ra-mi'.

A day in the pottery yard is a never-ending cycle.

***

Many days later, near mid-day Keshub exited the pottery yard into the Ra-eef' courtyard and stopped at the wash basin beside the steps. After working all morning treading clay, he washed his feet and splashed water to his knees to remove muddy splotches. He smiled a crooked smile and told himself he did not want to give Da-gan' cause to call him "dirt-stomper," too.

He climbed the stairs beside their stacked-stone house that snuggled into the hillside. Past the Ra-eef' grape arbors on the higher ledges, he reached the summit of Gibeon's hill. His eyes swept across the golden wheat fields of the valley below and the limestone hills in the distance. He had not seen the horizon in many days. He had missed it.

He jogged toward Sir Ghaleb's class for the first time since the last full moon. Cousin Micah still helped with wheat harvest. Lehab had attended recent days alone while Keshub worked in the pottery yard. Eskie and Ra-mi' had graduated and now worked their jobs in the family pottery business full time.

What apprenticeship would Baba choose for him in another year or two? He hoped it would not be in the pottery yard. Anything but the day-to-day numbing sameness of the pottery yard.

At archery practice Keshub pulled the bowstring and arrow taut. The slight dimple in the cedar wood shaft glared at him. Every imperfection influenced the arrow's flight, so he would observe the flight and try to compensate next time. He took careful aim to maximum tension and—Sir Ghaleb's shrill whistle signaled halt.

Down the line the Hittite soldier bent over Da-gan'. Red faced with a deep scowl and gritted teeth, he held one hand on a hip while he pointed to the trail to the village with his other. Da-gan' flung the bow and arrows in his hand to the ground, turned the other way, and ran into the olive grove.

Sir Ghaleb watched until Da-gan' disappeared around a thicket in the distance. He turned back and bellowed. "Men, how many times must I tell you these are weapons? They are not gewgaws.

Never, I repeat, never retrieve your arrows when others are still shooting!"

Yes sir! Keshub sympathized with the bully for once. There was so much to remember. Later, the old soldier paired Keshub with one of Lehab's classmates to walk through sword drill at half speed. If the bully had not been expelled for the day, would he have sparred with Da-gan'?

Chapter 9:
Keshub and Lehab

After class, Keshub walked beside Lehab in awkward silence in the scorching afternoon sun. He, Micah, and Lehab had been inseparable when they were younger. He did not remember what or who started the two of them down their path of resentment and distrust toward each other.

Lehab attempted conversation. "It is hard to get back into the drills when you have been out a while, is it not?"

Keshub's temper ignited. "I did not do so badly. I am still better than you."

Lehab dashed ahead and called back a challenge. "I will beat you to the steps, bragger boy!"

Why did I not expect this old trick of his? He would prove himself. He churned his legs and pumped his arms running full speed. Reaching for longer strides, he narrowed the gap between them, but Lehab reached the top of the stairs first.

Lehab placed his hand on the rock ledge beside the top step and turned to taunt with his tongue out as usual.

Keshub's eyes widened, and he yelled. "Lehab. Stop!"

Keshub increased his speed, drew his wooden sword from his belt, raised it above his head, and slashed with an audible whirr to the left.

His sword made a dull thud.

Lehab's brows collapsed inward, his mouth uttered a gasp, his shoulders and arms flinched.

"I-I...am sorry. There was no time to explain." Keshub nodded for Lehab to look left.

Lehab's eyes followed. The tail of a brown zig-zag patterned viper slithered into a crack near where Lehab's hand had rested.

"Thanks. I did not see it. I...thought you attacked me."

Moments later Keshub and Lehab entered the pottery yard.

Baba raised an eyebrow, one elbow sticking out of a wet clay jar. "You boys look pale. Is there something wrong, Keshub?"

When he hesitated, Lehab answered.

"Keshub saved my life, sir. There was a poisonous viper right by my hand. He knocked it away with his sword."

Baba withdrew his arm from the jar and stopped turning the wheel with his feet. "Keshub, I am proud of you."

Keshub raised his eyes to meet his father's. He did not reply.

Baba paused and wiped his hands on a wet rag. "Lehab, do you know that when a person saves your life you are forever indebted to that person?"

"No, sir."

"At the very least, Lehab, you must never again take more than your share of bread and leave Keshub with not enough. Do you understand?"

Lehab's eyes went wide, and he looked from Baba to Keshub. "Yes, sir."

Baba's dark eyes focused on first Keshub and then Lehab. "There will be no more feuding between you two, do you hear me?"

In unison, "Yes, sir."

"Many times in your lives you will need each other. Today was the first time, but it will not be the last. Decide now to value each other's differences as an addition to your own strengths. Find a way to work together and not against each other."

"Yes, sir."

"Ra-mi." Baba called across the pottery yard.

"Sir?"

"I have a change of plans. You will go for more water at the spring and then take a break. Keshub and Lehab, drink a dipper of water and get ready to stomp clay. Being face to face stomping clay builds friendships." Baba furrowed his brow, but his mustache quivered.

***

A few days later, Keshub answered his father's summons and stood before him while Baba checked off the list.

"The greenware stands dry and ready. The woodpile threatens to topple. The new kiln waits. Keshub, run to your Uncle Yaakoub's house and tell him tomorrow is the day. We are ready for firing day."

"Yes, sir!"

Later on the way home from delivering Baba's message, Keshub retraced the footpath the Ra-eef's had worn across the top of Gibeon's hill. He remembered the day Da-gan' had disappeared around a thicket halfway along their footprint-shaped hill.

He searched but did not find where Da-gan' might have hidden. Before he became a shepherd, he had explored much of the hill with Micah and Lehab. The ledges on its slopes and the dense growth in some parts of the summit offered many hiding places. Where had Da-gan' gone that day?

***

The next day Keshub and Ra-mi' kept the wood and dung chips coming. Uncle Samir and Baba, on hands and knees, packed the kiln, mumbling their strategies of placement for the delicate materials. Uncle Samir lit the fire with embers from the kitchen fire. Baba cocked his head toward the kilns and demanded total quiet. He touched the outside of the clay dome with a flat hand to test the temperature inside—until it became too hot to touch.

Finally, when the coals inside were white hot, Uncle Samir blocked the opening with stones and plugged air holes with mud. Then the most difficult time of all arrived. The waiting.

His father sat cross-legged in the afternoon heat with his head still tilted toward the kilns. At any sound in the courtyard, Baba barked, "Quiet!"

Keshub held his breath and tip-toed. Before firing day, the pottery yard buzzed with activity. Today, equal parts of silent hope and dread pulsated in the air around him. With nothing left to do, Keshub and Ra-mi' refilled all the water jars while the Ra-eef' family's good fortune rested in the glowing hot kilns. Would there be popping noises inside? Baba said an air bubble in the clay or a drop of water in greenware would make a disaster. Would there be many useless, broken vessels? Or would the Ra-eef' potters produce the sturdy pottery in demand in every household?

Tension etched deep lines in his father's face as he waited, helpless, while the fire did its work unseen. Keshub delivered soppy wet cloths sent by Mamaa to drape over Baba's head and shoulders. Uncle Yaakoub drew his brothers away from the kiln to sit together on the steps to the pottery yard. From there, they could watch and listen but also catch a bit of breeze.

At his mother's direction, Keshub set a water jar and gourd dipper next to Baba, dipped water, and extended it to his father.

Uncle Yaakoub wiped a brow. "The Hebrews asked the king of the Edomites for passage through Edom. He answered by gathering his army at the border ready to fight even though his army is sorely outnumbered."

Baba stared into the distance and passed the dipper to Uncle Samir. "Haydak told us we must be watchful. According to him, this is just the start of hearing about the Hebrews."

ᐊᔓᐃ

IN THE HEBREW CAMP IN THE NEGEV IN SOUTHERN CANAAN

Hosiah looked up from his task. His brother Elkanah sped toward him.

Elkanah halted in the shade of the henna-red awning of their tent. "Uncle Joshua sends word we must move out tomorrow. We must pack everything and be ready at first light."

"What is the hurry?" Hosiah combed his fingers through a bowl of dry manna to sift out small stones.

"The king of Edom and his army are over that ridge. They are preparing to attack us."

"I thought Moses negotiated with them for us to take the King's Highway through their land." He set the bowl of manna aside.

"Yes. He tried. But they would not listen nor budge. Now they are ready to attack us if we stay here."

Hosiah rose and placed his hands on his hips. "If we are leaving at first light, it is a good thing I filled all our water jars early today. I was trying to make less work for tomorrow, but you thought that was another of my foolish ideas."

Elkanah dipped his chin. "Your idea turned out not to be foolish at all but very wise. We have been spoiled by an abundance of water since Moses struck the rock several weeks ago. I am sorry I made fun of you. Where is Mother?"

"She is helping a neighbor who has a new baby. She will return soon, I think."

Elkanah glanced at the afternoon sun. "We must begin now if our cart is to be in its place with the Ephraimite clan at first light. Since father is not with us, the work falls to you and me."

Hosiah knew the routine. They had moved often. He dug packing gear out of their cart while Elkanah hurried away to bring their two oxen. They were a small household, but he mounded an amazing amount of stuff to pack tonight. He separated the things they needed for the evening and piled them near the door of their tent.

They would be tied on top of everything else tomorrow.

Hosiah muttered to himself. "At least we do not have to worry about packing food for the journey. Some call it 'the bland stuff'. But manna is there on the ground with the dew every morning. All we have to do is gather it."

Conflicting thoughts assaulted him. Why would a caring God take his father away in the prime of life? He had to admit, though, the manna God provided showed him God did care.

Mother returned from delivering stone-baked manna flatbread to a neighbor and took her apron from a peg on their tent pole.

"Mother, if we leave early, how will you cook tomorrow's manna?"

Mother splashed water into her cook pot. "I will bank the coals tonight, and we will have time for a small fire before sunup. If you boys gather manna at first light, I can make a warm porridge before it is time for our Ephraimite clan to start out. A drizzle of honey will make it just right for a quick meal. I will fry slices of cold porridge tomorrow night when we set up camp again."

Mother placed the cook pot in the sun to dry. "Thank you, son, for filling all the water pots this morning. Because of you, we will do very well. Others who are not so well prepared will soon be complaining."

Elkanah turned from where he worked with the oxen. "If they are not complaining about the food and water, they will complain about something else."

Chapter 10:
A Crouching Lion

A FEW DAYS LATER ON THE MORNING OF THE LONGEST DAY OF THE YEAR

Keshub breathed in the green of the meadow and the earthy smell of his flock at dawn. He had endured the assignment of carrying great quantities of water and treading squishy clay. He did not mind the tasks, but the confinement of the pottery yard walls stifled him. He stretched his shoulders and arms. For the first time in many days, he could stretch without knocking over pottery. He had time to gaze at the horizon. He could think.

The birds twittered nearby as the golden glow of morning brightened in the east. The twittering turned to tentative peeps and trills when the sun's red rim came into view. When its full rays burst over the hill and hit the morning dew, the valley sparkled with appreciation, and the birds crescendoed to full song. He relished the birdsong and the cool solidness of the rock he sat on. The fresh air and the morning breeze combed the tangles of tension from him. Today, he would officially become twelve harvests old.

For many days he had to concentrate on every step while carrying water. He had to focus on his feet to pick out unwanted bits from the rough clay. He kept his mind on chopping wood lest he injure himself or others. In the meadow he could think again and look beyond himself to the horizon. He took a long, deep breath and exhaled slowly.

Yesterday, he watched his uncles and his father stand elbow-to-elbow when Baba opened the kilns. When sturdy pottery came out of the cold ashes unbroken, the worry lines in the adults' faces disappeared, replaced by smiles of relief. Gran-baba Ra-eef' had taught them well.

Shaking himself from his thoughts, he looked up to check the flock. The sheep grazed quietly and licked the dew from each blade of grass. Upwind from them, he pressed his back against a large boulder. Something moved at the corner of his eye that should not be there.

He turned. Yes, from the shadow of another boulder, a low form stalked. The beast crept low to the ground toward a ewe on the edge of the flock—a lion unaware of Keshub's presence.

Keshub rose slowly.

The hunter advanced soundlessly, muscles rippling along his back.

Keshub sidestepped to draw closer, staying in shadow and choosing his steps to make no sound. The beast's long, low strides brought him closer to the ewe. Amber eyes and body the color of ripened wheat blended with the dry grasses. With every muscle tensed, the crouching lion crept closer. The ewe nibbled grass, unaware danger approached, silently.

Keshub calculated the possibilities. First of all, he must protect the flock. His encounter with a bear two moons ago flashed through his mind. The lion with its large paws and rippling muscles seemed unstoppable, but so had the bear. The bear was strong but not as fast as a lion.

This enemy would be so fast of foot and strong of jaw he could kill several sheep in only a few moments. At all cost, he must not panic the flock. He must not attract the attention of the lion or the sheep. A wrong move might cause his sheep to run toward the enemy.

His only option hung at his side—the stones in his pouch and the training Sir Ghaleb had given him. He made no quick movements. He kept his eyes on the lion while he laid his staff on the ground with his right hand. At the same time, he felt inside his pouch with his left hand. He picked two round stones from the five he had smoothed and shaped.

His right hand slipped the leather sling from his belt. Cautious side-steps around the edge of the flock brought him closer to his target. If his slingstone fell short among the sheep, he would scare his sheep into the hungry lion's mouth.

He moved by instinct. In one fluid motion he inserted the first stone and sent his sling whirring in a circular path over his head. The soft sound of the sling stone picking up speed over his head did not alert the sheep. They often heard him practice with it.

The lion did not break his stealthy stride. Easy prey was within his grasp. With the lion close enough to pounce, Keshub could wait no longer. The whirring stopped as the stone left his sling and silently crossed the distance between him and the hungry lion.

"Whack," the stone hit the lion squarely on the head. His head jerked backward.

Already Keshub had another stone in the sling making the whirring sound. The tawny hunter froze in mid-step, his head at an awkward angle, right front paw raised, poised on the edge of death.

Keshub's second stone smacked the animal on the rump with a thud that toppled him to the ground. With his last gasp of air, his golden sides expanded and collapsed while his tail flicked aimlessly—once, twice—and fell limp.

Keshub retraced his steps to his staff without taking his eyes off the lion. He approached the still body ready to retreat if there was any life left. A trickle of blood came from the sunken left eye socket. The other stared blindly. This enemy would hunt no more.

The sheep grazed, apparently with no thought of danger. Keshub swallowed down the fear in his throat and stared at the still form of the enemy. From life to death in such a short span.

He began to breathe again. He knew what he had to do next. He had seen Mother kill a chicken for roasting. He had seen Baba prepare a lamb for family celebrations. He took his small flint knife from its scabbard on his belt and slit the throat of the still-warm carcass.

The life blood of the beast flowed onto the rocky ground and made garnet puddles in the gray dust.

With unbidden tears, Keshub felt the beast's side with an open hand and drew back from the surprising heat. The tawny coat reflected the heat of sunlight, much warmer than he would have imagined. The short hairs of the fur were silky smooth and rough at the same time. How could this be? Beautiful *and* fierce. Awesome for his skill and strength and beauty, but hated and feared for the threat to his family's survival.

Keshub snapped branches from a nearby bush and covered the lion so the buzzards would not see him. He hoped the branches would keep the fur from being damaged by those scavengers before he could bring help to skin him. He smiled when he pictured Gran-mamaa Amara in a warm winter wrap from the pelt.

Chapter 11:
Longest Day Celebration

Keshub squared his shoulders and struggled to keep in step behind his long-legged brothers. They climbed Gibeon's hill in the glaring afternoon heat of summer to join the celebration on the threshing floor.

"So, Keshub is the big hunter now!" Eskie, Brother Number Three, clapped him on the shoulder.

Keshub rested his hand on the weapon he had used that morning to protect his sheep. Eskie's words of praise and the expectation they implied did not match how he felt. If the sun were setting that moment in mid-afternoon, he would still feel like *this was* the longest day of his life.

Since the episode with the lion, he had sunk into a swamp of conflicting thoughts. He had never used his skill to kill before. Training with pretend swords and slingshots always seemed like great fun—a game.

To measure up against his brothers, he had practiced daily

when he was with his sheep. He had carefully collected five almost perfectly smooth, round stones and had honed them to smooth them more. It was great fun to see the three-legged bear scared off from Micah's flock. But now he understood why Sir Ghaleb was always serious about the mid-day classes. Protecting his family was serious business.

These thoughts crowded for attention as he looked down on the harvest celebration from the west end of Gibeon's mount. Gibeonites would celebrate the harvest and watch the sun go down on the longest day of the year.

Eskie spoke twice to get his attention. "Come with me, little brother. We must tell Sir Ghaleb of your heroic deed this morning. He should know that his training protected our sheep again."

While Eskie told the morning's adventure to their teacher, Keshub felt no excitement in the telling.

The old soldier spoke softly. "Well done, young man. This is what our training classes are for—to protect and defend. You have learned well."

Keshub noted a smile on Sir Ghaleb's lips, but in his eyes there was something else—perhaps sadness, perhaps kindness. Or understanding.

Keshub acknowledged the hoped-for praise with a simple "Thank you, sir" before Sir Ghaleb turned away to start the archery competition.

Keshub paid little attention to the contest until the crowd hushed around him. The contestants had narrowed to two, Eskie and one other. The other archer hit the charcoal blackened center of a circular grass mat four out of five tries.

As last year's champion, Eskie shot last. His brother's first arrow struck the top edge, barely inside the black circle.

The crowd voiced a collective "Hunh?"

Perhaps the master craftsman's bow and quiver of specially made arrows was not such an advantage after all. Uncle Yaakoub had taken Eskie to Jerusalem last year to trade a yearling lamb for it, but Baba thought it a waste.

His brother's second arrow struck the black exactly opposite the first at the bottom edge and brought a similar response from the crowd. When Eskie's third and fourth arrows struck precisely inside the right and left edges, Keshub eyed his brother closely.

Keshub heard murmurs around him as excitement built. "Is he doing that on purpose?" and "Is he playing with us?"

Yes, he was. His brother wore an expression Keshub knew well—disarming goodwill with cunning beneath. Mother had a saying for it. "Boys, beware when your brother wears that look. He can talk you out of your woolen blanket on the coldest day."

The last arrow struck the exact center, and the crowd around Keshub broke out in wild cheers.

Sir Ghaleb came forward and congratulated the number two archer of Gibeon before turning to Eskie with a broad grin and a laurel wreath crown. Keshub cheered along with the crowd while dread weighted the pit of his stomach. By the time his competition arrived, he had overheard Eskie tell the story of Keshub and the lion several times. Men and boys from the village looked at him differently. They actually looked at him. Being an unnoticed nobody in the crowd had been more comfortable. Now they knew him and knew he was Eskie's brother.

The old soldier called his name, summoning him to hurl sling stones at a target hung from a tree. The weight in his stomach grew heavier.

From the chatter of the crowd, Eskie's voice rang out. "You can do it, little brother."

Keshub stepped to the line. The target failed to arouse excitement in him. The smooth coolness of the stone as he placed it in his sling felt like the cold weight in his stomach. Holding the stone in place, he took his stance and flexed his tense shoulders. He whipped the sling overhead, and set it to whirring. The sound took him to his near-dawn experience with the lion when he had moved by instinct to defend his flock.

The crowd's disappointed groan brought him back. His first stone sailed wide of the target and hit the tree with a thunk that barely registered with him. He rubbed sweaty palms on his tunic and hurled second and third stones. Only one made the target flap lazily in mid-air. Unable to look into the eyes of the spectators, Keshub turned away and sought a place at the back of the crowd where he could hastily wipe away a tear.

"How does it feel to be a failure, dirt stomper?" Da-gan' spat on the ground. "Your big brother bragged to everyone you are a sure shooter with your slingshot. Sure shooter, my eye. You are a loser—an embarrassment to your whole dirt-digging family. I guess you will pay when you get home."

Keshub had not seen Da-gan' sitting there in shadow. He did not feel like defending himself. He was not a loser. Embarrassed? Yes. Perhaps his brother was embarrassed, too, but the contest no longer seemed important. Keshub moved away from his tormentor without a word.

Later, Eskie, wearing a leafy wreath crown, sought Keshub out. "Kesh, I thought surely the Ra-eefs had a chance at two crowns today. What was the matter? The target was bigger than a lion, and you almost missed it altogether."

Keshub did not understand either. He responded with bravado he did not feel. "It must be because there were no eyes on the target, big brother. When I was spinning the sling this morning, all I remember seeing were the lion's eyes."

At the end of the longest day of the year, the Ra-eef' family gathered to watch the sun go down. Keshub's mouth watered when Mamaa and Aunt Sabah produced a basket dinner for the celebration. Still-warm flat bread and crisp vegetables to dip into a savory bean paste with olive oil and garlic.

Ezak arrived, hot and sweaty, in time to join in. "Baba, there were many people at Jerusalem's longest day market today, but trading was slow. The livery keeper warned us there had been a solemn procession at dawn. The whole city went down to Hinnom Valley."

Baba lowered his eyes and dipped his chin at Ezak's words.

Keshub jerked his head and frowned. *What happened at*

Hinnom Valley?

"About mid-afternoon King Adoni-Zedek spoke from the top of the wall. He declared the Hebrews were no threat at all, as if he himself were the reason why. Good news had arrived from the king of Arad in the southern Negev. Zedek shouted, beating his chest. 'The gods are pleased with us. The cowardly Hebrews are slinking south back into the desert.'"

When Baba and Uncle Samir escorted the ladies and young ones home in the twilight, Keshub remained among the young men. But after a short time of listening to the laughter and fun-making, he took his bedroll to the high rocky ledge near Gran-baba's resting place. A place as comfortable as anywhere, the quietness matched his mood better.

The limestone had soaked up the sun's heat, and the warmth penetrated to muscles taut since his early morning encounter with the lion. Westerly breezes from the Great Sea cleared his mind and promised heavy dew. The solitude provided a balm. His shoulders relaxed for the first time all day.

A few moments later Ra-mi' appeared. "Anything wrong, Kesh?"

"No. Just need time to think."

"I understand, brother. I will think with you."

Chapter 12:
Bitter Grief

Keshub complained to his sheep. "What else can go wrong today?"

In the full light of morning, his shorn and shaggy flock wobbled along behind him. With hand above his eyes, he confirmed grass near home was gone. Every day he took his charges farther to find enough. Because of his late start, there would be little of the precious dew when he found grass. He wagged his head from side-to-side thinking of the fancy Mr. Jiroft from Persia. The guest complained he did not get enough water for his camels.

He got all there was! The little spring across the trail from the pottery yard ran dry. Neither Keshub nor his brothers went to their sleeping mats until the night was half over. He counted ten trips to Gibeon's main spring, ein el-Beled. Until the night water guard said they had used their allotment for the next three days.

Finally, green appeared ahead—not much but enough for the day. With his sheep grazing around him, he leaned against a boulder.

"Those eyes. What pride and anger I saw there. He looked down his nose at Mamaa's lentil stew with dried mutton, too. Was it too simple? Too common? Not enough? Who in this life has never ever been told 'That is all there is.'? With those gold rings and silk tassels hanging everywhere, even on his camels, maybe he has not."

A sudden warm, moist sensation on his hand brought Keshub back to the present. His favorite lamb gazed at him with sympathy in his dark eyes. "Hey, Jho-ee. Thank you, friend."

He imagined the lamb understood him. Surely, the trusting dark eyes with white lashes said to him, "All will be well, friend." But Jho-ee was no longer a little lamb. If Keshub did not see the wooly one coming, Jho-ee's playful nudges could buckle Keshub's knees and knock him off his feet.

He took the wooly face in both hands and gave Jho-ee a well-deserved ear-scratching. When the half-grown sheep turned away to graze again, he leapt up and twisted his body in mid-air giving a lamb-like thanks. Keshub laughed.

He raised his eyes to the horizon, and sheep other than his own grazed nearby. He checked his own flock before sauntering over to find the other shepherd. He found him on a low boulder with his back toward Keshub and his head in his hands. Whoever he was, all was not well with him either.

A few steps away Keshub stopped. "Are you all right?"

When the shepherd jerked his head up and pushed his scraggly hair back with one hand, Keshub recognized the boastful son of Adoni-Zedek.

The Amorite wiped his eyes with the back of his hand.

"What?"

"Are you all right?"

"Of course."

Keshub was not convinced. Judging by the quivering lip, neither was bin-Zedek.

"Friend, do you want to talk about it?" Keshub checked his flock over his left shoulder.

"What possible good would talking do?"

Keshub eased down beside him. "It is very bad then—whatever is bothering you?"

"Oh, yes, very bad is right." Bin-Zedek sighed and wiped his nose on the hem of his tunic.

"My gran-baba would say, 'A load is lighter when it is shared.'"

With a sigh the Amorite shepherd propped his elbows on his knees and dropped his head. "It is my brother." He began to weep again with great shudders.

"One of the soldiers?"

Bin-Zedek shook his head and wiped his eyes. "No, Do'ni, my little brother."

"What happened?"

"He died."

"How?"

"It is unspeakable, boy."

Keshub did not know what to say, so he placed his hand on a grieving shoulder. "I am sorry."

After a moment, bin-Zedek spoke with his head still down. "He was the only one who looked up to me. He was always asking me questions. I guess Father did not have time for him either. Do'ni waited for me to return from shepherding each day—always glad to see me. He followed me about like an orphaned lamb."

Bin-Zedek rambled on. "My older brothers say I am a worthless nuisance. Father is always angry with me. My mother died when I was born. Do'ni's mother used to let me stay with her and Do'ni, but I did not belong there. Now she is distraught about the death of her only son. Do'ni was the only person alive who acted like he cared whether I lived or died."

After a long pause, bin-Zedek's head jerked upward. A look of terror came to his face. He stared into the distance as if he saw imminent danger. Keshub checked the horizon and then his flock for a threat to their sheep or to them. The source of bin-Zedek's fear did not lie on the horizon. Keshub remembered the lion's blind stare in death. This time Keshub saw the living—staring at death.

For the first time, bin-Zedek glanced at Keshub. "What if I am next?"

"Next? Is it a horrible plague?"

"It might as well be. But no, the menace is my own father."

"I do not understand."

"No, there is no way you could." Bin-Zedek's eyes darted here and there as he mumbled to himself. "I must make a plan. What can I do? Where can I go? I know no one who is not either afraid of or loyal to my father."

Keshub shrugged. "I know someone."

"You?"

"Yes. My brother has told us about an old man who saves a place next to him for my brother and uncle on market days. I only know that my brother Ezak heard him mutter about his dislike of your father. Ezak says the old man is kind. I think you could go to him, and he would help you. If your life is in danger, it is worth a try."

"It is, friend. And I will. What is his name?"

"Endo."

"Endo. Yes, I know him. He is that strange little man who sleeps on the street under his small cart. He pushes his odd assortment of possessions everywhere. Sometimes children make fun of him."

"Bin-Zedek, I still do not understand, but if I or my family can help you, we will. You can give a message to my brother Ezak on market days. He and Uncle Yaakoub are usually there."

"Friend, do not ever call me by that name again. Today, I renounce the name given to me by the one who sired me. I am no longer the son of Adoni-Zedek. In the future call me plain 'Zed.'"

"As you wish ... Zed. I have been away from my sheep too long, and I must go back."

Keshub returned to his peacefully grazing sheep and puzzled over Zed. He did not understand what had happened to the little brother, but Zed was grief-stricken, afraid, and helpless without a friend. Keshub left him somewhat comforted and with hope. He would talk to Baba about this.

He rounded up his sheep with a whistle and wave toward home.

When Jho-ee took a place beside his shepherd friend, Ram-ram lowered his head and horns to nudge the upstart aside and claimed his place as leader of the flock.

Keshub chuckled and side stepped to avoid being tumbled down the hill himself.

***

A few days later Keshub hurried home after Sir Ghaleb's class with Lehab beside him.

Da-gan' blocked the path.

"Hey, pottery boys. Have you been playing in the dirt lately? Is that why you look like girls when you shoot with a bow and arrow? Especially, Le-e-ha-ab."

"Back off, big mouth." Keshub planted his feet and rammed his hands onto his hips. "Unless you would like to *eat* some dirt today."

"Oh, yeah? And just who is going to make me?"

Keshub lowered his voice and stared. "Me, Keshub, of the potters of Ra-eef."

He squared his shoulders and advanced toward his challenger, his eyes boring into Da-gan's. "We are makers ... of the best pottery ... around here."

He stopped face to face with his tormenter, a hand-breadth apart. The bully loomed over him a hand-breadth taller.

"You cook your breakfast and your supper in our pottery. Your baba stores his grape harvest in our pottery. You can taunt all you want, but you will keep on needing ... our ... pottery ... every day of your life in Gibeon."

Da-gan' blinked and stepped back. "Well, the runt there still shoots like a girl." He took another step back, pivoted, and hurried down the path to his home.

When Da-gan' was out of hearing, Lehab whispered. "Man, that was brave. He is taller and bigger than you. Where did you get the courage to talk to him that way?"

"I do not know. I was not thinking. Maybe I was doing what

Baba would do if threatened. As soon as I talked calmly and walked toward him, his eyes changed. Then I knew he would not hit me. Friend Haydak said you can tell much about a person from his eyes. I think Da-gan' is not as tough as he wants us to think."

Keshub turned toward home. "But Da-gan' was right. We do need practice with our bows and arrows to keep up the good name of Ra-eef'."

Arriving at home, he and his cousin went immediately to their assignment to carry and stack wood. Eskie chopped with the sharp bronze ax Uncle Yaakoub traded for recently. Uncle Samir, Lehab's father, stacked.

Lehab rushed to his father's side. "Baba, you should have seen Keshub stand up to Da-gan' after class today."

"Oh?" Lehab's father turned to Keshub. "You do not look like you took a hit, Keshub. What does Da-gan' look like?"

He shrugged his shoulders and let Lehab tell the tale.

"Keshub walked right up to Da-gan', nose to nose. Well, Keshub's nose to Da-gan's chin and stared him down. Actually, he stared up, and kept talking. Da-gan' made fun of our being potters again and of my being such a terrible shot with the bow and arrow.

"Keshub told him we make the best pottery anywhere around here and that his family uses it every day. Keshub spoke slowly and must have surprised Da-gan'. I think the bully did not know what to do with Keshub's answer."

Eskie paused chopping wood. "Quick thinking, Kesh. How did you decide to answer the bully that way?"

He shrugged again with no reply.

Lehab answered for him. "He said he was not thinking. He said maybe Uncle Ishtaba would do the same in a similar situation."

"Hah, ha, ha." Lehab's father combed his hair back with his fingers. "You are right, Keshub. Your baba is the hardest person to get into an argument I have ever met. First he just listens. Then he just talks. He has been that way since we were boys."

Eskie leaned on his ax handle. "Uncle Samir, do you think these two could go hunting with me this afternoon? Sounds like they need some instruction and practice with their bows and arrows. And I have been itching to go hunting."

"Great idea, Eskie. Since we do not have a guest with camels today, Lehab can be spared at the livestock pen. As soon as we finish stacking what we have cut, you three may go. I expect roasted game for tomorrow's dinner, boys."

As Keshub stacked wood, Friend Haydak's words returned to him. "Look at the eyes."

A few days ago pride and arrogance glowed in the Persian's eyes. Fear had clawed at Zed's eyes.

In Da-gan's, hurt haunted at the edges.

Chapter 13:
Surviving the Heat

CRITICAL

IN THE HEBREW CAMP AT MT. HOR,
SOUTH OF THE NEGEV

"Yes, Mother?" Hosiah rubbed his eyes.

"Time to tend your sheep, son, before the tongue of the sun's thirsty rays get to the dew first. And take one of your largest spring lambs out of the flock. Neighbor Elishama will prepare mutton to dry today. He says we might as well take advantage of this heat, since we must camp here for thirty days to mourn the high priest's death."

"All right, mother. Will we have mutton for supper?"

"I think a mutton broth from the bones with manna dumplings would be good."

"Yum-m-m. I will look forward to that all day."

***

FOUR WEEKS LATER

Hosiah plodded beside their oxen on the dusty trail to Atharim. Their wagon clanked along with all they owned piled on top or tied to the sides.

"Hosiah!" His big brother pointed behind.

"What?" Hosiah gasped.

Elkanah delivered a message from Joshua to neighbor Elishama, leader of the Ephraimite clan. "We have been attacked! Uncle Joshua said to pitch camp immediately and stand your ground around the Tabernacle."

Elkanah yelled over the roar of activity amongst their neighbors. "The king of Arad attacked the Danite camp from the rear this morning. We must have let our guard down. The Canaanites poured over the horizon on both sides in an ambush."

Mother clasped her hands to her mouth. "Oh, no. Was anyone lost?"

"They surrounded and captured twenty-five families of the Naphtalites. Moses made a vow if God will deliver Arad into our hands, we will totally destroy them. "

"Will Uncle Joshua lead the attack?"

"Before first light."

The next night, Hosiah sat cross-legged on the looped-wool rug at the entrance to their tent among the Ephraimites. His older brother sorted through spoils from Arad his Uncle Joshua gave them.

"Hosiah, look at this." Elkanah held up a tunic of fine linen with embroidered edges. "It is too small for me. For you, perfect."

Hosiah ran his open hand over colorful stitching. "It is much too fine for shepherding. The one I am wearing is better. Anyway, new linen is itchy and stiff. I like the one I have because you wore it before me and softened it up, brother."

Mother chuckled. "The truth of it is, Hosiah, my brother Ahira wore it when he was a lad. Others wore the tunic in between."

"Can you trade the new one for something we need?"

"We will see. Or I could make a very fine apron from it for

myself. But look at this. This is what I am most excited about." Mother opened a large bag and scooped up amber colored grain with two hands. She smelled the grain with a look of pure delight.

Leaning toward her, Hosiah and his brother each took a whiff of the small hard grains—smaller than Hosiah's little fingernail.

"It smells—nice, I suppose." Elkanah rubbed his nose.

"What is it, mother?" Hosiah pinched a couple of grains and popped them in his mouth.

"It is wheat."

"Wheat?" Elkanah repeated. "What does it taste like, Hosiah?"

"Kind of bland, but it has turned gummy in my mouth."

Mother laughed. "We grind it to make flour for bread and bake it. In Egypt, my mother was a baker in the house of an important Egyptian official and baked bread with yeast every day. I helped her even though I was young. You cannot imagine how good bread made from wheat smells when it is baking."

Mother's eyes sparkled. "The night before we left Egypt, my mother's master came to us with tears in his eyes in the middle of the night and pressed upon us a large bag full of wheat from his storehouse. For a few days, mother baked flatbread for all around until the supply ran out."

"The man was crying, Mother?" Hosiah had to ask.

"Yes. God had sent the tenth plague to Egypt. We called it the Passover."

"Tenth plague?" Elkanah dipped his chin.

"Passover?"

"Yes. In the first nine plagues water turned to blood, hailstones destroyed the crops, and lice, locusts, and frogs or such invaded the land. But the tenth brought death to all first-born sons in Egypt."

"All of Egypt?"

Mother shook her head. "Except for our Hebrew families in Goshen. God had told Moses that every household should kill a perfect young lamb and paint its blood over and beside the doors to our houses. Everywhere God's angel of death saw the blood, he would pass over."

Mother hung her head and re-tied the bag closed. "I am sure my mother's master had a first-born son who died that night. It was a terrible night in Egypt. That is what it took for God to convince the pharaoh to let us leave."

Mother looked up and brightened. "Well, we have no more time for stories. Your Uncle Joshua said we must break camp before first light. Now that our Naphtalite families have been recovered, we must continue on the course Moses sets for us."

Hosiah squinched his face. "Mother, some of the boys say their fathers think we should attack other villages in the Negev and move toward the hill country."

Mother raised her chin. "I am sure there is no lacking of other ideas, but Uncle Joshua says that God speaks to Moses personally. That is why we follow Moses."

⊙₰ℊ

IN CANAAN THREE DAYS LATER, NEAR GIBEON

"Finally, the morning breeze comes from the Great Sea, so there will be heavy dew."

Beside a dry wadi, Keshub found a circle of green under a willow tree that remembered water ran there in the past.

He leaned against the trunk with his sheep at his feet and drew his victuals bag from the folds of his girdle. Elbow to elbow Mamaa and Aunt Sabah had packed one for each family member while he had carried water. In this heat, fresh cool spring water was best. No hot drinks needed for anyone but Gran-mamaa.

He smiled at Gran-mamaa's sentiment of their weather that morning. "Only ripening grapes and greenware like this hot weather. Unlike people, grapes get sweeter, and wet clay dries faster."

Keshub loosened the drawstring on his bag and peered in. Their supply of last year's raisins ran out days ago, but the return of the westerly breeze marked the beginning of the season of ripening fruit.

Watching his little flock, a lump came to his throat. He tried to swallow the bitterness. The memory of Jho-ee, his favorite lamb, remained fresh. Keshub had always hated butchering day. This year it nearly broke his heart. In truth, hot weather served their needs in a third way. Mutton dried faster. But dried mutton would never taste the same.

He blinked several times as he scanned the horizon. A runner, probably from Jerusalem, appeared from the southeast keeping to the stream bed. In that terrible heat, a runner meant urgent news.

Keshub advanced to meet the messenger. "Peace, brother." He extended his water flask to the Amorite messenger about Ezak's age. Sweat poured down him.

Keshub waited while the young man took short gulps of water between large gulps of air. Finally, he spoke. "News from Arad. It is gone, destroyed."

"Arad?"

"Yes, in the Negev south of Hebron."

"What happened?"

"The Hebrews. They totally destroyed Arad's people and their villages three days ago." The runner managed to gasp. "Adoni-Zedek said, 'Be ready. They may be coming our way next. Where are you from, boy?"

"I am a shepherd of Gibeon."

"You must warn Gibeon and the other villages of Aijalon Valley."

"I will."

"I will go to Bethel and Ai from here."

The runner handed Keshub the water flask and turned, calling over his shoulder. "Molech must be appeased. Call upon him yourself for protection."

The messenger jogged toward Bethel. In the heat, speed could not be his goal. He had to conserve his strength to finish the task.

Keshub watched him disappear around the bend of the dry gulch before he whistled to his sheep and set out for home. Even though he had an important message, he pushed down the impulse to rush his flock. His wooly charges would succumb to the heat if they were urged even to a slow, wobbly trot.

He had no choice but to say over and over to himself Gran-baba's most often heard advice. Be patient.

That evening, instead of a fire in the center of the Ra-eef' court-yard, he helped set about several of Ranine's new lamps to combat the dark, moonless night. The courtyard paving stones had soaked up the sun's rays and even at twilight were still uncomfortable for bare feet or sitting. He drew up his knees and arranged his tunic beneath him to avoid direct contact with the stones.

In the afternoon he had delivered the message to Beeroth, the closest of the three other villages of Aijalon Valley. Knee to knee with his father, he waited to repeat the message from Adoni-Zedek at the fire circle.

When Baba asked him to speak, Keshub gulped and hesitated, but took a deep breath when Baba rested his rough right hand on Keshub's knee. "A runner sent by the king of Jerusalem brought a message about the Hebrews. Three days ago they attacked the city of Arad in the Negev south of Hebron. The runner said, 'They destroyed everything, the people and the villages. Be ready. The Hebrews may be coming our way next.' That is all."

Neighbor Agh-taan, keeper of the main spring, raised his voice above the clamor. "We do not know the intentions of the Hebrews, but this attack is practically at our back gate. Now is the time to do what we can."

"Hear, hear," boomed the deep voice of neighbor Ra-gar'. "I say the people of Gibeon need an army and a wall like Jerusalem's."

Sir Ghaleb answered. "Neighbor Ra-gar', we have considered these things. But in our case, a wall has not seemed feasible because our spring is at the base of the hill."

"What about an alliance with the Amorites?" Ra-gar' shot back.

Sir Ghaleb looked from neighbor Agh-taan to Baba before answering. "We have not thought such an alliance would benefit Gibeon."

Ra-gar', father of the village bully, challenged Sir Ghaleb with a snarl. "Explain to me why help from the king of Jerusalem would not be a good thing, esteemed advisor in all things military."

Keshub bristled at the disrespect in Ra-gar's voice. He turned toward his teacher.

The old soldier lowered his head and cleared his throat. "We have fewer than fifty men who could serve as soldiers, and not enough of the rest of us to feed and clothe an army. If we make an alliance with Jerusalem, Zedek might take all fifty men. Then leave us ten of his strong-arms to protect us and order us about. Would we be safer?"

Ra-gar' sputtered and huffed but had no reply.

Keshub squirmed on the hard limestone floor. *When Ra-gar' comes to the fireside, does Da-gan' guard the sheepfold?*

While other villagers responded, Keshub watched how the breeze played with the flickering flame of the lamps. They cast strange dark shadows on their rock walls.

Baba inserted a voice of calm and reason. "Gentlemen, we agree we cannot stand up against a horde of invaders. What we can do is strengthen our position while we negotiate."

"How do we do that?" came from Nabi, the old one.

"Like what?" Ra-gar' demanded.

"What do you have in mind, potter?" came from another neighbor.

"First of all, we must consider water. Sir Ghaleb and I have discussed how many containers of water would be required to survive an attack even for a few days. For three hundred people and maybe more, the measure of water is astounding. My brother Samir may have the solution to this problem. Samir?"

Keshub had never heard Uncle Samir speak in this group.

"Men, I have inspected the rock surface on the hilltop." He cleared his throat. "Above ein el-Beled. I believe it is solid limestone."

Neighbor Ra-gar' blurted. "Practically the whole area is limestone. What has that to do with anything?"

"Well, yes, neighbor, uhm-hum, you are correct. The point though is that the limestone is solid and will hold water. Uhm-hum. *If* we can bore a good size cistern into that rock, and I believe we can, we can store enough water for several days." Uncle Samir's throat bump wobbled up and then down.

Low murmurs of doubt circulated around the courtyard.

Uncle Samir rubbed his chin. "Most of us have some experience with boring into the bedrock on the western slope where our forefathers sleep. We all know it is slow and tedious work. But I think we can do it together, *if* everyone is willing to give a morning or afternoon. Just like we take a turn guarding our spring, we can take a turn digging a cistern."

Murmurs continued but on a different note.

"When do we start?" came from a voice near the gate.

"I will be at the summit above the spring at first light. To anyone who can, I say bring your tools. We can get organized and start tomorrow."

"Thank you, Samir." Neighbor Agh-taan clasped his hands in front of him. "Surely, all of us can spare one morning every few days, if not more, to do the work that will benefit us all. We will consider food stock on the summit at a time when we know we can have adequate water. For tonight, let us go to our homes and consider what each of us can do."

The clatter of small rocks tumbling down the stairs from the summit startled Keshub and the others around the fireless circle. Ezak emerged from the darkness of the stairs to the summit and skidded to a stop at the bottom of the steps next to a clay lamp. He had skinned knees and elbows, and bits of grass and leaves clung to his tunic.

Baba rushed to Ezak's side.

"Excuse me, Baba."

"What is it, son?"

"The Hebrews."

"The Hebrews?" Multiple voices repeated in alarm.

"Here?" Some asked.

Ezak shook his head. "No. They are gone! Turned away from the Negev—back to the desert!"

Chapter 14:
Everything Changed

ABOUT TWO WEEKS LATER

Keshub hopped from one foot to the other at the steps to the pottery yard waiting for cousin Micah to arrive. He greeted his double cousin with a soft shove. "Micah, it has been too long. How is the shepherding?"

"Shepherding is good. I still like it better than farming and milking cows every evening. Sheep are friendlier and not nearly as big. You are back in the pottery yard?"

"Yes, in the afternoons. We have several orders for storage jars. Mornings, I work at the cistern."

Lehab leaned in to whisper. "Does Haydak's arrival yesterday have anything to do with this family council?"

"Maybe." Keshub chirped in unison with Micah.

Baba quieted the family.

"Mother Amara, please take the seat of honor." Baba gave his arm to his mother to guide her to a hide-covered stool.

"Friend Haydak and brother Yaakoub, please join us."

The always-smiling Haydak ambled forward with the gait of one more comfortable riding a camel than walking. He carried a large oddly shaped bundle and placed it beside Gran-mamaa's stool.

Keshub winked at Micah, savoring the secret he had kept. Uncle Yaakoub swiped at his eyes with the back of his hand and joined Baba.

Keshub frowned. *Uncle Yaakoub? Why was he there?*

Baba nodded to his caravanner friend.

Haydak pointed to the odd bundle and addressed Gran-mamaa. "Good wife of Ra-eef', please accept my personal gift to you and grant me my request."

Haydak made a deep bow despite his immense girth. "From long years of association, I know you, dear woman, and your family to have a rare combination of compassion and uncommonly high degree of integrity. And you have within these walls a gem of womanhood in your granddaughter Isa'na."

Gasps and squeals of surprise from the women interrupted the old caravanner.

From the deep pockets of his caftan, Haydak produced a gold medallion set with a turquoise stone and hanging from a leather cord. "With deepest humility, I offer this dowry in behalf of my nephew Yah-ya bin-Krafkaar to you and her father Ishtaba for the hand of the lovely Isa'na."

The whole family took in a collective gasp. Keshub nodded his approval and elbowed Micah whose mouth gaped open.

Haydak held Gran-mamaa's right hand to place the medallion there. "I speak for us both when I say our highest honor would be to join our families and the lives of these two young people for all time."

Gran-mamaa placed her other hand firmly on the caravanner's and nodded.

Haydak raised his voice. "We have agreed to celebrate this union when my nephew and I return from Egypt."

Baba and Haydak exchanged a formal kiss to either cheek.

Micah gave a side-wise smirk and pointed Keshub back to the front as Uncle Yaakoub stepped forward.

Baba bowed low to Gran-mamaa and then to his brother Yaakoub.

Keshub's wrinkled brow shot a silent question back at Micah's broad smile.

Baba lowered himself to one knee and took his mother's and brother's hands. His voice cracked, and he ducked his head to swallow. "Mother-love, and brother Yaakoub, our lives are already eternally intertwined. The bond could not be stronger than it is. Together we have watched over our children and delighted to see them grow to be diligent and worthy of our trust, even into the next generations of Ra-eefs."

"Brother Yaakoub, on behalf of my first-born son, Ranine, please grant our request for the hand of your daughter Rachel—."

Keshub dropped his jaw. He turned to Micah while exclamations of surprise from the rest of the family interrupted Baba.

The courtyard filled with the smiting of hands and the women's trill of glee.

Keshub launched a playful fist to Micah's mid-section in silent acknowledgement of both their hard-kept secrets.

Baba extracted something from a bag behind Gran-mamaa's stool and continued as soon as there was quiet enough. He held two perfectly matched pottery ewers. He handed one to his brother and the other to Gran-mamaa. "Please accept this dowry made by my son's own hands to confirm our unbreakable bond and provide for him a help-mate for all time to come."

With tears in his eyes, Uncle Yaakoub took the water pitcher and extended his hand to help Baba stand.

As Keshub's father and uncle embraced, Keshub extended his left hand palm up in front of his cousins. Micah and Lehab stacked their hands on top, and each repeated with their other, palm down, before they gave their stacked hands a vigorous bounce.

Gran-mamaa's voice rang clear and strong as she called the four young people to her. The caravanner's bashful nephew produced an arm-length bough of cedar. Bowing to gran-mamaa, he presented her with the fragrant branch he had recently plucked from a cedar of Lebanon. Gran-mamaa caressed the aromatic reminder of her childhood home and brought it to her nose. Her wrinkled lips stretched across her teeth as she acknowledged Ya-yah's gift.

The couples knelt shoulder to shoulder before her while she pronounced a formal blessing on each couple in turn, waving the branch over their heads. "May you continually grow in respect for your mate and in dependence on one another. May you be fruitful and multiply."

Gran-mamaa's blessings brought on more high-pitched trills and cheers.

Baba tried to speak but could not get everyone's attention. Finally, he whistled like a shepherd, and the courtyard quieted. "We will celebrate Ranine and Rachel's wedding feast at the full moon after olive harvest. For now, let's eat."

Mother Danya and Aunts Raga and Sabah' produced reed trays filled with hand-held savories wrapped in flat bread or steamed in grape leaves along with melon slices and grapes from Ra-eef' gardens and vineyards.

Keshub pulled on Micah and Lehab's arms and nodded toward Gran-mamaa. "Let's see what is in the lumpy gift from friend Haydak."

He knelt at Gran-mamaa's feet and pressed her to open her gift.

She laughed and reached out to tousle his hair and his cousins'. "Yes, my beloved 'trio of trouble' grandsons. That is the name your gran-baba called you when you were still crawlers. Together you have always been the most curious, most energetic triple delight to your old gran-mamaa. We will open Haydak's surprise together."

Gran-mamaa turned to Lehab and Micah on her left. "You two, help me bring this bundle to the fore. Keshub, bring friend Haydak here so I can thank him."

Keshub returned leading the giver, who had been sampling the foods set out. "Here he is, Gran-mamaa."

Gran-mamaa leaned forward and felt of the strange bundle. "What have we here, my Bedu friend?"

The barter-master laughed. "Something to keep your idle hands from mischief, my dear woman, from a friend forever indebted to you."

Seeing that the bundle was tied closed with a single leather cord, Keshub spoke up. "May I untie it for you, Gran-mamaa?"

"Yes, do, Keshub, but do not break the cord. I can make use of it in any number of ways."

When the caravanner laughed loudly, he drew the attention of others to the opening of the peculiar gift. Keshub untied multiple knots and drew back to wind the cord into a round wad while his cousins loosened the covering. When the cloth unfolded onto the courtyard floor, several balls tumbled out and rolled in all directions.

Gasps of amusement erupted. The younger Ra-eef' children squealed with delight and scrambled over the courtyard to retrieve Gran-mamaa's odd gifts.

Keshub placed one in the lap of his bemused grandmother.

Since her hands saw better than her eyes, her expression immediately changed from a question to beaming delight. She lifted her friend's gift to her nose and announced, "Leather cord! And it has been dyed."

To her Bedu friend she asked, "Is it red?"

"Yes, madame. Your nose is keen indeed."

Gran-mamaa sparkled with laughter. "Old friend, what a wonderful gift. Plaiting I can do even in the dark."

She continued in a whisper heard only by the old trader and the three cousins nearest her. "With this gift you will brighten the darkness of what is perhaps my last winter."

While Haydak reached out a hand to his friend, Keshub looked at his cousins and shook his head. Surely Gran-mamaa could not know this.

Uncle Yaakoub urged his family to return home. They had a considerable walk by the light of the full moon. While the rest of the Ra-eefs dispersed to their quarters, the two newly-betrothed couples also parted to their regular quarters.

CR80

IN THE HEBREW CAMP EAST OF THE SALT SEA

"Eee-i-ah-agh!" A desperate scream came from neighbor Elishama's tent next door.

Hosiah and his mother jumped.

More screams followed. Some female voices, some male.

Hosiah looked up from the Senet game board he held in one hand. His other hand paused in mid-air with the ivory dice shaped like the pyramids of Egypt. He shuddered, lip trembling. "Is it the snakes, Mother?"

"Very likely, son." Mother wrung her hands in fear and worry. "There are so many snakes in this place. So many families are tending their loved ones or in mourning, we cannot move on."

Mother shuddered and did what she always did. She turned to practical matters. "I must go to them. I will take the manna scrambled with rosemary and dried mutton I made for supper. The whole family will be in shock and fear of what comes next. They will need our help."

"Yes, Mother." Hosiah put away his only possession that belonged to his father when he was a boy. "I will bring water for them. They will need more when the fever comes on."

"Thank you, Hosiah. That is thoughtful. Where is Elkanah?"

"He went to see Uncle Joshua at the tent of meeting. He will be back before supper."

Mother changed to her new apron. "Good. Get the water, but be careful. The snakes are almost the same color as the ground. You cannot be too careful."

"Yes, Mother, I will." After a pause, "Mother?"

"What, son?" She took up the dish of manna.

"What will we have for supper?"

"We have plenty of manna bread left from this morning. We

102

can have a little honey with it, too."

Mother started toward the neighbors' tent where low moans of grief and anguish had replaced the screams.

Later that afternoon his mother returned. "Hosiah, our friend Elishama already has fever. Like your father, he knew his time was near because of what happened thirty-eight years ago. If he lives until morning, he will not be able to move his arms or legs."

"Where was the snake, Mother?"

"Behind their ox cart in the shadow of their tent. The snake bit their son Enan, too, when he tried to kill it."

Mother explained her plan. "I will cook for them until Mrs. Elishama can leave their bedsides. I will bring home portions for our supper. You may eat the manna fresh from the hillside with the morning dew as you tend your sheep. Adding a fresh rosemary leaf would be tasty. I have seen much of the 'crown of the hill' growing in this area."

"What about Enan, Mother?"

"He got less of the snake's venom, son. They are keeping him still and watching him carefully."

"Mother!" Elkanah shouted and waved as he neared. "Uncle Joshua said God answered Moses' prayer for a cure! It should be ready by tomorrow evening. Uncle Joshua summoned the bronze workers and the carpenters to do the work."

"Bronze workers? Carpenters?" Mother shook her head.

Hosiah shrugged. "How can they help?"

Elkanah turned palms up. "Uncle Joshua said the carpenters will craft a tall wooden pole and attach a bronze likeness of the snakes on it. Moses will erect the snake's likeness in the middle of the camp for all to see. Anyone who has been bitten must turn and look at the symbol of the serpent lifted high. Anyone who does will be healed."

Hosiah stood with mouth open. He could not process the logic of the cure.

Elkanah threw his arms wide. "Uncle Joshua says to tell everyone. 'Look and live!'"

Chapter 15:
A Father's Anger

SEVERAL DAYS LATER

Keshub gripped two handles of a round-bottomed gufa filled with limestone rubble. Afraid the reed basket's handles might break from the weight, he shifted the gufa onto his forearms and arched his back for balance.

"Boy!" Ra-gar' boomed another demand. The village bully's father and Neighbor Agh-taan worked thigh-deep inside the hollowed-out limestone bowl that would become a cistern for Gibeon. "Bring me the water bag. I am parched. And be quick about it."

Keshub emptied the gufa at the rubble pile and pivoted. Without missing a stride he sprinted to the goat-skin bag hanging from an ancient olive tree.

Inside the depression, Ra-gar' stood scowling. One hand on his hip, his other hung limp with a basalt stone hammer.

"Pour the water, boy, so I can drink it from down here."

"Yes, sir." Keshub removed the stopper from the pour spout and grasped two handles, which on the goat had been legs. Keeping one foot on ground level, he stepped down onto a narrow ledge.

He extended the water bag at arm's length and poured a small stream for the surly neighbor. Every muscle strained to keep the water steady for the gaping mouth of dirty yellow teeth.

Keshub wavered as his foot began to slip. He tensed every muscle to keep his arms high and the water stream steady.

The hateful eyes of the bully's father darkened and his scowl deepened.

Keshub's sandaled foot slipped off the ledge. The water jerked aside to douse Ra-gar's head and shoulders. Keshub flailed the air, and the bag flopped to the floor of the rocky depression. Ra-gar's huge chest broke Keshub's fall. The demanding neighbor dropped his hammer and howled.

Stunned, Keshub sat up at Ra-gar's feet and reached for the bag still pouring out water.

"You worthless Hivite." Ra-gar' lashed out and landed a backhand blow to the right side of Keshub's head.

Keshub reeled from the force of the blow, but scrambled to pick up the bag before more water wasted.

Neighbor Agh-taan moved between Ra-gar' and Keshub to prevent more blows.

From where he rested on the rim, the old-timer Nabi, intervened with a croaky voice. "That is enough, Ra-gar'. The boy is not your slave. Or your son."

Keshub clambered to the rim of the soon-to-be cistern and sat for a moment. When he lifted his eyes, the horizon swayed. He lowered his eyes and blinked rapidly before he tried another look at the horizon he loved. The distant hills stood steady as they should. A few days ago from this same vantage point he had identified a group of refugees arriving. All ages, they had walked and carried heavy burdens. They were families from east of the Jordan River, fleeing in fear of the Hebrews.

Today, Keshub squinted and spied travelers again in the hazy distance. Immediately alert, he summoned Sir Ghaleb's teaching on how to identify approaching visitors.

He rose slowly, with his head still throbbing, and called down into the cistern. "Neighbor Agh-taan, we have visitors again. Important ones, I think. These visitors are not like the refugees who came and relieved me of my new linen tunic, sir. You may want to see for yourself."

While Agh-taan scrambled out, Keshub described what he saw. "These travelers are coming quickly. One is mounted on a donkey. The other four appear to be soldiers carrying spears. The bronze tips catch the sunlight. I think they are not wearing armor, maybe leather doublets."

Neighbor Agh-taan huffed and put his hands on his hips. "Good eyes, Keshub. You are right. Soldiers carrying only small packs, means a short trek. Or they expect hospitality. They come from the direction of Jerusalem. A man riding a donkey has to be a rich man or an official."

Keshub squinted. Could the rider be his friend Zed's father?

Agh-taan picked up his tools and tool bag. "Since there are only five of them, they are not an attacking force. Perhaps they have a peaceful purpose."

"Should I run to tell my father, sir?"

"Yes, do. Tell him I will meet him at the spring."

"Yes, sir." Keshub returned the bag to the olive tree and trotted more slowly than usual down the trail to home.

He crossed the courtyard and mounted the steps to the pottery yard one at a time since his head still hurt.

"Baba, we have visitors again, probably from Jerusalem. Neighbor Agh-taan asked you to meet him at the spring."

Later that evening, Keshub formed a scoop with a torn piece of warm flatbread wrapped around the end of his index finger. He held the bread in place by his thumb and middle finger. Ready to dip into the field bean stew, he gazed at Baba's right hand. Every male of the household older than ten harvests watched to take their first dip of stew.

Instead, Baba paused with his hand and bread scoop in mid-air.

"Ranine, what have you done to your hand?"

Keshub returned his hand to waiting position on his knee.

Ranine shrugged. "The chisel slipped, and I scraped my knuckles on the wall of the chamber." He worked part of every day to enlarge a chamber for himself and his bride at the back of their house where it nestled into the hillside.

"Perhaps Keshub can be spared to help you in the afternoons. After supper, show your hand to your mother. She will want to treat that cut with an ointment."

"Yes, sir."

Keshub's eyes returned to Baba's hand, his own hand poised and waiting.

"Keshub, neighbor Agh-taan told me what happened this morning at the cistern."

Still holding his flatbread, Keshub felt the right side of his face with the back of his hand and winced at the soreness. "Uh, uh, I think I was clumsy, Baba."

"An accident, son. Both neighbor Agh-taan and the old-timer said you are doing a fine job. Ra-gar' is your elder. You must continue to show respect to him even if his actions show no respect for others." Baba finally jabbed his bread into the stew.

Keshub followed Baba's example, observing the custom of eating in silence, but winced with every chew. Before the last swipe of stew, Baba rose from the dinner mat and exited the courtyard through the main gate. Baba did not return until several guests arrived from the village. Among them was neighbor Ra-gar' with a red face.

Soon, Baba took his seat. "Neighbor Agh-taan, everyone wants to know about our visitors from Jerusalem. Please tell us what you learned."

Baba's voice sounded strained and his words clipped. *Is Baba angry?*

"Friends and neighbors," the chief keeper of the spring of Gibeon lifted his voice. "An emissary from the king of Jerusalem came today. He said Adoni-Zedek himself will visit us soon. He will extend an offer of an alliance. Several other city-states around us have already joined."

Agh-taan directed his gaze at Sir Ghaleb. "He asks our young men to volunteer in his army. He said early recruits have the advantage to advance more quickly in rank."

"Did he have news about the Hebrews?" A neighbor from the village whom Keshub had worked with on the cistern voiced their greatest concern.

"Yes. He said the Hebrew multitude has avoided contact with the Moabites and the Ammonites on the east side of the Salt Sea by taking a trail on their eastern border."

"Where are they heading, Agh-taan?" another villager asked.

"Rumors persist they plan to invade our Canaan land. But according to the emissary from Jerusalem, Adoni-Zedek is confident the Hebrews will be stopped before they cross the Jordan River."

Keshub rubbed at the ache in his jaw while Agh-taan continued.

"Sihon, king of Heshbon, is a distant Amorite cousin to Zedek. Sihon claims the land north of the Moabites along the east bank of the River. The Hebrews, if they intend to come here, will have to go through Sihon's territory."

"One Amorite is worth three Hebrews in any battle on any day." Ra-gar' boasted, though his voice was not so bombastic as usual.

No one commented, but Baba's jaw hardened, and he glared at the braggart.

The end of neighbor Agh-taan's nose twitched when he spoke. "Zedek thinks the villages of Aijalon should join the alliance with him and the kings of Hebron, Jarmuth, Lachish, and Eglon. He says we will all be stronger. If one is attacked, all will come together to defeat the enemy."

Agh-taan rubbed his nose. "The emissary asked that we have an answer ready when the king comes at the full moon."

Keshub jerked his head up to detect Ranine and Baba's reactions. That was the same time they had planned for Rachel and Ranine's wedding celebration.

The old-timer cleared his throat noisily. "How many stout young soldiers will he bring to negotiate a treaty?"

Agh-taan chuckled. "The emissary said he will travel with about twenty men and will require our best lodging for himself and four others. His soldiers will camp nearby."

He pointed his twitching nose at Baba. "Neighbor Ishtaba will provide for Zedek and his two servants since the Ra-eef' guest lodging is the largest in Gibeon. Who of you can offer hospitality to Zedek's other two officials?"

Ra-gar' curled his lips into a wicked smile that showed his yellow teeth and blurted out. "I am sure the good men of Jerusalem would prefer to spend the night in the home of an Amorite, someone of their own kind. I will gladly give lodging to them all."

Agh-taan, whose family had lived next to the spring of Gibeon for five generations, accepted Ra-gar's offer. "Thank you, neighbor. Hospitality for Zedek is already decided. You will house his two officials."

The old-timer dropped his head to hide his mirth. Ra-gar' grimaced but did not argue further. At Baba's nod, Keshub tapped Ra-mi' and Lehab on the shoulder to go to their rooftop sleeping quarters. His older brothers stayed at the fire circle since they were counted among the men now.

As they left the fireside, Keshub heard Sir Ghaleb take up the discussion. "Men of Gibeon, thanks to everyone's contribution of time, tools, and strength, we are making progress with a cistern on the summit. A parapet along the east rim is also progressing...."

As they climbed the stairs, Keshub whispered to Ra-mi' and Lehab, "Did you hear that?"

"What?" Lehab asked. He slept on the roof with his cousins now.

"The full moon. That is when Ranine and Rachel will come together now that they are betrothed. The king of Jerusalem is coming at the same time. What will we do about that?"

Ra-mi' and Lehab shrugged.

After light snores came from Lehab, Ra-mi' confided to Keshub.

"I heard Baba speaking to Ra-gar' outside the courtyard this evening. I was bent over emptying the wash basin onto Gran-mamaa's rose bush beside the guest quarters. They did not know I was there."

"What did Baba say?"

"He said, 'Ra-gar', if I ever hear of your striking Keshub again, I will not be responsible for my actions. You will regret it to your last breath.'

"Then Ra-gar' said, 'You threaten me, Hivite?' And Baba said really quietly but angrier sounding than I have ever heard him, 'Not a threat—a promise.'"

Keshub marveled at what he had never thought possible. "Baba promised Ra-gar' a fight?"

08&90

IN THE HEBREW CAMP EAST OF THE SALT SEA

Hosiah whispered to himself. "Longsuffering wears thin on Mrs. Elishama."

"What did you say Hosiah? I thought I heard you say something." Their neighbor's son roused from his un-tired sleep.

"Nothing, friend. I am too accustomed to talking to my sheep and expecting no response."

Enan rolled his head on his pillow. "Oh, to be on the hillside with my sheep again, Hosiah. Sorry lad that I am, I did not find it pleasant when I went out six dawns of seven. I should have been grateful to be out of hearing of my mother's infernal yammering." Enan tried to sit up.

Hosiah gave him a hand. He stayed with Enan while Mrs. Elishama took a short break from caring for him. Enan got less of the serpent's venom than his father. Mr. Elishama had died the next day before Moses raised the bronze serpent on a pole near the tabernacle. Enan's condition had not progressed as rapidly.

Enan's mother returned and began the moment she saw her son. "Enan, you are awake. Please, son, listen to the mother who bore you. I beg you, look at the serpent and live. Do not cause your poor mother to waste away and die of grief for having lost both my men."

"I am all right, Mother."

Mrs. Elishama clasped both hands to her breast. "No, son, you are not well. You have not suffered the rapidly progressing symptoms of the poison like your father did. But as surely as I am standing here, you are growing weaker before my eyes every day."

"Mother, I will soon be better. I can do this. Hand me a dipper of water, please, Hosiah."

Hosiah held a gourd dipper to his neighbor's lips while Enan's claw-like hands tried to help.

Mrs. Elishama hurried on. "No, you are not getting better. Listen to your poor mother for once. You are slowly getting worse. You are dying in your stubbornness just as surely as your father did."

"I said I am all right, Mother. Leave me alone."

"Son, I cannot leave you alone. How can I stand by and not speak? My cousin's neighbor was healed this morning. They were afraid he would die before morning. Please, son. Listen to me. Look and live!" Mrs. Elishama knelt sobbing with bowed head, hands folded in prayer.

"Look and live? Nonsense! What can one look do?"

Mrs. Elishama wailed her grief, sobbing and swaying side to side.

"All right," Enan shouted. "I do not believe it will help me, but I will look to stop your continual nagging every blessed day."

Hosiah handed Enan his crutch and helped his friend struggle to his feet.

Enan hobbled to the opening of their tent. "See! I am looking. Are you satisfied, Mother! I am looking at a useless bronze snake. On a wooden pole. I do not believe such nonsense can heal me, but I am looking!"

Enan stared at the back of his red and swollen hand where two closely spaced wounds festered. "I am looking ... at my hand ... that has had no feeling in it ... for days."

Enan whispered, and his eyes took on a new brightness. "I have ... feeling in my hand again! And the wounds ... are shrinking before my eyes."

He flexed his fingers open and closed. "Mother, I have feeling in my hand. And my feet, too!"

He dropped the wooden crutch. "I do not need the crutch! I am healed!"

"Thanks...be to God." Enan sank to his knees. "I was stubborn. I called the cure a flimsy superstition. I thought I could get better on my own. I did not think it possible a mere look could help, but when I looked, God had mercy on me and healed me."

Mrs. Elishama's pleadings turned to praise. "Who is like You, O Lord, working wonders before our eyes?"

Enan bowed his head. "Oh what a wretched...sinner I am. Oh what an awesome God we have!"

Chapter 16:
Baba and His Guest

A fortnight later Keshub scratched his shoulder and squirmed inside the stiff new flax cloth garment.

"Keshub, stand still." Mother's dark eyebrows dipped inward, the sure sign of a short supply of patience today. "I have no time for your fidgeting."

"Yes, Mother, but it itches." Flecks of rough flax stem embedded in the homemade cloth tortured him.

"Never mind the itching. Hold out your arms." Through fish-bone pins held on one side of her mouth by pursed lips, Mother mumbled. "We have no time for scratching. You have to wear Ra-mi's tunic for the king today since yours is on its way to Sidon on the back of a refugee. Ranine's wedding is in two days and you will have to wear your own."

Keshub extended his arms at shoulder level, and tried not to squirm within the loathed new garment.

Mother loosely outlined his body with pins in the coarse cloth.

"Your father said the refugees had more need of your other new tunic than we did. He thinks it kindly of them to leave their tattered old tunic. I am not so certain nor as generous as he is. Ouch!" Mother inserted her finger in her mouth to lick where the pin had pierced.

"Your gran-mamaa will stitch along these pins, although it seems she sees less every day. I would do it, but there are so many other things I need to do. You must warmly embrace her and kiss her pin-pricked fingers in thanks."

"Yes, Mother," in sing-song fashion.

"Nothing would please her more. Now slip this over your head and watch out for the pins."

"Ouch!...Ouch. Ugh. I am glad that is done." He put his old tunic back on. "I would rather shovel limestone rubble all day than be fitted for new clothes." He mumbled as he turned to go to work on the summit.

Mother Danya called after him with a smile in her voice. "Keshub, your gran-baba said 'You will find in life, you do not always get what you want.'"

He waved good-bye without looking back. "Yes, Mother-dear."

In mid-afternoon Keshub swept rubble in the new chamber his brother Ranine prepared for his bride. Low murmurs came from his parents' chamber nearby where Baba washed off the evidence of the raw material of his trade. *Does Baba hate a new tunic as much as I do?*

Keshub overheard a snippet of their conversation as he lugged a gufa of rubble out. "I will not pretend to be anything but a humble potter before this beast of a man. In truth, the likes of him should be...."

Keshub questioned the force of the words he heard. "A beast of a man"? *Adoni-Zedek? What did Baba know of the king that would cause him to describe the man so?*

Finally, the twilight hour arrived. Keshub's mouth watered at the aroma of roasted lamb stuffed with rosemary sprigs while he scratched his shoulder with one hand. Ra-mi's new tunic itched him no less than his own. He cupped one hand over the lighted wheat straw to carry fire to each pottery lamp nestled in their niches in the wall.

Keshub had not seen Lehab and his family since mid-day when they set out to Uncle Yaakoub's house for an over night visit. *Where were his brothers?*

"Our guests are arriving, son. Open the gate for them." Mamaa retreated behind the kitchen wall, raising her scarf to her head.

Keshub pushed the courtyard gate open, stepped aside and held it.

Baba entered first, followed by two stout soldiers who positioned themselves on either side of the gate. They stood as statues.

"Welcome to our humble home, sir." Baba turned with a slight bow to bid his guests enter.

Adoni-Zedek, with close-cropped beard and mustache covering fleshy jowls, strode in clasping his leather girdle with one hand. The index finger pointed proudly to its large bronze buckle studded with turquoise stones. His mantle of scarlet draped over one muscular shoulder. Leather greaves covered his thick hairy shins to the knees. His tunic was fine linen.

Keshub eyed the king's tunic. No little brown flecks in the finely woven fabric. He tried not to scratch at his own. The king's two other servants entered behind him and stood against the wall next to the statues.

Neighbor Agh-taan, in his own new tunic and hardly scratching at all, led the local delegation of Sir Ghaleb with his bronze sword at his side, and Uncle Yaakoub wearing his usual smile of good humor. No doubt, the family would hear the retelling of the visit from the king of Jerusalem until they all had the tale memorized.

Keshub closed the gate behind him and stood between the two soldiers. While they stared straight ahead, he inspected the hilt of a bronze sword in its sheath next to him. *What would it feel like to hold a real sword?*

The king of Jerusalem swaggered around the Ra-eef' perimeter, head held high, while Baba and the other men stood waiting. With one arched eyebrow, the king looked down his broad nose at his surroundings.

Keshub remembered the first time he met bin-Zedek, the king's shepherd son. Zed had thrown back his shoulders in much the same way.

The king completed the circuit of the courtyard and removed his cloak, extending it without looking. The younger of the two statues, about Eskie's age, lurched to receive the scarlet cloak before it fell to the limestone floor.

Zedek's first words were, "Surely your home belies your claim of poverty, sir."

With a slight nod, Baba directed him to Gran-mamaa Amara standing at the half wall. Gran-mamaa stepped forward with head draped, holding the family's best pottery ewer, Ranine's wedding gift. She stared, chin up and eyes wide open, in Zedek's direction and began pouring. Isa'na, with covered head bowed and downcast eyes, held a pottery basin beneath the king's extended hands to catch the water.

Keshub sucked in a quick breath. Something evil burned in Zedek's eyes when he eyed Keshub's sister.

Keshub had not understood why his friend Zed feared his father, nor why Baba had called the king "a beast of a man." Now, he too, feared the man for the evil he saw simmering in those eyes.

Perhaps Baba saw the look also, for immediately he called Zedek to his place of honor at the straw mat on the courtyard floor. Baba snapped his fingers and nodded his head to Keshub indicating Gran-mamaa's stool.

Keshub grabbed the stool and hastened to position it beside Baba at the place of honor.

The king sat alone on his lofty perch while Baba invited his other guests to sit on the grass mat. The common-folk custom of sitting on the floor proved the inappropriateness of the king's short tunic and greave-clad lower extremities

How will the king reach the food? And when will the soldiers eat?
Keshub rubbed at his shoulder and took a place opposite the king.

Mother brought a small bowl and placed it before the king. Gran-mamaa followed with their best large pottery bowl filled with the same goodness for all the others. After he passed the bread, Baba cleared his throat and began eating silently. Zedek with one eyebrow arched high waited for his older servant to pick up the king's bowl.

The scrawny manservant, who was perhaps Uncle Samir's age, tore a piece of flatbread and took a small bite of stew from the king's bowl. He considered the piece of roasted lamb for a moment and sunk his teeth into the crusty flesh. Both eyebrows shot up. With cheeks bulging, he chewed slowly, tilting his head and nodding to the king.

Keshub understood and smiled. Mamaa surely knew how to season a roasted lamb. The king attacked his food. When the bowl was empty, Mother replaced it with another full one.

Keshub's mouth hung open. *Two bowls? Full? Whoa. Kings eat well.*

Across the mat, Zedek licked his fingers, wiped his mouth with the back of his hand, and un-wedged a sliver of mutton from his front teeth with his fingernail. He kept his eyes on his bowl and chewed noisily, except for a moment when Mother served him. Isa'na had not appeared to serve again.

When supper ended, Baba directed the men to the fire circle while Keshub swung the courtyard gate open. Baba personally greeted the men of Gibeon and several from other villages in Aijalon Valley.

Zedek's two officials arrived with neighbor Ra-gar'. The Amorite of Gibeon strutted among the Ra-eef' guests introducing his own guests in fine linen caftans and leather girdles.

Ra-gar' bowed low when he met the king of Jerusalem.

Baba, without words, caught Keshub's eye and nodded toward Gran-mamaa's stool.

Keshub trotted to obey and placed the stool beside Baba on the right.

"Take your yoke and jars to the spring. Get more water for the livestock and guest house."

"Yes, sir." He rounded the half wall to the kitchen and found Mamaa sitting leaning against the other side. He had suspected Baba's order held more than a need for water.

"Keshub, after you check the guest house and livestock pen for water, take a load up the back steps of the pottery yard. Leave the water there and take the back trail to join your brothers in the grape arbor above the orchard."

Baba's guests settled around the fire, as Keshub crossed to the courtyard gate, grabbed his cloak from a peg, and exited with the yoke across his shoulders. Two soldiers stood on guard outside the gate with two more guarding access to his family's guesthouse nearby. Across the caravan trail, Zedek's other soldiers camped near the small spring. A lamb roasted on a spit over their fire.

The evening star shone bright in waning twilight as Keshub filled the water jars on his yoke. He lugged the familiar load up the back steps to the pottery yard. Easing the water jars onto the floor, he proceeded up the rough back trail to the first grape arbor above the kitchen garden level. In shadow he paused to listen to the men below and pulled his cloak close to keep out the chill.

Neighbor Agh-taan queried the king who towered above his seated audience. "If you provide training and housing for an army for Gibeon, where would such an army be trained and housed and how many would be needed?"

Others had questions as well. The king of Jerusalem became red in the face. He sputtered his answers. He paced back and forth. Finally, Zedek stopped his pacing and squared his feet and shoulders with hands on his hips.

In the grape arbor, Keshub held his breath.

Zedek snarled with gritted teeth and spat out his words. "You country people obviously have your own odd way of doing things, but let me tell you this."

The king stabbed a finger in Baba's direction and bellowed. "You are but men. We of Jerusalem have a far superior force behind us. We have Molech as our god. He is a consuming fire. The sooner you recognize your weak condition and your need of his protection, the better off you will be."

In the arbor, Keshub looked up at the North Star overhead and whispered aloud. "Baba is not afraid of the Amorite god."

Baba replied in a strong but even tone. "Thank you, king of Jerusalem, for your counsel. We of Aijalon Valley will reply to your offer when we can reply with one voice. Please enjoy your night's stay in our humble guest quarters. I ask your man-servants to take one of the lamps from the wall to light your way as you go."

Zedek jerked his head as if he had been struck. He was dismissed. After a slight hesitation, he pivoted and stomped across the courtyard. He grabbed his scarlet cloak from one of his servants while the other hastily opened the gate so Zedek could stride through without hesitation.

Ra-gar's guests also rose and followed behind the king of Jerusalem. The cloakless servant exited behind Zedek's men—but came back and grabbed the lamp, bobbing his head in humility. In the arbor, Keshub silently clapped his hands to see Adoni-Zedek's exit with face the color of raw liver. Uncle Yaakoub fastened the gate closed behind the king and his entourage.

Neighbor Ra-gar' rose to his feet and blustered. "Potter, you have dismissed the great Amorite king of Jerusalem!"

Baba replied in an even tone as the full moon arrived on the horizon. "He is a man who proclaims to be king of Jerusalem. How great he is, I do not know yet. My father Ra-eef' would say, 'The measure of a man is not in how tall he is or how bold he is, but in the depth of his wisdom and integrity.'"

Neighbor Ra-gar' stomped out.

Uncle Yaakoub had the gate open by the time Ra-gar' got there.

"Keshub." A hoarse whisper from the darkness made him jump.

"What?"

"Up here."

No mistaking Eskie's voice. He rose to follow.

Eskie laid a finger on his lips and led the way up the stairs before whispering. "Baba thought it would be unwise for Zedek to see how many men of soldiering age live here. Mother provided sumptuously for us as well. Otherwise the aroma of roasted lamb would have been our un-doing."

At the upper grape arbor, Keshub joined all his brothers, and Ra-mi' handed him his bedroll. By the light of the full moon, he followed the length of the sandal-shaped summit to arrive at the threshing floor on the west end. Keshub flipped open his bedroll, stretched his chest and arms, and soaked up the amazing brightness of the moon and stars. He had been excited to meet the powerful king of Jerusalem, but the king's eyes had left Keshub strangely unsettled.

No wonder his friend Zed was afraid. Now he understood a little better why the son of Adoni-Zedek wept for a dead brother and for himself.

Can Plain Zed escape the evil burning in his father's eyes?

Chapter 17:
First Trip to Jerusalem

TWO DAYS AFTER THE KING'S VISIT

Keshub inserted two sturdy cedar rods through the frame of Gran-mamaa's stool to make a carrier for her.

Mamaa called from behind the half wall of the kitchen.

"Yes, Mother?"

"Is Gran-mamaa's stool ready?"

"Yes, Mother."

"I am almost out of water here. Go to the spring, son, so we will have water for tomorrow morning, and hurry. We are almost ready to walk to Uncle Yaakoub's house for the wedding. Put on your cloak. It is cold."

"I do not need my cloak, Mother. I am fine."

"The wind is increasing, son, and the air is getting colder. Wear ... your cloak."

"Yes, Mother."

When he neared ein-el-Beled, Da-gan' leaned over the water

filling his own jars. He wondered again, What is Da-gan's problem?

Keshub spoke before Da-gan' knew he was there,. "So, your mamaa ran out of water before suppertime, too."

Da-gan's shoulders and back muscles tensed beneath his crudely patched homespun tunic. Without turning, he spoke in a low monotone. "No. She ran off years ago with a caravanner."

"Oh." Keshub did not know what else to say. "I am sorry."

Da-gan' rose from the spring with his water jar. Without meeting Keshub's eyes, he shouldered past, chin high, jaw set. "Yes. Me too, high and mighty dirt stomper." He strode away—cloakless.

With jaw dropped, Keshub followed Da-gan' with his eyes. The name-caller disappeared among the stone houses that clung to the ledges of Gibeon's hill. Keshub fingered his woolen cloak. No wonder Da-gan' always seemed angry.

***

By moonlight Keshub and his cousins placed their bedrolls together on the threshing floor.

Eskie, Brother Number Three, rubbed his stomach and stretched slowly. "Well, well, boys, tonight Ranine and Rachel were married, and we had roasted lamb for the second time in three days!"

Keshub turned onto his side to face the warmth of the fire and pillowed his head on his hands. "When will Haydak and Yah-ya return?"

Ezak tucked his arms under his blanket and drew the edge up to his chin. "What will the next report of the Hebrews be? Yesterday, Uncle Yaakoub and I talked to Mr. Endo at market. He said the Hebrews are negotiating a peaceable passage through the territory of the Amorites east of the Jordan. According to Endo, Sihon king of Heshbon says he will not negotiate."

No one replied.

Keshub tucked the end of his blanket snuggly at his feet before he pulled the wool to his eyes. He stared into Ra-mi's brave little fire dancing and dodging in tune with the wind. *There are too many changes. Too many serious things to consider.*

⋈⋈⋈

Two days later, Keshub returned from Sir Ghaleb's school skipping down the stairs from Gibeon's summit with Lehab at his side. Baba, Uncle Yaakoub, and Ezak sat at the fire circle deep in conversation—in mid-afternoon.

When Keshub reached the last step, Baba swept his arm toward a vacancy at the circle across from Uncle Yaakoub. "Keshub, we need to talk to you. Lehab, go to your chores, please."

Standing in the place Baba indicated, Keshub tried to read their expressions. "Me, Baba?"

"Yes. Sit down, please."

"Yes, sir."

Uncle Yaakoub leaned back and smiled. "Keshub, I need another helper to go to market in Jerusalem."

Ezak nodded.

Baba filled in details. "Son, you will spend the night at Yaakoub's house and return home tomorrow evening. Get your bedroll and help load the donkeys."

***

In the gray light of morning, Keshub's breath made smoke in the chill air. He thrilled to follow his uncle and brother up the hill on the southeast rim of Aijalon Valley. He gazed backward a moment at Gibeon with wood smoke rising. The halter rope on the donkey beside him tugged at his hand. How often had he gazed this direction at the stack of mountains against the horizon? Today he would pass by the same mountains to enter Amorite territory and see Jerusalem at last.

The heads of three Ra-eef' donkeys bobbed up the hill before him, laden with pottery packed in coarse reed baskets with wheat straw padding. He quickened his pace going down hill into

Amorite territory on the other side.

Along the way, other travelers joined them from side trails that led to neighboring villages—ones he had barely heard about. Some carried their goods on their backs and some led their own donkeys. As their little procession grew, Keshub's excitement grew. *Do all roads lead to fabled Jerusalem?*

At mid-morning they crested the last peak, and sunshine bathed Mt. Moriah nestled among other mountains. He could not take his eyes off the wall that circled Jerusalem on the southeastern slope. Much larger than Gibeon, the Amorite stronghold spilled down the slope like the golden silk scarf the caravanner from Persia draped around his neck last summer.

A line of travelers, including himself, plodded down the slope bearing burdens or driving livestock. Behind him sheep bleated. Below him, a basket of recently harvested olives swayed with the gait of its owner.

The stream of travelers crossed the wadi between the two mountains, and ended where Ezak pointed. "See Gihon Spring and the marketplace below the city gate?"

At the wadi in the Hinnom Valley below Jerusalem, Uncle Yaakoub stopped at a pool. "Haloo there, friend. I have my young nephew with me today. He will stay with our donkeys when we bring them back, since your son is no longer with you. That is, if you are willing to keep our donkeys as usual."

"That is good, friend. Without my son to help me, I am limited in how many donkeys I can lodge here."

"I understand. Keshub is a good worker. He will tote water or whatever you need."

"Ah, you are a kind man, friend."

"Well, I have been leaving Ra-eef' donkeys in your care for many years. It will be good to help. How is your son? Have you seen him since he joined Zedek's army?"

"He did not join by choice, friend. He was healthy when he came home for a short time a few days ago—and hungry. A soldier's life is hard. I do not see him often and worry much."

Uncle Yaakoub waved good-bye. "I will send the donkeys back with my nephews after we unload."

The man raised his voice. "And for your kindness, you will pay nothing today. I insist."

On the dusty road up to the market near Gihon Spring, Keshub's head tilted back to take in the wall that loomed over them. From the top of the wall Zedek's soldiers paced. Armed with bows over their shoulders and spears in hand, they peered down on the market and the arriving crowd. Some of them looked no older than his brother Eskie.

At the marketplace teeming with activity, Keshub halted behind Ezak and Uncle Yaakoub who greeted their friend Endo. The little old man with a scraggly beard waved them toward a wide space against a low wall beside a small wooden cart. Endo greeted his uncle as an old friend. Perhaps everyone his uncle met soon became an old friend.

When his uncle introduced him to Endo, Keshub found himself enveloped in the man's arms and cloak that smelled of wood smoke and body odor.

"Thank you, thank you for sending Zed to me." One kiss to either cheek would not do. The old man kissed Keshub on both cheeks multiple times.

The little old man's cloak, fashioned from mostly drab homespun patches, had a few squares of finely spun cloth dyed henna red or golden acorn brown. Some squares bore embroidered embellishment.

Ezak came to his rescue. "Keshub, help me unload here."

Keshub gladly pulled himself away. Soon Ra-eef' wares stood displayed in even rows, taller vessels near the wall, on a cowhide on the limestone floor of the market. Keshub followed Ezak against the flow of travelers to return the pack animals to the liveryman.

"I am Keshub, sir. Do you want me to fill the water troughs first?"

"Yes. And keep the pen clean, too. The dung heap is yonder, and the jars and yoke are beside the trough."

Keshub draped his cloak on the livery fence and took up the yoke with Ra-eef' water jars attached. All morning, he alternated between the two tasks given him by the livery owner. He had tended enough animals in the Ra-eef' livestock pen that he had no expectation for the trough to stay full or the dung to stay picked up. At mid-day someone called his name.

Holding an oak pitchfork full of fresh dung, he turned. His friend, the scrawny son of the king of Jerusalem, leaned on his forearms against the livery fence.

"Zed! I hoped I would meet you again. Wait there."

Propping his pitchfork against the fence, Keshub ran to the livery owner where he repaired a halter near the road. Keshub raised his voice to be heard above the roar of a sled scraping by loaded with heavy timbers and pulled by six stout horses.

"Sir, may I take my lunch now?" When the liveryman agreed, he jogged to his cloak and threw it over one shoulder. He pointed with his thumb toward a rock overlooking the wadi.

Zed shouted above the roar behind them.

"What are you doing here, Keshub?"

"My uncle and brother are at market today—next to Mr. Endo. The liveryman's son is now in your father's army. He needed our help, and we needed him for our pack animals. So I am working here today. What about you?"

"I returned my sheep to the fold. Now, I am useless for the rest of the day. No one wants to hire me because I am the king's son, but the king ignores me. My soldier brothers say I will never make a soldier." Zed shrugged.

Keshub opened his victuals pouch and offered raisins in a normal voice since the noisy transport ceased somewhere behind them. "I met your father."

Zed's eyebrows shot up. "You did? Where?"

"He came to Gibeon seeking an alliance. He ate dinner in our courtyard and stayed in our guest quarter."

"Did Gibeon agree to the alliance?"

"Baba told him we were not ready to make a decision."

"Then your father told my father no. No one around here tells my father no and lives to tell it. Was he angry?"

"Yes. Very angry."

"Someday I would like to meet the man who said no to my father."

"You would be welcome in Gibeon, I am sure." Keshub ate his last raisin and returned his victuals bag to its place at his waist. "Perhaps I should finish my work. My brother may return for our donkeys soon."

Zed stood and turned to wave good-bye. His eyebrows shot up in alarm, and his face blanched. The same fear had clamped on Zed's face in the summer. What alarmed him so?

Keshub whirled to see the menace. Behind him, men, directed by Zedek's soldiers, hauled on ropes to erect heavy timbers into a rough frame. They worked in an area cut out of limestone, possibly a quarry. He sized up the firewood standing nearby, enough for five firing days in the Ra-eef' courtyard, but he did not know what it meant.

Zed laid a hand on Keshub's forearm. The force of his grip startled Keshub. "I must go to the market and speak to Endo. I hope to see you soon." Zed hurried away.

Keshub retrieved the pitchfork and puzzled over what had caused Zed such alarm.

The livery man came to lean on the fence. "Who were you talking to?"

"My friend Zed, sir."

"Is he Zedek's son?"

"Yes, sir."

"Friend, huh? Well, if anyone needs a friend, he does."

"Sir. May I ask a question?"

"What is it?"

"What are the soldiers building over there?" He nodded over his shoulder to indicate the timbers being erected in the distance.

The man took a step backward, dipped his chin at Keshub, and stared. His throat bump bobbed as he swallowed. At last, he shook

his head slowly side to side and walked away without a word.
   Fear welled up in the pit of Keshub's stomach.

Chapter 18:
Trouble Brews in Jerusalem

Keshub propped a pitchfork against the livery fence in the Valley of Hinnom. His brow wrinkled as he lifted the yoke and its double burden of water jars to his shoulders. *What is so unspeakable?*

By the time Ezak came for the donkeys, he had filled the water trough again. In the Jerusalem marketplace he helped his brother fill the donkeys' packs with traded goods. Pottery had been traded for, among other things, a sack of wheat, a bag of new season raisins, a coil of rope, a flint knife. He hefted the knife to feel its weight and tested its sharp edge with his thumb. *Someday.*

Uncle Yaakoub and Mr. Endo talked beyond his hearing. The old man's long drooping mustache quivered and jumped with the force of his words.

Eight of King Zedek's leather-greaved soldiers stomped into the marketplace carrying spears. Their leader barked a command, and they spread out by twos around the spring. Their scowls targeted the recent refugees from Heshbon who cowered amongst their meager belongings.

Ear-splitting whistles from four more Amorite brutes on the wall of Jerusalem demanded the attention of everyone in the market. King Adoni-Zedek appeared with his scarlet cloak over one shoulder. The mid-afternoon sun at his back flashed from his polished bronze helmet and from the bronze spearheads of his henchmen.

Keshub squinted. The king must have planned for the effect to dazzle his onlookers and make them think his presence brought a golden light. Keshub shivered remembering the firey darkness he felt in the king's presence in their courtyard.

Zedek bellowed. "Citizens of Jerusalem and merchants of the area, we welcome you to our beautiful Gihon Spring marketplace. Because these are perilous times, we must address new and dangerous issues." Zedek paused.

Keshub shifted his position so the sun would not shine directly into his eyes.

"I speak now to the wave of homeless people who are flooding our land. What cowardly instinct overwhelmed you that you could not stand your ground and fight the Hebrews in the homeland you fled?"

Keshub tipped his head back to stare up at the evil snarl on the king's face.

"If there is a real man among you who will join the army of Jerusalem, you and your family will be fed. Otherwise, move on now!"

***

A few hours later, Keshub's footsteps sent small pebbles skittering down the stairs from the summit. He struggled to keep his balance while he supported his brother on the steep decline. Beside him Ezak sucked in an audible breath through clenched teeth with each step. His right arm draped across Keshub's shoulders.

Keshub kept his eyes on the light from the fire circle below them. Since the shadow of Ra-eef' orchards and vineyards fell across much of the hand-hewn path, the weak light of a crescent moon gave little aid.

Only Baba waited up. He rose from his place at the fire and met them at the bottom of the stairs. He assisted Ezak on the other side. "What happened?"

"I stepped in a hole, Baba, coming over the summit. The waning moon hid behind a cloud for a moment, and I did not see the next step. I am glad Kesh was with me. The ankle hurts much, and I needed him to help me get home. But I do not think anything is broken."

"I am glad you were there, too, Keshub. Lay out your brother's bedroll here beside the fire."

Keshub un-rolled Ezak's woolen blanket while Baba summoned Mamaa and brought Gran-mamaa's stool. Keshub and Baba settled Ezak onto his mat with his injured foot elevated on the overturned stool. Mamaa brought both of them a bowl of still-warm stew and a handful of flatbread. He and his brother wolfed down the hearty fare.

"Do you have good news from market?" Baba stirred up the fire.

"No good news tonight, Baba." Ezak wiped his mouth.

"How so, son?"

"First of all, you remember our friend Endo?" Ezak chuckled and gave Keshub a sidewise glance. "When he met Keshub this morning, he nearly smothered your son Number Five with thanks for suggesting Plain Zed should seek out Mr. Endo. The old man takes great delight in his friendship with the king's son. Plain Zed came to him this afternoon quite upset. I do not know what the boy talked to him about—"

"I do." Keshub frowned. "Sort of."

"What do you mean, son?"

"Baba, Plain Zed found me at the livery and sat with me while I ate my victuals at mid-day. When he turned to leave, he saw behind us a sight that made his face drain of color."

After a pause, Baba demanded. "What did he see?"

Keshub turned his palms up. "I do not know what the meaning was. But soldiers building a structure of rough, heavy timbers in an old rock quarry in the Valley of Hinnom struck Plain Zed with terror."

Baba's eyes darkened and his brows came together. "I see. Thank you, son."

Ezak whistled air through his teeth as he shifted his foot's position. "Baba, both locals and refugees from the east crowded the market today. The refugees are Amorites, mostly, and supposedly near kin to the people of Jerusalem. They have many needs. Endo almost gave away his store of castaway household goods and acorns."

Ezak combed his hand through his hair. "In mid-afternoon, we thought we might load our donkeys and start home in time to be here for supper. That was when Zedek appeared at the top of the wall and made an announcement."

Ezak shook his head and his curls flopped back onto his forehead. "Zedek called the refugees cowards for fleeing instead of fighting. He told the men they should 'Join my army and be fed, you and your family, or move on now.'"

"I can imagine the panic that caused." Baba gazed into the fire.

Keshub blurted. "You have not heard the worst yet, Baba. If the homeless stay inside the city or in the marketplace outside, they will be hanged at sunrise!"

"Yes. The refugees are exhausted already and now must move on. Mr. Endo himself sleeps in the street and has for years. So Endo was irritated by Zedek's announcement, but he said there are plenty of places with softer ground than the streets of Jerusalem." Ezak winced.

Keshub leaned forward. "There is still more, Baba. Zedek said tomorrow will be a day of fasting for the citizens of Jerusalem. Every family is to bring to the Temple of Molech what they would have eaten on that day. Right, Ezak?"

"Yes, little brother. Even worse, they are to bring all their sons who are old enough to grow hair on their lip to enlist in the army of the god Molech. Any who do not appear by the evening twilight will feel the wrath of the fire of Molech."

Keshub leaned in with hands on knees. "Baba, Mr. Endo tore at his hair like a mad man, and paced like a caged animal. After a while he threw all his things into his cart with no thought to any kind of order."

Ezak pursed his lips and clenched his square jaw. "Mr. Endo made Uncle Yaakoub and me promise to meet him tomorrow night on the edge of the forest above the Valley of Hinnom before the moon rises. A large oak with the nest of an eagle is there. Endo says we must come, but now I cannot. What do you think, Baba?"

"Son, I must speak to Yaakoub about this before I answer. These are treacherous times that require us to give more than we ever imagined possible. We do not know Endo's purpose in meeting. We can only guess why he is insistent." Baba scratched the back of his neck. "If that is all, Keshub, you must get to your bed."

Keshub rose to obey but stopped at the bottom of the stairs.

Baba crouched at the fire, banking the white coals for tomorrow's fire.

Ezak already snored.

"Baba?"

Baba pivoted toward him. "What is it, son?"

"Something I forgot to tell you." Keshub crossed the courtyard as he spoke. "About the day I found Plain Zed weeping near his sheep. It was a few days after the longest day market and celebration."

"Yes, son. I remember it well." Baba rose and turned his back to the glowing embers. "What do you know about Plain Zed?"

"I know he feared his own father—afraid 'he would be next' he said. I told him about Endo because he needed someone who would help him without his father knowing."

Keshub shook his head trying to make sense of what he had seen and heard, and looked squarely into his father's eyes. "I still do not understand, Baba, but Haydak the caravanner told me to look at the eyes. I saw King Zedek's eyes up close when he made threats in our courtyard. I do not understand why Plain Zed is afraid of his own father, but I saw something to fear in that man's eyes."

Baba drew him into the folds of his caftan and spoke with a hoarse voice. "Fifth Son, be glad for the innocence of youth. I fear, though, you will very soon grow up too quickly. Off to your mat now."

"Yes, sir."

***

After midnight the next night scudding clouds revealed and then hid the waning moon. Keshub stayed in shadow at his uncle's side on the ridge above the Valley of Hinnom. He had seen the dark looks exchanged between his father and uncle at the mention of this valley. *What unspeakable secret does the valley hide?*

Uncle Yaakoub leaned against the oak tree across the trail with one sandaled foot hiked onto a low boulder at its base. He pulled the cowl collar of his cloak past his mouth to conceal his breath-smoke.

Keshub drew his own homespun cloak closer and thrust his hands into the sheepskin vest underneath. Uncle said they could not be too careful in concealing their presence. Along the trail below, a few campfires burned down and dimmed with the lateness of the hour. No one moved about them. If the camps were for refugees expelled from Gihon marketplace, they had not moved far.

In the distance, cartwheels rumbled a low roar.

Uncle Yaakoub planted both feet on the ground and stood erect with a hand cupped behind an ear. His soft words could have been mistaken for the sighing of wind in the trees. "That may be Endo's cart coming this way."

The rumble grew louder. Uncle Yaakoub gave a hand signal

to get into the position they had planned. When the cart neared, the eagle on his nest shrieked an eerie cry. Still in shadow, Uncle Yaakoub stepped onto the trail.

Mr. Endo stopped and lowered the hand bars of his two-wheeled cart so it rested on its short back legs. He greeted Uncle Yaakoub with a kiss to either cheek and hushed words. "Thank you for coming, friend."

Keshub stepped to the other side of the cart ready to push. He rested his hand on the sideboard and jumped when a hand wrapped around his wrist. "What?"

"Sh-h-h, Keshub." Plain Zed lifted Endo's patched cloak that covered the contents of his cart and wriggled out the back end.

Uncle Yaakoub approached. "Boys, stay in shadow until we start down on the other side."

"Yes, sir."

Keshub stepped to Plain Zed's side. "I thought you would be coming with us tonight. Did you have any trouble getting away?"

"A little. I will tell you later."

Mr. Endo retrieved a crooked walking stick from his cart. He and Uncle Yaakoub turned toward the top of the ridge. Keshub and Zed each lifted a hand bar and put all their strength into pushing the cart up the trail. Every palm-size rock became an obstacle to the wooden wheels. Keshub whispered. "Whoa. Mr. Endo must be stronger than he appears. I had considered him a weak little old man."

"I had not considered him at all, until recently. Tonight, I have put my life in his hands."

When they descended the other side of the hill, he and Plain Zed had to change their stances. Keshub leaned back and planted his feet heel-first to keep the cart at a steady speed. About half way to Gibeon, Uncle Yaakoub called a rest stop. Keshub leaned against a tree beside the trail next to his friend. In the darkness, Endo's cloak rose from the cart and a form emerged and stepped to the ground.

Chapter 19:
The Unspeakable

In dim moonlight the patchwork cloak rose from the bed of Mr. Endo's two-wheeled cart.

Keshub sucked in his breath.

"Zed, where is Mr. Endo?" A voice as soft as lamb's wool floated on the night's breeze.

Keshub froze with mouth open and eyebrows aloft.

"I am here, ma'am." Mr. Endo emerged from shadow and walked the mysterious young lady a distance away. Her caftan caught sparkles of moonlight.

Keshub shot a glance at Zed. "Who is that?"

"She is my little brother's mother, Layla."

"The one that died?"

"Yes, Do'ni. She found me packing a knapsack and guessed my reason. She hates my father as much as I do and insisted she come, too."

"How did you get away?"

"After I returned my sheep to the fold today, I volunteered to carry water and clean the livery man's stable. I said you told me he needed help, and I had nothing better to do."

"He was not suspicious?"

"No. He was too distraught taking care of his son. Soldiers brought him home with a broken leg last night. I worked until dark, then hid in the shadow below the rock where we had lunch yesterday."

Keshub nodded. "And you joined Mr. Endo when he crossed the wadi, but what about Do'-ni's mother?"

"Endo smuggled her out in the crowd Zedek's soldiers forced out of the city the hour before sundown."

***

Dawn arrived to Aijalon Valley as Keshub and his friend stepped back from pushing Endo's cart with its mysterious cargo.

Uncle Yaakoub pointed to the sandal shaped mount that dominated the east end of the valley of patchwork fields. "Follow the caravan trail to the main spring, ein-El-Beled. Continue around the Mount of Gibeon until you pass a smaller spring and the Ra-eef' potters' guesthouse. Kesh and Zed will take the shortcut and meet you there."

Keshub and his friend followed Uncle Yaakoub to his home nearby.

Aunt Raga welcomed them with hot flatbread, cow's butter, and barley porridge with raisins and honey.

Keshub licked his lips at the sight of a rare breakfast served near a fire. "Cow's butter? Aunt Raga, please tell cousin Micah I will never again show him sympathy for having to milk cows for Farmer Khalil. Having cow's butter on hot flatbread would be payment enough."

As Aunt Raga refilled his bowl of hot mint tea, Zed wiped a greasy chin. "Good lady, thank you for this delicious fare. Mr. Yaakoub and your family are most fortunate every day to have the best welcome I have ever had in my life."

Aunt Raga's face dimpled as she acknowledged Zed's compliment with a nod. She exchanged a pleased look with Uncle Yaakoub before she scurried back to the kitchen fire.

Uncle raised his voice enough to be heard in the kitchen, too. "We may not get such a feast every day, Zed, but my wife is a very good cook."

After draining his bowl of mint tea, Uncle Yaakoub pushed himself up from the grass mat. "Men, time for you to relocate to the Ra-eef' courtyard. Avoid being seen as you cross the summit. We do not need questions we cannot answer from the villagers."

"Yes, sir." Keshub grabbed his knapsack and swung it into position as Aunt Raga thrust his bulging victuals bag upon him.

"Give this to your mother and do not tarry. It is not often I can send my sister cow's butter."

"Yes, ma'am." Keshub looped the drawstring around a wrist, raised his eyebrows, and licked his lips. "What will Mamaa do with such a treat?"

He and Zed set out on the well-worn path through newly sown winter wheat fields sprouting single blades of bright green. He led their climb to the summit. Keeping to shadow, he avoided passing the cistern where Gibeonite villagers continued their cooperative digging effort.

At the top of the Ra-eef' stairs, Keshub whispered his plan. "Stay hidden by this pomegranate bush. If no one is in the grape arbor, I will signal for you to hide there while I speak to Baba."

Zed nodded.

Keshub skittered half-way down the mount and inspected the narrow ledge woven with bare branches of grape vines waiting for the return of warm weather. He waved to Zed, all clear. When he reached the courtyard, he heard the clattering of pottery loom weights. His mother and aunt chatted at their upright looms in the warm sunshine while Gran-mamaa braided red leather strands.

With his sore foot elevated, Ezak looked up from his mat where he whittled a long-handled spoon. He nodded his silent question,

"How did it go?"

Keshub gave him an affirmative nod.

"Mother, Aunt Raga sent cow's butter." He pressed his victuals bag into his mother's hands and turned toward the pottery yard before she could ask for explanation.

His brothers and Baba worked clay at different stages as always.

"Baba."

"Keshub, you are home!" Baba rose from his place at the wheel where he had a fully coiled cook pot. "Ra-mi', take over smoothing this pot inside and out for me."

Ra-mi's face lit up. "Yes, sir!"

Baba wiped his hands on a wet rag as he accompanied Keshub to the courtyard. He asked in hushed tones, "Is everyone all right?"

"Yes, Baba. But we had a surprise, too."

"A surprise?"

"Yes. Mr. Endo met us near the ridge above the Valley of Hinnom, but he was not alone."

"Was Plain Zed with him?"

"Yes, but there was someone else, too."

Baba dipped his chin, and concern etched his face. "Did someone follow Endo? How did you get away?"

"Nothing like that, Baba. We expected Mr. Endo and Plain Zed, but Zed's friend insisted she had to come, too."

"She?"

A crisp knock sounded at the courtyard gate. Keshub opened the gate and held it back for Baba to see.

Mr. Endo leaned on his crooked walking stick and bowed from the second step. "Sir, I am Endo, recently a merchant of Jerusalem and friend of your brother Yaakoub. If I may, I have need to talk to you, out here."

Baba dropped the wet rag on a peg in the wall beside the gate and joined Endo.

Keshub followed, and Ezak hobbled out the gate to the top step and closed the gate behind him. At the bottom of the steps next to the caravan trail, Endo's cart tilted on its back legs.

Endo drew Baba to the cart and rested his hand on the side-board. "Sir, we brought an unexpected passenger who needs your help. She is in grave danger if she is found by King Zedek, as are we. I wanted you to meet her and let you decide if you can help us."

"Who is she?"

"She is one of Zedek's harem, sir."

Baba raised one eyebrow. "To lodge her cannot be my decision alone. Keshub, ask your mother to come, please."

"Yes, sir." He took the steps up to the gate by twos.

Ezak swung the gate open. Keshub bolted across the courtyard. "Mother, Baba needs to talk to you, outside."

His mother rose from the grass mat at her loom and raised her shawl to cover her head. Endo bowed low when she approached.

"Danya, this is Endo from Jerusalem. You must hear his tale, too. Endo, start at the beginning, please."

"Madame." Endo bowed low again to Keshub's mother. "Perhaps you have already heard of Adoni-Zedek, king of Jerusalem?"

Mother's nose flared almost imperceptibly, and she lowered her chin in assent.

Aha, King Zedek gets no meat next time, if ever he chances to take another meal in this courtyard. Keshub tried not to smile.

Endo turned questioning eyes to Keshub. "I brought Zedek's son. He was with Keshub."

Keshub nodded over his shoulder. "He is hidden in the upper grape arbor now."

"Good. When Zed gathered his few things in Zedek's palace yesterday, this young woman saw him and guessed his mission. She insisted she had to come along, for she hates Zedek with a white hot passion known only by unjustly bereaved mothers."

The patchwork covering in the cart moved, and indeed, rose up. Large dark eyes flooded with tears and swept by long lashes appeared. Slender fingers bearing henna tattoos gripped the side-board.

"Please help me. I implore you. Do not turn me away." The young woman placed one hand, embellished with twining vines and budding flowers, over her mouth and gulped back a sob. "He cast my darling little son in Molech's fire."

Baba, with his own sudden tears streaming, turned to Mamaa. "The beast of a man put his own son in Molech's fire?"

Keshub froze. *In Molech's fire? The king put his own son, Zed's little brother, in the fire? The Valley of Hinnom. The huge amount of firewood. The awful deed is unspeakable. Who could explain such a horrible thing?*

Mamaa reached over the sideboards and put her arms around the grieving woman whose sobs racked her body. "You are safe now, dear. Sob all you need."

Keshub's arms felt like wood as he peeled back Endo's cloak covering the cart.

His mother helped the young woman dressed in finest linen dyed a soft blue step down. Flecks of gold thread in the cloth reflected sunlight as she stepped from the cart.

"What is your name, dear?"

"Layla, ma'am."

"Layla dear, come with me." With her eyes on Baba's, Mamaa nodded toward the guest quarters a few steps away.

Baba swiped at his eyes and shoved the door open. Layla entered its semi-darkness, dabbing at her tear-streaked cheeks.

Mamaa followed, but turned back. "Keshub, please fetch one of Ranine's lamps. Ask Ezak to tell your gran-mamaa I have been called by a neighbor in need."

"Yes, Mother." Still numbed by the shock of what he had learned, he returned moments later with the lamp.

Mamaa gave him the guest house water jar. She gripped his shoulder with a warm hand and leveled her eyes with his. "Son Number Five, there is so much in life we do not understand. Keep looking toward the kindness of the sun's rising and setting. Perhaps tomorrow will be a kinder day."

Keshub blinked rapidly as he turned toward the spring. When he returned with water, he knocked softly. Hunched dozing next to the door, the old merchant from Jerusalem rumbled like a bee hive beneath his odd cloak. At least Keshub assumed it was Endo. Mamaa peeked out and motioned him to enter and place the jar on its shelf near the door. She followed him out.

"Keshub, I need you to stoke the kitchen fire and place a cook pot with water in the fire. If Gran-mamaa or Aunt Sabah' ask questions, tell them I will be longer than I thought. After that, go to the pottery yard and bring two handfuls of rough clay from the wadi and a flask of olive oil."

***

That afternoon while Baba returned to the pottery yard and Mamaa wove at her loom, Keshub carried out the plan they had made. He wheeled Endo's emptied cart into the recess of the livestock pen behind part of the guest house. Not quite hidden, but unobtrusive.

While Gran-mamaa napped and Aunt Sabah' tended to her little ones inside the house, Keshub lugged bedrolls and water through the courtyard and up the stairs. He delivered them to the cleft where his family stored foods preserved in wine vinegar. The secluded natural hideaway had been the site of his best daydreams as a lad.

With nothing left to do but wait for twilight, he refilled his water flask and climbed to the arbor where he left Plain Zed in the morning. He found his friend curled up asleep in his blanket in a little alcove between two grapevine trunks.

Best idea I have had all day. Keshub crawled into his own bedroll with daylight filtering through the arbor. In moments he slept.

He woke later to see the weave of bare grapevine branches and blue sky. What?

"Hey, sleepyhead." His friend spoke in a hoarse whisper.

"Zed?" Leaves rustled as he raised himself to lean against the hard wall of the ledge.

"Here." Plain Zed wriggled out of a bed of fallen leaves. He disentangled himself from his cloak, stood to his feet, brushed dried leaves off, and grinned. "Best daytime nap I ever had, Keshub."

"I am glad, friend." Suddenly his head felt too heavy for his shoulders, and he dropped his chin to his chest. "How have you survived, Zed? Knowing what your father has done?"

"I have tried to focus on the good I see in others. I have told myself I have his blood in my veins, but I have a choice between good and evil." Plain Zed's chin quivered. "Friends like you make the difference, Keshub."

He swiped at his eyes with the back of his hands. "This will be your home for a few days until a caravanner going to Sidon happens by. That is where Endo says you and he should go."

"Sidon?" Zed tilted his head and nodded. "I have never seen the sea, but can anything be more fearsome than what I have left? Perhaps I will become a sailor. I should think my small size would be an asset on a seagoing vessel."

Zed extended a hand to pull his host to his feet. "But come with me, I want to show you something."

Keshub followed about ten long strides along the ledge to the end of the arbor. He knew the area well, though it had been a long while since he had played at made-up adventures there. A fence made of pruned out vines and twigs divided the Ra-eef' grape arbor from a tangle of natural growth.

Zed pointed beyond the fence and squeezed between the fence and the rock face of the ledge. Keshub followed, pushing thorny limbs and hanging stems of ivy aside. When Zed stopped a moment later, Keshub glanced back the way they came and detected a faint path.

Zed pointed to the ground. Pistachio husks lay scattered about at their feet. He pointed to a place knee high beside a boulder. Keshub bent low to peer into the late afternoon shadow. He reached out and pulled from a rock crevice a tattered woolen blanket and a small leather bag. *Who has made a little nest here and spies down on the Ra-eef' pottery yard and courtyard?*

Chapter 20:
A Tale Unraveled

On Baba's left at the dinner mat, Keshub licked his lips antici-
pating the aroma of flatbread cooking over the fire. He had been
salivating since he delivered dinner to the upper arbor for their
secret guests.

"Ezak, please introduce our guest."

"I am happy to do so, Baba. This is Mr. Endo, our friend from
Jerusalem. He has saved a prime booth space for Ra-eef' pottery
for many moons. We welcome you, Mr. Endo, to our home."

"Thank you, Ezak." Endo shrugged his patchwork cloak behind
his shoulders and with open palm pointed to Keshub. "And I met
this young lad just two days ago."

Mamaa delivered her favorite bowl filled with parched wheat
and fresh spinach with herbs, olive oil, and a *generous* amount of
chopped dried mutton. When twilight waned at the end of the
meal, Keshub sipped from his bowl of hot water flavored with
dried apricot.

Mr. Endo set their secret plan in action. "Sir, I beg your pardon?"

"Certainly. What is it?" Baba tilted his head.

From his seated position Endo made a slight bow. "Thank you, kind sir, for indulging my penchant for sleeping in the open air. The cleft Keshub showed me is most suitable."

"You are welcome. Is there anything else you need?"

"There is. An old man feels the need to bed down with the sunset. May I ask Keshub to help me to my quarters?"

"Certainly. Keshub has set our lamps on several of the ledges to help you find your way." Baba acted his role well and nodded to Keshub.

With a glance toward Ezak, Keshub followed Mr. Endo out the gate to where Miss Layla waited in the guesthouse. When she handed him her small bundle of belongings, almost no trace of henna tattoos remained. His face must have shown his surprise.

Miss Layla smiled shyly. "Your mother is amazing."

"Yes, she is." He smiled and followed Mr. Endo through the courtyard. He climbed the stairs carrying a large bundle of their guests' combined belongings. Baba's voice faded as he told the familiar story of their family migrating from the northland around Mt. Hermon.

Keshub watched the old man's every movement until they reached the upper ledge where Plain Zed waited. Mr. Endo removed his patchwork cloak and extended it to Keshub. Keshub donned the odd garment and pulled the hood up.

The Jerusalem merchant wrapped himself in a tattered woolen blanket from his bundle Keshub had carried.

Keshub lifted his eyebrows and shrugged before descending the stairs in his best imitation of the older man. With slightly stooped shoulders, he nodded as he passed by the gathering at the fire circle. He gestured a sleeve toward the outside gate.

According to plan, Baba would nod and talk to distract the others. At the guesthouse by the caravan trail, Keshub scratched at the wooden door, afraid a knock might be heard by others. When the door opened, he stepped inside and removed Endo's cloak. The dim light of the oil lamp cast shadows across the small room.

Miss Layla layered the patchwork cloak over her own, tied it under her chin, and pulled the hood over her long dark hair.

Keshub whispered. "Let me see." Backing up, he took note that the cloak drug slightly more on the floor than it had when he or Mr. Endo wore it. "Can you walk on tip-toes through the court-yard?"

"I will try."

"You have not been in the courtyard yet. Are you clear about the layout and where you should go when you enter?"

"Yes. Veer right along the half wall to the stairs."

"Yes. There are lighted lamps beside the steps, but it is still dim. Be careful."

Keshub opened the door only enough to allow Miss Layla to squeeze through. He followed her out with the oil lamp but waited until he heard her push the courtyard gate open. When she closed it, he pulled the guesthouse door closed, too. The lamp and the sliver of moonlight lit his way. He followed the fence of the live-stock pen to the back stairs of the pottery yard. From there a lit-tle-used trail scaled the first ledges through the seasonal vegetable garden.

Keshub kept low and in shadow to join Mr. Endo and the secret guests on the upper ledge. "Is there anything else you need?"

Plain Zed flung his arms open wide and whispered. "What more could a man want? To finally be out of Adoni-Zedek's house-hold is a priceless gift."

Mr. Endo smiled. "Miss Layla has retired to the space at the back of the cleft. We are all tired, but I have need to talk once more to your father. Could you ask him to tarry at the fire for a moment when the others go to their beds?"

When Keshub re-entered the courtyard from the stairs, he sat beside Lehab at the fire circle. Uncle Samir was in the middle of the familiar tale of the balky donkey from his childhood. Since Keshub knew what came before, he slapped his knee and joined in the laughter while stealing a glance toward Baba.

When his brothers and Lehab went to their bedrolls on the rooftop, Keshub hung back. "Baba."

"What is it, son?"

"Mr. Endo wants to speak to you."

"I wondered why you did not snuff out the lamps. Get him, son. We do need to talk."

Moments later, he and Mr. Endo joined Baba at the fire. Across the courtyard, Ezak snored softly where he had bedded down to avoid the painful hobble to the rooftop. Before Keshub reached the boys' sleeping quarters, Baba spoke in a tone Keshub had rarely heard from his father.

"So you are Endo who has befriended my brother and son at market. Now you have either befriended or kidnapped the king's son and a woman from his harem. You have involved me and my whole family in your plot."

Keshub stopped with one foot on the next step.

Baba stirred up the dying embers of the fire. "Forgive me, but I must ask you plainly, what are your motives?"

"You are right, kind sir. I have put you and your family in danger, and you have a right to know the full story."

Keshub sank onto the stairs—unable to remove himself from hearing Endo's tale.

"Sir, my story began ten plus five years past at this season of waning daylight. When light reached its weakest point that year, and darkness reached its strongest, I became a man bereft of pleasure and all other thoughts but one."

Mr. Endo extended his hands to the warmth of the coals. "I was a widower and metal smith worker near Beersheba. My days were pleasant with work, but my nights were my joy. I had a daughter who was comely and chaste. Her name was Rabia. We lived with cousins and aunts aplenty, so I believed she was protected in my absences. Do you have daughters, sir?"

"I do." Baba pulled his cloak close.

"Then perhaps you understand me. On the darkest day of the

year and the darkest day of my life, a dastardly man of power and renown chanced to see my daughter. He took her by force and carried her away while I was beating out bronze buckles on my anvil at the forge." After a catch in the old man's voice, he paused a long while.

Keshub's ears strained to hear.

"I left the forge, and everything I knew, to follow after my captive daughter. When I found her in Jerusalem, I learned the man who stole her from me was Adoni-Zedek."

"Aye, I have met that beast of a man." Baba stirred the coals and orange sparks rose from the fire.

Keshub clenched his fists. He, too, had met the man whose eyes held sparks like those rising from the fire.

Mr. Endo wrung his hands together and leaned down on his knees. "Then you also understand I was powerless to rescue her, though I considered it many times. Soon she was with child. I had only one opportunity to speak with her. She feared she would not survive childbirth, and she made me promise I would always stay close by to watch over my grandchild whether it be girl or boy."

The old man raised his head. "She said to me 'Dear Baba, the father is evil, but the child is innocent and will need you someday.' The boy you are hiding is the child. I began to have hope again on the day he introduced himself to me as 'Plain Zed.'"

Baba cleared his throat. "Does the boy know?"

"No. I have not told him."

"I think you should. Tomorrow morning. The rest of the family knows only about you staying in the upper arbor. We must not risk anyone else seeing Plain Zed or Miss Layla. And you must seclude yourself because we cannot chance being asked questions we cannot answer."

"I understand. I hope my little band can join a caravan going to Sidon as soon as possible."

Baba paused. "I hope you have what you need for the evening. We will decide later what else we can do."

"Keshub has provided everything."

"He will take you back to the arbor now and extinguish the oil lamps. Right, Keshub?"

Startled, Keshub answered. "Yes, sir."

Early the next morning, he delivered fresh water to their guests on the ledge.

Plain Zed met him with a wrinkled forehead and brows drawn together. "Keshub, someone came to the nest beyond the twig fence in the middle of the night."

Keshub sucked in his breath and whispered. "Did you see him? Or her?"

"No." Plain Zed shrugged. "I only heard the visitor. There were muffled sobs."

Fear grabbed him. "Do you think the visitor could know you were there?"

"I think not. We were all very tired."

Something clicked in Keshub's thinking as he descended the stairs. Two unrelated thoughts began to make sense.

***

In late afternoon three days later, Keshub delivered a covered dish to the upper grape arbor. His brother number two's ankle was enough better to do his whittling with their guests.

"Is it not truly amazing, Keshub?" Plain Zed sat cross-legged whittling a pot hook.

"Sh-h-h." Mr. Endo and Ezak looked up from their whittling.

Nearby Miss Layla stitched a piece of homespun cloth Mamaa had provided her.

Plain Zed ducked his head and whispered. "Only a short while ago I was friendless and hopeless in the palace of a king. Now I have friends who have risked everything for me and a grandfather, too. Though I am in hiding I can do useful work, and I am happier than I have ever been in my life. Whatever else happens, I can face it."

Mr. Endo rose to take the hot victuals to the cleft where the little band of refugees would eat together later. "Whatever else happens we will face it together, son."

"Thank you, Gran-baba. My own father has never called me son."

With a sudden sniff, Miss Layla gathered her work and rose to turn away, wiping fresh tears. She pushed past Mr. Endo and bent low to enter the cleft.

Ezak swiped at his own eyes and used his crutch to go down the stairs. "I will return tomorrow."

Plain Zed blinked rapidly. "Friend, you probably do not know the privilege you have of growing up in a family such as yours. Please tell your mother the food is most excellent. I have not eaten finer in the palace of a king."

Keshub chuckled. "I will tell her, and I would guess you will have choice meat in your stew tomorrow night."

Keshub lowered his voice. "Have you detected any more visitors to the nest beyond the fence?"

***

Before morning light five days later, Keshub climbed the stairs to the arbor with fragile cargo—a lighted lamp, a flask of oil, and a bag with three more lamps. He stopped on the ledge below the hideout. Mr. Endo and Plain Zed appeared from the arbor shouldering their bedrolls.

Mr. Endo whispered. "Is everything ready, Keshub?"

"Yes, sir. The caravanner and his men are stirring. They will soon load their camels. Is Miss Layla awake?"

"I am here, Keshub." Coming from the cleft on the other side of the arbor, Miss Layla appeared wearing a homespun tunic and a woolen cloak with a hood covering her hair.

Keshub recognized the cloak as his mother's. Miss Layla carried a bundle looped over one shoulder. She could have been one of the refugee women he had seen in Jerusalem. The henna tattoos left no trace, no hint of her former identity.

Keshub held his lamp high. "Follow me, but please be careful. The stairs are steep."

Mamaa waited at the courtyard gate to hand each traveler a victuals bag. Keshub hurried to open the gate and held his lamp for his mother descending the few steps to the caravan trail.

Baba waited for them at Mr. Endo's cart, but disappeared in the direction of the little spring across the trail. Keshub positioned his lamp to help Mr. Endo pack Miss Layla's meager belongings in his cart.

Eskie, Brother Number Three, handed out filled water flasks to each departing guest. In gray light, Baba stepped from behind the reeds and bushes that grew around the little spring. He led a Ra-eef' donkey. Ezak walked beside him. He had exchanged his crutch for a walking stick.

"Danya. We need a word." Baba spoke with a catch in his voice.

Mamaa's hands flew to her mouth when she saw her second-born geared up for travel. "Ezak?"

"Mother, I am going with Mr. Endo."

Mother reached out and touched Ezak's cheek. "Why, son?"

"With the danger of being seized for their armies, I cannot go to market in any city in Canaan. There is no job for me with Ra-eef' pottery. Baba is sending me off with a load of Ranine's lamps to give me a start as a merchant in Sidon. And perhaps I can help Mr. Endo and the others get settled there."

Ezak's brave smile trembled. "Who knows? I may be back to get more pottery when the fear of trouble in Canaan dies down."

Keshub's eyelids prickled with tears he tried to blink away.

***

On his way to the summit to carry rubble for the digging of the cistern, Keshub turned to the horizon. He swallowed a lump in his throat to see ten camels winding toward the pass of Beth Horon on the northwest rim of Aijalon Valley. A small cart and Brother Number Two's pack donkey brought up the rear.

Near noon, Keshub retrieved his slingshot, victuals bag and wooden sword. He waved good-bye to the men digging the cistern to attend Sir Ghaleb's class. All morning he had ruminated on a plan to confirm his hunch about who the nestling near the upper arbor could be. His secret guests had not detected another visit in the time they had spent there. Perhaps the nights of no moon had kept the pistachio eater away while the danger of falling was so great for anyone traipsing along the ledges.

Keshub nervously fingered the drawstring of his victuals bag as he approached. Several boys from the village arrived together for class. Da-gan' lagged behind the group. The others huddled together to eat their victuals. They left no room for a disagreeable bully.

Da-gan' slunk by and sat alone.

Nearing, Keshub lifted his shoulders and lowered his chin to pump up his resolve. He made a friend of one Amorite. *How hard can it be to make another?*

Loosening the drawstring of his victuals bag, his raisins and almonds became visible. He approached Da-gan's back with hand extended as if the bully were the balky donkey in Uncle Samir's story. He dropped to the ground on one knee beside Da-gan'. "Want a raisin or almond?"

Da-gan's eyes darted to meet Keshub's. Keshub lowered his own and took a raisin for himself. He tossed it in his mouth before he met Da-gan's eyes.

Da-gan' shifted his focus to the food and reached out, unhurried. He selected an almond and raised his sad dark eyes to Keshub's before he brought the morsel to his mouth and crunched.

Keshub wrinkled his brow, selected an almond, and turned away to insert it. "I wondered how you knew I stomped dirt for a living?"

Da-gan' stopped crunching.

Keshub turned back. "Have another one," and took one for himself. "Something else I wondered. It must be awful lonesome at night for a night watchman's son."

Chapter 21:
The Bully

Keshub eyed his shaggy-haired arch enemy above their crossed swords. He tensed every muscle, ready for sword practice to begin on the summit of the hill called Gibeon. Cold-season sunshine filtered through low-hanging branches of an already ancient evergreen oak. With his head tilted up he stared a challenge at dark eyes glaring down at him. He must not gulp down the fear rising in his throat. This name-calling bully might see or, even worse, hear his discomfort.

He had to be quicker and smarter than this opponent half a head taller than himself. Wooden swords or not, Da-gan' was notorious for his angry lunges and disregard of the rule of no contact.

Sir Ghaleb, the Hittite soldier who trained Gibeon's boys and men to defend their wide green valley, limped among the pairs. Left hand resting on the hilt of his bronze sword, the teacher stopped beside Keshub. "Da-gan', try to make it through sword practice without being sent to the pomegranate bush to sit the rest of the day."

Da-gan's eyes widened. His nostrils flared, and his lips pressed together. He glared through the crossed swords and pushed back harder.

"Yes, friend," Keshub mocked with a thin smile and raised eyebrow. "I ask you to be gentle with me. I would like to live to be thirteen harvests old." He kept his knees bent, ready to spring. With all the arm power gained from lugging multiple yokes of water daily, he leaned into his crossed sword.

Da-gan's squinty eyes and flared nostrils eased a bit.

Good. Maybe he had Da-gan' confused. Did the bully want to beat the snot out of his favorite target? Or did he want the friendship Keshub offered today when he shared his morning victuals?

Sir Ghaleb's piercing whistle split the air.

Keshub sprang to his right before the sound subsided.

Da-gan's eyes popped wide. He pivoted to his left and swept his sword across to deflect Keshub's first lunge.

Keshub engaged his opponent with flicks of the wrist. His sword clicked and scraped. Trying to gain an advantage with this scowling hulk, he leapt to his left and lunged again. Da-gan's backhand blocked the attack and swung wide.

Keshub's hand burned from the shock of their swords' contact. He smiled tight-lipped through the pain. "You are strong, friend." Gripping tighter to the hilt while he shifted his feet, he swiveled his wrist and redirected his sword tip to the bully's torso, never taking his gaze from Da-gan's.

His towering adversary set his jaw and bared his teeth. He shuffled backward. Reversing his backhand, he slashed downward from right to left.

Da-gan's earlier backhand still stung Keshub's hand. The impact of the enemy's forehand reverberated to Keshub's elbow, and his funny bone did not laugh. Whoa. This sheep herder is strong! He must keep away from Da-gan's right-hand slash. "Hey, big fellow, take it easy on a scrawny runt like me." Keshub grinned and flexed his right elbow.

Da-gan' flashed a cruel smile as his power arm continued its jarring follow-through.

Keshub grasped his hilt with both hands and crashed down with all his might to meet his opponent's extended backswing. Da-gan's grip loosened. His sword tipped downward. He reached with both arms trying to catch his wooden sword.

Keshub cross-stepped to his opponent's vulnerable left and lunged in to touch Da-gan's mid-section. "My advantage." He claimed victory and laid his sword flat across his thighs as he bent, hands on knees, gulping big breaths. "I thought you had me there. Your forehand slash is gruesome, friend. My elbow still feels funny."

Da-gan' stooped to retrieve his sword. His face reddened, and he bared his clenched teeth. "Lucky lunge, dirt-boy."

At the sneered reference to the Ra-eef' family's pottery business, the heat of anger rose within him. Keshub snuffed out the flame with determination. He would outlast the bully with offers of a truce. Rubbing his right elbow, Keshub reached for his water flask and offered it first to Da-gan'. "Take a swig, and let's try another round."

Da-gan' shoved Keshub's hand aside with the broadside of his wooden sword. "Let's get on with it, dirt digger. You need to find out who you are dealing with here."

Keshub gritted his teeth to keep from returning a nasty remark. When Sir Ghaleb's whistled signal interrupted their third round, Keshub heaved a sigh. They were one and one.

He thrust his sword through the golden-brown girdle at his waist and, in spite of the cold weather, wiped sweat from his brow with the sleeve of his flaxen tunic. He bent to retrieve his shepherd's staff and homespun woolen cloak.

Picking up Da-gan's as well, he fingered its threadbare condition. Extending the dirty hooded cape and then the oak rod, he gasped. "Friend, that was the hardest workout I ever had."

Da-gan' grabbed his staff and flimsy cloak and stalked away. Keshub sauntered toward the assembly area at the top of the trail to the village that spilled down the slope of Gibeon. Cousins Lehab and Micah fell into step beside him.

Micah whistled. "Da-gan' looked like trouble."

"He was. I caught him off guard in the first set and made him angry. After that, I had all I could do to dodge his forearm slash."

"Da-gan' did not go to the pomegranate bush, so he must have followed the rules." Lehab adjusted the bow slung over his shoulder.

"He did. He did not kill or maim me. I count that as a victory."

Sir Ghaleb, whose name meant victory, blew out a shrill signal for quiet among the boys in his charge. "Men, welcome our new students from Beeroth and Keariath Jearim. Tomorrow will be an important day. I will announce my new fulltime assistant and form platoons. Each of you will be assigned to a platoon."

Keshub exchanged glances with his cousins.

The old Hittite soldier moved among them demanding their attention with his deep voice and clipped accent. "Men, we know from reliable sources that a vast army and a mysterious people camp in the desert two day's march east of Canaan. That means the horde known as Hebrews are a mere three-day march from here."

***

On the morrow, Keshub squared his shoulders as he stood between his cousins, Micah and Lehab. He could not be prouder. The old Hittite soldier had named his assistant. Keshub's older brother Eskie, Number Three son of Ishtaba, stood at attention beside Sir Ghaleb. Keshub strained to hear his teacher's platoon leader assignments. How many platoons would there be?

"Whe-e-et! Atten-tion!"

"Platoon Six will be led by Keshub, son of Ishtaba."

Keshub's mouth dropped open. Micah nudged him with an elbow.

Cousin Lehab pinched him. "No, you are not dreaming, Cuz. Go stand with the platoon leaders."

To the side, Eskie instructed platoon leaders while Sir Ghaleb called names to form platoons. Keshub, still numb from the honor and the weight of responsibility, jogged toward the boys—Eskie said to call them men—assigned to him. Platoon Six, under the old oak.

A loose bunch of tousle-heads waited for him. He gasped and dropped his head as he ran to face his men for the first time. Oh, no. Da-gan', a head taller than anyone else, stood apart from them all. Would Keshub be able to lead a platoon that included his name-calling nemesis?

***

A few days later, Keshub leaned against the stacked stone wall that enclosed the crowded Ra-eef' family courtyard.

Beside him, Micah pushed off the cold limestone. "Did the whole village come for your sister's wedding to a caravanner?"

Haydak, the thick-girthed uncle of his sister Isa'na's bridegroom, led the dancing with surprising energy. Weaving in and out, his multi-colored striped turban bobbed back and forth amongst the wedding guests.

Keshub shrugged and raised his voice to be heard above the merrymaking. "Maybe. But they brought food. Come on, after we visit the layout of foods, let's move up to the grape arbor ledge where our bedrolls are stored. Too crowded here."

"Good plan."

At the top of the steps to the rooftop sleeping quarters, Keshub secured a handful of raisins and pistachios in the new striped girdle at his waist. He had found his mother weaving gray-green and acorn brown yarn on her upright loom a few days ago. His girdle still gave him a whiff of the mint leaves used for dye. In his other hand he held flatbread roll-ups of honey and cracked wheat.

Micah ran up the last steps with girdle bulging, crunching almonds. "I never saw so much to eat."

Keshub led the way to the grape arbor, one more level up, where

157

only a few yellow leaves clung to the vines. He plucked at some and spread them on the ground. Laying the rollups on the leaves, he licked the stickiness from his hand. "We do not get sweets often."

Micah spoke through a mouthful. "My mamaa brings out the honey when one of us has a cut or a cough."

Keshub spread his bedroll, folded wide enough for two to sit on, before he plopped down and scanned the courtyard below. "Look at Da-gan' near the kitchen. He is stuffing his girdle full. I wonder who cooks at his house. You know he does not have a mother."

"Then he or his baba must cook, unless he has a neighbor who will." Micah licked his fingers.

"It must be hard for them not to have a mother in the house."

"You are sympathizing with that bully who calls you names under his breath every day?"

"Well, yes, a little. But I still would like to hit him in the nose sometimes for his dirt name-calling. I might try it if I thought I could reach his nose and back off without getting my own nose flattened."

Eskie arrived with Ra-mi' and their cousins. He rolled his eyes and put a finger in one ear to muffle the wedding sounds. "The threshing floor?"

"Yes!" Keshub and the others agreed in unison and grabbed their bedrolls.

The moon alternately lit their way and hid behind fast-moving clouds, but Keshub and the others knew the way. On the west end of their footprint-shaped hill, Keshub and the Ra-eef' grandsons descended to the threshing floor on the first ledge. He flipped out his bedroll. Feet first from one end, he wormed into the cozy cocoon of homespun woolen blankets to escape the cool, brisk wind.

From inside his bedroll, his older brother Eskie turned on his side and propped his head on a hand. "Who knew our friend Haydak the caravanner was a dancer?"

Ra-mi', always the quiet brother, poked kindling into a small fire in their midst. The wind shoved the flames this way and that.

Keshub shifted in his bedroll to face the hoped-for warmth. "Yes It appeared our plump caravanner had more fun than anyone." The star Toliman shone brightly above the southern horizon. Baba said its name meant *the heretofore and the hereafter*. "What will life be like for, Isa'na, and for us now that she is married to a caravanner?"

Eskie gazed at Ra-mi's brave little fire. "Our new brother-by-marriage hardly ever talks. I have not heard his plans."

"What will life be like for any of us if the Hebrews keep coming this way?" Cousin Lehab fed kindling to Ra-mi'.

Barely poking a finger out of the warmth just beginning to build inside his woolen wrap, Keshub pointed to the star. "Baba believes there is a Star Namer behind that star. Perhaps the Star Namer knows. We cannot know until the Hebrews attack."

Eskie scratched his scraggly chin hair. "Baba always ends a discussion of the Star Namer with 'We prepare for what we can prepare for. We endure with integrity what we cannot prepare for.' It is the enduring that worries us all."

Ra-mi' placed one last wrist-size length of wood into the fire and turned to his bedroll.

"We are nearly finished digging a cistern out of limestone on the summit. We are better prepared to withstand an attack than we were." Keshub rubbed his nose to warm it.

"We still have to carry water to the summit to fill that gaping hole." Lehab muffled from inside his homespun bedding.

In the distance, music and laughter continued to pour over the quiet hillside lulling Keshub toward slumber. Sudden silence popped his eyes open.

He jerked his head toward Eskie. "What stopped the celebration?" Storm clouds overtook the waxing moon. Outside their fire circle, darkness grew heavy.

Eschol shrugged. Keshub pulled his woolen blanket closer under his chin. Hurried footsteps sounded from the crest of the hill. At the top ledge above, his elder brother Ranine's face appeared out of darkness, grotesque and mysterious behind a lighted torch.

Dark shadows wavered over his youthful features, aging him.

Number One son of Ishtaba recovered enough breath to speak and called down with a loud voice. "Refugees are arriving at our spring from Amorite territory across the Jordan. Many refugees. Heshbon is destroyed."

"Heshbon?" Keshub sifted through the mental images gained from many caravanners' stories.

Ranine descended the first few ledges. "Yes, Heshbon. And Sihon, their king, and all his army are dead. The Hebrews have taken their cities and are destroying everything. They say refugees from the surrounding areas are pouring across the Jordan at Jericho like cattle stampeding. They vow no one is safe here in Canaan either."

Keshub sat up, stunned. Ranine's words refused to sink in. Now the Hebrews were only a two days' trek due east of Gibeon!

"Kra-ka-Boom!" The ground shook, and the air crackled.

Keshub jumped up and rolled his mat and blanket with fat raindrops splashing his back. The rain turned to cold stinging needles as he clambered up to an overhanging ledge. His knees tucked under his chin, Keshub wriggled in place where each of his shoulders was under the armpit of an older brother. In spite of the coolness of the night and the dampness of his garments, he felt too warm in close quarters. The six of them made their own heat ... and fragrance.

The rain settled down to a steady pace as Ranine tapped the ground with his rain-drenched torch. "The celebration ended when the watchman at the spring sent a message to neighbor Agh-taan. A stream of refugees began arriving at dusk. They are camping near the spring and in Neighbor Agh-taan's olive grove. They say Sidon is their destination."

When the wind and lightning subsided, Ranine rose. "Mother will worry less if we are at home. Now that the thunder and flashes of lightning are far from us, we should go. Baba may need us."

A walk in the rain sounded good to Keshub.

Yah-ya, his sister's new husband, met them in the courtyard.

"Keshub, your baba said you are needed at the spring to carry water. Eskie, bring your bronze axe. Ra-mi' you can help start the refugees' fires.

"There are many. Some are injured, and some are ill. Most have little more than the clothes on their backs. The guest quarter is ready for the ill. They need to get out of the rain."

Eskie slapped Yah-ya on the back. "So, the bridegroom, who seldom has spoken in our presence, is giving up his lodging on his wedding night."

"The refugees need our help, and more are arriving. Who knows how many will come and how long they will stay?"

Keshub shouldered his yoke. What would all this mean for Gibeon?

Chapter 22:
The Platoon

Keshub's breath made smoke in the crisp morning air. Why did his breath look like smoke on a frosty morning? He wondered about many things as he climbed to the summit lugging the goat-skin water bag. Would Gibeon ever return to normal? Surely two recent weddings in his family and a flood of refugees from the east were not normal.

After a few days' rest, the refugees had moved on toward Sidon. Some long-time Gibeonite families had moved on with them. While the refugees camped near their spring for a few days, work at the cistern had slowed. He had carried many yokes of water for the camp, for families just like his own in many ways. They were like his family, except they had no home. And they did not know where they would find one.

Keshub stopped and shifted the water bag on his shoulder at the top of the stairs. He surveyed his family homestead below. In the courtyard, ten natural limestone ledges down, Mamaa' tended the kitchen fire. Ra-mi' tended the fire in the pottery yard while Baba and Ranine worked the clay.

He quickened his steps, ready to get back to work at the cistern. What would the Hebrews do next? Fear lurked behind the talk at the spring and at the evening fire circles. Only a few moons back, Haydak, his favorite caravanner, warned Gibeonites to be watchful of the strange people who shunned contact with others. At the time, they camped on the edge of Canaan south of Beersheba. They were closer now, east of the Jordan—way too close.

Keshub hung the filled goatskin water bag on the nearest gnarled olive tree and took up his position at the lip of the deepening cistern. He frowned. The cistern was the result of fear. Of the Hebrews on the other side of the Jordan River? Or of the Amorites in the surrounding hills? Which threat was greater?

Perhaps fear was normal. A farmer tilled, planted, harvested, and stored up grain for fear of starvation. Surely, fear produced some benefit.

When he stood before his platoon of nine on the summit, fear squiggled in the pit of his stomach. Da-gan' challenged every order with a scowl and muttered his name-calling. How could he earn the respect of the other eight with Da-gan's opposition? Da-gan' mostly kept his name-calling under his breath, but the others heard.

Keshub shook his head. If he could beat the bully at sword drill every time, surely the bully would concede. But try as he might, Keshub's quick footwork seldom won more than one out of three sets against the bully's brute force.

He peered into the shadowy bowl cut into solid limestone using only basalt hammers and chisels. Below him, three men huddled around a new tool.

"Keshub. I need water." Uncle Samir grunted as he set up the new tool Haydak had brought from Egypt.

Keshub ran to fetch the water bag. Oh the marvelous things friend Haydak found on his travels. He had waved good-bye to Haydak and his two camel handlers at dawn three days ago. In

Keshub's imagination, he rode a camel behind Haydak to Damascus by way of the Jordan crossing at Beit Shan. He had never been there, but he had constructed vivid images in his mind from the tales of many caravanners.

He glanced northeast, in the direction of Damascus, and spied through the haze the tip of Mt. Hermon, the fabled benevolent old man in a white shawl. The caravanners said snowmelt from its slopes fed the Jordan River.

"Keshub, water."

Keshub extended the bag to his uncle.

"For the hole. Pour about two mouthfuls. Aim it at the point of the auger." Uncle Samir's brow knit in concentration.

Keshub determined to keep his mind on the cistern and the new iron invention friend Haydak had paid dearly for.

Uncle Samir's eyes fairly glowed as he explained to the other men from the village how it worked. Uncle Samir guided the weighted shaft. "Steady, men. Begin slowly and gradually increase speed."

The two held either end of a wide ox-hide strap about three arms' lengths long. Between them, half the leather strap wound around the shaft of the iron auger.

"A little more water, Keshub."

He tipped the bag again, and the auger's shaft began to grind. First one and then the other of the strap-men made the shaft turn. Their muscles bulged with the effort.

Keshub swiveled his head back and forth in rhythm. One man pulled and made his end of the strap longer. The other provided firm resistance as his end grew shorter and shorter wrapping onto the shaft. Back and forth the strap-men pulled.

"More water, Keshub." With his whole body, Uncle Samir fought the moving shaft to keep it weighted and straight. Faster and faster went the relay between the two men below him until the shaft screamed at a high pitch. The auger drilled into the limestone as if it were a flint knife cutting butter.

"What a fine treasure Haydak found for us!" Uncle Samir's

voice sounded eerie coming from within the pit.

Catching a glimpse of his uncle's face as he repositioned the auger to drill another hole, Keshub chuckled. "I think you are like a boy with a new whimsy to play with, Uncle."

"Boy, if you think this is play, we will let you try your weakling hand at it. This is work," growled one of the strap men. He stripped to the waist in a slant of sunshine and positioned himself again.

Sweat poured down the man's bare chest, but at ground level, Keshub pulled his lamb's wool vest tighter and hunched his shoulders against the cold wind. "Sorry, sir. I meant no offense. It is plain to see you are working hard, despite the look of great pleasure on my uncle's face while he gives all his strength in the effort."

"Apology accepted, son. It is plain to all Gibeonites that the demon of laziness does not dwell in the home of the Ra-eef's."

***

When the sun arced to its highest point of the day, Keshub stowed his tools at the cistern. He jogged the short distance to Sir Ghaleb's school and sought his brother Eskie.

Sir Ghaleb's assistant checked equipment at the archery range.

"Eskie?"

"What is it, little brother?"

Keshub checked over his shoulder to be sure they were alone. "How can I get Da-gan' to stop calling me names? How can the others respect me when he does not?"

"Stay steady, little brother. Your best strategy is not to lose your temper."

"If I were bigger than him..."

"You are not bigger, but you are faster and you have more endurance. Get your men in formation. Let's see what I can do about this. I have an idea."

Keshub joined his platoon gathered at the oak tree. Da-gan' stood an arm's length away from the others. "Line up, men. Lehab here." He stepped off a long pace. "Micah, here." Another pace,

"Da-gan' here. The rest fall in line as before."

Eskie trotted to Keshub's side. "Platoon Six, your assignment today is to run."

"Hunh?" chorused several in his young platoon.

"Run the length of Gibeon's plateau, then down to the threshing floor before returning here. Stay in line, and carry your staff and gear. This is not a race. As much as a fighting man needs skill with weapons, he needs the other men with him. And he needs endurance. Now, go. Follow your platoon leader."

Keshub led an easy jog through the gray-green olive orchards of the east end and followed a trail marked by many previous footsteps. Running felt good. The pounding of nine other pairs of feet muffled behind him when they entered the deep green pine woods at mid-point. He had gathered fallen pine needles here to soften Gran-mamaa's bed. In a small clearing he slowed and circled wide. "Halt, men, but run in place."

Da-gan' and another struggled to keep the pace.

Keshub began to have hope. He slowed his in-place gait and skirted the clearing, allowing stragglers to catch up. Heading to the west end, he made up a chant. "Left, right, left, right. To the west, to the sea. Out of sight, running free. Left, right, left, right."

His platoon's footsteps echoed in the woods as they passed through. He stopped at the top limestone ledge above the threshing floor with hands on his knees. "Going down, give the man in front of you the space he needs. Keep a steady pace, but do not hurry."

Keshub pointed. "Micah, go first and wait at the threshing floor for all of us."

Micah sat on the edge and eased down to a boulder on the next level. As soon as Micah launched himself over the next ledge, Keshub waved another man to follow. He directed Da-gan' to descend last, ahead of himself. Da-gan' heaved himself over the edge, slid to a foothold, and planted his rod before jumping to the next level. One ledge after the other, he kept moving.

Keshub descended last and joined his men. "That was the easy part, right? Are we ready to climb?

Groans escaped from several.

"Remember. Speed is not our goal. Getting to the top, together, is. Use your shepherd's staff to help you and to help the man behind you if he needs a hand."

"When you are ready, Micah, lead us to the top, and wait there for the whole platoon."

Keshub gauged the strength of each would-be soldier by how easily, or not, he scaled each ledge that was nearly twice his height. Da-gan' and he were the last to grab onto a bush and dry tufts of grass to aid their climb. Da-gan's routine did not include carrying water for a large family like Keshub's. It showed. On one particularly steep ledge, half way up, Da-gan' slowed, struggling to keep the pace and fell far behind the others.

Keshub waited behind Da-gan' on the ledge below. To his right a few paces, he found another route. He negotiated the next level and towered above the still-struggling Da-gan' whose red face poured sweat.

Keshub braced his feet and extended his staff.

Da-gan' eyed the staff and then Keshub. Da-gan' hesitated.

"Take it. We are platoon mates. We help each other."

Da-gan' grasped the staff and pulled his belly onto the ledge.

"Good. Let's keep going. Only a few more to the top." Keshub turned, smiling to himself, and scaled the next ledge ahead of the biggest, strongest, and slowest man in his platoon. Would this change Da-gan's attitude? Would the platoon accept his leadership?

Chapter 23:
Nothing But the Jordan

Three days later Keshub sloshed down a gulp of water and turned, grabbing his cloak at the rim of the cistern. A common Bulbul, startled, whirred from ground to treelimb and scolded, "*Wheet-ru-Tweet!*"

Keshub jogged to his platoon at the oak tree. No taunts from Da-gan' in the last three days. Would he finally face his nine men without his stomach doing flips in his mid-section? Up ahead, cousin Lehab talked with the boy from Beeroth, and two others tossed a sling stone back and forth. Even Da-gan' stood among the others talking to cousin Micah. Good. More evidence Da-gan's attitude was changing.

"Kesh. Come here. See what I brought." Micah's black eyes sparkled as he bounced in place and wore a pleased-with-himself smile.

Beside him, Da-gan' bit his lip. Was Da'gan' trying not to smile? Keshub tugged his cloak closer to shut out the wind. "What is it?"

Micah shot a glance at Da-gan' who stepped behind the tree.

168

"Yesterday Sir Ghaleb said platoons three and six will run to the threshing floor today. I know he said it is not a race, but have you seen how tall and long-legged the men of that platoon are? We might be embarrassed if we are too much slower than they are. Da-gan', bring it out." Micah stepped aside.

Keshub tilted his head and puzzled, Uncle Yaakoub's ladder? Da-gan' dragged short lengths of sturdy oak branches lashed to two longer ones. Uncle sometimes used the homemade device to scale the ledges on the shortcut to Micah's house on the south face of Gibeon's hill. Da-gan' peered between two rungs with a question on his brow.

Micah helped Da-gan' support the heavy ladder. "Da-gan' and I will carry it. We can all scale the steepest ledge faster. Right?"

"Maybe, but you two will have to lead going out and bring up the rear on the way back."

"We will." Micah elbowed Da-gan'. "We will be a team."

Da-gan' actually smiled.

"I will check at platoon leaders' meeting to see if we are allowed to do this. I will be back."

***

After military training school ended, Keshub still smiled. Not only had Sir Ghaleb approved the use of the ladder, but also he commended Platoon Six for innovative thinking and working together. Platoon Three had completed the run ahead of them, but not by an embarrassing distance.

Keshub paused at the top of the rough-hewn stairs to the family courtyard. A cold wind whipped at his tunic. He tucked his hands under his arms for a brief warm-up and scanned the horizon. In his shepherding days, when he was only eleven harvests old, he dreamed of life beyond the horizon. Now that he was twelve, he had not lost his desire to travel, but he had far less time for daydreaming.

From the hills to the northeast, a caravan headed this way on

169

the trail that came from the Jordan crossing at Beit Shan. Only five or six camels? Would there be guests at dinner? At the Ra-eef' pottery yard, Baba's black hair streaked with gray and Keshub's black-haired elder brother Ranine bent over their work. Ra-mi, brother number four, stomped gray wadi mud to change the sticky stuff into smooth, elastic clay.

Keshub fidgeted. Sometimes Baba needed him to work the mud, too. He would so like to be assigned to meet the visitors from afar. "Baba, a caravan is coming from the northeast. What do you want me to do today?"

"Check with your mamaa. She may need more water if we have guests."

"Yes, sir."

On his second trip with the yoke to the small spring across the trail from their homestead, Keshub took in a quick breath. Now that the string of camels drew closer, he knew them. His favorite caravanner had departed only a few days ago. Haydak returned now the same way he went. This could not be good news.

Keshub set aside his yoke and half-filled water pots at the spring. He raced up the back stairs to the pottery yard and slowed only to take the narrow path among the fragile greenware drying in the sunshine. "Baba!"

Baba's pottery wheel stopped. "What is it, Keshub?" He looked up with one hand inside smoothing the cook pot he formed and one outside caked with wet mud.

"Haydak is returning! He is urging his camels to a faster pace than usual. Why would he come back so soon without the other caravanners he usually travels with?"

Baba sprang up and grabbed the wet rag always nearby. He rubbed most of the clay residue from his hands and forearms and grabbed his sheepskin vest.

"Ra-mi, cover your basin of mud and finish smoothing this pot. I will meet Haydak."

Keshub stood waiting with his father at the bottom of the steps to the courtyard. Baba's brow furrowed with worry lines.

Haydak bin-Khanjar's usual smile had deserted his deeply lined weathered face. He rode his favorite camel, Khali, who declared her distress at being spurred past her usual easy gait with a prolonged growling burrrr-ump. Haydak reined her to a stop near the livestock pen.

Keshub and his father strode to meet them, and Keshub took hold of Khali's rein. Discontent smoldered in her deep amber pools fringed with long dark lashes.

At Haydak's mild command to kneel, she obeyed but expressed herself with a great audible whoof of breath. Baba clasped his friend's hand and helped him dismount. Khali, too, lurched to her feet—tall hind quarters first, then front legs. She gave a pouty nudge to the caravanner's shoulder.

Keshub patted and stroked the disgruntled camel's neck and stalled leading her away. Knowing the news could not be good, he strained to hear Haydak's words.

"The Hebrews have defeated Og of Bashan at Edrei, my friend. We have no doubt they will invade Canaan next."

Keshub's mind reeled as he led Khali to the livestock pen. Invade? Here? Numb, as if his limbs were made of wood like his sword, he helped Haydak's handlers unload their packs and camels.

Cousin Lehab, with curls flopping in his face, called from the gate to the pen. "Keshub! Your baba says to come. He has a job for you. He says to come quickly. I will help here."

Keshub pitched the vine-tied wheat straw bundle he carried to Lehab and ran to the courtyard gate. Inside, Baba and Haydak bent over a small fire. Mamaa had brewed tea. The two men sipped and stared into the fire.

Keshub hesitated but had to interrupt their thoughts. "You called me, Baba?"

Baba shook his head and, with a far-away look, tore his eyes from the flame. "Yes, son. Run as quickly as you can to Uncle Yaakoub's house. Take the quickest path across the summit. Tell your uncle I need him to come to the fireside, tonight. It is important. You may stay for supper there and come back with your uncle."

"Yes, Baba." Keshub welcomed the task to run ... and think. He grabbed his shepherd's rod and ran to the stairs leading from the courtyard to the summit. Ten ledges up at the top of the stairs he paused to regain his breath. Baba's voice sounded calm, but both his and Haydak's brows were creased with worry lines. What did any of them really know about the Hebrews?

Running as if Hebrews pursued him, he sprinted a shortcut through the ancient olive grove. At the east-west path he had run with his platoon today, he eased to a jog. A vision of Micah and his ladder pulling Da-gan' into a faster run, made him chuckle. In the end, with his tongue hanging out, Da-gan had hazarded another smile.

Half-way down the main path, Keshub branched off to Uncle Yaakoub's house. Among the pines the wind was calm. He stopped a moment with hands on his knees to catch his breath. Eerily, the wind roared in the tree tops. He imagined the roar of an invading horde.

A black-winged dove hopped to the ground nearby and eyed him with a side-wise stare. "C-o-o-o, c-o-o-o."

Keshub started off again, and the dove took flight with the peculiar rattling sound doves make.

What did he know? The very mention of Hebrews drove fear into the hearts of the refugees he had carried water for. In the hot, dry season the message-runner he met in the wadi said the Hebrews defeated the king of Arad and destroyed their cities. He said the king of Jerusalem expected the Hebrews to come here next.

Keshub emerged into the blustery wind from the pine woods on the south side of the long narrow hill. Directly across the valley, lay his uncle's house and livestock pens. Using his handy staff for balance, he clambered down and sprinted across the valley through winter wheat fields bright green with new growth.

His sister's new husband tended the pack animals outside the stable. "Yah-ya, where is Uncle Yaakoub?"

Yah-ya straightened. "In the tack room. What do you need?"

Keshub tossed an answer over his shoulder as he headed for the tack room. "I have a message for him from my father."

In the lean-to beside their small rock-walled courtyard, he blurted. "Uncle, my father says he needs you at the fireside this evening. It is important."

"Is this about pottery?"

Keshub shook his head. "No. It is friend Haydak. He is back with news that the Hebrews have defeated Og of Bashan."

Uncle Yaakoub rocked back on his heels and blew out a slow breath. "So, now there is nothing between Canaan and the Hebrews but the Jordan River."

***

Keshub huddled between his brother Ra-mi' and cousin Lehab as early darkness descended on the Ra-eef' courtyard. Cold winds whistled around corners and through undetectable spaces in the rock wall that enclosed the Ra-eef' homestead. The coldest part of the year crouched over them like a stalking lion.

All the Ra-eef' men, including a new son-by-marriage, huddled around the fire with Haydak. Neighbor Agh-taan and Sir Ghaleb arrived at the same time.

Baba stood to greet his closest friends. "Thank you for coming. I thought you two should hear the news first. Tomorrow will be soon enough to tell the rest of the village."

When they settled into the fire circle, Baba turned to Haydak. "Friend, you left us for Damascus just six days ago. Tell us the disturbing news that caused you to return."

The caravanner folded his hands together and settled them atop his ample waistline. "The Ra-eefs are my dearest of friends and now family, too. I thought it not kind of me to bear my tale to Damascus before sharing it with you. All of you know the first already. The Hebrews have for a time been settling into the areas they captured from Sihon and the Amorites."

The wind died. Now only the crackling and hissing of the fire accompanied the caravanner's deep voice and somber words. Keshub pulled his lamb's wool vest closer around him while he stared at the flames dancing among the logs.

"Five days ago their army marched along the road toward Bashan. It seems the Hebrews had no fear of the giant king. Surely they had heard Og's iron bed measured longer than two men lying head to foot and wider than a man is tall. If they heard, the story did not stop them from rousing the giant from his bed."

Hairs on Keshub's arms stood up straight.

"Og took their challenge. He marched out with each of his giant sons leading a battalion. The two armies met at Edrei in a valley east of the hills that line the Jordan."

Haydak shook his head. "Somehow the Hebrews must have outwitted Og's army. Perhaps Og and his sons were too confident of their stature and strength. Perhaps they believed their god who required child sacrifice would protect them. Perhaps the Hebrews set an ambush."

The caravanner stroked his short beard. "We do not know because no man of Og's army survived. The Hebrews struck down Og, his sons, and his whole army."

"Everyone?" neighbor Agh-taan gasped.

Haydak nodded. "Even now the Hebrews are taking possession of the land of Bashan. Another flood of refugees is crossing the Jordan near Beit Shan. That is where I was when I heard the news."

The old trader took a deep breath and placed a hand on each knee. "There is one more curious tale to tell."

Baba leaned in. "Yes? Go on. We would hear it."

Keshub hunched his shoulders and hugged his knees to his chin. He exchanged a side-wise glance with cousin Lehab beside him as Haydak began.

"I chanced to take tea with a man in Beit Shan who had talked to a Hebrew, a Hebrew boy."

Neighbor Agh-taan squared his shoulders and tilted his head toward the caravanner. The flat tip of his nose dimpled as he spoke.

"Even the refugees who flooded by us in a panic had rarely seen a Hebrew. None had actually talked to one. I questioned every family at the spring to try to sort out myth from fact."

Haydak pursed his lips and nodded. "Right. The Hebrews have shunned all settlements except to attack. Curiously, they have skirted by Moab and Ammon's territories without event. But they now dominate on Jordan's east bank."

"What about the boy, sir?" Keshub's curiosity urged him to speak.

"He was a boy about your age, Keshub. The man who told me this tale was named Maydan. When he met the Hebrew, Maydan shepherded a small flock on the back side of the blue hills of Moab."

"Are the hills really blue, sir?" Lehab blurted.

Uncle Samir sitting on the other side of Lehab placed a hand on cousin's knee in quiet rebuke.

Haydak defended Lehab. "It is all right, friend. I like to see curiosity in a boy. Lehab, the hills always appear to be blue in the distance. Perhaps the air in that place makes them so."

He lowered his voice and spoke more slowly. "But here is the tale Maydan told. Early one morning about two moons past, the man shepherded on a hillside at the far reaches of the territory of Moab. When he heard other sheep bleating nearby, he investigated from the crest of the hill.

"Before the Moabite's eyes, a most strange sight appeared. On the ground the morning dew sparkled like sunshine began in a dewdrop. As the droplets disappeared, a strange substance appeared—like flattened grains of wheat in size but white in color."

Keshub searched Haydak's lined face and pictured his words.

Haydak stared at the fire as if the story were written there. "Not far away a shepherd boy knelt and gathered the white substance into a leather pouch. Besides bagging the strange stuff, he ate a few grains at a time."

The caravanner raised his gaze to Keshub. "The Moabite shepherd did not want to frighten the lad who had not yet seen him. He stopped with one knee to the ground and leaned on the other.

'What is it, son?' He pointed to the strange substance lying on the ground."

Keshub squirmed to a cross-legged position.

"The boy looked up with kind and intelligent eyes, not at all afraid. He answered with a smile and dancing eyes as if to share a great joke. 'That is what it is, sir.'

"Puzzled, Maydan repeated his question more slowly, for the young boy spoke with a difficult accent. Maydan pointed to the strange substance on the ground." Haydak extended his index finger.

"The boy laughed and repeated 'That is what it is, sir. We call it 'what is it?' because we do not know what it is. We only know that the Creator of heaven and earth, who is our invisible God, supplies us with what-is-it six mornings out of seven.'"

Keshub leaned forward with hands on his knees.

"Maydan questioned, 'Why only six out of seven, boy?'

"'Why? Because the seventh day is holy, sir. On the seventh day God rested after he created all that we behold. God set the seventh day aside as holy, a day of rest for us, too. Is it not so for the people of your land, sir?'"

"He called the stuff what-is-it?" Lehab's dark locks flopped this way and that as he shook his head.

Haydak grinned and shrugged. "This is the tale Maydan told. He went on to say 'As we talked, the what-is-it disappeared like the dew, slowly at first. When I looked around me, suddenly the mysterious foodstuff vanished.' Maydan turned back to ask more, but the boy had rejoined his flock. There was no more opportunity."

The old trader gestured as if holding a bowl. "As Maydan looked into the dregs of his tea that day, he said, 'It does not take a prophet or soothsayer to get the message. A people who are fed by the hand of Creator God each day are not ones to have as your enemy.'"

Haydak slapped his knees. "Maydan sold his sheep the next day and moved his whole family to Beit Shan. After hearing the news from Bashan on the day I saw him, he was considering where to move next."

Baba cleared his throat. "So, friend Haydak, you believe this man Maydan's tale to be true fact?"

"Yes. I do. I have talked to many men in my life of traveling. I believe I have the ability given me by my Bedouin heritage to discern men's character. I looked deeply into Maydan's eyes, and he returned a steady gaze. I can say with certainty his meeting with a Hebrew lad happened as he said."

Haydak extended his left hand, palm up. "This also explains why the Hebrews have discouraged caravans from approaching. They have need of nothing."

Baba rubbed his chin with thumb and forefinger before he spoke. "You have heard our friend. Rumors have swirled about us for months that the Hebrews were coming to Canaan. Now they are less than two days away, apparently with an appetite for conquest." Baba leaned his elbows on his knees.

"This is the time for decisions. We who are heads of families must decide what is best for our offspring. Our friend says we are not safe here. Tomorrow night our friend will give his report to the rest of Gibeon. Yaakoub, brother, can you be here again on the following night with an answer for you and your family?"

"Yes, brother, I will be here."

Keshub sucked in a breath and fear gripped him. He wanted to see the world outside Aijalon Valley but not this way. Was it possible some part of the Ra-eef' family would become refugees? Like those who straggled by their spring recently—homeless, hungry and weary?

Chapter 24:
Let Every Man Decide

From the bottom of the dark pit he helped dig in solid lime-stone, Keshub raked up rubble. News that the Hebrews were near spread quickly. More Gibeonites showed up today to help dig the cistern. Would the cistern allow them to survive a few days and negotiate if invaders came to Aijalon Valley?

Keshub bent his knees and hefted a new gufa with his last load of rubble for the day. His aunt, Lehab's mother, had woven this round-bottomed, flexible reed basket for extra strength. She said hauling chipped limestone wore out a gufa in less time than it took for baby chicks to hatch.

He lugged the heavy load up the spiral of narrow steps in the wall of the cistern and broke into sunshine at the rim. At the slag pile nearby, he dumped the load. He wiped his brow and grabbed his cloak and water bag hanging nearby.

At the bottom of the cistern, Uncle Samir worked in shadow with two of their Gibeonite neighbors. His voice sounded eerie and hollow. "We have made good progress, men."

Uncle Samir and the two men climbed to the rim and retrieved their tunics and cloaks. A cold gust of north wind quickened their movements. Keshub held high the almost empty goatskin water bag for each of them to get a drink.

Uncle Samir sat on the solid rock rim, feet dangling. "Tell folks we will be ready to fill the cistern in a few more days."

"Yes, sir." Keshub stashed his gufa and trotted to join his platoon.

* * *

After dinner in the Ra-eef' courtyard, men of Gibeon arrived for the evening swap of information. In summertime their full-length homespun tunics looked nearly the same— hen's egg white. Mamaa said flax cloth does not take up dye easily. On a winter evening, the men pulled close their woolen capes dyed in a variety of earth tones. Green from fig tree leaves, blue-gray from mint leaves, and the most common, golden brown from acorns. Neighbor Agh-taan had the only yellow girdle and scarf, colored by pomegranate skins.

Keshub and cousin Lehab chose a place against the rock wall of the pottery yard. Keshub pressed his back into the stored-up warmth from the sun. Older men were given seats in the first ring around the fire. Haydak repeated what he had learned in Beit Shan.

Neighbor Agh-taan spoke next. "Friends, we also have received news today from other travelers stopping by our spring that the main Hebrew camp is now at Shittim."

Keshub gasped. If the Hebrews entered Canaan from Shittim, Jericho would be the first city in their path. After that, a day's walk due west would bring the Hebrews to Gibeon.

Baba's deep, quiet voice and unhurried words redirected Keshub's clamoring thoughts. "Neighbors, I have said to my own brothers and sons each man must decide for himself and his family what he will do. No one will decide for all. So I believe our time together is best spent by saying, sirs, what possible actions do you see before us?"

"We can all pack up" offered one neighbor, "and flee like the refugees we have seen streaming by."

Another threw up his hands. "We can go to Jerusalem or Lachish. Both have walls around their cities."

Baba turned to the caravanner. "Friend Haydak, you talked with one refugee in Beit Shan and saw others. What do you say is the plight of a refugee?"

"The refugee I took tea with had fled from one supposed danger and arrived at a place of greater danger. Even then he was casting about for where he could flee this time."

"Keshub?" Baba called from across the courtyard, and all eyes turned to the fifth son of Ishtaba.

Keshub sat up straighter. "Yes, sir?"

"Come here beside me."

"Yes, s-sir." What had he done that Baba would call on him in this way? He wove through the assembly of men seated on his courtyard floor. In the dim light of the fire and Ranine's lamps flickering in their niches, he tried not to step on anyone's hand or garment. The sudden silence of the gathering threatened to choke him.

Baba made room for Keshub to kneel beside him. "Tell them what you told me after market day in Jerusalem at the last full moon." He scanned the circle of men. "Before the defeat of Sihon of Heshbon."

Keshub swallowed with difficulty and his voice squeaked. "The king of Jerusalem stood at the top of the high wall above Gihon Spring. He called the refugees cowards for not staying and fighting in their own country. The king said they could stay in Jerusalem if the men joined his army."

Keshub gained courage and breathed deeply. "No one would be allowed to sleep on the streets. If they tried, they would be hanged at sunrise. Everybody had to leave the city before sundown because the gates would be locked at that time."

The old-timer Nabi scratched his nose with the back of his hand and then waggled his index finger. "Goes without sayin', that man is the orneriest man I ever saw. And I have seen a plenty."

A few chuckled. Others nodded.

"The fact is," Neighbor Agh-taan waved his hand to include everyone there. "Any community has only limited resources. For all of us, last year's stores are dwindling, and barley harvest is still two full moons away. There is a limit to what we can give to others before our own families go hungry. I am not suggesting we become misers and turn away the needy, but I am saying there are limits to what we can do."

"What about an alliance with the Amorite kings?" boomed neighbor Ra-gar'. "When are we going to accept their offer of help in our defense and join Zedek's army?"

Sir Ghaleb stroked his short beard with one hand. "Neighbors, you all know I was a soldier in my youth. When I was a lad, I thought soldiering was all about the glory of the battle won and the fame that comes to the brave and victorious. Even before an opponent near cut my leg from under me, the glory of battle had dimmed for me."

Ra-gar' harrumphed.

The old soldier cleared his throat. "I saw women and children who had no man to provide food for their mouths or clothing for their backs by the sweat of his brow. I saw whole cities reduced to rubble and the stored grain taken as the spoils of war. The survivors of the destroyed cities combed through the rubble for anything of value. If they found something to barter, there was no bread to buy."

Keshub's hero looked down at his hands. "I came to think, and I live with the guilt of the thought every day, that it was kinder by far to leave no survivors than to leave survivors with no hope of their surviving."

He stared into the fire. "I began to hate my job and myself for the pain and grief I caused."

The old soldier's voice broke, and Keshub remembered stroking

the still-warm lion on the longest day of the year. He had regret-
ted having to kill the beautiful beast that threatened his flock.
When Eschol had reported Keshub's victory to Sir Ghaleb that day,
Keshub had sensed the old soldier's empathy.

"Sirs, I hope you know I would fight for Gibeon to the death,
but I would not venture out to seek battle in no wise."

Ra-gar' snarled. "So our all-wise military adviser says sit and
wait to be attacked?"

Baba nodded. "You are right neighbor Ra-gar' about one thing.
We must decide what we can do and probably soon. However,
tonight the question is simpler. The question, for each of us to
answer for himself and his own family, is, Do we stay? Or do we
go? No one will think less of any man for deciding it is right for
him and his family to leave Aijalon Valley."

Ra-gar' grumbled and fumed as he stalked out, but the rest of
the men of Gibeon left the courtyard with chins lowered and little
to say.

The following evening Keshub pressed shoulder to shoulder
next to Lehab and Micah behind their fathers at the fire circle.
Being closely packed staved off the shivers that threatened him,
from the cold and from the dread of their fathers' decisions. The
courtyard wall sheltered from the brunt of the sharp north wind.
The smoke from the fire blew one way and then another. Was the
fire unable to decide which way to go?

While the men exchanged greetings, Keshub whispered to
Micah and Lehab, "Do you know yet what your babas have
decided?"

Both cousins whispered, "No, do you?"

"I can only guess we will stay because Gran-mamaa Amara
is not well. Her cough seems to be worse every night. We are all
afraid for her."

Baba, eldest brother of three Ra-eef' sons, cleared his throat
and confirmed Keshub's assessment. He added a hopeful note.
"Perhaps even the Hebrews will need pottery if they come to
Aijalon Valley."

Uncle Yaakoub turned both palms up. "I cannot imagine living in a city or what I would do there to provide for my family. We will stay."

After Uncle Yaakoub's announcement, Keshub extended his open left hand, palm-up in mid-air, across cousin Lehab's lap.

From the other side of Lehab, Micah laid his right hand on top. Keshub held his right hand up with two fingers crossed. When Uncle Samir announced his family would stay, Lehab broke out a smile and placed his hand on top of Micah's. Keshub and his cousins piled on their other hands till they resembled a stack of flatbread. Jostling shoulder to shoulder, he bounced their hands before breaking apart.

"Ranine?" Baba asked.

"We will stay, Baba, to help defend. If we survive the threat of the Hebrews, there will always be a need for pottery. I can starve here as a lowly potter doing what I love as easily as I can starve somewhere else doing who knows what? Besides, where else would be a better place for my first-born to arrive?"

"Will the family have a new potter in the coming year?" Uncle Yaakoub slapped Ranine on the back.

Ranine dipped his head. "We shall see."

When the merriment died down, Yah-ya cleared his throat.

Keshub reasoned that Yah-ya had the easiest decision to leave because he was not established in Gibeon yet. Life on the trail would be hard for his sister Isa'na, but Yah-ya had been caravanning since he was Keshub's age. What would Yah-ya decide?

"It would be the easy way out for me to continue working for my uncle on the caravan. But with my beloved Isa'na to consider and the possibility of children in the future, I cannot see caravanning as anything but a hazard for her. I will stay to help defend Gibeon. If the Ra-eef' family business has a place for me, my wife and I would like that. If not, I will find work with neighbors in the valley."

A moment of stunned silence followed before whistles and cheers of encouragement broke out. Hope dawned in Keshub's heart replacing the dread. He whistled and clapped along with his cousins next to him.

Eschol pounded Yah-yah on the back. "Who knew the bashful bridegroom was an orator, too?"

Wrapped in his bedroll later, Keshub considered their plight. What changed? How could he feel happy now? Their situation had not altered. No part of the threat of danger had diminished.

The un-walled village of Gibeon still stood vulnerable to attack. Their water source, one of the most reliable in Canaan, bubbled up surrounded by valuable farming land. Gibeon could not hope to escape attack if the Hebrews invaded. How could his family and Gibeon possibly survive an attack?

Chapter 25:
Preparing for Attack

In the frosty morning air several days later, Keshub's breath made smoke as he arrived at the main spring at the foot of the east slope. "Good morning, sirs."

Farmers congregated nearby to sharpen their farm tools and hear the latest news. Baba Nabi, the old one, cleared his throat and croaked. "Mornin', lad."

Some of the men also attended Sir Ghaleb's new mid-morning class on the summit to sharpen their skills for battle. His brother Eskie said many had attended when they were boys. Keshub filled the jars suspended from his yoke and huffed up the path from the spring to the cistern on the summit. With the digging completed, he helped fill the gaping hole they had dug.

Going up, he met a man new to Gibeon who stepped aside with empty jars to allow unhindered passage. "Good morning, ... neighbor."

"Good morning, son of a potter. What is your name?"

"My name ... is Keshub, sir." He kept his eyes on the steps to the summit.

"I am glad to make your acquaintance, Keshub."

Later on his way down, Keshub stepped aside for the new neighbor trudging to the summit with his own yoke and double load.

The man continued as if there had been no pause in their conversation, "I am Jabal ... and not a sir .... That is no one ... has ever called me sir before. When my son is born, ... I will be a sir to him." He flung the last words over his shoulder.

On Keshub's next climb, they met again. "And if the babe is a girl, I will be a sir to her. The time is near, so we shall soon see."

Pouring sweat and making steady rhythmic progress in warm winter sunshine, Keshub directed a question over his shoulder. "Where are you from, Jabal?"

Little by little Keshub learned Jabal was a farmer and recent refugee from Moab. When Jabal took a short break, Keshub joined him. "How can you devote so much time to carrying water? Most of the men can make only a few trips before they have other work more pressing."

"I have no other work at present. I have asked neighbor Agh-taan to inquire for me. I hope a farmer who is too busy to gather at the spring in the mornings will hire me soon. I have a strong back and willing hands. Until I have work that will buy bread, I will repay the kind folks of this village by toting water."

At evening fire circle, Jabal arrived with another newcomer about Eskie's age. He introduced the man to Baba and neighbor Agh-taan before they took a place next to Baba. Jabal nodded a greeting to Keshub as Baba's deep voice gained their attention.

"Men of Gibeon, we have news of the Hebrews from a young man who arrived from Moab today."

The Moabite placed a calloused hand over his heart to introduce himself. "I am Jabal. This very day I met a fellow refugee from Moab at the spring." Here Jabal placed his right hand on the knee of the younger man beside him. "In fact, he is my wife's cousin, Ramath. Cousin, please tell us what you know about the Hebrews."

"I will. Until five days ago, I worked as a cook's helper for King Balak of Moab. This is what I know. I saw Balak's teeth chatter in fear when he heard the Hebrews defeated our neighbor Sihon, king of Heshbon. But he panicked when the Hebrews also soundly defeated Og, the giant king of Bashan. Og's men were the best and most powerful of any I saw visit King Balak. The Hebrews defeated and utterly destroyed both kings, their armies, and their cities."

Keshub stared into the fire. The fear in the eyes of the refugees from Heshbon still haunted him.

Ramath rubbed his hands on his knees to keep warm. "Since the Hebrews moved to Shittim, practically at our tent's door, Balak has squandered much treasure in fear of them. He sent his princes with a number of Midianite elders to consult a well-known sooth-sayer—twice. The seer lived on the Euphrates River far to the north and east.

"I helped load the camels when Balak's sons set off laden with gold and silver to pay the soothsayer's fee. Balak promised great riches if the man would come and curse the Hebrews. The first delegation led by Balak's third son failed entirely. The seer refused to come. He said he could not curse a people God has blessed."

Keshub craned his neck to see Baba's reaction. Baba's eyes narrowed and his forehead wrinkled a question as the Moabite continued.

"Balak was furious at the first report and sent his eldest son with more men and more camels laden with more riches than the first time. Finally, the seer agreed to come, but according to one of his own servants, strange and unexplainable things happened on the way."

Keshub jerked to attention at the mention of strange and unexplainable things. Were they good things ... or bad?

The cook's helper lowered his chin, wide-eyed. "I slogged to the edge of Moab on the Arnon with the set-up crew that went ahead of King Balak to meet the soothsayer. For two days cook had me digging fire pits and building stone ovens. King Balak arrived, wearing enough gold chains and medallions to make a camel balk, in time to receive Balaam the soothsayer."

The Moabite raised his chin and eyed the stars. "We had prepared a feast to outdo all feasts. The noisy celebration disturbed even the cliff swallows on their nests that night. While I tended the cook's fire, Balaam's younger servant came to heat his master's bed warmer. He gazed into our fire, just as we are doing tonight, and asked, 'Have you ever heard a donkey speak?'

"He was a young lad, and I laughed at his silly question. I asked him, 'No, have you?' To my surprise, he answered, 'I did today.' He shook his head, completely serious. 'Karishma, my master's donkey, spoke today. Master took a fancy to her and bought her from a Persian caravanner mostly because her name meant 'miracle.'"

Neighbor Nabi hooted. "Young man, you expect us to believe a donkey spoke? You do not look like a simpleton, but donkeys do not speak, not even if they are from Persia and are named 'miracle.'"

Neighbor Agh-taan inserted, "Son, what about the Hebrews?"

"Sir, I am getting there."

Keshub blurted. "I want to hear what the donkey said," then ducked his head. How had he dared speak?

Baba cleared his throat. "Ramath, please continue, but be aware it is getting late."

"Yes, sir. The young man at my kitchen fire said the donkey named Karishma had shied twice before she suddenly lay down on the trail in a narrow passageway. His master beat her with a rod all three times to make her get back in line with the caravan. On the third time he said 'her braying turned to words in our ears.'"

Ramath nodded to Keshub. "Like you, I had to ask, 'What did the donkey say?' The lad quoted, 'What have I done to you to make you beat me these three times?' The seer railed at her for making him a fool and said 'If I had a sword in my hand, I would kill you right now.'"

Baba Nabi cackled. "And then her master would walk. Who would have made him the fool then?"

The Moabite cook's helper chuckled. "The lad said, 'You will not believe what happened next.' I told him I was not sure I believed what I had heard already. Then he described seeing a bright light in the narrow, shadowed passageway. A light so bright he had to shade his eyes. He heard a rumble like thunder, and his master Balaam fell facedown and answered the rumbling with 'I have sinned. I did not realize you were standing in the road to oppose me. Now if you are displeased, I will go back.'"

Baba's forehead creased with more questions, but he did not interrupt. Keshub scratched his head. Who spoke from the bright light?

Ramath shifted his position. "Now for the part about the Hebrews. For the next three days, I drove an oxcart that carried wood as Balak and his court escorted the soothsayer. Each time we reached a high overlook where we could see the Hebrews' camp at Shittim below, the king of Moab commanded, 'Curse the Hebrews, and I will reward you with riches.' The master of delay would say, 'Build me seven altars,' and Balak would order us to start stacking stones."

Keshub adjusted his position on the limestone floor to wake up his sleeping limbs as Ramath continued.

"The soothsayer would go some distance away and bow low with his face to the ground. When he came back to the altars we had made, he would make a big speech that sounded like a blessing instead of a curse. Balak would rant in protest. The owner of the talking donkey would shrug, 'Must not I speak what the Lord puts in my mouth?'"

"Balak was persistent. He sent us to three other mountain tops and sacrificed many cattle and sheep. In the end he was stomping mad. For all the show and his pleading for curses, Balaam gave him no curses. Every pronouncement was a blessing on the Hebrews and bad news for the rest of us because 'the Lord their God is with them.'"

"I had been thinking already about following Jabal and my cousin since I have no other family. So when I heard the soothsayer's words, I took the first opportunity to leave."

Baba stroked his short beard. "Thank you, Ramath, for your report. We hear so much that is rumor borne by panic, but panic and rumor are no good basis for making decisions."

The next afternoon snowflakes floated in the light breeze. Low clouds hovered over the Valley of Aijalon. When Keshub and his cousin Lehab skittered down the stairs from the summit, Baba and Uncle Samir had their heads together with Eskie at the fire circle. Keshub nodded to his cousin in the direction of the courtyard gate and Lehab followed.

At the woodpile Keshub picked a branch as thick as his wrist and laid it on the chopping block. He checked the sharpness of the bronze ax and arched a blow. Uncle Samir and Eskie usually took turns chopping with the bronze ax while he stacked and carried. He pressed his tongue to one side between his lips as he concentrated.

"Halloo!" Uncle Yaakoub startled him when he appeared leading five of their best pack animals. He led them to the livestock pen and shut them in.

Keshub waved as his uncle disappeared around the guest quarters. He placed another log on the chopping block.

Soon Eskie leaned over the wall of the pottery yard and called down. "Keshub, come now. Baba wants to speak with you." He returned to the courtyard, so Keshub could not ask what Baba wanted.

Keshub raised an eyebrow and shrugged a silent question toward Lehab. Was he in trouble?

Lehab turned palms up and shook his head.

Keshub whirled his cloak over his shoulders and took the steps by two. Inside the gate, "You called for me, Baba?"

"Yes, Keshub. Sit down, please."

"Yes, sir."

Uncle Yaakoub came right to the point. "Keshub, I need a new apprentice to go to market with me in Jericho."

"Me, sir? To Jericho?"

"Yes, you, Keshub. You are the best man for the job."

Baba lowered his voice. "Keshub, you are also the only man for the job. We believe our older young men are in danger of being forced to become soldiers for the Amorites. Neither Eskie nor Yah-ya can go to market anywhere in Canaan at this time. When you go to market, Eskie will go with you to the ridge above Jericho, but no farther."

Uncle Yaakoub took over. "You and I will sell our wares in Jericho and return home. Eskie will camp on the ridge and will be our first-hand observer of the Hebrews' camp across the Jordan. He and neighbor Agh-taan's son Bildad will swap places every three days. You and I will re-supply them when we go to market. Do you have any questions?"

"When do we leave, sir?"

"At first light tomorrow. Bring your bedroll. You begin the job now by filling the water troughs in the livestock pen for our donkeys. Then come to the guest house to help make up the packs for market and for the lookout post."

"Yes, sir."

"You may go now." Baba nodded.

On Keshub's way to the gate Uncle Samir asked, "Brother, what about the young Jabal? Neighbor Khalil needs more help than we can give him."

Baba answered. "We do not know how good a worker he is."

Pivoting, Keshub felt compelled to interrupt. "Baba?"

"Yes, Keshub? What is it?"

Though Baba's back was to him, Keshub detected the arched-eyebrow tone. "Please excuse me for interrupting, sir, but Jabal is a very fine worker, I think. He is strong and quick and most cheerful in attitude. He has been working harder than anyone in carrying water to the cistern. He told me 'Until I can work for hire to buy bread, I will repay the kindness of the people of Gibeon by helping fill the cistern.'"

"Thank you, son." Baba replied in a softer tone. "We will look into that. Now go to your task."

"Yes, sir." Keshub plunged out the gate and down to the livestock pen. "Lehab, I am going to Jericho! Tomorrow!" In his imagination, he was already on the trail.

ℭℛℰℴ

IN THE HEBREW CAMP AT SHITTIM

Hosiah skipped a pyramid-shaped ivory token on his Senet game board made of acacia wood. With all his chores done, he lounged in the winter sunshine on the carpet before their tent.

"Where is Mother?" Elkanah demanded as he neared.

"She is inside." Sudden fear gripped him when he eyed his older brother's face. Hosiah scooped up his game and rose to follow Elkanah inside through the tent flaps.

"Mother, a plague has started on the other side of the camp. Uncle Joshua said to stay inside and pray. He said, 'Do not go out for anything until you hear from me or Kemuel.' Moses is talking to God at the Tabernacle."

"Do you think God is angry with the grumblers again, like when we had all the snakes?" Hosiah shuddered.

"Uncle Joshua said the cause is more serious than grumbling this time, little brother. Some of our people have participated in Baal worship with Moabite women."

Mother took their hands. "Boys, kneel with me. The God of Father Abraham and of Moses has brought us this far. He will not forsake us now."

Wails of grief rose up, first in the distance, and then nearer. After a few moments with bowed heads, Mother quoted in a firm voice the law God gave Moses on the mountain.

"You shall have no other gods before me."

Hosiah and his brother joined her with the prompting of a squeeze from her hand in theirs.

"You shall not make for yourself an idol."

"You shall not misuse the name of the Lord your God."

"Remember the Sabbath day by keeping...."

Hurried footsteps sounded, going toward the Elishama family's tent. The familiar voice of Enan, son of their neighbor, rang out. "Mother, Kemuel says the plague has suddenly stopped because Phinehas took quick action .... Yes ... Mother, I must tell our neighbors, too."

A moment after Enan left their tent to tell other neighbors, Mother stifled a sob with the back of her hand. "Boys, do your afternoon tasks. I will see if any neighbors need my help."

Hosiah picked up his water jar. *Thank you, God, for not using snakes this time to discipline your people.*

Chapter 26:
First Trip to Jericho

In gray light at the first cock's crow Keshub yawned as he rolled his bedding and tied a bundle for the trek to Jericho. He would be ready when Uncle Yaakoub arrived. In the courtyard he rubbed his hands together to warm them above the kitchen fire.

Mamaa thrust a bowl of hot rosemary tea into his hands. She cleared her throat and raked a tear from her eye. "Drink it, son. And remember, you are not yet big enough to ignore your mother's wishes."

He moistened his cold flatbread in the steaming liquid and ducked his head. Why would she be reluctant to see him go on the biggest adventure of his twelve years?

Following behind his uncle and Eskie, Keshub halted at the ridgeline trail in late morning.

Uncle Yaakoub called out. "Check your packs and your animals. The rest of the trail descends to the Jordan Valley floor. Tighten cinches if needed."

Keshub checked the pack on the donkey in his charge and pulled the leather belt tighter across its round belly.

"Remember to look behind us often for rain clouds. A small shower here at the top of the ridge can quickly cause a rushing torrent in the wadi below. If we see rain behind us, we must move up the ravine to higher ground until flash flood waters have passed us by."

Uncle Yaakoub came to inspect and inserted a finger between the cinch and the donkey's belly. "Very good, nephew. Tight, but not too tight. Our animals are our first concern on the trail. Think of Raja here as your best friend. Talk to her. She will be a good listener."

Uncle tilted his head and gave a crooked smile. "Probably, she will not speak like Karishma the Persian donkey did."

On the downward trail, Keshub munched a few nuts and dried figs. "Raja, this is my first time to come this way. I have dreamed of seeing Jericho since I was a small lad. Today is the day!"

At mid-afternoon Uncle Yaakoub stopped again. "We will see Jericho around the next bend. Keshub, stay with the pack animals while Eskie and I scout the area over this ridge. We must find the best position for a lookout post."

While he waited, Keshub surveyed the deep ravine and the wadi far below. The trail followed the ins and outs of the canyon wall well below the ridge.

He jumped at the scream of a black-winged eagle as the powerful bird broke over the ridge above him, light feet and legs dangling. The raptor rose with broad wings stroking the air until he stretched and soared with ease. "Whoa, Raja, we are at the height of eagles here."

Eskie and Uncle Yaakoub clambered back over the rocky ridge and skidded down. Eskie thumbed over his shoulder, eyes flashing, "We found just the right place, Kesh. I will have full view of the valley."

Big brother swept a hand across the horizon, painting an extended picture. "The city of Jericho, the Jordan, the plains of

Moab on the other side, and the Hebrew camp at Shittim. Did you see the eagle take flight?"

"I did."

"His nest is about two stones' throws away beyond this ridge. He will be my neighbor for three days at a time until Agh-taan's son changes with me."

Uncle Yaakoub stayed with the donkeys. Keshub leaned into the climb for balance and lugged supplies behind Eskie up and over the ridge to a wide three-sided bowl-shaped ledge. "Where can you see Jericho?"

"Up there." Eskie scampered up the left side of the bowl and lay flat on his belly beside a boulder the size of their guest house.

Uncle Yaakoub whistled.

Keshub scrambled with hands and feet, with Eskie right behind him, to rejoin his uncle on the other side. The sun slipped over the north-south ridge behind them where they had stopped for lunch.

Uncle Yaakoub pointed to an inconspicuous stack of three rocks under a scrubby bush near the trail. "Bildad will look for this sign and know where to find you, Eskie."

"Yes, and Bildad will signal with the caw, caw of a crow. I will return with the squeeh-ee-yew of a cliff swallow. Appropriate, do you agree? Me, the cliff swallow who lives among eagles. Kesh, you may need your own signal."

Uncle Yaakoub handed Eskie a broken branch from another bush nearby. "Keshub, let's get on down the trail a way before the long twilight turns to dark."

Eskie waved with the broom. Then bent over and swept out their tracks on the ascent to the ridge.

Keshub cupped his hand to whisper to his donkey. "Raja, friend, I have pretended to see Jericho when I played in the cleft above Gran-mamaa's orchard. Now I will."

Raja's ear twitched, and she flicked her tail.

Moments later, the Jordan Valley opened up before him with Jericho, its high walls, the palm trees, and the gushing spring. Both he and Raja were speechless.

About half way down to the valley floor, his uncle stopped at a small level area with a blackened fire pit. "We will sleep here and head on down at first light."

Keshub ate from his victuals pouch, flatbread and dried mutton. He washed down the traveler's fare with water from his flask. He chewed slowly and marveled at the massive walled city in the dim twilight. Too soon the shadow of the ridge behind them cast a shroud of darkness over the city of his dreams.

Inside his bedroll, Uncle Yaakoub snored.

Keshub could not sleep yet. On his belly, chin on his hands, he looked down on Jericho and stored up his impressions. Hundreds of small cook fires cast a faint glow inside the walls of the city. The only light in the rest of Canaan came from a few campfires scattered along the valley floor and several concentrated outside the gate to Jericho.

He found an offending stone under an elbow and tossed it at the dying embers of their fire. What makes the fire in the middle of the Hebrew camp so strangely bright and unmoving? He turned to his back. Sleep overtook him as he marveled at the lighted under-bellies of the few clouds over him.

By first light of morning, Keshub strained his water-carrying muscles to help Uncle Yaakoub lift packs onto their animals. By the time the sun appeared, he plodded stiff-legged beside his donkey down the sharp decline. The City of Palms beckoned.

"Raja, to a boy whose home hugs the side of a hill in a pleasant green valley, Jericho seems a different world. Yesterday, I left Aijalon Valley wearing her bright green winter robe of wheat and barley grasses growing in the fields."

Keshub swept his hand toward the Jordan Valley. "Today, we have no chill wind at our backs from the great sea. Instead, the air is warm and still."

He removed his cloak and stowed it. "Raja, even the trees are different. Those palms around the spring look like soldiers wearing elaborate headgear. And over there the palms are in such orderly rows, they make an orchard very different from the olive and fig trees of Aijalon Valley."

Raja did not comment. Of course, he had seen it all before.

"And the city! Those thick golden walls reflecting the morning sunshine jut above the top of the palm trees like a giant crown."

At the gushing spring of Jericho, Keshub stayed with the animals while Uncle sought a place to set out their wares. At a small pool, he gaped with head back and mouth open at the steep base that supported the thick walls of mud-brick. "Raja, for many days Gibeonites broke their backs and their tools digging the simple cistern on Gibeon's summit. Even so, our defenses are nothing compared to Jericho's. Our natural limestone ledges are easy to climb. Surely there is no way an enemy could enter this city except through the gate."

When Uncle Yaakoub returned, he had secured a place near the steep road up to the city gate. "Anyone coming down from the tell will immediately see some of the best pottery in Canaan. Perhaps when you are more experienced with pack animals, we can get a stall in the market inside the first wall. But this is a good place, too."

Keshub hobbled the pack animals in grass nearby while his uncle unpacked their wares.

Uncle Yaakoub greeted everyone who sauntered by with his hearty 'halloo'. He exchanged news of Canaan and the Jordan Valley when people stopped.

A man with a large bag of dried dates draped over his shoulder talked with Uncle a long while. When he exchanged his dates, bowed, and carried away Ra-eef' pottery, Keshub had to ask. "How do you know what is a good trade, Uncle?"

"People offer what they have to trade for what they think is of equal or greater value. If I agree too quickly, they will think they offered too much, and they will be unhappy after the trade. We make a friend when both of us are happy with the trade."

Keshub packed the bag of dates, harvested from the palm trees nearby, into empty pack frames waiting for the trip home.

A linen merchant traded for six Ra-eef' pots, and Keshub rearranged the remaining pots. "I think new linen is itchy stuff, but my mother will be very happy with your trade."

When he tended the booth alone for a short time, a customer inspected the pottery closely. "Hello."

When the man looked up and moved on without a word, Keshub muttered to himself. "Did I say something wrong?"

He asked Uncle Yaakoub about the no-sale later. "Keshub, you will meet all kinds of people and receive all kinds of responses. Hello is a perfectly good opener. Try it again with the next five customers and see what happens. The pottery is excellent and will sell itself if the customer wants it."

In early afternoon, Uncle Yaakoub drank from their goatskin bag and held it toward Keshub. They had sold all their wares. "While I make up the packs, take the donkeys to drink at the pool below the spring, and fill these two water bags. One for us and our animals and one for your brother, the cliff swallow."

Keshub returned leading five donkeys. Together, he and his uncle lifted the lighter packs into place on the animals' backs. Uncle Yaakoub tightened the cinches and took special care to pad the strap across the donkeys' breasts. "The weight of their packs and the steepness of going up the trail home will cause great pressure here, Kesh. Even the stoutest and most agreeable pack animal will balk if there is anything that causes irritation in this area."

"Yes, sir."

Uncle Yaakoub took the reins of the lead donkey. "We have one more night of cold victuals on the trail before we get a hot meal. So, let's get started."

The long twilight began before they reached the outcropping near Eskie. In the faded sunlight he came to the trail to meet them. "Hello, fellow travelers. I apologize that I cannot show customary hospitality of a meal and a night's lodging to visitors."

Keshub wrinkled his brow.

Eskie explained. "A fire and smoke, little brother, could reveal my position to people in the valley below or to passers-by on the trail."

Uncle Yaakoub handed Eskie the full water bag. "We cannot be too careful about keeping your position a secret. Your report will be welcome in three days when you return. Kesh, let's get a few paces closer to home before we camp for the night."

By the time the sun rose the next morning at his back, Keshub trudged up the rocky trail halfway up the canyon above the Wadi Qelt. He shook his head. His brother had told him the trail was steep, the canyon deep, and the plant life bleak. "Raja, the contrast between Aijalon Valley and the Jordan Valley could not be more stark."

By mid-morning his legs burned from the climb. When they reached the north-south ridgeline, Uncle Yaakoub called halt in the oak forest with its drab cool-season garb.

Keshub donned his cloak again. "Raja, we made it. Our trek is an easy downhill-walk from here—through rich green wheat fields. You can even take a munch here and there, friend."

Three days later at the evening fireside, Keshub squirmed through the usual local topics. He sat up straighter when Baba dismissed the villagers, saying the Ra-eef' potters had family matters to discuss. The villagers did not know about their spies, yet. Sir Ghaleb and neighbor Agh-taan left with the others, but returned to hear Eskie's first report.

"Neighbor Agh-taan, your son Bildad will find our lookout nest most hospitable. The rain clouds do not reach our lonely perch. Every day I observed clouds hanging blue wispy curtains at the ridgeline while I sat in the shadow of the rain."

Keshub rubbed his hands together as much in excitement for having seen these things himself as to keep his fingers warm.

Eschol turned to Uncle Samir. "I had not understood before why there are few trees and only scrawny bushes on that side of the ridgeline trail. The rain clouds stopped at the ridgeline most of the time. The nights were cold, but the days were warm and almost always sunny. With the water Bildad brought in and what I left with him, he will have plenty."

Eskie nodded to Baba and Sir Ghaleb. "Now I will tell what the lookout sees when he looks out. The Hebrews are still quite far away beyond the River. I can tell their camp is, indeed, large and, from the distance, looks something like an eye."

Lehab leaned back. "An eye?"

Eskie nodded. "There is a distinct center to it. What is in the middle, I cannot tell. But there is a ring around that center—a vacant space left between the large center and the tents around it.

"At night a huge column of fire marks the Hebrew camp. I would hate to gather the wood each day for that fire each night."

Eskie shifted his position and cast a glance toward Baba. "The only other thing to report is about the other lookouts."

Baba arched one eyebrow as Eskie went on.

"On my second day I saw a young man cross the river to watch the Hebrews from a mountain on the other side. A replacement arrived daily after that. I believe they were spying for King Zedek. Each day the replacement went to the riverbank and drew out a small boat hidden in the dense thicket. What did our friend Haydak call that thicket?" Eskie looked to Uncle Samir.

Uncle Samir lifted his chin and supplied the word. "Zor."

"Yes. The new lookout rowed across the Jordan, secured the boat in the dense growth of the Zor and hastened to the top of the nearest mountain. Another spy descended, hurried to the boat, and crossed the river to climb the trail that rounds the base of my perch."

"Thank you, son." Baba turned to neighbor Agh-taan. "Our sons will give us important first-hand information."

"We cannot assume the Hebrews will stay where they are, but we also cannot put all other things aside until we know what the Hebrews will do next. For now we must all double our efforts to fortify the summit and be ready for an attack while we carry on making a living for our families."

Keshub bit his lip at the thought of Aijalon Valley overrun with enemy attackers.

C</S>

IN THE HEBREW CAMP AT SHITTIM

Hosiah puzzled over why the leader of the tribe of Ephraim went from tent to tent in their camp. "What is neighbor Kemuel doing, Elkanah?"

Elkanah stowed the leather envelope he had used to deliver Uncle Joshua's supper of bits of dried mutton steamed with manna. "God told Moses and Eleazar to order a census of all our men who are twenty years old or more."

"Does that mean there will be another battle soon?" Hosiah dreaded the thought.

"Probably, little brother."

Chapter 27:
Who Is the Enemy?

Keshub wriggled farther down into his warm cocoon of mother-woven wool and smiled. The biggest dream of his life had come true. He had seen Jericho for himself as Uncle Yaakoub's assistant. In the courtyard where his brothers and cousin slept to escape the sharp winter wind, no one else stirred. Baba's snore rumbled within the house. An ever-so-faint lightness to the dark told Keshub dawn was not far away. There would be a crust of ice in the water vessels.

From the house he had not slept in since he was much younger, except when sick with a fever, Gran-mamaa coughed. "Ka-hu-ah. Ka-hu-agh." She coughed more lately, though she sounded better that morning.

Mamaa squinch-squinched by in leather sandals as she emerged from the depths of the house dug into the hillside. She scritch-scratched at the kitchen fire to stir up the coals, then added fuel with a soft plunk.

The wood smoke tickled his nose. There would be warm tea

and cold flatbread for dipping soon. He should rise and help but lay there soaking in the sounds and smells of their home in the early morning.

Lehab snored next to him and Eskie nearby, but not Ra-mi'. Was he awake, too? Was he also pretending to sleep? No, a faint sound came from the pottery yard. That must be Ra-mi' stirring the fire there. Brother number four loved everything about the work of a potter.

Baba's footsteps sounded next, solid, firm—like the man he was, like the man Keshub hoped to be. Keshub lay very still to see if his father would awaken him like when he was a child sleeping inside the house. A moment later, a soft, warm puff of air reached his exposed ear.

Baba whispered. "Kesh. Time to get up, son."

"Hu-uh? Oh." Rubbing his eyes a moment, he rolled over, scrambled to his feet, and rolled up his bedding.

Faker, he told himself.

"Keshub, come here and give your gran-mamaa a warm hug." The gravelly voice demanded attention.

He rolled his eyes but smiled and complied. He encircled Gran-mamaa and the rich fur robe she shivered under. She wore fur from the lion who stalked his flock at dawn many moons ago on the longest day of the year. Gran-mamaa's shoulders felt thinner than the last time. "Do you like your robe, Gran-mamaa?"

"Yes. Thank you, Keshub. This is the finest garment I have ever owned. What a proud day when you protected our sheep and brought it home for me. When I am gone, I want each of my grand-sons to have a girdle made from this fine fur. Then every time any of you girds up you will know your Ra-eef' family heritage is with you. Be true to your heritage, Keshub—and I know you will."

"Yes, Gran-mamaa."

He wanted to protest Gran-mamaa's passing from among them. Instead he wrapped his arms around her again and held on gently lest she break.

Mamaa called from the cook fire. "Keshub."

"Yes, Mother?"

"Come get Gran-mamaa's tea, please—and your own."

"Thank you."

"You are welcome, Fifth Son."

By the time it took to drink a bowl of warm tea clasped between his two hands, the tempo of the day began. His younger cousins jostled each other as they grabbed their victuals bags and staffs and hurried to the sheepfold. Not so long ago, he had a flock to tend each day.

Baba and his pottery crew climbed the steps to the pottery yard. Mamaa knelt at her loom to weave, and Aunt Sabah' fed her little one while she waited for water to heat to wash his soiled clothing. Gran-mamaa, dwarfed by her fur robe, huddled on her stool in the warm sunshine and braided red leather cord into a fine rope.

Keshub waited for Uncle Samir, but, deciding to go ahead, shouldered a bag of tools. He would help build a lookout post on the summit today. Half way up the stairs at their early garden ledge, he stopped in mid-stride. Someone was sick. He laid his load of tools on the steps and rounded a lattice ready for pole beans to grow on.

Rachel, his brother Ranine's bride, bent double.

"Rachel? Are you all right? Do you need help?"

She straightened and offered a weak smile while wiping her mouth with the hem of her apron. "No, Keshub. Thank you for your concern, but I am very well. In fact, I am with child."

"With child?"

"Shush. Not everyone knows yet."

"You are going to have a baby?"

"Yes. We are so happy, but we are waiting a while to let others know. So, please do not tell. Your mother and Gran-mamaa know."

"Do you need some water?" He offered his own.

"Thank you, Keshub. I should have brought my own. This has been happening a lot."

"Keep the water."

"Thanks."

Smiling, he had to ask, "How does Gran-mamaa know? She cannot see."

"Oh, she can tell. She has required a hug every morning since the wedding celebration. She said it warmed her up, but I think she wanted to be the first to know by feeling me growing."

"Yes, that sounds like her."

Keshub returned to his tools. Rachel knelt to thin and weed seedlings. He waved good-bye and winked.

A few days later, Keshub returned from his second trip to Jericho with Uncle Yaakoub. He plodded beside his clip-clopping friend, Raja, and emerged from the ridgeline forest into the wide Valley of Aijalon. The flat-topped, footprint-shaped hill of Gibeon stood alone below them, surrounded by green fields. On the valley floor, at the far end of neighbor Agh-taan's wheat field, Keshub squinted to take in the Ra-eef' homestead. A donkey stood at the fence of the Ra-eef' livestock pen.

Keshub raised his voice to be heard over the clip-clops. "Whose animal could that be?"

Uncle Yaakoub kept the pace and flung an answer over his shoulder. "Only one animal—not a caravanner. See the two men leaning against the wall of the guest house?"

Keshub squinted. "Soldiers do not lean unless they are waiting for someone. Right?"

Uncle Yaakoub waved an arm with a flourish. "Probably someone grand and important who rides a donkey. Who is important, rides a donkey, and has soldiers guarding him?"

Keshub allowed Raja to chomp a mouthful of the lush wheat grass beside the trail. "Do you think another emissary from Adoni-Zedek in Jerusalem has come calling?"

Still half way across the wheat field, Uncle pointed. "Did you see the soldiers grab their spears and snap to attention?"

Baba and his guest rounded the corner of the guest house. The guest pivoted toward Baba and hunched forward.

Keshub's eyebrows shot up. "Baba's guest appears angry. Is he wagging his finger in Baba's face? Uh-oh, wagging a finger in Baba's face is not a good thing to do."

The angry stranger vaulted onto his mount and spurred the animal to a hasty trot.

Uncle laughed. "Sorry, soldier-boys, leisure time is over. Hope you are rested enough to keep up with the jackal you are guarding."

Keshub waved to Baba who ambled out to meet them at the little spring.

Uncle Yaakoub lifted his voice. "Are you needing a little fresh air and a walk-about, brother?"

"That is exactly what I need." Baba stopped with his fists jammed onto his hips.

Keshub brought his animals abreast of his uncle's.

Uncle arched his brows high and tugged his mouth in a downward curve. "Who was that?" He could not keep his good humor out of his voice.

"He was another official emissary of Adoni-Zedek." Baba clipped his words and tossed his head. "Sometimes I think we are in greater danger being neighbor to that fiend than any other threat."

Uncle nodded while a smile played hide and seek behind his beard and mustache. "What did he want?"

"He wanted the same thing the other one wanted but had a different approach. He wanted to buy an alliance by paying us to make palm-size talismans of Molech for Zedek. He wanted to sell them in the marketplace in Jerusalem. In his first offer he would pay us after each market day for the number sold."

"Hum-mm." Uncle Yaakoub put his hand to his short beard and tilted his head. "What was the second offer you turned down, brother?"

Was Uncle Yaakoub teasing his big brother? Afraid Baba would send him off to other duties, Keshub tried to be invisible. He fell a pace behind Baba.

"He brought out a leather pouch and rattled it, leering like the ghoul he was. When I did not respond, he took a few gold coins out and said he was authorized to pay in gold now for a delivery of talismans before the next full moon. I refused again."

"Of course, you did." Uncle's grin grew wider.

"I told him this is a small family business, and we do not have enough workers to manage a job this size at any price. I did not tell him we would not lower ourselves by making a deal with such a despicable person as Zedek."

"Of course, you did not. That would be rude."

Baba hardly paused. "I also did not say I would not even consider dirtying my hands to make something as useless as a clay talisman of Molech. Zedek would use them to continue scaring the people of Jerusalem into submission."

"Hear, hear, brother." Uncle Yaakoub clapped his older brother on the back and laughed. "It is good to see you still have your integrity."

Uncle Yaakoub lowered his voice—his tone now serious. "While we were in Jericho, word came that the Hebrews attacked the Midianites on the other side of the Jordan. The Midianites have been close allies with the Moabites lately. That must be what happened when Eskie reported a large number of Hebrews left their camp geared for battle several days ago. This time they took women and children as slaves."

Keshub jerked his head to read his uncle's expression. Did that mean everyone else beside women and children were destroyed?

ೋഇ

IN THE HEBREW CAMP EAST OF THE JORDAN RIVER

Hosiah stacked wood beside the kitchen fire.

"Mother!" Elkanah slowed as he returned from helping Uncle Joshua at his tent across the camp.

Mother pushed aside the flap that covered the doorway to their tent. On the Persian rug under the awning at their doorway, she wiped the dust of fresh ground manna on her plainest apron. "What is it, son?"

"Uncle Joshua said Hosiah and I must fill our water jars tonight and gather extra manna tomorrow morning."

"Did he say why?"

"He said we will have more mouths to feed tomorrow."

"More mouths?"

"Mother, he said he did not have time to explain because he, Moses, and Eleazar were dividing the spoils taken from the Midianites."

"Well, then, we must wait until tomorrow to see what Joshua means. Boys, get more water. I will finish grinding manna to thicken the soup of dried mutton on the fire. Supper will be ready by the time you return."

"Mmm-m. Dried mutton in a thick gravy! That is my favorite, Mother." Hosiah rubbed his stomach as he headed to a nearby spring with his brother.

The next morning Uncle Joshua arrived with two Midianite captives. He readied to leave. "She has not talked yet. She looks strong. Perhaps in time she will be a great help to you, Magdalyn."

"I hope the child will be a pleasure to you." Uncle Joshua turned away to resume his duties at Moses' side.

Mother turned back to their tent. A young Midianite girl knelt on the carpet near the entrance with head held high but eyes downcast. She held a small child who sucked her thumb.

Mother whispered. "The girl reminds me of myself when your father was killed suddenly last year. Please get her a bowl of water, Hosiah. Place it on the rug in front of her. She will drink it when she is thirsty enough."

Mother stooped in front of the young girl and the child clinging to her.

The child peered out of wide, dark eyes through tousled strands of black hair plastered to wet, tear-stained cheeks.

"Hello, little one. Are you hungry?"

Mother produced a nicely browned manna griddle cake left from breakfast. The child's eyes showed immediate interest.

"Hosiah, please bring the honey pot."

"Yes, Mother."

Soon the young child sat on his mother's lap receiving small pinches of griddle cake dipped in honey.

The young woman knelt nearby, unmoved. Mother patted the child's leg then gathered strands of dark hair off wet cheeks. "It will take time, Hosiah. But we have plenty of time to get acquainted with the new members of our household."

Hosiah turned away with a smile. Mother loved helping at birthings and tending other folk's babies. Now she would have one in their own household.

Chapter 28:
News from Mt. Nebo

Keshub placed his fingers at his lips and practiced the bulbul's call as he trod the trail through the oak forest. The early morning light struggled to penetrate the thick canopy of evergreen leaves.

He pulled his sheepskin vest close and squared his shoulders. He told himself he was not really afraid, but he had never come this way alone before. He had shivered at a lion's roar at night on the clay dig not too far from here. Would he ever forget the lion slinking toward his sheep in the meadow? The morning of the longest day of the year seemed so long ago now.

Baba cautioned him this morning. "Peer around the bends to check for other travelers on the trail. Leave the trail and hide until you are alone again." Baba had arched his eyebrow for emphasis.

Keshub had drawn water for a few caravanners who travelled with young slaves in their party. Was Baba afraid of his being stolen away as a slave? Of course, Zedek's notorious young soldiers might do the same.

Keshub stopped at the place to leave the trail for the climb over the ridge to Eskie's lookout perch. He shifted the heavy water and victuals bags and gave the cheerful call of the bulbul. *Wheet-ru-Tweet.*

Eskie did not answer with his cliff swallow's call.

Keshub called again but still no answer. His heart leapt to his throat. Something was very wrong. What had happened that Eskie was not there? Was he taken captive by Zedek's men?

He scrambled up the incline clawing at the dirt and rocks, but slowed as he reached the top. He raised his head only enough to expose his eyes and surveyed the lookout post and the camp on the ledge below.

The sun neared the mid-day point, and Eskie was not in his place watching over the Jordan Valley. Keshub's heart nudged his throat again.

His brother sprawled on the cold, hard ground with his knapsack as a pillow. In broad daylight? Was he injured?

Keshub wriggled on his belly across the narrow peak to keep a low profile. Once out of sight of the main trail, he slid recklessly down the slope, clutching at protruding rocks to avoid a freefall. Nearing Eskie, a familiar snore halted his fear for his brother and whipped up sudden baba-like anger. He is asleep? In the middle of the day?

With his sandaled foot he tapped Eskie's twice before he roused. "What is this, Eskie? Asleep on duty?"

Eskie turned away blocking the sun with his arm across his eyes. Little brother poked harder this time.

"Huh-unh? Oh, Kesh. Leave me alone." Eskie brought up his knees inside his tunic.

Why would Eskie act this way? He left Eskie lying there while he found the rosemary branch and returned to the trail to brush out his obvious footprints on the other side of their ridge. He returned and climbed to the lookout position. What was happening in the Jordan Valley?

He scanned the whole valley. Everything looked the same until he focused across the Jordan. At the mountain nearest the river and the Hebrew camp, frenzied movement drew his attention. Men climbed up and down and all around that mountain like ants around an ant hill.

Baba would need an explanation. Keshub got the goatskin water bag and stood over Eskie pouring drop by drop on his face.

"What? Bildad? Why?"

"You did not hear my signal. If you had, you would have known I was not Bildad. Wake up and tell me what has happened. I must return to report to Baba soon. I brought your new supplies. Bildad is injured and cannot come."

"Umph." Eskie turned onto his back.

"If you were one of Zedek's spies, you could be executed, big brother." Keshub prodded Eskie's foot harder.

Eskie was half awake with droopy eyelids and yawning, but Keshub could not waste too much water, so he turned to the victuals bag. Surely food would wake his brother. Mamaa had sent him a whole roasted duck's leg. Lucky fellow. Keshub would volunteer to roost with eagles all day for such a feast. The rest of the family got bits and pieces in a lentil stew.

Keshub held the lookout's new victuals bag open. "Eskie, wake up and eat this duck's leg, or I will eat it for you."

Miraculously, Eskie sat up. "A duck's leg? For me?"

Keshub thrust the delicacy at his brother.

Eskie grabbed it and gnawed.

Keshub pointed toward the Jordan. "What is happening there on that mountain across the river? Men are crawling over it like hornets around their hive."

Eskie swallowed, then gulped water from the full water bag. "You will not believe it when I tell you, little brother."

"But you must tell me, and make it quick. I brought you victuals for three more days. We hope Bildad can walk by then. If not, Baba will decide what to do next. I must return by dark. So, tell me. What has happened?"

"All right." Eskie wiped his chin. "At mid-morning yesterday I said to myself, 'I know that young man going there.' I talk to myself aloud to remind myself who I am and why I am here. Otherwise, lookout duty would be like being in a prison."

Keshub nodded. "Yes, Mamaa says her Number Three is the Ra-eef' grandson who most loves to talk."

Eskie shrugged. "You see, for days I have considered the possibility of accompanying a spy from Jerusalem across the river so I could see the Hebrews closer up. I turned over ideas of how I could approach one of them. I could not simply overtake Zedek's man on the trail because that would reveal I had come down the same wadi. Several days ago I chose a place to meet a spy from Jerusalem."

Still chewing, Eskie tightly closed the victuals bag and tucked it into a niche of a boulder. He nodded over his shoulder for Keshub to follow. He crawled up the incline to the lookout spot on one hand and one elbow and turned onto his back. He pointed with the duck's leg. "I climbed down that steep cliff there by way of some narrow ledges and avoided the sheer drops."

When Keshub turned, his eyes popped wide and his jaw fell.

Eskie took a gulp of water. "I knew it would be dangerous, but the risk would allow me to intercept Zedek's spy before he reached the Zor and his hidden boat. Since I knew the young man who went by on the trail, the right time had come to act on my plan.

"I grabbed my knapsack with water and food inside, slung it over my shoulder, and placed my bow and quiver over my other shoulder. I clambered down." Eskie shrugged and concentrated on stripping every morsel from the duck's bone.

Keshub eyed the large rounded boulder where Eskie pointed and could not believe him. "How?"

Waving the bone, Eskie turned onto his belly and wriggled into position to see the valley below.

Keshub crawled up beside him.

"I mostly slid on my bottom until I reached a ledge below. When I got there, the rest was easy. Before the spy from Jerusalem had reached the valley floor from the wadi trail, I crossed through the date palm grove south of Jericho." Eskie crunched the cartilage on the bone's end.

"Zedek's spies walked along the far edge out of view of Jericho. If I could go through the grove on an angle with their lookout mountain straight ahead, I would intersect his path."

Keshub traced Eskie's path as he spoke, and prickles of excitement ran up his backbone.

"When I reached the far side of the grove, I stayed behind cover until the man had passed and was only a few paces down the trail." Eskie licked his greasy fingers.

"I whistled softly. The young man turned, raised his bow, and seated an arrow onto his bow string in one fluid motion."

Keshub shook his head. How was he going to tell all this to Baba?

"I stuck my head out from behind a palm tree and said, 'Impressive, man. Jebus is your name, right? You are son of the skilled artisan who made my own bow.' Then I stepped into full view holding up my bow to show the truth of my words and kept talking."

"Eskie, you could have been killed."

Big brother shrugged. "I said, 'How I wish I could afford to use only arrows made by your father. Too bad, I must make my own replacement arrows. They are pitiful substitutes at best, although I am getting better at it.'"

"You know Baba will be furious, Eskie."

"The spy lowered his bow and arrow but held it ready. He said, 'You need a sharp iron knife. Flint knives cannot be so sharp or precise.'" Eskie sucked on the joint end a moment.

"I took a step closer and introduced myself. I told him I lived in a country village near Jerusalem. I had seen him demonstrate my bow and arrows the day I traded a yearling lamb for them. I said to him, 'You can imagine my disappointment to find the bow, as excellent as it is, is only as good as the bowman using it.' His bow arm relaxed a little at that." Eskie inserted the softened joint end into his jaw teeth and crunched down.

"So I told him my father had sent me to find out more about the Hebrews, and I had been watching from one of the ridges for several days. I nodded and shrugged in a general direction so I would not give away our position."

Keshub shook his head back and forth. What a great risk his brother had taken.

"I laughed and told him, 'I have to say you fellows have a better plan. A boat and a perch on that mountain top there must give a better view of the action. Do you mind if I go with you today?'

"When he hesitated, I said, 'Oh, I can stay out of sight until your friend leaves if that is what you are thinking.'"

Keshub shook his head, and a chuckle bubbled out. "Eskie, you have more gall than anyone around."

"It is talent, little brother. Jebus from Jerusalem answered, 'You seem to know our mission already, so I would not be divulging any secrets .... Sure. Why not? Let's trot or I will be late reporting to duty.'

"So I said, 'Let's go! And thanks.'"

"Eskie, Baba will be so angry when he hears this. You may go to bed without dinner until the next full moon. It is lucky you will not see Baba until after his anger has a chance to cool. So tell me the rest and make it quick, I have to head home soon."

"Yes, you do. I will talk as fast as I can.

"I followed Jebus into the Zor. There were thorny vines and brambles growing everywhere, and we saw a very large cat print. When we reached the bank of the Jordan, Jebus pulled a small boat from behind tall canes growing near the water.

"Keshub, tell Baba Jebus said 'As soon as Mt. Hermon begins to thaw, this will all be under water. After another full moon of spying, we can take a break while the river floods.'

"Jebus found a rope submerged there and took up the slack until I could see it was strung across the river and tied to a tree on the other side. He directed me to help him pull hand over hand. Otherwise, we would have ended up far down the river on the other side because the water flowed swiftly.

216

"When we got to the other bank, I helped Jebus hide his boat in the Zor, and we hurried to the foot of their lookout mountain. He called it Nebo. I hid and waited while he went up. The other spy came down and left the way we came.

"Then I followed the clear footpath to the top and joined Jebus who was lying on his belly peering through a bush. I slithered up beside him to see the most incredible sight of my life."

Chapter 29:
A Close-Up View

Fully awake and full of duck, Eskie pointed. "Little brother, from here you see the Hebrews are a dark smudge at the foot of the blue hills. On Nebo the view was like standing over an ant hill or like watching the Ra-eef' flocks graze on the hillside across Aijalon Valley from the pottery yard."

Lying prone beside him at the perch, little brother removed a pebble from under his elbow and tossed it aside. "Baba is going to be angry that you crossed the river, but what did you see?"

Eskie turned from lying on his belly to his side. "Hebrew tents covered the whole valley floor between several mountains of Moab. The tents lined up in rows with wide lanes from the center point, like my fingers splayed out." He spread his fingers apart to demonstrate.

"What was in the center?"

"Another tent, but much larger and black. A fence of white curtains, whiter than anything I have ever seen, surrounded it. Here

218

and there the sun continually flashed from fittings for the framework of the fence. I said to Jebus, 'Surely it cannot be, but that sparkles like gold or silver.'"

"What did Jebus say?"

"He said, 'I will not report that to Zedek. He would have us storm the gates of Hades for that much gold.'"

"What else did you see?"

"The cloth fence had an entrance on the side facing the rising sun. The gate was a handsome red color. Between the red entrance and the black tent two large fixtures stood in an open area. One appeared to be a basin. Men carried and poured, what must have been water, into the basin." He turned back onto his belly and propped himself on his elbows, considering his next words.

"A curious thing happened while I strained to take it all in. An intense shaft of light flashed from the basin and pierced my eyes— almost as if I were gazing directly at the sun and as if the light had sought me out. I rubbed my eyes with my fists and looked again, but the piercing light was gone." He swallowed to clear his throat.

Keshub stared back at him with huge eyes.

Eskie forced his usual tone of bravado. "The other fixture was an altar for sacrifice, perhaps made of bronze. An amazing sight, Kesh."

"And now you have to stay three more days. I will tell Baba what you have told me, but not as well as you would."

"Kesh, there is more. I will try to make it shorter because you have to return home by dark, but Kesh, I heard their two leaders speaking to each other."

"What? How? How did you get so close? Baba will be furious." Little brother forgot to whisper.

"Calm down. I did not go into their camp. How simple do you think I am? They came to Nebo."

"What? They came to the mountain you were watching from? That mountain where people are running all over searching for something?"

"Yes. At first we saw many people in the Hebrew camp come

together in a crowd. They were quiet for a long time. Jebus and I agreed for so many people together in one place, there was an awesome silence. We also agreed yesterday was a very different day for the Hebrews than any we had observed before. But I have not told you about the cloud."

"The cloud?"

"All day a cloud hovered over the large tent in the middle of the Hebrews' camp. Suddenly the small cloud became a cloud like no other cloud I have ever seen, appearing to stand erect and tall. I turned onto my back to look for the top as it shimmered in the afternoon sunlight.

"I whispered. 'Jebus, do you see what is very strange about that cloud?'"

"He answered, 'You mean beside standing up and looking like it reaches to the heavens? What?'"

"I said, 'There is no shadow.'"

"'No shadow?' he said."

"Compare the shadow cast by the grove of palm trees."

"Jebus whispered back, 'You are right.'"

"I said, 'A cloud like that would cast a long shadow if it really were a cloud.'"

Eskie raked his hands over his scrubby beginning of a beard. "Well, things began to happen more quickly at that point. From Mt. Nebo we heard the multitude cheer mightily. The sound of the combined voices of our enemy was like the roar of a lion near enough to pounce. Chills raced up my spine. But soon the crowd changed to moaning and wailing. After that two men emerged from the multitude and walked toward us."

"Toward you?"

"Yes. We did not understand at first, but when it became clear they were coming to Nebo, Jebus signaled 'Let's go!' We turned onto our backs and slid down. As soon as we could stand without being seen, we scrambled down as fast as we could go on the trail to the Zor."

He pursed his lips considering how reckless his words would

sound. "When we reached the bottom of the mountain, I motioned to Jebus, 'I will be right back.' I crouched low and kept behind large boulders and bushes until I circled the base to get a better view of the two men coming our way. I crept as close as I dared, so I could see them through a crevice between two large boulders."

From the corner of his eye, his little brother shook his head back and forth. Keshub's mild disapproval would not compare to what Baba would vent.

Eskie turned to his side again to look his little brother in the eye. "The older man had white hair and beard flowing over his shoulders like the snow covering Mt. Hermon. The younger had gray hair and a short beard. Tears streamed down his rugged face while the older one spoke. 'Remember, Joshua, the Lord Himself will cross over ahead of you. He will destroy these nations before you, and you will take possession of their land. Be strong and courageous. Do not be afraid, for the Lord your God goes with you; He will never leave you nor forsake you.'"

"Whoa. You heard him say that?" Little brother's eyes were as big as full moons at the horizon at harvest time.

"Yes. The old man's voice was as strong as thunder. After a kiss on either cheek, the older man turned and climbed to the top of the mountain. The younger knelt with hands clasped and head bowed, but I did not wait any longer. I ran like the wind to rejoin Jebus."

Keshub rubbed his arms as if he were suddenly cold.

"We put as much distance as possible between us and the Hebrews. But by that time, twilight arrived—too late to go through the Zor. Cat tracks or not, we huddled inside the Zor near the thicket's edge. We swapped turns watching the mountain top and listening for the big cat." Eskie forced down a shiver.

"About midnight I unfurled my bedroll to get some sleep while Jebus watched. Thunder roared and lightning cracked. I jumped. We both witnessed the flash that struck Nebo and was over in a moment. Only one clap of thunder with no rain to follow—just a thunderous amount of wailing and mourning from the Hebrew camp." Eskie unplugged his grapevine stopper from his pottery flask and took a long draw of water.

"At first light, Jebus and I found the trail through the Zor to the river where we searched for the rope tied to a tree. We both pulled with all our might to take up the slack on the submerged rope and pulled the boat across the river to us. We jumped in and kept pulling until we reached Canaan. When we turned to look back, several men searched Mt. Nebo."

Keshub frowned. "The day is half gone, and they are still searching. Do you think they are searching for the white-haired leader?"

"If they are, they must not be finding anything. If he were there, they would have found him by now." Eskie shook his head. What happened last night when lightning struck?

"On this side of the river again, Jebus had second thoughts about admitting he left his post early. He did not think anyone would believe what he saw—the pillar cloud that cast no shadow or the lightning on the mountain top."

"Will Baba believe your story?" Little brother arched the family eyebrow, just like Baba.

"It is true, little brother. I could not make up a story this strange. But now I must tell you about Jebus. He and I rested a short while in the cover of the date palm grove. Jebus vented his frustration. 'I hate Zedek. I hate Zedek's so-called god Molech. What am I doing going along with everything that oozing, pustulous boil of a man says? He killed his own son. What kind of man does that? Molech, schmolech. Zedek uses that garbage to scare people into doing what he says. I wish I knew what else to do. Leave Canaan, maybe. What about you, Eskie?'"

"Jebus sounds like Baba, Eskie. How did you answer?"

"I agreed with him without thinking. 'My father hates Zedek, too.' I said. 'He refused an alliance with him, twice.'"

Little brother lowered his chin and raised an eyebrow—just like Baba would do.

Eskie combed his fingers through his hair. "Jebus said, 'Really? How did he do that and live to tell it?' I had said too much already and shrugged."

"Jebus asked me, 'Did you say where you are from, Eskie?'"

Both Keshub's eyebrows shot up. "Uh-oh. Did he figure out we are from Gibeon?"

Eskie tucked his chin. "Yes. He asked, 'Are you from Gibeon?' Before I could answer, he said, 'I admire anyone who stands up to Zedek and gets away with it. I do not know anyone else who has.'"

"Keshub, it just came out of my mouth, 'Then you should meet my father.'

"And Jebus said, 'I think I already have. If your father will not agree to an alliance with Zedek, are you going to fight the Hebrews alone or are you leaving Canaan?'"

"I told him neither."

He asked, "What are you going to do?"

Keshub glanced at the sun and shook his head slowly back and forth.

Eskie plunged on. "I told him I did not know, but we have always been neutral, and we would like to remain that way. I know I should not have told him so much, but I felt I could trust him."

Arms folded, Keshub kept on shaking his head and staring.

"That was when Jebus said, 'Neutral is not in Zedek's vocabulary. Your father and Gibeon's reputation for having trained fighting men gives you an advantage that holds Zedek back from forcefully annexing Gibeon .... So you are a lookout for Gibeon? Your secret is safe with me. In fact, I wish ...'"

"That was when I heard someone coming and cautioned Jebus with a finger to my lips. His replacement had arrived. Jebus kissed me on both cheeks before he rose and placed his fist over his heart with a nod. Then he turned to meet his fellow soldier."

"How did you get back here?" Keshub turned back to his belly to view Mt. Nebo again.

"I stayed where I was a bit longer, and then slithered like a viper on my belly half way through the palm grove before I stood. I wanted to flee as fast as I could. Instead, I walked as if on a mission of importance toward the foot of the trail back to Gibeon."

Keshub slid on his back from the perch down to the bowl-shaped ledge. He retrieved his water bag and Eskie's empty victuals sack. "What *will* Baba say, big brother, when I tell him your story? You will owe me for this."

"Yes, I owe you, Kesh."

Little brother grabbed the rosemary broom at the top of the ridge and slithered on his belly across the peak until he was out of sight.

Eskie turned back to scan Mt. Nebo. More important, what will Baba do about a coming invasion?

Chapter 30:
A Flood Coming

Three days later, Keshub shifted his knapsack and the goatskin water bag as he peered up and down the trail. No other travelers in sight. He signaled, "Wheet-ru-Tweet."

"Squee-eeh-yew."

That would be Eskie, the cliff swallow, from his nest among the eagles. Keshub scrambled up the steep ridge on all fours to balance the heavy knapsack and water bag on his back. At the top of the ridge, he lowered the heavier water bag and waved to his brother. All along the trail, he devised a plan to wring some pleasure out of Eskie. He would make his scoundrel of a brother pay for his recent reckless exploits.

Keshub had expected Baba's explosion. He traveled by moonlight across the valley and through neighbor Agh-taan's wheat field. He entered the courtyard, breathless.

He had blurted out, "Eskie crossed the Jordan and saw the Hebrews up close!"

"Eskie did what?" Baba's deep voice raked over Keshub and echoed off the courtyard walls. Even cousin Lehab awoke.

When the whole family emerged from their hillside dugout, Baba lowered his voice. He simmered below boil through the rest of Eskie's tale.

Now on the last ridge above Jericho, Keshub descended back to the trail to pick up the broom tucked behind a rock at the trail's edge. This time he swished away his tracks up to the ridge and kept a low profile to ease over the peak.

Taking up the water bag again, Keshub mostly slid down to the bowl-shaped ledge where Eskie sat cross-legged as if he were at Mamaa's dinner mat. Expecting victuals fresh from home.

Keshub understood and sympathized, but still, he had borne the brunt of Baba's anger. He deserved a little revenge. He shook his head and exaggerated his sadness. "Bildad is not better, Eskie."

"I figured that when I heard your bulbul signal and not his crow's caw. What victuals did you bring?"

"He sent his apology that you have to serve as spy three more days. That will make nine days straight."

"As long as needed. What victuals did you bring?"

"Bildad's ankle must be badly wrenched. His baba does not think it is broken. You should see how swollen it is."

"Yes. Yes. What victuals did you bring?"

Keshub rummaged in his knapsack. "Mamaa feels ever so sorry for you—having to eat so much cold flatbread and all."

"What. victuals. did. you. bring?"

Keshub smirked. "Would you care to guess what our mother sent out of pity for your having spent so-o much time with no one to talk to on this lonely perch?"

Eskie sucked in his cheeks, exaggerated a sunken stomach, and clasped his hands together. "Wha-at?"

"Flatbread and..."

"And what? What? I am starving!"

"Mamaa sent cow's butter...a-and...a leg of lamb."

"A whole leg of lamb?" Eskie grabbed the leg and chomped

down. His eyes rolled back, then closed as he savored his new provisions.

Still chewing, "Did you say cow's butter?"

"Yes."

Grasping the leg in one hand, Eskie wiped his mouth with the back of his other. "Where did we get cow's butter? We do not have cows."

"From Farmer Khalil. You know he is ill and says he will not be with us much longer. But he is so happy now that Yah-ya is doing his leather work. Cousin Ra-heeb' and Jabal, the Moabite refugee, are managing the farming. The butter and some cheese, too, were gifts. You missed the big celebration when Uncle Yaakoub and Ra-heeb' asked Khalil for his daughter Keturah."

"I missed it? Aw-w. How many roasted lambs?"

"Four. Lehab shot a goose, too."

"Oh, no. I missed a goose, too? What about the gift? What did Ra-heeb' give Farmer Khalil?"

"A donkey."

"A donkey ... for a wife." Eskie crooked a grin.

While his brother devoured the leg of lamb, Keshub settled beside the massive boulder at Eskie's perch. Baba had told him to stay over night and come home at morning light. The ant-like comings and goings around Jericho seemed normal, calm.

In late afternoon after a nap, Eskie joined Keshub at the perch. "Have you seen anything interesting?"

"Only the people stopping at the spring among the palm trees and those going up to and down from the gate of Jericho. And I see the eye-shape of the Hebrew camp, sort of."

"Wait until dark, you will see the strange light. At first I thought it was a fire—burning up endless piles of firewood, every night. I have come to realize that cannot be. We potters of Ra-eef' know firewood and how much is required. The Zor would be bare near them if it were so. Besides, it is impossible that bright light is a wood fire."

Keshub nibbled at a rib of roasted lamb as shadow from the

ridge overtook Jericho.

"Keep your eyes on the cloud over the Hebrew camp, Kesh. Watch it change as darkness arrives."

With the last rays of sunlight, the cloud reflected the orange sunset. Instead of fading with the sunlight, the cloud increased from a glimmer at dusk to a glowing light reaching high into the night sky.

"Whoa." Keshub rolled over to his back to see the top of the amazing cloud, his voice a hoarse whisper. "And whoa again. Eskie, next to the light of the Hebrews, the Big Bear and North Star are not as bright as usual."

"Yes. I have noticed that, too. They cannot compete with the light over the Hebrew camp, I think."

The next morning Keshub took up his near-empty knapsack and the branch for sweeping and bid good-bye to Eskie at the perch. He scrambled up the outcropping that shielded the perch from view of the trail and raised his head only enough to peer over.

Eskie called out a caution. "Kesh, wait."

He stopped, and squirmed away from the peak before turning. "What?"

"When will Ra-heeb' claim his bride?"

Keshub shrugged. "Oh, after the barley is threshed." He eased over the top with a wave.

***

Two fortnights later in their Ra-eef' courtyard, Keshub dipped his warm flatbread into steaming mint tea. A staple at every meal in other seasons, flatbread in the season of near starvation was reserved for dipping on cold mornings. Until barley harvest, Mamaa would use the last stored-up grain carefully.

"Ummm." Next to him Eskie cupped his bowl with both hands, then made an exaggerated frown. "Three more days at the perch until I eat my next warm meal, Kesh. That nine days between warm meals while Bildad's ankle healed seemed like an eternity."

Mamaa scuffed across the courtyard bearing two knapsacks. She extended a sagging sack to Keshub. To Eskie she held out a bag stuffed to near overflowing. "I am sorry, Keshub, there is not enough grain left to make flatbread for everyone, but Eskie needs it. I know you understand."

"Yes, Mamaa, I do. I know you worry about Eskie when he is spying on the Hebrews all alone, but I think he is glad he can help." Keshub shoved his brother number three on the shoulder. "He likes sitting amongst eagles and thinking his lofty thoughts."

Baba neared and cleared his throat. "Eschol?"

"Yes, sir?" Eskie dipped his chin and lowered his eyes. He had heard many times already how angry Baba had been two fortnights ago. Baba had not called him Eskie since.

"Keep your lofty thoughts on this side of the Jordan River, son. No more adventures. You will be there to watch from the perch only and report what you see. Remember that."

"Halloo!" Uncle Yaakoub stuck his head in the gate. "Anyone going to Jericho with me?"

Keshub shouldered his knapsack and headed to the livestock pen with Eskie scurrying right behind him.

Outside the gate, Eskie whispered. "I did not tell Baba I have talked to Jebus again.

Keshub jerked his head and stopped to face his errant brother.

"Do not fear, little brother. I stopped Jebus at the mid-way campground below our perch. He still does not know where our lookout post is. He is a good man, Kesh. He confirmed my observations that absolutely nothing out of the ordinary has happened in the Hebrew camp since the day we spent together on Nebo."

***

Early the next morning, Keshub followed Uncle Yaakoub and his donkeys to the spring surrounded by palm trees.

Uncle Yaakoub halted and spoke to a crippled man sitting beside the road.

The man laughed with a happy cackle. He gave a gaping, sunken smile and nodded. He had no teeth.

Uncle Yaakoub bypassed their usual spot and led his train of donkeys laden with goods to the foot of the gravel ramp. He did not hesitate. He plodded up the steep road to the iron-barred gate.

Were they going to enter Jericho today?

Uncle Yaakoub spoke to an official at the gate and paid a vendor's tax before they entered with their six pack animals. Inside, Uncle Yaakoub looked right and then left and chose left.

Keshub followed—into an entirely different world. The street before him curved with the bend of the outer wall. On the left, small, dark houses appeared to be two single rooms built against Jericho's outer wall, one on top of the other. A narrow stairway on one side led to an upper room. The same stairway, in many cases, also led to a neighbor's upper room.

On the right, houses clung all a-kilter one above another to the further incline of the tall hill Jericho was built on. Had the houses sprung up there on their own like mushrooms clinging to a dead log in the forest?

Keshub stroked Raja's long soft ears. "Everything is the same color. The houses are the color of dirt, the same as the dusty street. Children's garments are the color of dirt, and their faces are smudged with it. Their eyes are sad, too."

The smells took his breath away. "Raja, I never before appreciated open space and a stiff breeze. Oh to be at the threshing floor on Gibeon's hill right now."

Keshub gulped at the sight of one particular child, the age of Uncle Samir's youngest. The child wobbled on a raised threshold in a soiled loin cloth. His silent tears made rivulets down his cheeks.

Uncle found an open area down the lane for their booth.

Keshub helped lift packs off the donkeys and untied leather cords to open them. Out of sweet-smelling wheat straw, he brought pottery and whittled pothooks and long-handled spoons. He set larger pieces at the back against a limestone retaining wall.

"Keshub, take these three donkeys back the way we came to the old man I spoke to near the spring. Tether the animals near him as he directs. He will watch them for us. Come back to get the others."

"Yes, sir." When he reached the gate and fresh air reached his nostrils, he inhaled slowly. He sidestepped to avoid fresh animal droppings. Even that smelled better than the air inside those walls.

The old man squatted exactly where he was before. "Sir, my uncle told me to bring these animals to you for your keeping. Where would you like me to take them?"

"What is your name, sonny?"

"Keshub, sir."

"Well, Keshub, first of all I am not sir. I am Deyab. Second, meet my grandson. Tadjhe!"

"Yes, Gran-baba?" A two-generation-younger replica of his grandfather appeared with teeth and strong legs.

"Show Keshub where he can leave his donkeys, son."

"Of course, Gran-baba. Over here, Keshub."

Keshub followed the lad a short distance away to a patch of grass and a small spring-fed pool. Raja stood still while he tied a wide cuff of leather around both front legs below the knees.

Tadjhe held the lead rope.

Keshub looped a narrower leather cord between the two cuffs to allow Raja a short stride for grazing. He rewarded her cooperation by rubbing her gray back and shoulders where a black stripe made a cross.

Raja responded with a nudge of her muzzle and a soft ee-Aw-w.

After hobbling two more, less willing, donkeys, Keshub straightened and grinned. "Thanks for the help. I think the animals know this is my first time to be in charge. I will bring three more in a bit."

As they rejoined Deyab, Tadjhe looked up with big brown eyes. "Will you be in Jericho overnight, Keshub?"

"I hope not," came out of Keshub's mouth unbidden. Before he could apologize for the offensive sound of his words, Deyab cackled.

"It is a foul place, is it not?" The old man squinched up his wrinkled, leathery face.

"Yes, sir, I mean Deyab. It is. Do you live there?"

"Me? Oh, no. There is too much Bedouin blood in me for that place. It is too tight with too many people, too dark, and too much like rats in a cave for me."

Keshub agreed and waved. "Thank you, s-, I mean Deyab. I must go back to get our other animals."

"I will be right here, Keshub. Hold your nose and watch where you step." The old man cackled again.

At their booth, Uncle Yaakoub had a customer. His nod was all Keshub needed.

He led the three animals away.

The same toddler wobbled on his threshold again.

Such big, pitiful eyes and such sadness Keshub could not imagine.

After he left the donkeys with Deyab and Tadjhe, he passed the sad-eyed lad a third time. Keshub drew a dried fig from his pouch and stretched out his hand.

The child stared at the morsel for an instant. Then he snatched it as if it might disappear if he delayed. The dirty hand went straight to his mouth. After a small bite, the lad gave all his attention to chewing.

Keshub slipped away. The rest of the day he stood at his uncle's side or carried a clay vessel for a new owner. All of Jericho was not as squalid as his first impression.

The first impression, however, stuck with him.

***

At mid-afternoon he stretched his shoulders back and inhaled deeply of clean, fresh air. "Raja, I am very glad to be heading home."

Uncle Yaakoub whistled a tune as he led the way up the trail to Eskie's perch.

Raja's ears twitched toward Uncle.

Keshub rubbed gently behind her long, pointy ears. "Uncle Yaakoub must be glad for fresh air, too."

Keshub patted Raja's neck. "Does a lighter burden for the return make you glad, Raja? The luscious melon we bartered for, from a Jordan Valley garden, will make Eskie glad."

That night the warm woolen blanket and the fresh, chilly breeze on his cheeks made him glad—glad to be a Gibeonite. What about the child in the doorway whose eyes followed him every time he passed by? Why did he have such big, sad, unblinking eyes?

CBSO

IN THE HEBREW CAMP

Hosiah lowered a fresh jar of water into its place in the shade of their awning. He stabilized the narrow-bottomed crock with a ring of readily-available limestone rocks. "Yes, Mother?"

"Please take Zu-zu away from the tent and play with her. Co-zi' and I are overwhelmed by how many neighbors have brought me their manna to bake today. We cannot watch her properly, and she might get too near the fire. Please, son."

"Of course, Mother." Hosiah put away his Senet game and retrieved a soft sheep's skin ball from his belongings in their tent.

"Zu-zu! Do you want to catch the ball?"

"Baw!" squealed the toddler and ran toward him.

Hosiah backed away to lead her to a safe distance. He tossed the ball underhanded to her. The homemade toy went through her toddler hands, and hit her chest.

She flinched as the ball fell to her feet. Swaying unsteadily, the child bent to pick up the ball with both hands.

"Catch me, Zu-zu!" Hosiah skipped away glancing over his shoulder.

Zu-zu giggled as she ran with a toddler's gait. "Baw!"

He looped back and danced with arms flailing the air to evade Zu-zu's pursuit. His mother and the young Midianite woman knelt kneading bread on two flat boards nearby.

"Zu-zu is good for us all, Co-zi'. My son enjoys having a little sister. Hosiah is twelve now. And I love having a little one around again. I am sorry for the loss of your sister, but I am glad you and her child are safe with us."

Co-zi' looked up with a half-smile and returned to kneading the manna bread in front of her.

Chapter 31:
Two Spies

Keshub munched a dried fig and tossed in an almond for crunch. "The smell was awful, Lehab. Jericho was a dirty, sad place. I felt sorry for the people there, and I felt rich in comparison if just for the fresh breezes of Aijalon Valley. Fresh breezes and our family, they make us Ra-eefs rich, I think."

"Keshub, you sound like one of the caravanners. A little travel has made you a philosopher."

"Boys," Uncle Yaakoub called from the lead donkey. "Get ready to move out. Check your cinches and packs. Next stop, Jericho's spring."

Keshub rose from his haunches and joined the three donkeys in his care.

Eskie's and Lehab's heads bent together inspecting Farmer Khalil's two donkeys. Some of the pottery going to market had the farmer's leather goods and cheeses packed in them and around them.

Uncle Yaakoub reported to Baba after the last trip to Jericho. "The barley fields in the foothills of the Jordan were yellow-green and almost ripe while ours in Aijalon Valley were still green. Folks there will be needing storage jars a-plenty. I can sell all we can carry."

Keshub patted Raja on the neck and jostled the pack holding Gran-mamaa's seven-strand, braided, red leather rope. Gran-mamaa had warmed under her middle son's praise when Uncle Yaakoub predicted a high price for such fine workmanship.

"What do you think, Raja? Will the buyer be a horseman or a rich man with a fancy wagon? Or maybe a caravanner who will resell Gran-mamaa's fine handiwork in a far-away place?"

Pack steady, Keshub scratched Raja's head behind her ears and clumped along beside her at the end of the line of Ra-eef' donkeys. "Uncle says we will wait until just the right person makes an offer for the red rope."

Uncle Yaakoub signaled halt before the last bend in the trail where a full view of the Jordan Valley would open up.

Eskie whistled a piercing *squee-eeh-yew* to signal Bildad over the ridge at the lookout perch.

Bildad's caw-caw answered, and Eskie left the trail burdened with three day's provisions.

The Ra-eef' train moved on with hardly a pause.

As Keshub neared the place where his brother left the trail, Eskie returned from depositing his gear at the peak.

He paused backing up the steep incline with a rosemary branch for a broom and cupped a hand around his hoarse whisper. "Kesh. Bring me another melon from Jericho. That was good eating."

"We will try, brother." Keshub waved and kept plodding. He rounded the bend below Eskie's perch, and Jericho came into full view in the valley below.

He whispered. "Raja, as smelly and sad as it was inside, that city is still an amazing sight rising so high and mighty above the palm trees."

CRSO

IN THE HEBREW CAMP

(On about the first day of the first Hebrew month of Abib)

Hosiah arrived at Joshua's tent near the Tabernacle at mid-morning.

Uncle Joshua presided in the shade of the awning to his abode and addressed the leaders of the twelve tribes. "Men, it is time to move from here. Go through the camp and tell your people, 'Get your supplies ready. Three days from now you will cross the Jordan to go in and take possession of the land the Lord your God is giving you for your own.'"

The men dispersed, and Hosiah stepped forward with two hands extended, carrying a leather envelope. The freshly gathered manna, with bits of rosemary and dried lamb stirred in, was still warm.

Uncle Joshua drew aside the leader of the tribe of Judah. "Caleb, send me your best two young men as quickly as possible. They will cross the Jordan and enter Jericho to report the attitude and readiness of the land. I have Moabite clothing that will help them ease in and out without too much notice."

Caleb stroked his white beard and nodded. "I know just who. Salmon, son of Nahshon, and Othniel, son of Kenaz. I will send them immediately."

Hosiah had heard the story many times of Caleb's and Uncle Joshua's spy mission thirty-eight years ago. His uncle and the other oldest man in the camp had been close friends for over forty years. They had believed the God of Israel would give them victory. Now the only survivors of that whole generation parted with a kiss to either cheek.

Hosiah handed his uncle the pouch of warm food and took up a sagging water bag. He returned lugging a full water bag from a nearby spring as two men dressed in rough garments were leaving his uncle's tent.

Hosiah shouldered the tent flap aside and hung the heavy water bag on the tent pole.

Uncle Joshua tied the flap open and entered. He took up his half-eaten food, now cold. "Tell your mother thank you for this morning's meal. Tell her I said it was delicious as always."

"Yes, sir."

"Your mother may have heard already from the leader of our Ephraimite tribe. Kemuel will be passing the word we will move out in three days. I will come tomorrow to see if there is anything your family needs."

"Yes, sir."

Excitement bubbled up in Hosiah's chest as he jogged back to their tent at the west end. Skirting along the edge of the vast camp, he neared the dense thicket. He had heard the roar of a lion deep in its tangle twice. Now the Jordan River overflowed and trees, shrubs and thorny vines stood deep in flood waters. In three days, they would cross that flood? How would they accomplish what looked impossible?

Across the river the fortified city of Jericho rose like a crown above the tops of the palm trees near it. The Amorites of Heshbon and Bashan had fortified cities, too. The Hebrew army had destroyed them. In the warm sunshine, Hosiah shivered. He lifted his gaze to the high ridge above the Jordan Valley. At what price would his people gain the land promised to Father Abraham?

⊂⊃

AMONG THE CANAANITES

Keshub rose early hearing Jericho's gushing spring and fringed palm fronds rustling in a faint breeze. He helped load the Ra-eef' donkeys and inserted a finger between cinch and rounded belly.

Raja swished her tail.

Keshub took that as an affirmative and shuffled behind Uncle and Lehab up the gravel ramp into the gaping maw of the oldest city in Canaan.

Inside the first wall, Uncle Yaakoub claimed a good, wide space against a retaining wall. The stacked-stone wall supported the slope below Jericho's second wall of mudbricks.

Keshub and his cousin unloaded packs, set up their booth, and delivered their donkeys to Deyab. On his return from the spring, he elbowed Lehab beside him. "The children are quite different here this time. They seem happier. Uncle Yaakoub said they would be—because of the barley harvest. He says the children were starving when we were here at the last full moon."

His cousin Lehab gawked wide-eyed and open-mouthed, just like he did on his first time in Jericho.

Keshub stopped in the crowded lane to pick up a tightly wound ball of rag strips and tossed it back to a young boy playing in the street. Keshub scanned the area searching for the sad-eyed boy who ate his dried fig, but did not see him. Back at the booth, he helped Uncle Yaakoub by pulling out the pottery customers pointed to and by rearranging the remaining stock.

Lehab returned from carrying a clay jar to the home of one customer with a big smile and a wooden treasure. "Look at this, Keshub! A game called 'goat's knuckles.' We can play it together."

"How do you play it?" He examined the acacia wood game board about as long as his sling and a little wider than his hand.

"I roll the goat's knuckles on the ground to learn how many moves I get to skip my colored pegs along these three rows of squares. You do the same on your turn. The first one to move all his pegs down the first row, back on the second and down the third row opposite where he started, wins."

"What did you pay for it?"

"I traded the new belt my mother wove for my first trip outside Aijalon Valley."

"Will your mother be angry? How will you carry your lunch pouch if you have no girdle to tuck it into?"

Lehab shrugged. "Aw, I will pick wildflowers for Mamaa when we return. And my pouch has an extra-long drawstring cord. I can put my arm through and hang it on my shoulder."

Uncle Yaakoub whistled softly behind them. "Boys, put that

away and pay attention to customers."

"Yes, sir." Their two voices answered at once.

At mid-morning Keshub took a customer to Uncle Yaakoub to finalize the trade. He waited with hands folded together at his waist until his uncle finished talking to an angry man with hands on his hips.

The man glanced up and down the lane. "My barley harvest was stolen from me by the king's strong-arms. They *allowed* me to keep hardly enough to replant next year and certainly not enough to feed my family. The king stores all the grain in Jericho's inner vaults and doles it out as he wishes. Those who can pay are charged exorbitant prices."

The citizen of Jericho tossed his head and turned both hands palm up. "The masses who have nothing else to pay except their labor literally become slaves. They do the king's bidding to feed themselves and their families."

Keshub pondered the man's words. What must it be like to be so poor you sell yourself for bread?

During a lull in activity at their booth, Lehab gave Keshub an elbow poke. "A little boy over there has been waving at you and trying to get your attention for some time now."

"Really? Where?"

"Over there." Lehab pointed across the narrow lane to a house against Jericho's outer wall. "Do you know him?"

Keshub smiled and waved. "Sort of. I gave him a dried fig when we were here before. He seemed so sad. Uh-oh. Here he comes!"

The child darted across the busy lane on stubby legs and did not stop until he clasped his arms around Keshub's knees.

"Hey, little fellow. I am glad to see you, too." The child had the same sad eyes he remembered, though now a shy smile stretched his lips. "But I think your mamaa will be looking for you." Keshub took the little fellow's hand to lead him in the direction he came from. "Let's go back now."

A cry of alarm came from across the lane. "Jho-ee! Where...?" A young woman of Aunt Sabah's age eyed Keshub and approached with chin down and elbows pumping.

Keshub had seen the same look on a mother ewe protective of her newborn lamb.

The woman confronted Keshub in the middle of the lane. "Why do you have my nephew with you?"

"I am sorry, ma'am. He ran across to me."

Jho-ee leaned toward Keshub and held out his arms as the young woman picked the child up.

His aunt turned away in a huff to deny the child's wishes. "Do you know my nephew?"

"Ma'am, I only saw him when we came to market here once before. He cried in a doorway back yonder. He seemed so sad. I gave him a dried fig. Sorry to cause any trouble."

Sudden tears came to the young woman's eyes. "My sister died. He lives with me now."

An approaching cart demanded his attention. Keshub scooted out of the lane to make space for the cart and ended up in front of the house Jho-ee came from.

"Fi, fi," Jho-ee extended a cleaner hand than before, opening and closing.

The young woman laughed. "Jho-ee, you little beggar!"

Keshub shrugged. "I would be glad to give him another fig if you agree."

"It is his nap time, but ... Well, all right."

Keshub produced a dried fig from his pouch and held it out. "I once had a favorite lamb named 'Jho-ee."

Nibbling on the fig already, little Jho-ee's eye-lids drooped half way closed. His aunt silently mouthed "Thank you" and turned to go.

Later, Keshub waved to Jho-ee's aunt working in the afternoon sunshine on her roof.

She smiled and returned his wave.

As the sun glided half way to the western rim of Jordan Valley, Keshub and Lehab watered their donkeys and filled water bags at the spring.

Keshub led the last three donkeys back inside to be loaded with their packs. At the booth, Gran-mamaa's leather rope was gone. "Did you pack up the leather rope, Uncle? Or did you sell it?" "We sold it! Two men bought it." Uncle Yaakoub gave a thumb-to-forefinger signal to indicate a very satisfactory price.

"I wonder who?" Looking around, Uncle nodded toward the house across the lane. He spoke under his breath. "There they are, over there."

Keshub followed his uncle's glance to where Jho-ee's aunt led two men up the stairs of her house against the outer wall. One of them had Gran-mamaa's braided red rope looped over his shoulder.

Keshub shrugged. He had hoped for a caravanner. These men looked ordinary.

"Let's join Lehab and see how far up the trail we can go before dark, Keshub."

"Yes, sir. I am ready." Keshub trudged along the descending gravel ramp behind his uncle. Near ground level, shouting and a loud clank rang out behind him. Looking back, the barred outer gates of Jericho had closed tight behind a platoon of soldiers bearing shields and spears with bows slung over their shoulders.

The men thundered down the steep road.

Keshub grasped the animals' lead ropes near the halter to steady them and moved the donkeys aside to make way. The toll takers disappeared behind heavy inner wooden doors slamming shut.

Keshub patted Raja's neck to calm her. "I thought they closed the gates nearer dark."

Uncle frowned and nodded. At the spring, he asked the old man, Deyab.

"Aw, the king is jumpy with the Hebrews camped so close by. Something or somebody spooked him, so he clapped the gates closed a little early. I thought with the barley harvested and the river flooded, we could relax for a few days. All the uncertainty is bad for my business."

Darkness arrived by the time the Ra-eefs reached the campground half way up the trail to Eskie's perch. Keshub made a small campfire while Lehab and Uncle unloaded, hobbled, and fed their pack animals. He ate his now meager victuals with a few dates added and wriggled into his bedroll. He stared at the mysterious light marking the camp of the Hebrews across the Jordan. All quiet except for Lehab's light snore, a voice spoke from darkness.

"Uncle."

Even half expecting Eskie to join them, Keshub started. He turned and rested on his elbows.

Uncle Yaakoub put a finger to his lips and joined Eskie outside the circle of firelight.

"There has been a great increase of activity in the Hebrew camp today, Uncle. Two men crossed the Jordan at mid-morning. They crossed near Gilgal, the small village at the wide shoals where the water is not moving as rapidly. Even so, they had to swim with their belongings in a bundle on their shoulders. I cannot say for sure, but I think they are Hebrews."

"Where did they go?"

"They took a round-about route but ended up at Jericho in the early afternoon and entered the gate."

Uncle Yaakoub kept his voice low. "Two men came to our booth today about that time. A strange encounter. They wore old clothing typical of a tradesman and hardly looked at me. They never spoke.

"One pointed at Gran-mamma's red rope. I told him it was very valuable thinking he could not afford it. He showed me two small wedges of silver. I was suspicious to see Egyptian silver in the hands of men in near rags and told them the rope was worth three times that much.

"The other man took out a wedge about the same size. 'If you have four of those,' I said, 'we have a trade.' And they did. They walked away with Gran-mamaa's rope. And that is when I saw they wore new sandals. I think their clothing was a disguise. They likely were your Hebrew spies, Eskie."

"Perhaps so, Uncle. When the gates suddenly shut, I thought you were still inside. I was much relieved when you headed up the trail toward me. But I think the two Hebrews are still inside Jericho. In three days I will return home with more to tell, I am sure."

Keshub clutched his blanket to his chin. He pictured again two men following little Jho-ee's aunt up the stairs to her roof. Were the new owners of Gran-mamaa's red rope Hebrews? The enemy?

Chapter 32:

On Jordan's Stormy Banks

In the Hebrew camp, Hosiah sprinted along the water's edge carrying Uncle Joshua's empty leather meal pouch. The Jordan River flowed by carrying debris from upstream. A single sandal of some unfortunate soul wedged in the bough of a salt-cedar tamarisk tree. He slowed to a jog as he neared their tent in the Ephraimite camp. "Where is Mother?"

Co-zi' stopped her rhythmic grinding of manna in the small mortar and pestle she held in her lap. She turned to the tent and nodded.

Elkanah paused using a flint stone scraper to hollow out and smooth a log to make mother a new kneading trough.

Hosiah held back the tent flap, and Mother emerged. "What is it, Hosiah?"

"An official message from Uncle Joshua. He says to the whole camp 'When you see the ark of the covenant of the Lord your God, and the priests carrying it, you are to move out from your positions and follow it.' Then he said, 'Consecrate yourselves, for tomorrow the Lord will do amazing things among you.'"

Mother clasped her needlework to her bosom. "So, it is time. After forty years, how unreal that the time really has come to enter the Promised Land."

Hosiah puzzled. What amazing thing would God do? A flooded river blocked their way.

Unlike Mother's calm appearance, Co-zi' looked up with tears. Her trembling hand cupped the dark head of Zu-zu, napping at her side. "Mum, what will happen to Zu-zu and me?"

Mother knelt down and hugged her frightened friend. "You and Zu-zu have been with us for two months. You are now part of this family. Whatever happens, we are in this together."

Hosiah had seen other Hebrews ordering their Midianite captives about with harsh words and even lashes. Co-zi' and her niece seemed more like family. Having been a slave herself in Egypt at such a young age, Hosiah was sure his mother would never use that ugly word.

Mother straightened with hands on her hips. She surveyed all their household possessions, much of it still packed in the oxcart. "Elkanah, bring the large wash pot to the fire. Hosiah, fill it with water from the river. We all must have baths. While Co-zi' and Zu-zu bathe inside the tent, I will give you boys a haircut out here."

Mother turned to Co-zi and held up the linen garment she had been decorating with colored threads. "Co-zi', this is for you."

While Co-zi' gaped, Mother ducked inside the tent and came back with a small linen garment the right size for Zu-zu. "Hosiah, do you believe you were this size once? Still like new, I should have given it away long ago. I would like Zu-zu to have a fine new garment."

At supper Hosiah scratched the back of his bare neck and took his place between Mother and Zu-zu.

Mother placed before them manna flatbread for dipping into curds of milk. "Before we begin, I ask each member of the family to thank God for something He has provided."

Mother nodded to Elkanah to go first. "I thank our God for Uncle Joshua who leads us now that Moses has died."

"I thank God for the cloud that goes before us to lead the way." Hosiah gently squeezed the small hand beside him. "Zu-zu, what are you thankful for?"

Zu-zu smiled shyly and turned to bury her head in her auntie's lap.

"Co-zi', what are you thankful for?" Mother's gentle voice encouraged the shy young woman dressed in a festive new garment.

Co-zi' fingered the colorful stitching across the yoke of her new garment. "Mum, I am thankful I am in the hands of a kind woman such as you."

"And I am thankful God has brought me this far by trusting Him for each day. I know He will not leave us now."

"Mum?"

"What is it, Co-zi'?"

"What about the Canaanites?" Her hand came to her mouth where her lips trembled. "I saw the battle two months ago. Not many ... of my people survived. Just Zu-zu and I ... from our family."

Mother reached out and took Co-zi's hands. "Co-zi', it is not for me to say. Every person, whether Hebrew or Canaanite, is ultimately accountable to the Creator God alone. I can only tell you what Father Abraham said long ago, 'Will not the Judge of all the earth do right?' and what dear Moses wrote for us not long ago. 'He is the rock, His works are perfect, and all His ways are just. A faithful God who does no wrong, upright and just is He.'"

Hosiah looked up at the cloud now taking on its evening glow over the Tabernacle. Could he place a simple trust in what God says He will do, like his mother? She never seemed to worry about the how.

CRSO

In Gibeon, Keshub shivered even though warm spring sunshine had bathed Aijalon Valley all day. He sprawled beside Lehab on the steps to the pottery yard. Baba sent him there to block the men arriving for the fire circle from entering the pottery yard full of fragile wares.

Seated at the fire on the courtyard floor, Baba cleared his throat. "Men of Gibeon, the Hebrews have not moved in two moons from their camp at Shittim. We have a report that their leader of many years died about that time."

Baba gave Eskie a piercing black-eyed stare with a slightly arched right eyebrow. "We have posted a lookout above Jericho for more than two moons. We now have a definite indication they are planning to enter Canaan. Our lookout can tell you what he saw."

Keshub stretched his neck to see brother number three sitting cross-legged between Baba and Sir Ghaleb at the head of the fire circle.

"Jericho has been shut up tight for the last four days since two Hebrew spies entered the city. I, myself, saw the men swim across the Jordan and go through the city gate. We think Uncle Yaakoub actually talked to them in the market, although he did not know it at the time. They were disguised as tradesmen."

"But wearing new sandals and paying for the red rope with wedges of silver." Keshub whispered in Lehab's ear.

Eskie squared his shoulders. "Jericho shut up tight that afternoon. The king's men searched the roads and fords looking for them. They found nothing."

Eskie leaned forward, hands on his knees, and lowered his voice. "Even after sundown, the men of Jericho ran this way and that with their torches. In the dim light before dawn, two men climbed down a rope that hung from a window in Jericho's wall. They did not go to the river but to the hills. For two days, they hid at the top of a ravine below me. At dusk on the evening of the second day, they crept undetected to the shoals and swam across."

Wood shifted in the fire and sent yellow sparks flying upward. Eskie turned to Baba.

"That was yesterday. Bildad arrived to replace me right on time, but I could not leave this morning for thinking something was surely about to happen in the Hebrew camp."

Eskie cleared his throat. "And I was right. By mid-morning the Hebrews broke camp and moved closer to the river. They came in a long, wide, slow-moving mass of people, oxcarts, flocks, and herds to the river across from Gilgal. And the cloud moved with them."

"The cloud?" A Gibeonite neighbor questioned.

"Yes, sir. The whole time I have watched the Hebrew camp, a cloud always stays over them. Beginning at dusk with a strange glow, the cloud intensifies into a shimmering white light by night. At first I thought they built a huge fire each night, but I have come to know it is the cloud itself that gives light. Yesterday, either the cloud moved with the camp, or possibly, the camp moved *with the cloud.*"

"But the river is flooded, right?" asked another neighbor.

Eskie scratched his chin. "Yes, it is out of its banks all along the way. The Zor along the river is standing in water with many bushes and trees showing only the topmost branches. At the shoals where the river widens to twice its width, the water flows more slowly. I saw their spies swim across. Surely, there is no way such a mass of people with children and flocks and wagons could cross as those two men did."

"We will see what happens next." Baba's voice remained calm, but worry lines creased his brow, accented by shadows cast by the fire. "We have heard warnings about the Hebrews since this time last year. Our friend Haydak, the caravanner, was the first to caution us about their intention to invade Canaan. All year long we have heard from caravanners, and then refugees, as the Hebrew threat loomed nearer."

Neighbor Ra-gar' boomed out his sarcasm. "We have wasted a whole year. We should have joined up with King Zedek of Jerusalem and the Amorites long ago. Now we have, at most, two moons before they attack, while the Jordan is flooded."

Nabi, the old-timer, raised his scratchy voice and pointed a crooked finger at Ra-gar'. "Many did not believe it, but my Baba said when those Hebrews left Egypt forty years ago, the Red Sea opened up for them, and they walked across on dry ground."

"What! That is a ridiculous tale told by silly old women, and men, afraid of the rattle of a leaf blown by the wind." Red-faced Ra-gar' blurted. "I will believe all the myths I have heard about the Hebrews when the sun stands still!"

Tight-lipped, Old Nabi crossed his thin arms across his chest but made no reply.

Baba repeated. "We *will* soon see. Moving to the shoals surely indicates they intend to cross. Maybe we have until the dry season begins and the flooding stops, and maybe we do not."

Eskie shook his head and placed his hands on his hips. "People fled Gilgal on this side of the Jordan and headed to the hills at the sight of the Hebrews on the other bank. Jericho is shut up tight with lookouts on top of the walls and at the fords."

Baba cleared his throat. "Starting tomorrow, we are sending two men to our lookout post. The folks at Kephirah are sending a young man with Eschol so there will always be two watchers. If anything happens, one can come home immediately to bring word, and one remains to continue watching.

"Our neighbors at Beeroth and Kiriath Jearim also will provide a man for our five-man rotation."

Keshub nodded with new understanding. Sir Ghaleb and Baba had their heads together late into the night after the fire circle many times recently.

"Samir, brother, we need the wood-gathering crew at the ridgeline trail tomorrow. Our military man will tell you why." Baba turned to Sir Ghaleb.

Keshub whispered to Lehab. "I will be on that crew." When he was not traveling to market with Uncle Yaakoub, he had worked with Uncle Samir hauling wood to fire the kiln.

Sir Ghaleb took up a blackened stick from the fire and raised his chin. He surveyed the men he had personally trained to defend Gibeon. "Men, we need the earliest possible warning of the Hebrews advancing into Canaan."

He slashed two long black lines on the white limestone of the courtyard floor. "The first line is the Jordan River. The second parallel line is the ridgeline trail between Jerusalem and Bethel on the sunset side of the Jordan."

Keshub tapped Lehab's knee and whispered. "Let's move to the wall in the pottery yard so we can see what he is drawing." He scrambled to his feet and rounded Ranine's work station. At the wall overlooking the courtyard, he leaned on his forearms and mouthed. "We have been to the ridgeline."

Lehab cupped his hand to Keshub's ear and whispered. "Some here have never been out of Aijalon Valley."

Sir Ghaleb peered their way and tapped his stick. "We are here in Aijalon Valley below the ridgeline on the sunset side halfway between Bethel and Jerusalem. Rainfall on our side of the ridge gently flows toward the Great Sea. On the other side of the narrow trail, rain crashes from the height of the ridgeline to the depths of the Jordan Valley below and flows into the Salt Sea. Flash floods gouge the wadi canyons ever steeper."

The old soldier scratched two black lines, Y, connecting the ridgeline and the Jordan River, and glanced up. "We know the enemy will advance up the wadis."

Keshub placed the end of his sash on the wall and used it as a little padding for his elbows.

"This line is the Wadi Qelt. It flows from Jerusalem and empties into the Jordan River near Jericho. The shorter line is the Wadi-el-Gayeh. It begins near Bethel and Ai in the hills to our north and flows into the Qelt here."

Sir Ghaleb twisted a large charcoal dot with his charred stick on the Wadi Qelt near Jericho. "Our lookouts have been here on a ridge above Jericho. If troops advance up the trail along the Qelt toward our lookouts, our men will fall back to a signal fire laid and ready here above the Wadi Qelt. It will be very important that our fire-builders leave an ample supply of dry tender in place for a quick-starting fire."

Uncle Samir nodded.

"When our lookouts light the first signal fire, we in Gibeon will know to prepare to move to the summit. One of our lookouts will start home with the message of who, how many, and their speed of advancement."

Neighbor Agh-taan leaned in. "The one who stays ... what will he do?"

"That lookout will fall back and stay in hiding above the trail to see which fork the enemy takes." The old soldier traced the movement with his blackened stick. "If the enemy continues on the main trail toward Jerusalem, our lookout will remain in place and watch for further developments.

"But if the Hebrews come up Gayeh, our lookout falls back to another signal fire laid here below the ridgeline trail. He will wait. If the Hebrew army continues on the Gayeh trail, they are heading for Ai. If they turn to follow the trail that branches away from the Gayeh, they will be coming here. Our lookout will set the second signal fire and return to Gibeon as fast as he can."

Baba placed his hands on his knees. "When we see the second fire, we will know to get everyone on the summit."

Keshub's hero and his father's best friend leaned back and gazed at his students. "Are there any questions?"

The fire burned down to low blue and yellow flames wavering over whitened logs. Keshub could not think what would become of Gibeon if a second warning fire were lit. "What about our lookout, Sir?" His tremulous voice surprised even himself.

The old Hittite droned a monotone answer. "It is possible he will be pursued by the enemy. If he is fast of foot and stays in the underbrush and shadows of the ridgeline forest, it is possible he could reach Gibeon. He might cause the advancing enemy to delay their attack while they pursue the lighter of the signal fire."

The old soldier suddenly looked older when he glanced at Eskie. "Does anyone else have a question?"

No one did.

"We already know our best defense is being prepared with enough food and water and firewood on the summit. We will be buying time to negotiate with the invaders." Baba's calm voice redirected Keshub's fear of the unknown to something solid to do. "Water is supplied by the cistern we dug and filled. Some food supplies and some firewood is in place, but we need more. So, until we see the signal fires, we go about our daily tasks and get ready on the summit.

"The barley harvest is our most strategic need. The farmers need help from anyone available to bring in the ripened grain as quickly as possible. Also, my brother Samir needs extra hands, axes, and donkeys to gather wood for the summit and the signal fires. See him if you are available."

Baba lowered his chin. "Make sure your assigned area behind the wall on the ledge is livable for your family. Some have not built a rain shelter. We have several more weeks before the dry season begins. You will be out in the rain if we must go to the ledge. You cannot rely on anyone else to have space for you."

Neighbor Agh-taan raised his voice. "Ishtaba, I believe we need a night watchman on the summit amongst the belongings there. Some folks have reported things are missing from where they put them."

Baba turned. "I am sorry to hear that, neighbor. Our resources will be stretched thin by all we must do already, but you are right. I hope you will make those assignments just as you make the assignments for a watchman over the spring and for keeping a lookout on the crest each day."

"I will." Agh-taan nodded, then raised his voice. "Men, come see me at the spring tomorrow to get an assignment."

"Is there anything else?" Baba asked.

"Yes, brother," Uncle Samir craned his neck to survey the crowd in their courtyard. "I will be at the spring at sunrise if you want to go with the wood gatherers."

Baba, the calmest head in Gibeon, dismissed the gathering. "Go to your homes, men, and comfort your families in these uncertain times."

Keshub, at the pottery yard wall, jerked his head toward Eskie. "Lehab. Follow me."

All through the evening, he had itched to ask Eskie about the rope. With Lehab in tow, he pulled Eskie aside. "Could you tell what color the rope was that hung in the window of the wall where the spies came down?"

"No, I was too far away to tell the color, but I spoke to Uncle Yaakoub about where the window is positioned on Jericho's wall. He thinks the position lines up with where he set up the Ra-eef' booth that day. He definitely sold our rope to two strange men who may have been Hebrews in disguise. And you saw the same two men carrying the red rope into a dwelling against the outer wall. We are convinced the rope of escape was red."

Keshub led the way up the stairs to the rooftop sleeping quarters. The low hum of conversation ebbed away as the men of Gibeon left, and the Ra-eef' grandsons wriggled into their bedrolls.

Lehab whispered to Keshub. "I say your baba is preparing for the Hebrews to cross a flooded river. What do you say?"

"I say he does not want to be unprepared *if* they do." In the chill of the moonless night, fear seeped into Keshub's thinking. The pounding of his heart threatened to drown out the light snores from his brothers and cousin.

He had traveled the terrain Sir Ghaleb described many times. Would the lookout above Gayeh have time to get away after he lit the second signal fire? Not knowing if the signal fire lighter or his family could survive an attack, Keshub's heart threatened to leap out of his chest.

Turning to his left shoulder, he spied the small cluster of stars that made a cross near the southern horizon. He forced himself to breathe slowly, drawing in the calming effect of gazing at the night sky.

His gran-baba had passed down the teaching of an ancient wise man in the north land when Gran-baba was a lad. The old man taught about the Creator God who wrote His story in the stars.

Baba recently had pointed to the southern cross constellation. "Perhaps these five stars are a boundary mark. What you cannot know, you must trust to the one who does know."

Keshub centered his gaze on the bright star called *Toliman* next to the cross. Baba said its name meant the *heretofore and the hereafter.*

Baba and Gran-baba hoped the Star Namer watched over the potters of Gibeon.

Keshub considered again what Eskie heard the white-haired old man say before he went up on Mt. Nebo and disappeared. "The Lord Himself will cross over ahead of you. He will destroy these nations before you, and you will take possession of their land."

Keshub squirmed to his back. If the lighter of the signal fire survived to reach Gibeon, would Baba succeed in negotiating with the enemy? *What you cannot know, you must trust to the Star Namer who does know.*

Eskie heard the old man at the foot of Mt. Nebo quote the Hebrew God. "Be strong and courageous. Do not be afraid, for the Lord your God goes with you. He will never leave you nor forsake you."

Keshub shivered and clamped his elbows to his side and his fists to his chin. Was it the Hebrew God who caused the cloud to give light over their camp?

Is their God the One who knows the heretofore and the hereafter?

He locked his jaws to keep his teeth from chattering.

Is the Hebrew God the Star Namer?

Chapter 33:
Crossing the River

Keshub pursed his lips and shook his head in disgust as his shoulders squared at the afront. Some of the men crowding into his family's home leaned against the half wall in front of the kitchen fire pit. Sandaled feet squashed soft pink blooms. Had they not seen Gran-mamaa's spring flowers that bloomed there?

Others stood in the pottery yard and leaned forward on the short wall that separated it from the courtyard. He and Lehab had moved fragile greenware away from the area before Baba allowed anyone to go there.

Keshub, hunched shoulder to shoulder with his cousins on the top step to the rooftop. Other boys their age crowded onto every other step.

Uncle Samir struck a bronze plate three times with a hide-bound basalt hammer to get everyone's attention.

Baba's deep voice held their attention. "Men of Aijalon Valley, we welcome you to Gibeon. As most of you know we have had a lookout watching the Hebrews on the ridge above Jericho for many days now. I want you to hear the first-hand report of what happened yesterday on the banks of the Jordan. Eschol."

Eskie stood and straightened his shoulders, while murmurs subsided. "Baba, Sir Ghaleb, and men of Aijalon Valley, I would not have believed what I am about to tell you if I had not seen it with my own eyes. Before our lookout friend from Beeroth left our perch above the Jordan Valley yesterday, the Hebrews took down their tents and loaded their oxcarts."

"They dismantled the large tent in the middle of their camp last and loaded it onto six oxcarts. Removal of the last layer of the big tent revealed a fixture draped with blue cloth. The blue-draped object received special treatment. Four men, two abreast, approached slowly toward two poles protruding from under the covering, front and back. The poles ... flashed in the sunlight."

"You say the poles flashed in the sunlight?" Neighbor Agh-taan leaned in with a frown.

"Yes, sir. I believe the poles are covered with gold. The four men hesitated a long while, it seemed, before lifting the mysterious object. Each man bore one end of a pole on his shoulder. Together, they proceeded to the flooded river's edge. The east end of the Hebrew camp moved first but stayed a long distance behind the four men and their strange burden."

Beside his cousins, Keshub sucked in a breath and put a hand to his mouth, waiting.

Eskie gulped. "Our friend from Kephirah will confirm my report when he arrives tomorrow. The Hebrews *crossed* the Jordan River."

Gasps of alarm came from those who had not yet heard the news. "They are in Canaan already?"

"That cannot be, can it?

"How? The flood is at its worst!"

After a nod from Baba, Uncle Samir struck the bronze once more.

Eskie shook his head. "I can only tell you what I saw. At

mid-morning, the four men bearing the blue-draped furnishing stepped into the edge of Jordan's flood waters. And a loud rumble like thunder made the ground tremble where I lay.

"I scrambled to remove myself from the depression we have made at our lookout perch. A boulder the size of our guest house tilted, then tumbled down the ridge and came to rest at the half-way campground below us. Uncle Yaakoub and his crew often camp there."

Keshub gasped. He had lain beside that boulder. He pressed his shoulder into Lehab's and turned to him. He and his cousin stared into each other's eyes, questioning. They had slept at that campground. What force could move such a giant boulder? Had there been even a tremor in Gibeon yesterday?

Eschol gave his earlobe a tug. "By the time I got over my fright and returned to my position, I found a great surprise. The men shouldering the gold-covered poles had stopped in the middle of the river. They stood still ... on dry ground. The water from upstream had stopped flowing."

"The water stopped flowing?" One incredulous neighbor spoke above the murmurs of many.

"Yes, sir. The water stopped."

Another neighbor demanded. "They stood on dry ground? What happened to the water coming downstream?"

"I do not know what happened, only what I saw and what our friend from Kephirah will confirm tomorrow night. In the distance toward Mt. Hermon, up the river, I could see a great amount of water as if it were piled up while the water below the Hebrews drained rapidly away. By the end of the day, almost all had drained into the Salt Sea."

"What happened next, Eskie?" Lehab called from beside Keshub on the stairs.

"Well, cousin, like I said, the four men bore their burden half way across the river on dry ground and stopped. Next a large number of men armed for battle crossed ahead of the rest and stood battle ready to protect the others as they arrived in Canaan."

"Did the king of Jericho have his army there to meet those invaders?"

"The city of Jericho is locked up tight. No one is coming and going since the Hebrew spies visited them. Jericho's army seems to be camping on the top of the wall while they keep watch."

"How were the Hebrews armed?" The voice was Sir Ghaleb's.

"It seems they had mostly bows and arrows, spears, and axes with perhaps leather shields."

The Hittite soldier leaned back. "Probably, most of those weapons came from Heshbon, Bashan, and the Midianites—the nations they destroyed in the last four moons."

The old soldier's words struck Keshub like lightning as a gust of spring wind sprinkled a shower of white petals from Ra-eef' fruit trees. The enemy would add precious few weapons to their arsenal here. In the scant light of the crescent moon peering through scudding clouds he pictured Gibeon overrun by an overwhelming enemy.

Keshub shook his head to clear the terrible thought and brushed at a petal blown onto his cheek.

Baba's deep voice, always steady as a rock, halted the rising panic in the pit of Keshub's stomach. "Men, I refuse to believe, yet, there is no other outcome to our situation than what happened to the Amorites east of the Jordan. Let's hear the rest of Eschol's report." Baba brushed away a single petal landing on his cheek and turned to his number three son.

Eskie hooked his thumbs in his girdle. "In the afternoon when the last Hebrews crossed, several men shouldered stones as big as they could carry from the middle of the river and mounded them outside their camp near Gilgal. Then the four men, standing in the middle of the river from early morning until twilight, finished crossing the river. They marched the covered furnishing borne on golden poles directly into the large tent already erected in the middle of the camp.

"The Hebrew camp covered the valley floor next to Gilgal. They made the exact same orderly formation of tents around the large central tent, as when the sun rose over them at Shittim. And the Jordan River waters crashed back into a rushing flood again."

"Whew!" Uncle Yaakoub whistled. "How do we resist a people whose God stops the mighty Jordan for them?"

Eskie nodded. "That must be what the people of Gilgal thought, too. Few had stayed when the Hebrews arrived across from them at the shoals. When those brave few felt the earth tremble and saw the waters cut off, they fled with all haste out the back of their village. They headed for the hills. By the time the Hebrews arrived at Gilgal's doorstep, no one was there to greet them. The Hebrews took Gilgal without the slightest resistance."

Baba thundered above the murmurs of alarm. "You heard this report, first hand. The Hebrews are in Canaan. Our plan is to be prepared to take refuge on this hilltop with water and food supplies for several days while we try to negotiate a treaty."

"If you intend to go to the crest of Gibeon when we see two signal fires, you must prepare now."

Baba turned to neighbor Agh-taan. "Do you have a night watchmen for the summit, neighbor?"

"Yes, every night."

Baba looked to Samir. "Samir, brother, are the signal fires laid on the ridges between here and Jericho?"

"Yes, they are. Smoke from one fire will mean they are coming up the Wadi Qelt. Two will mean they are coming to Gibeon."

"Do you need more men to bring in wood for the summit in case of siege?"

"Yes, definitely. And we have another signal fire to build on the west end of our hill to warn our sister villages that the Hebrews have been sighted coming our way."

Baba turned to the farmers of the group. "How goes the barley harvest? Who still needs help?"

Several responded with "aye" and a raised hand.

Baba asked those farmers and Samir to step toward the pottery yard wall. "Before you go, please see these men who need your help. If we all work together, we will be ready."

Keshub had only moments to talk to cousin Micah. "How is it with you, Micah? Is our barley harvested?"

"Almost. Two more dry days and we will finish, I think. As soon as the threshing is done, we will have a wedding celebration at the threshing floor. I hear you two are on the wood-gathering team."

Lehab, looking toward the stars and shaking his head, droned. "Yes. We are not sure how much will be enough, so I think we will be woodcutters and toters for a long time to come."

Uncle Yaakoub approached with a lighted torch for their over-hill trek home. Micah turned with a wave. "I will see you after the threshing."

Keshub returned the wave without Micah's optimism. Was Micah not listening? Could the Ra-eefs count on anything past tomorrow?

***

His breath tore at his throat as Keshub thrashed through under-brush. Thorns slashed at his legs in semi-darkness as searing fear gripped his mind. Cold air burned his lungs. His heart pounded wildly in his chest urging him on. He ran for his life, ignoring the shouts that dogged his path. A horde pursued. He thrust aside a branch. Thousands of feet pounded the earth behind him. So many, the earth beneath him trembled.

A voice urged. "Faster, Keshub. You must keep going. You can do this."

Up ahead, Baba beckoned. "Keshub, come."

"Keshub!"

"Huh-unh? What?" Suddenly awake, had he heard a voice or dreamed it?

"Keshub!" A hoarse whisper originated from the stairs.

Suddenly alert, Keshub rolled over to see Baba barely visible in the dark, peering over the parapet from halfway down the steps.

"Yes, sir?"

"Come. We need you. Get dressed. Quickly."

"Yes, sir." He scrambled to his feet, rolled his mat and blanket together, and stowed it in its place. In the dark he wound his girdle around his middle and fumbled with his sandals. He gave up and carried them to the courtyard. At the bottom of the steps he grabbed his pouch and cloak from their pegs in the wall.

Baba's head showed above the half wall that shielded the kitchen fire from view.

Keshub rounded the end of the wall where Baba stirred up the coals and added kindling. From within the Ra-eef' house, Ranine's oil lamps glowed. Soft voices and intermittent moans alerted Keshub.

"You need wood, Baba?" He knelt to tie on his sandals.

"No, son. I have wood. Rachel's baby is coming, and it is too soon. You must run to your Uncle Yaakoub's house to fetch your Aunt Raga. Rachel wants her mother to be here. Go as fast as you can, but be careful, too. Do not take any chances. With the clouds and only a wisp of moon, you could easily take a fall. We do not need you to break a leg or your head."

With barely any light from the newly laid kitchen fire, Keshub took the dipper full of ice cold water Baba handed him. "Yes, sir. I know the way well, but I will be careful, as you say." He took a long drink, and handed the dipper back.

Baba brushed his hand through his hair with a strange expression—a softer, helpless look that Keshub had never seen before.

"Be off, son, and...be careful."

Keshub trotted to the stairs. "I will, sir."

A slice of moon played hide and seek behind the clouds. But he knew the way to the summit—every stone, every bush, every limestone terrace. He crossed the east end of the summit easily. He had played as a lad among the ancient olive trees there.

On the path across the summit to the south side he was less sure. He wished he had brought his staff to feel for the rocky ledges where no intermediate steps had been hewn. Even without it, he was soon on the valley floor and running full speed toward Uncle Yaakoub's home.

He entered his uncle's courtyard and took a gourd dipper from its peg near a water jar beside the door. He tapped the side of the jar gently with the dipper—clonk, clonk. He waited a moment and tapped again.

"Uncle Yaakoub!" He whispered.

"Keshub?" Uncle appeared rubbing his eyes.

"Yes, sir. Baba says Rachel is having her baby. She wants Aunt Raga to be there with her."

Fully awake, Uncle turned to get Aunt Raga who stood two paces behind him and heard the message herself. "I will be ready in two shakes of a lamb's tail."

As she turned away, Uncle called after her. "I will wake Yah-ya and Isa'na and saddle a donkey."

Uncle grabbed his cloak from a peg. "We will take the valley path and be there as quickly as possible. You go back over the summit and tell them we are on our way."

"Yes, sir." Keshub drank a dipper of water before hooking the wooden handle on its peg.

He was off in a trot and covered the level ground with ankle-high spring wheat tickling his every step. The slice of moon that hid behind scudding clouds all night chose the right moment to give its brief light when he climbed the dangerous south slope. Clouds rolled in again when he reached the olive grove on the east end.

He felt his way along in the clearing. He could become disoriented in the most familiar area and fall from a ledge.

He stopped in mid-stride. A sound to his right ... drifted up ... from the ledge below the summit. He sucked in a breath and held it. He knew where he was. The sound may have prevented the fall Baba had feared.

He stood motionless, exhaling without a sound. What was the sound he heard? A footstep? A click? From farther away, a different sound—a soft snore. Was neighbor Agh-taan's night watchman asleep on the job?

Keshub stayed frozen and held his breath again to hear the

slightest movement on the ledge below.

There. Someone moved among the temporary shelters. Only a person up to no good would be so stealthy. Was it the thief of Gibeon?

Keshub waited. The canopy of clouds thinned for a moment allowing starlight through. A hulk moved, faintly darker than the darkness around it on the ledge below him.

Without thinking, Keshub launched himself over the summit's edge with a loud "Ee-yie!"

The broad, flabby shoulders of the bent-over thief broke his fall.

"Thief! Thief!" Keshub gasped to alert the sleeping watchman and anyone else in hearing distance.

"Wha?" The only sound the flailing thief made.

Keshub, straddling the broad back, grasped at the neck opening of the thief's tunic while the watchman stood back with club raised.

Sir Ghaleb reached over Keshub's shoulder and grabbed the thief by the hair of his head.

Another Gibeonite neighbor appeared with a torch.

Keshub scrambled to his feet as Sir Ghaleb lifted the shaggy head of ... Ra-gar'.

The burly Amorite who had favored an alliance with Zedek, the child sacrificer of Jerusalem, snarled. "Hivite."

"Keshub?" Sir Ghaleb puzzled. "What are you doing here at this time of night?"

"Rachel is having her baby, sir. I went to Uncle Yaakoub's to fetch her mother."

With one foot on Ra-gar's back, Sir Ghaleb reached out a hand to Keshub's shoulder. "I see. You can go home now. We will take care of Ra-gar'. You have solved a mystery tonight, son."

Neighbor Jabal, the Moabite refugee, held a torch high. "Tell your father my wife and I will come shortly to help in any way we can."

"Yes, sir. I will." By the time he reached his mat on the rooftop sleeping quarters, first gray light nudged away the blackness of night. What else could happen today?

CRSO

Returning from a sacred assembly at the Tabernacle on the fourteenth day of the month of Abib, Hosiah peered up into Uncle Joshua's calm countenance. Uncle had read Moses' instructions for celebrating the Passover. "Mother told us about the night God caused Pharaoh to order the Hebrews to leave Egypt. She was a little girl at the time."

Uncle Joshua nodded. "Exactly forty years ago."

"Brother-in-law, Elkanah has chosen our Passover lamb."

Hosiah rubbed his stomach. "I found hyssop growing on the hillside yesterday and helped Elkanah lay the fire and set up the spit for roasting."

Uncle Joshua angled a smile to Hosiah's mother. "Magdalyn, your boys are most efficient."

Mother patted a hand over her heart. "All this brings back strong memories of when I was a little girl. I saw my mother and father making the same preparations in Egypt."

Uncle Joshua raised his eyes to the afternoon sun. "Aye. And I was more than twenty years older than you."

"Brother-in-law, you remember Mr. Elishama who was head of the Ephraimite clan? His widow and her son will join us to make eight of us. There should be no problem to eat all the Passover Lamb tonight."

"We will begin at twilight."

At the appointed time, Hosiah held the halter and stroked the soft, wooly lamb near the entrance to their tent.

With his two nephews beside him and a year-old lamb without blemish before him, Uncle Joshua prayed.

"Lord God of all that live and breathe in Your creation, Your servant and these families come before You on this sacred occasion in the month of Abib in the land of Canaan. We come before you with heads bowed to commemorate Your mighty hand and outstretched arm that brought great terror and miraculous signs and wonders to deliver Your people out of Egypt.

"You have told us we are Your people by no merit of our own, for we are a stiff-necked people. We are your people only because You have chosen us.

"Lord God, we place our hands on the head of this innocent lamb, confessing our daily willfulness and unworthiness of Your blessing. Lead us in Your ways and guide us to do Your will."

The lamb's soft pink tongue licked Hosiah's hand that held the rope around his neck. Each Hebrew-born person present took a turn with bowed head to place hands on the lamb's wooly head.

"In solemn obedience to God's command..." Uncle Joshua performed the duty of head-of-household at twilight.

The lamb tried to bleat one last time before life left the pink-rimmed eyes.

Dark red blood flowed onto Hosiah's hand. He dropped his chin to his chest. *God of Heaven, my sin caused this lamb's death.*

Chapter 34:
Close But Worlds Apart

As the sun peeped over the blue hills of Moab, Hosiah rolled out of his warm sheepskin bedroll. Ever since the battle with the Midianites, when Co-zi' and Zu-zu came to live with them, he had slept here under the small wagon beside their tent. He had found this his favorite part of the day when the sun's rays met the morning dew and diamonds danced on every surface.

He smelled wood smoke and heard mother moving about at their fire. He rounded the oxcart and tent. Steam rose from a water pot nestled into the glowing coals. Mother dipped some for him and added a few rosemary leaves.

He stretched and yawned before taking the small bowl. "Mother, I am still full from eating so much lamb last night. I may never be hungry again." He blew on his rosemary tea and took a cautious sip.

Mother handed him a wide-mouthed pottery flask hanging from a leather cord. "Goats milk yogurt. When you find pasture, add a few grains of fresh-picked manna to it for a little crunch. Please do not go too far with your flock, though. We are aliens in this land."

"Yes, Mother."

"You must shepherd both our flocks today since Elkanah has taken the handcart to the twelve-stone monument to get a share of the spoils from Gilgal. There will be such a crowd, there is no telling how long he will wait in line.

"And while you are out, pick as much rosemary as you can carry. I used all I had when we roasted the lamb last night."

Hosiah gulped the last drop of tea. "I will. What are we having for dinner?"

"Co-zi' and I are expecting several neighbors to bring manna for me to bake this morning."

Hosiah girded up his sash and tucked in his small pouch and sling shot. He suspended the container of yogurt from the sling shot. Inconvenient to carry, but he would eat it soon.

"Bye, mother!"

"Good-bye, my growing-taller-and-not-a-little-boy-anymore son. God speed."

CRSO

Keshub rolled out of his bedroll on the roof, alone. He was late. The sun shone a hand-width above the ridgeline. Surely his roof-mates rose at first light. Did Baba let him catch up on the sleep he missed?

He rubbed his eyes with the heels of his hands. What was the sound that woke him?...Ah, yes! The baby!

"Wa-ah! Un-wa-ah! Un-wah!"

Murmurs floated up from the house and courtyard below. Gran-mamaa Amara laughed—followed by a deep cough. She had her wish for a great grandchild.

Keshub skittered down the stairs to the courtyard.

At the fire circle with Baba and Eskie, Gran-mamaa cupped her crooked fingers around a pottery bowl with steam rising. "Good morning, Sunshine."

Baba turned his head. "Catching up, are we? The wood-gathering team is half-way to the ridgeline by now." Baba's smile made the remark no rebuke.

Eskie smirked. "On Zedek time, little brother? Out all night and sleeping all day?"

Baba motioned for Keshub to sit across the fire from him. Mamaa appeared with a small bowl of tea and another of yogurt as he folded his legs beneath himself.

"Thank you, Mamaa." What kind of unusual gathering was this—meeting mid-morning when there were chores to be done?

"Keshub."

"Yes, sir."

"We have bad news."

He stopped with his bowl half-way to his mouth and raised his eyebrows, glancing at Baba and then the others.

Gran-mamaa's already-wrinkled brow was drawn with deepened worry lines.

Mamaa shot a look toward Baba and muttered. "He is only a boy, Ishtaba." She turned slowly back to her kitchen fire.

Eskie gulped his hot tea with none of his usual mirth.

"Neighbor Agh-taan just left. He said Bildad's ankle is sprained again." Baba started softly, but raised his voice more for the explanation. "He cannot return to the lookout perch. We have young men from Beeroth, Kiriath Jearim and Kephira along with Eskie, but our plan to have two men on the ridge only works with five in rotation."

Was Baba explaining for him or for Mamaa and Gran-mamaa?

Baba took a deep breath and hesitated. Then he lowered his head. "Keshub, we need you again."

Shaking his head slowly from side to side, Baba had the same helpless expression Keshub saw the night before. Baba raked his hand over his gray-streaked mustache, his mouth, and his short beard, but he spoke loud enough to be heard across the courtyard.

"Fifth Son, you are only ten harvests plus almost three. Already, you have done the work of a man because you were needed. You have been to Jericho many times now. You know the way. You know about the signal fires because you helped lay them. You are the logical choice to fill in for Bildad."

Keshub bit his lip, suppressing rising excitement. With effort he kept his voice low and calm. "Yes, sir. When do I leave?"

Baba nodded toward the rooftop. "As soon as you get your gear and victuals. Eskie will go with you to introduce you to the other lookouts and be with you through your first time on duty. Eskie is ready now."

On the rooftop Keshub buried his face in the woolen blanket to allow the ear-to-ear grin he felt. Me? A spy for Gibeon?

By the time the sun arced toward mid-day, Keshub walked single-file behind Eskie on the trail through the forest to the ridgeline. Unlike his first trek with the clay-gathering crew almost a year ago, Keshub kept his brother's pace easily.

Eskie was unusually quiet. At the ridgeline trail, Eskie peered in both directions from behind cover. "I have seen single messengers as well as whole platoons of soldiers running this trail between Ai and Jerusalem. It is safer to avoid both."

On the downhill side of the ridgeline, Eskie raised a hand to signal stop. "Baba said to check the signal fires every time we go by to see that all is still in order. We must proceed from here with greater caution."

Keshub checked signal fire two while Eskie surveyed the path ahead along the Wadi-el-Gayeh.

On the trail again, Eskie spoke over his shoulder. "Little brother, I will do the talking and introduce you to our neighbors and fellow spies when we get to the perch. Understood?"

"Understood."

Later, at the site of signal fire one, the closest to the perch, big brother raised a hand of warning—two fingers, then pointed down.

Two men on the trail below? Keshub eased behind a boulder beside his brother until Eskie gave the all-clear sign of thumb and forefinger together. "Zedek's soldiers from Jerusalem are at the half-way camp below us. So far, they do not know about our perch. We want to keep it that way."

At mid-day they met their neighbor spy from Kiriath Jearim on his way home to Aijalon Valley. Keshub felt the young man's unvoiced question as he eyed Keshub from head to foot. Unbidden, Keshub scratched his mouth and upper lip. He still did not have hair on his lip. Maybe a little fuzz. Was he experienced enough to be a spy for Gibeon?

Late afternoon arrived before Eskie whistled *squee-eeh-yew* like the cliff swallow to warn of his arrival. He handed Keshub a broken branch, and together they swept themselves over the ridge to the bowl-shaped ledge below the lookout perch.

Eskie pointed Keshub toward the resting area and slithered on his elbows and belly up the slope to a position next to the other two spies.

From the nest below the perch, Keshub shook his head at the open sky where the house-size boulder had been. With the boulder removed by the recent quake, three spies could lie side by side now. What must the jolt have felt like to have dislodged a house-sized rock?

At first, Eskie and the other two whispered with pointing and nods about the Hebrews. Then Eskie must have told them he had brought his little brother because they turned and frowned at Keshub.

Was Eskie convincing them to give Keshub a chance to prove himself? Several times they turned to reevaluate their first doubtful impressions.

What was Eskie telling them?

When deep darkness arrived, all four spies huddled together below the perch wrapped in their bedrolls. Each ate the cold victuals he had brought from home.

Obeying Eskie's instructions, Keshub ate silently and listened.

Eskie drank from his water flask and wiped his mouth. "What do you think the Hebrews were doing today?"

"It looked to me a bit like a market around that pile of s-stones they erected on the day they cros-s-ed the river." The spy from Kephirah had a missing tooth in front and chewed slowly.

"Seven days since the people of Gilgal fled to the hills." The spy from Beeroth had only one continuous bushy black eyebrow.

"Seven days the Hebrews have not removed any spoils."

"The Hebrews-s are not looting like you would ex-spect." The gapped-tooth spy's sibilants whistled. "Too orderly for that."

"You are right. But today, after five days in the land, they hauled wagonloads of stuff out to the rock pile at the river." The single eyebrow undulated.

Eskie leaned his elbows on his knees with clasped hands. "We met our friend from Kiriath Jearim on the trail. He said they had a large assembly and celebration yesterday. Is that right?"

"Yes-s-s. Fires-s were lit all over the camp until well pas-st midnight."

The other spies kept glancing Keshub's way, but saying nothing. He squared his shoulders. No one had spoken to him since he arrived.

The eyebrow spy lowered his chin. His dark eyes peered out from where the brow bunched together over his nose in deep furrows.

What had Eskie told them at the perch? Eskie remained serious, expressionless, not at all Eskie-like. Was Eskie playing a game with them?

The spy from Kephirah hissed. "S-so Kes-s-hub. How many bears-s have you killed?"

"No bears, sir. I did scare one off once."

His questioner smirked at Eskie until Keshub added, "It was a lion I killed."

The eyebrow from Beeroth looked at Keshub sideways. "How many were in the gang of robbers you caught?"

Surprised, Keshub frowned at Eskie who had dropped his head, shoulders shaking.

"That, too, was only one, sir. I was lucky to be on the summit and able to jump down on him from the ledge before he knew I was there. He was much too strong for me otherwise."

In the moonlight the two spies smiled broadly while Eskie covered his mouth and rolled over backward with muffled laughter.

The spy from Beeroth launched a pebble to Eskie's shoulder. "I thought sure your brother was an out-and-out liar, Keshub. Turns out, he is only a great stretcher-of-the-truth."

"Yes, sir. Our Gran-mamaa says Eskie received far too great a portion of imagination with the desire to talk."

"You need not address-s us as 'sirs-s,' Keshub," whistled the spy from Kephirah. "We are all only young blackbirds-s s-sitting here on our perch together."

Beeroth rose to his feet and turned away. "I will take the first watch."

Keshub wound his girdle around his victuals pouch and tied it to use as a pillow. He shook his head at how quickly the others snored already. Unable to sleep yet, he stared at the stars on the southern horizon, just above the eagles' perch.

A shiver of excitement raked over him. The hairs stood on the back of his neck and arms, tingling.

Was he too young to do this job as Mamaa and Gran-mamaa thought? He would do his best to prove them wrong and make them all proud of him. He felt his upper lip. Yes, a little fuzz there.

CR&SO

Hosiah scurried to help as his brother Elkanah neared. "What did we get?"

Elkanah pushed their hand cart with all his might while the wooden wheel dug deep tracks in the sandy soil. The sun had slipped down over the ridge above the Jordan Valley into the long twilight.

"Elkanah, I was beginning to worry."

"I am sorry, Mother. Uncle Joshua needed help. By staying until the end, we got some of the leftovers no one else claimed."

With the cart almost emptied, Mother wrapped her arms at her waist. "How nice to have olive oil and barley again. And not one sign of a weevil, so the grain must be freshly harvested."

Mother smiled his way. "I am glad you found fresh rosemary this morning, Hosiah. We will nestle it into the grain to keep out the weevils."

"One last thing, Mother." Elkanah smiled from ear to ear.

"What is it?" Hosiah and his mother spoke at the same time.

"Close your eyes, Mother. You, too, Co-zi' and Zu-zu. Hosiah, come help lift this heavy thing."

All their eyes closed except Zu-zu's. The toddler peeked through her fingers.

Hosiah bent his knees and reached into the cart.

Together they lifted a bulky heavy object covered with cloth.

Hosiah struggled with clenched teeth to set it down in front of Mother.

Elkanah stepped back. "Open your eyes, Mother. Unwrap your surprise."

"Well, this cloth is wonderful! I think it is silk. And what a beautiful color of yellow. I have not seen anything so bright since I was a little girl in Egypt."

Elkanah rolled his eyes and grimaced. "Leave it to mother to be so excited about the wrapping she has no thought for the surprise inside."

"I am getting there, son. I am getting there." She folded back the fine silk, and her eyes got as big as the full moon rising behind her.

"Oh, my!" She clasped both hands to her mouth. "God is so good! It is just what we need. A large mortar and pestle for grinding grain—and it is hewn out of black basalt rock. See, Co-zi'? We can grind grain for three or four batches of bread at once. Now we really can start a bakery!"

Uncle Joshua appeared from the lane between Ephraimite tents looking weary and carrying a large jar. "Hello. I brought you something no one else claimed. Probably, none of the men knew what it was because many have never seen the stuff before."

Uncle Joshua chuckled. "A Danite murmured 'Foul stuff, nice jar.' I almost did not stop him from emptying the contents on the ground. He swapped with me—an empty jar for this one."

"What is it, Joshua?"

"Magdalyn, close your eyes and smell first."

"What? More surprises?"

Mother obeyed and inhaled. Her eyes flew open, and she squealed like a young girl. "Sourdough starter!"

Hosiah took a turn to smell and examine the strange sour-smelling slimy stuff in the jar from Gilgal.

Zu-zu expressed her doubt best of all, a squinched up nose and down-turned mouth, "Yech!"

Mother laughed. "Just you wait, Zu-zu. You will love the bread I will bake for you."

"Magdalyn, there is one other thing I must tell you." Uncle Joshua's serious tone foretold trouble. The leader of the twelve tribes of Hebrews cleared his throat. "There will be no more manna."

Hosiah shook his head to be sure he heard aright. No manna? What will it mean for us to have no manna?

"Does everyone know?" Mother tucked a stray strand of hair behind her ear.

"No, everyone else will learn in the morning. We will eat the produce of the land from now on."

After a moment's thought, Mother gave her head a quick nod. "Well, the Two Widows Bakery will go into production this very night. There will be hungry children to feed tomorrow. Hosiah, get us more water from the spring. Elkanah, we will need more firewood before morning."

"Co-zi', dear, please begin grinding our new supply of barley on our new grinding stone. I will tell Mrs. Elishama. She and I have been secretly planning a partnership bakery for some time."

Mother untied her apron and folded it. "Then I will visit our neighbor who has two almost-grown daughters. Perhaps they would be willing to help us. I hope we can keep someone grinding all night. By morning we will be well supplied with freshly baked flatbread. By noon tomorrow we will be baking the first batch of Promised Land Sourdough loaves."

Uncle Joshua shook his head. "Magdalyn, you continually amaze me. Here I was worried what the people's reaction would be. You have reminded me these people are resilient and resourceful. I am also reminded God will work everything out according to His plan."

Hosiah waved good-bye to his uncle and headed to the spring with a goatskin water bag. No manna tomorrow? The people have complained they were tired of manna. Will they also complain because they have none?

Chapter 35:
Justice

Keshub placed hands at hips and challenged his big brother. "What?"

"Run. There is no place to run to. Just run in place."

Keshub eyed the scant flat area of the spies' nest—his three-day home high above the Jordan Valley. He had to admit Eskie was the most experienced spy of Gibeon. He, the newest.

"You will thank me later. We cannot lie here in the sun all day without moving. I learned my lesson the hard way when I first started spying. I had to take breaks to run on the ledge below our nest. When I did not, the climb back up the trail to Gibeon made my lungs and legs burn like fire, and I felt like an old man. So, Keshub, run."

All day Keshub swapped places with Eskie and the spy from Beeroth, the one with the continuous black eyebrow. Keshub either draped his body at the rocky perch watching the enemy or ran, grumbling to himself, in a flat space big enough for three bedrolls.

On his belly at the perch, he gazed down on all those below him. Two of Zedek's men from Jerusalem lay prone and peered over a precipice to Jericho and the Hebrews below them. Men of Jericho stood above the palm trees at every square bastion and lookout post built into the magnificent high walls of Jericho. They kept watch on the threat to all Canaan at Gilgal. Keshub estimated the distance from Jericho to the Hebrew camp at Gilgal—about the same as the distance from home to Uncle Yaakoub's across Aijalon Valley. He observed another market day near the Hebrews' pile of stones. Eskie said twelve Hebrew men carried them from the middle of the river on their shoulders.

Keshub tried to imagine seeing the raging flood before him changed in a moment to dry ground, allowing easy passage for the Hebrews.

He inspected the familiar campground below where Lehab and he had camped with Uncle Yaakoub. Zedek's lookouts leaned against a boulder the size of the Ra-eef' guest house. Did they know about the earthquake? Did they know that stone toppled from here only a few days before?

At mid-morning of Keshub's second day, Eskie leaned on his elbows at the perch and opened wide his hands. "So far, it looks like," and then he remembered to whisper, "this could be another day of 'nothing happening.' Those Hebrews must be a patient lot."

He paused. "What is different? Oh my! Kesh, come look!"

Keshub scrambled up beside his big brother. "What?"

"What do you see different?"

"Different? Umm. The whole valley looks the same."

"Except, there is no cloud."

"No cloud? Oh-h! You are right!"

"The strange cloud that did not cast a shadow. That cloud seemed to be leading them when they moved up to the Jordan from Shittim. And again when they shouldered the golden poles and bore a large burden draped in blue into the river. It is not there this morning."

"What does this mean?"

278

"I have no idea."

Keshub took the mid-morning watch while Eskie ran as if a horde of Hebrews chased him. Their friend from Beeroth had left to report on his two days of spying. Keshub raised onto his elbows. Something new down below. He picked up a pebble the size of his little fingernail and threw it squarely at his brother's back.

Startled, Eskie halted and turned.

Keshub signaled with rapid hand motion to come.

Eskie clawed at the incline, then slithered into the groove his body had made in the last three moons.

Keshub pointed to Gilgal.

Hebrew men assembled on the edge of their camp nearest Jericho. From out of the mass of Hebrews a column of men emerged.

Eskie raised himself on his forearms. "Heavily armed. Many of them. With helmets ... spears ... shields."

Keshub sucked in a breath and held it, straining to hear. A faint continuous eerie sound hummed in his ear.

Eskie counted. "Seven men blowing rams' horns. Marching out of camp."

Keshub whispered. "Followed by four men carrying a chest by poles on their shoulders." He turned to his brother. "The one you described when they crossed the river?"

"Yes, but draped with a blue covering that day. Now we can barely look at it with the blinding sunlight reflecting off its surface. I thought the poles were covered with gold." Without turning, he nudged Keshub. "Now it looks like the whole chest is gold."

Keshub nodded with brows drawn, trying to commit the scene to memory so he could give details to Baba tomorrow. He took up the thread. "After the golden chest, more men with helmets and spears."

"Yes. Looks like a rear guard for the golden chest. Let's listen awhile, little brother."

The column of Hebrews with their golden chest snaked toward Jericho. As they neared, the blare of the trumpets increased.

Eskie nudged again. "Look at Jericho. See the panic as the soldiers of Jericho run here and there on the rim of the wall."

Armed men sprinted to join the watchmen on the wall the width of two oxcarts. On the side nearest the advancing Hebrews, defenders of Jericho stood four men deep.

Big brother, Sir Ghaleb's star pupil, pointed out Jericho's strategy in a whisper. "Archers alternate with rock hurlers and stand slack-armed until the enemy comes within their range. See those long poles?"

"Yes."

"They will reach down on the outside of the mud-brick wall with the poles to dislodge any ladder-climbing attackers. But I do not see the Hebrews carrying anything like a ladder, do you?"

"No."

"See the campfires at the bastions?"

"Yes?"

"Now they heat pots of oil to be poured down onto anyone who tries to scale their almost impregnable wall. The people of Jericho have the most impressive wall in Canaan. Still, they are not taking any chances."

After the initial flurry of activity to prepare for the advancing Hebrews, the men of Jericho waited, battle ready. The slow-moving column of Hebrews angled to march parallel to the wall—out of reach of archers and rock hurlers.

"Jericho's men are spreading out, Eskie."

"Yes. Ten paces apart on the whole wall, they are stretched too thin. A trained army could attempt to scale the wall in three or four places at once. Even though the Hebrews would suffer casualties, I believe they could succeed eventually."

"I do not see that most of the Hebrews are a trained army." Keshub raked his hair off his forehead. "Other than those close to the gold chest, a good many of their weapons appear to be farm tools. Shepherds' crooks and wooden pikes for goading cattle or sheep, just like ours in Gibeon."

"Sharp eyes, little brother."

"Do they really believe they can take Jericho?" Keshub drew in a deep breath. When the Hebrew column completed the circle, like a shepherd's girdle, around Jericho, the trumpets stopped.

Eskie rubbed his hands together. "This is a stare-down. The Hebrews on the plain and the Canaanites on the wall are facing each other. Poised for action."

Keshub held his breath. The trumpets blasted their eerie music again, and the fore guard led off. "They are leaving?"

The Hebrews returned to Gilgal following the gold chest with the sound of trumpets fading.

"Why are they leaving? Why did they just march around Jericho and go back home?" Keshub scowled and shook his head.

The defenders of Jericho sent up a mighty cheer as if they won a victory. A few hurled some of their precious stockpile of ammunition toward the slowly retreating Hebrews.

Eskie muttered "Save your ammunition, men. They may come back."

Following Eskie's lead, Keshub turned onto his back and slid down into the nest.

Eskie scratched his head. "What did we just see?"

Wide-eyed, Keshub shrugged and shook his head.

Early the next morning, after a fitful night of uneasy sleep, Keshub tied his bedroll to his knapsack to make the trek to Gibeon. Eskie ran in place on the ledge, while at the perch their friend from Kiriath Jearim, who arrived late yesterday, gazed eastward.

Eskie whispered as he slowed to a trot. "Keshub, ask Sir Ghaleb about what we saw the Hebrews do yesterday. Ask if he has heard any such strategy from his days in the Hittite army."

"I will." Keshub took up the broom to sweep away his tracks on the other side and bent low to approach the crest. He slithered across on his belly to inspect the trail below.

That night in Gibeon Keshub lay on his belly, in his spy position, but beside Lehab at the parapet of their rooftop. He gave his report to Baba and Sir Ghaleb at the main spring earlier. Baba said there was not time for a spies' report tonight. What could be more important than what is happening in the Jordan Valley?

Keshub propped up on his elbows and looked down on the Ra-eef' courtyard.

More men from Gibeon than usual arrived as the waning half moon rose over the eastern horizon. Sir Ghaleb arrived, causing a lull in the low rumble of conversation.

Keshub stared.

The old soldier carried a heavy bag and led Ra-gar' the thief by a short rope attached to Ra-gar's left ankle. Neighbor Jabal, the Moabite, followed behind the prisoner holding a rope tied to the thief's other ankle.

The thief's hands clasped behind him, tied at the wrists by leather cord.

Micah joined his cousins and flopped down beside Keshub.

"Hey, cousin, do you still miss your sheep? You have seen many things lately."

Keshub shook his head. "Micah, shepherding represents the peaceful good old days in my dreams. Most days of spying are utter boredom *while nothing happens.*"

"So far, *nothing is still happening* in Aijalon Valley." Lehab shook his head as Baba quieted the men.

Baba raised his voice. "Regarding the Hebrews, we sent runners today to announce a council of the villages of Aijalon Valley at mid-day tomorrow. We will meet at the threshing floor on the west slope. Any citizen may attend. I urged each village to send several representatives. We must decide what to do next."

Baba turned toward Ra-gar' and his voice hardened. "Now, the men of Gibeon must deal with a thief amongst us. Anyone may stay, but this is Gibeonite business."

Everyone stayed.

Baba cleared his throat. "Life hangs by a thread in this valley...

"If crops produce, if livestock thrives and reproduces...

"If wives and children are strong and healthy...

"If the work of our hands is successful and has value...

"And if we are diligent and frugal with what we have...

"We may live to see the next sunrise.

"Sometimes people are diligent and frugal, but circumstances overwhelm them. When that happens, I have witnessed generous neighbors of Gibeon contributing so that no neighbor has starved in our midst."

Ra-gar' grimaced and met Baba's eyes.

Baba's black eyes narrowed and bore holes into the sorry carcass of the thief. "You, Ra-gar', have been accused of stealing. If we had not caught you and if we had not returned the stolen items to their owners, your thievery could have caused others to die."

Baba surveyed the courtyard before he glared into Ra-gar's sullen face. "We men of Gibeon work for the survival of our families. A council of your peers has been diverted from that priority to decide your fate."

Stone-faced, Ra-gar' pulled on his bindings and stared into the fire.

"Neighbor Agh-taan, please go first."

The largest landholder and caretaker of ein-el-Beled, the major spring of Gibeon, focused on the thief. "Ra-gar', your guilt is not in question here. The theft of specific items from our emergency supplies on the summit had been reported already. You were caught in the act."

Micah elbowed Keshub at the parapet.

Keshub nodded and shrugged. What was he thinking when he attacked a man twice his size?

Neighbor Agh-taan pointed at the thief. "At the time you were caught, you had a pouch of salt with another man's mark tucked in your girdle. A search of your home uncovered a stash of grain, oil, blankets, and honey. Clearly identifiable markings of the true owners were found on the blankets and on the containers."

The head of the oldest family in Gibeon leveled a stare. "Therefore, this council has determined you are guilty and deserve punishment. Sadly, your son is implicated, too. Whether by the force of your will or by his own, we do not know which, he has helped conceal your crime. But either way he will suffer the consequences of your acts."

Keshub shuddered. What *would* happen to Da-gan', the thief's son? The bully who learned his behavior from a bully father had warmed to Keshub's offer of friendship. Where was he now?

Baba nodded and turned. "Thank you, neighbor. I ask Sir Ghaleb to speak for the council next."

Sir Ghaleb squared his shoulders. "I am a military man. In a time of war, justice must be swift. We have enemies within striking distance. Therefore, we *are* in a time of war. The punishment should take place swiftly to deter others from committing selfish acts that distract us from preparing to meet the enemy. If guilt can be proven, the punishment for theft is always ... swift death."

Keshub sucked in his breath and heard a rustling of leaves on the ledge above him. He rose to all-fours and pushed to his feet. Stealing away from his cousins on the rooftop, he crept up the stairs to the grape arbor ... to join Da-gan' hiding there.

Da-gan' held his hand over his mouth, eyes wide as the men in the courtyard held his baba's fate in their hands.

Keshub eased down beside him without a word.

Sir Ghaleb raised a hand to quiet the group. "The military question is only how to render the punishment—by the sword, by the axe, or by the rope."

The thief's son gulped noisily.

Silence vibrated in the courtyard until Baba spoke. "Neighbor Nabi, as our most senior citizen of Gibeon, what do you say?"

Shaking his head from side to side, Nabi spoke with difficulty. "Son, this is a serious offense. In the olden days, I have seen a thief branded on the forehead and exiled. You would forfeit all but the possessions you can carry on your back."

After another pause, Baba turned to Uncle Samir. "Brother, do we have another option?"

"We do." The man who supervised the digging of the community cistern on the summit nodded vigorously. "We do, though it is the most difficult on our part. We propose to make Ra-gar' a ward of the community to serve with hard labor for a period of one year.

After one year of diligent servitude, he will earn the privilege of living among us a free man again or going where he wishes."

Uncle Yaakoub crossed his arms on his chest. "Tell us what you have in mind, Samir."

"With this option, Ra-gar', you would begin work immediately to chop wood for use on the summit. A fulltime wood chopper would speed up the preparations for our defenses. Later, we may want to dig out a larger pool at one of our springs to hold more water for the dry season."

Samir paused and surveyed the men of Gibeon. "This option is not without difficulty. All of us would be responsible for his keeping. We would have to provide food and clothing for the thief and his son while his labor is devoted to the good of the community. Since the whole community must be involved, I believe this option must be approved by a vote of the men of Gibeon."

"I hear you, brother." Baba nodded and swept a hand left to right. "Men of Gibeon, show by raising your hand if you believe this option has value to us."

After a few moments, most slowly raised their hands.

"Ra-gar', you have heard three options. Death, branding and exile, or one year of forced servitude. Which ... do you choose?"

Ra-gar' jerked his head up with a hint of a sneer. "I choose the third option," and dropped his head again, dimpled cheeks telling of his concealed smile.

"Say it!" Baba's deep voice boomed.

Keshub, shoulder to shoulder with the thief's son, flinched and felt the son trembling.

"Say what?" The miscreant stared into Baba's hard eyes.

Baba demanded evenly. "Repeat in full the charges against you and the punishment you have chosen, thief. First, the charge, Ra-gar'."

With head up, but eyes lowered, dimple gone, Ra-gar' obeyed. "For stealing from my neighbors, I choose one year of forced servitude."

"You do realize, Ra-gar', that if at any time in the next year this council determines to do so, one of the other two options can be brought to bear."

Ra-gar' met Baba's eyes. "Yes."

"All right." Baba still stared into Ra-gar's eyes. Slowly, he turned to address Sir Ghaleb. "Friend, I believe you have something to say at this point."

"Men of Gibeon, we need a means of restraining our prisoner and public servant. Therefore, I offer..."

The old soldier plunged a hand into the bag beside him and produced a clank. "My own shackles for the public good."

Keshub pushed up to sit with hands on knees. Why does he have shackles? The old soldier lowered his head. "I grew up in a noble man's household. My father was his gardener. The man's son and the cook's daughter were my best friends.

"When I was a young man, he obtained a position in the army for me. When I returned several years later, I had been promoted to captain and assigned to protect my benefactor. By that time he was second to the king of the Hittites.

"My benefactor's son who was my friend fell among bad company. The cook's daughter learned of our friend's desperate plan to avoid a creditor he could not pay. She came to my quarters at midnight.

"She begged me to go after our friend, the son, and to prevent him from carrying out an attack against the creditor. As protector of my friend's father, I was obliged to do what I could to guard my benefactor's reputation, if not his son's. But when I arrived, an act of murder had already been committed.

"My friend carried his unsheathed sword with his creditor's blood on it. Foolishly, I thought I could reason with my friend and help him. When he saw I was witness to his deed, he became more desperate and struck out at me."

Sir Ghaleb cleared his throat and glanced down. "His sword severed the flesh of my left thigh, and he called out for help.

"When others arrived, he told them I was the murderer. I had no defense except my own word. Who did they believe? A noble man's son or a gardener's son?

"To his credit, my friend had me carried home and fastened to my bed by the shackles you see. After several weeks of careful tending by our mutual friend, I walked again with the limp you have seen.

"When I was almost well, the noble man came to me in my quarters where I sat in shackles. He was truly a kind man. He knew the depths his son had sunk to and guessed the story had not all been told. Because of him, I had been nursed back to health rather than allowed to die of my wound."

Sir Ghaleb raised his chin. "He asked me to secretly leave Hittite territory and, in fact, to come here to Canaan. He asked me to observe the powers dominating Canaan and gather information regarding the intentions of the Egyptians. I did this faithfully for many years until the death of my benefactor last year."

Keshub had never heard the old soldier speak so long, and never about himself. The Hittite soldier swiveled his head toward Baba. "Since then, I have had no other loyalty but to the people of Gibeon and to the family of the man who welcomed me as a friend and confidante when I first arrived in Gibeon. I am speaking of your father, Ishtaba. Ra-eef' was the finest man and finest friend I have ever known. He would be so humbly proud of you and your brothers."

Baba's eyes glistened in the firelight as he accepted the heavy bronze chain and ankle cuffs offered. He stood and clapped the bronze cuffs onto Ra-gar's ankles.

While Ra-gar' stared at the physical evidence of his future for the next year, Baba Nabi cleared his throat. "Ishtaba, I believe Ra-gar's son deserves better than to be housed with his shackled father. That boy has borne the brunt of his father's bitterness since birth. My quarters are small, but I have room for one destitute young man who has no fault in whose son he is."

"So be it, Neighbor." Baba agreed.

In the grape arbor watching, Da-gan' hung his head while Uncle Samir addressed the men of Gibeon.

"Ra-gar' will be near the spring when the sun comes up. If you bring him wood to chop, you will pay for the work with food for him and his son. If he works hard, pay him well. If he is a slacker, pay him what he is worth."

Baba adjourned for the evening.

Sir Ghaleb and neighbor Jabal escorted Ra-gar' to his hovel— shuffling along in borrowed shackles.

Keshub put a friendly hand on the jutting shoulder bones of Da-gan's back. No words could console the silently sobbing son of the convicted thief.

Chapter 36:
Jericho

Keshub could picture every word of his big brother's report on the next night.

Eskie sat with elbows locked, straight arms extended to his knees. "After Keshub left yesterday, we watched an exact repeat of what my brother and I saw the day before. By mid-day, the Hebrews had marched around Jericho and returned to Gilgal with no other action."

Eskie turned to Sir Ghaleb. "I left the perch later than usual this morning to see if day three would be another repeat. It was. That makes three times the Hebrews have placed a noose around Jericho's neck and walked away. What can it possibly mean, Sir Ghaleb?"

"I do not know, son. I have never seen any battle strategy like it. The only thing I can guess is that they want to wear down the defenders of Jericho and scare the wits out of all of us who are watching."

Uncle Yaakoub held both hands up. "They already have us prepared for the worst, so I suggest a diversion is in order. Everyone is invited to a wedding celebration at the threshing floor in four nights. Now that we have harvested and threshed the barley, we invite you to celebrate the marriage of my son Ra-heeb' to the daughter of Farmer Khalil. Please come."

"You know I will be there. I never miss a marriage celebration." Nabi, the oldest citizen of Gibeon, cackled.

"You never miss free food, Nabi." Another neighbor clapped the old man on the back.

The night air in the Ra-eef' courtyard, thick with tension, seemed less oppressive as Keshub counted on his fingertips. "Eskie, on our present schedule, I think I will return for the celebration. But you will miss another feast. Too bad, so sad, brother."

Keshub dodged the brotherly jab that came his way.

The next morning, he started early for his second three-day assignment. He neared the Wadi Qelt trail about mid-day and crouched behind a boulder. A spy from Jerusalem trotted by to deliver the daily report to Zedek.

Keshub shook his head remembering the day he first met Plain Zed, the unloved son of Zedek, king of Jerusalem. How little he knew about the world outside Aijalon Valley then. He had thought surely the world beyond his own horizons was exciting and marvelous.

Resuming his downhill trek, he quickened his pace. How naïve he had been when he turned ten plus two harvests old. Looking into Zedek's eyes and helping Plain Zed escape from Jerusalem had introduced him to evil. Meeting the mother of a child sacrificed to Zedek's god Molech had opened his eyes to a world of cruelty. Keshub swallowed with difficulty and rubbed his eyes.

Peering around a bend in the trail, he sighted the spy from Kiriath Jearim and stepped out to meet him. "How goes it at the perch?"

"They marched around Jericho again and went back to Gilgal."

"That makes four days, right? What can it mean?"

Kiriath Jearim grimaced and shook his head.

At the up-and-over point to their spy's nest, Keshub whistled the bulbul's call, *"Whe-et—ru-Tweet."* With the usual precautions, he joined the young men from Kephirah and Beeroth on their bellies at the perch.

"What is happening?"

"Nothing." The Beerothite raised his single eyebrow.

"Apparently the ex-s-citement is-s over for today. I think I will take a nap." The spy from Kephirah slid down and rolled out his mat in the nest.

Alone with the young man with one eyebrow, Keshub attempted conversation. "What is your name, friend?"

He scowled and lowered his eyebrow. "Du'bo." His tone less than friendly.

After a short while, Du'bo turned with that continual frown he wore. "How old are you, anyway?"

Keshub sensed the challenge. "I am almost ten harvests plus three. One year ago I was a shepherd and had never been outside Aijalon Valley. Since then I have worked full time in my father's pottery business. I have dug clay from a rocky precipice in these hills, helped my uncle lay the signal fires, and helped sell pottery on several trips inside Jericho."

"You have been inside Jericho?"

"Yes."

"So your brother said you have killed a lion and captured a thief. Is that really true?"

"Yes."

"Humph. I am ten harvests plus seven, and spying here is my first time outside Aijalon Valley."

"Have you apprenticed for a life's work?"

"Mostly, I am a farmer's helper. I do odd jobs for anyone who has work, though."

"What about your family?"

"There are only my mother and myself. My baba died ten harvests back from a cut on his foot from a flint sickle that turned to blood poisoning." He spat over the precipice and grimaced, making his one black eyebrow curve down over one eye and arch high over the other. "He was a farmer's helper, too."

Keshub decided to ask no more questions. The young man seemed lost in his own thoughts.

Later, Keshub licked his fingers as he ate his victuals from home. Trying not to stare, he noticed how meager the Beerothite's supper was and how tattered his garments.

What could he do? Mamaa sent just enough for his own needs until he returned home. Considering the young man's apparent bitterness, Keshub did not want to make matters worse by appearing to offer pity. He would do nothing—this time.

As the Beerothite geared up to leave their nest the next morning, Keshub gave him a message. "When you give your report to my father at the pottery yard, please also see my mother. Tell her my stomach feels better after eating the roasted barley yesterday."

"Humph. I will." The young man shrugged as he looked up and down the wadi trail before disappearing over the ridge.

Keshub chuckled. *I believe Mamaa and Gran-mamaa will take one look at that boy, hear my nonsensical message, since they know I had no roasted barley yesterday, and insist on feeding him before he goes on to Beeroth. Beware, Du'bo, of the kindness of those two women. You may have to change your outlook on life after meeting them.*

Moments later, the spy from Kephirah signaled. "Come see!"

Keshub scrambled to the perch. Day five played out before them. The same as day four.

Late in the afternoon with nothing happening, Eskie arrived, and boredom left. "I had the best day off from spying. I trod the good green pastures of Aijalon Valley and bagged two hares. I hid in the reeds of the northwest pond and shot two ducks with my Jebusite bow and homemade arrows."

Eskie leaned back and puffed out his chest. "Mother was so pleased with my hunting success that ... She sent us a whole leg of roasted lamb! An apology for my missing another feast!"

As the sun went down on day five, Keshub patted his full belly. He took in a deep breath and held it a moment. "Bu-r-r-p." Maybe Du'bo the Beerothite would get some, too.

Day six. The s-spy from Kephirah had left the perch. Keshub lay side by side with Eskie and shook his head as the Hebrews returned to Gilgal, again. "Eskie?"

"What?"

"What do you think will happen to us if the Hebrews attack Gibeon?"

"Umm. If they attack us..." Eskie stared toward the distant blue hills. "...The men of Gibeon will gallantly stand in a line along the foot of our hill with clubs, hoes, axes, cattle goads, and one bronze Hittite sword to slow our attackers. Our few archers will occupy the first terrace and will use every arrow we have to stop as many Hebrews as possible before they reach our first line of defenders below us."

Eskie continued in a monotone, his head bowed. "But it will not be enough to stop them. There are too many of them. They will step on and over our bodies where we fall and will advance to the summit, if they wish."

Eskie bit his cheek. "There the old men of Gibeon and the sisters, wives, and mothers will roll the pitiful pile of stones we pretend is a wall ... down upon the advancing Hebrews ... until there is no place to hide. And it will not be enough to stop them. There are too many of them."

Keshub gulped noisily and could say nothing for a long while. "Do you think it will come to that?"

Eskie raised his head. "No, I do not. Baba is desperately casting about for another option. No one but him believes there are any options but two. We fight and die, or we surrender to their mercy and most of us die."

Keshub grasped onto the ray of hope Eskie offered—Baba believed there was a way out. What could possibly prevent the destruction of Gibeon and their family? Would Baba find a way?

Chapter 37:
Conflagration

As the sun rose over the blue hills, Keshub tied his rolled-up mat and blanket above his knapsack for the trek home. He munched the last of his raisins and almonds, delaying his return to Gibeon until the Hebrews marched, if they would.

The eagle returned to her nest clutching a fish in her sharp talons. Mother eagle ripped pieces from between her feet and fed a piece to each of her squawking, gaping chicks.

Eskie whispered hoarsely over his shoulder. "Here they come again."

Keshub clambered up and settled in his groove to watch. "They are starting out earlier today."

As the leading column of armed Hebrews closed the gap between them and the hindermost part of the column, they completed the circle, surrounding Jericho.

Keshub reared up on his elbows to leave. Would they stop a moment and head back to camp as they had done six days in a row?

He sucked in a breath. The trumpets kept on blaring. The marchers kept marching—around Jericho. *Are they marching around again?*

Eskie whispered. "Everything is the same. Seven trumpets blasting. The golden chest flashing in sunlight borne on the shoulders of four men .... Two times around ...."

Keshub moved his forearm back and forth to dislodge a grain of grit... "Now a third circuit?"

Past mid-morning, Keshub elbowed Eskie. "Should I go and report this? Or wait and see what happens next?"

Eskie turned his hands palm up. "Baba wants to hear when something happens, and something is happening now. We do not know what, yet. I say, you wait as long as you can and still reach home before dark. Baba will be worried that you are late, but you will have a more complete report."

Eskie looked to their friend from Kiriath Jearim for agreement on the plan.

He shrugged and nodded.

Keshub brushed off the area he leaned on and settled in. Nearing noon, the Hebrews completed four circuits, and still they marched.

Eskie whispered. "You should go now. If anything big happens, I will bring the report tonight by starlight. I think I know every rock, bush, and twist in the trail."

"All right, but without a moon the steep trail will be very dangerous. Be careful, big brother." Keshub turned to slide down into the nest, grabbed his gear and broom, and started toward the ridge.

"Keshub."

"What?"

"You be careful, too, little brother."

"I will." He peeked over, right then left, and slithered across.

On the steep, dusty trail toward home, he trotted as he had seen Zedek's men do. Soon his strong legs resisted the incline with the burning Eskie had described, but he pushed on.

On the trail above the el-Gayeh, he met the spy from Kephirah—

with the gapped tooth. Keshub paused to catch his breath while Kephira neared.

"Hello. Why were you running? What is-s the hurry? Why are you s-so late s-starting out today?" Kephira, smiling, searched Keshub's countenance. "What is-s happening at the perch?" He frowned and tilted his head sideways.

Keshub gulped air. "The Hebrews did not return to Gilgal after one loop around Jericho. They completed four and started a fifth circuit before I left at mid-day."

Kephira whistled an odd lop-sided whistle through his teeth.

Keshub waved and pushed himself to run again, pressing to reach home before sunset.

The sun sagged halfway into the Great Sea on the western horizon when Keshub stumbled out of the forest and into Aijalon Valley. A wisp of smoke rose from his family's homestead.

Forcing one leaden foot attached to a burning leg in front of the other, he staggered through neighbor Agh-taan's wheat field beginning to show heads of grain. If he stopped here, would he be able to go on? *Keep going, Keshub. Keep going.*

He reached the pool below Gibeon's main spring and collapsed onto the soft grass beside the bubbling water. Pausing to catch his breath first, he lowered his mouth to drink directly from its cool, fresh goodness.

He raised his eyes to see Baba and neighbor Agh-taan running toward him.

"Keshub! What has happened?" Baba knelt.

"Baba!" He gulped, then blurted. "I waited as late as I could to start home ... because the Hebrews did not stop marching today. They began their fifth time around Jericho ... then I had to leave. I am sorry I do not have more to report." He raised himself to sit beside the pool.

"All right, Fifth Son. Come and rest in the courtyard by the fire. You are soaked with sweat. You must not catch a chill."

"Ishtaba, I will go to the wedding at the threshing floor and tell the others Keshub is here."

"Thank you, neighbor. Mother Danya and I will come soon if Keshub is all right."

Baba extended a hand to help Keshub stand and walked beside him to hold him upright.

"Baba, Eskie said he may come home in the dark of the moon if he has important news."

Baba took in a sharp breath.

"Baba, I can hardly lift my legs."

"You are exhausted, son."

At the steps to their courtyard, Keshub's knees buckled.

Baba swept him into his arms and mounted the courtyard steps. "Danya!"

CRSO

By the time Ishtaba reached the top step, Danya had the gate open wide. He carried his youngest son, head hanging to one side, arms limp. Ishtaba laid him on a mat near the kitchen fire.

He stepped back to put his arms around his panic-stricken wife who pulled toward her son.

"Is he hurt, Ishtaba? Let me see!"

Keshub drew a deep, relaxed snore that must have come from his inner-most being.

Danya relaxed and smiled. "All is well with our son after all." She changed him into a dry tunic and covered him with a wool blanket.

Ishtaba stirred up the fire. "Please go to the wedding celebration, Danya. There is no more we can do for Keshub now. I will stay here."

He nodded toward the threshing floor on the other end of Gibeon's mount. "Your sister Raga needs you. While she weeps at the marriage of her son, she needs you to lead the ladies in the traditional trill of delight. No one can do that better than you, Danya."

Danya smiled and nodded. She grabbed her shawl.

Ishtaba stood at the gate and waved as his wife hurried down the camel trail toward the west end threshing floor.

Alone in the courtyard with Keshub snoring, Keshub's words came back to him. "Eskie may come home if he has important news."

Raising his eyes to the star *Heretofore and Hereafter* just above the crest of Gibeon's hill, Ishtaba whispered. "Have patience, Eskie. The trek is too great a risk with no moon. We will still be here tomorrow."

Later in the evening Ishtaba occupied his idle hands with whittling, catching the wood shavings to add to the tender jar for starting fires. Nothing complicated. Maybe a stirring spoon. He could not concentrate on the task in his hands. What was happening at Jericho?

Mother Amara arrived home from the wedding. Borne regally on her little stool with inserted shepherds' staffs by Samir and Ranine plus two men from the village. "Is everything all right, Ishtaba?"

Mother's gravelly voice concerned him. "Yes, Mother. All is well in Aijalon Valley."

His mother eyed him without comment and toddled off to her sleeping mat.

Nearing midnight Ishtaba awoke where he lounged against the half-wall beside Keshub. His family entered the courtyard, returning noisily from the celebration.

Mother Danya crossed to check on her fifth son. She pulled his blanket to his chin and smoothed the forelock that fell onto his brow from his widow's peak.

Satisfied, she turned to deal with leftover food and the aftermath of wedding preparations. "Ishtaba, I will only be a moment here. You can go to your mat."

Ishtaba cleared his throat. "I want to sit up a while longer. You go ahead."

The household quieted until Samir and Ranine reappeared in the courtyard.

"Baba." Ranine spoke quietly, his clay-calloused hands fidgeted by his side.

Ishtaba rose to his feet, instantly alert. "What is it, Ranine?"

"Come look."

Ishtaba followed his son and Samir up the steps from the court-yard to the summit. Half way to the top, his brother pointed in the direction of Jericho.

Ishtaba turned and inhaled sharply. The eastern horizon showed a strange orange glow. At the top of the stairs, Sir Ghaleb faced the eastern glow. He confirmed the fire could only be at Jericho.

Arms limp, Ishtaba sat with the others watching in silence on the dark hillside.

After a while, Ranine fetched woolen blankets from the court-yard below.

Ishtaba could not tear himself away from their silent vigil.

He slept briefly leaning against an ancient olive tree. He opened his eyes and whispered. "Oh, no. What catastrophe could light up half the sky that way?" The conflagration in the east was not a dream. A fire of unimaginable magnitude consumed—Jericho?

He combed his hands through his hair and rubbed his fore-head. Exhaustion flooded over him, and he raked his hand down his face and beard. Concern for his family and for the people of Gibeon overwhelmed him. And now more and more, other people of Aijalon Valley looked to him for wisdom. He, a lowly Hivite potter.

Looking up through the leaves of the olive tree, points of star-light twinkled. The weight of his responsibilities pressed against him like a double load of wet clay from the wadi. How could he provide for his family and protect those around him? He whis-pered. "I need help."

After a few moments of restful sleep, Ishtaba awakened to hear his brother Samir calling.

"Ishtaba! Come quickly!"

Leaping to his feet, Ishtaba joined the others on the lip of the summit.

"What?"

The early morning grayness dimmed the eerie orange glow. A drift of black smoke darkened the horizon.

"Look there! Coming across the wheat field, is that...?"

"Eskie!" Ishtaba broke into a run to meet another exhausted son bringing news from the spy's perch over Jericho.

Ishtaba led, scrambling down the stairs from the mount to the courtyard. He startled Danya and Mother Amara at the kitchen fire.

He clattered across the courtyard, through the gate, and down the steps. When he reached the spring, the brightness of the rising sun shone through a shroud of blackness—a smoky reminder of sure devastation somewhere to the east.

Eskie neared. He reached the spring, fell to his knees and uttered not a word. Finally, he wept silently.

Ishtaba knelt facing his number three son.

Wiping his eyes and drawing his hand down over his thin mustache and onto his chin stubble, Eskie spoke. "Jericho is no more, Baba. The Hebrews marched around it seven times and stopped. When there was a mighty blast of the seven trumpets, the people shouted. Except for the trumpets, it was the first sound we heard from them in seven days."

"And then?" Ishtaba reached out a hand to Eskie's shoulder.

"Baba ... the walls collapsed. Those walls, so beautiful in the morning sunlight, fell. They were so high and so strong, protecting so many people inside. *The Hebrews shouted,* Baba. Then the walls ... collapsed. Fell outward.

"The plastered glacis', that no man could scale, was buried beneath an enormous amount of fallen mud brick debris. Before the dust settled, the Hebrews climbed the rubble and marched straight into the city.

"They destroyed with the sword every living thing in Jericho— every ... living ... thing. Except for one small house on one portion of the wall that still stood. A few people were captured from that house and removed before the Hebrews set the whole city on fire."

"And that is what was burning all through the night." Uncle

Samir slowly brushed his hands through his hair and stopped with both hands on his head, looking eastward. "And is still burning now." His arms fell limp to his side, and he dropped his head.

"Baba?"

"Yes, son?"

"Because of the fire raging behind me, I could easily see the path in front of me through the night."

For the second time in just a few hours, Ishtaba directed his eyes to the southern sky. Was the Star Namer watching over them? Helping them?

To the others, Ishtaba breathed out his conviction. "It was not the Hebrews who brought down Jericho. Their God fights their battles for them, and my boy came home safely by the light of Jericho's destruction."

In his heart Ishtaba reasoned. Can the one who knows 'the *heretofore and the hereafter*' be the same as the God of the Hebrews?

Chapter 38:

On Being Invincible

Keshub shifted his pack with bedroll, water bag, and victuals.

Mamaa stood at the kitchen fire wringing her hands with tears falling.

One hand on the leather strap of his pack, ready to leave, his stomach fluttered with excitement mixed with dread. This would be his first stint at the perch since Jericho fell, then burned.

At the courtyard gate, Baba rested his clay-roughened hand on Keshub's shoulder. "Be extra cautious, Fifth Son."

Before the morning sun removed the chill of night, he started out through the wheat field with green heads of grain. Two days ago the Hebrews marched around Jericho seven times, and shouted. He shook his head. How could the proud city just fall? What would that look like? He quickened his steps. He would see the destruction before the day ended.

In the olive grove by the trail going up to the ridgeline, spring buds scented the air. A whole flock of songbirds tried to out-do one another expressing the joy of another spring morning in Canaan.

Keshub shifted his heavy load. The birds did not know the fear and dread that lodged in his heart and in the hearts of his Gibeonite neighbors.

He scanned the horizon ahead. No signal fires burned. A good sign. That meant no attack force had left the Jordan Valley for the interior of Canaan. What would the Hebrews do next?

At mid-morning Keshub neared signal fire two and left the trail to inspect the fire crew's work. Crouching, he surveyed the visible segments of the trail below that followed the in and out contours of centuries of erosion.

He crept to Uncle Samir's pile of precisely placed firewood. His uncle had chosen a place hidden by a large boulder from the el-Gayeh trail below. Keshub tipped his head back to see the peak of four small pine trees hewn and tipped together.

Uncle Samir said they would provide shelter for the kindling and tender below until needed. The pines would billow black smoke, visible a long distance, when lighted.

Keshub lay prone on the ground and belly-crawled under. He reached under the four-square stack of crossed logs the size of his arm. Inside the stacked logs, Uncle had made an assemblage of spindly pinewood kindling, branches the size of his thumb, some upright, the length of his body.

Uncle had cautioned. "As important as the wood is, air is more important. Pack the wood too tightly, and it will not burn."

Under the spire of kindling Keshub touched the loosely piled tender—small sticks no larger than his little finger, dried grass, and small pine twigs with needles still attached. Dry, as it should be.

He reverse wiggled out and raised one side of a flat rock next to the pile. A leather pouch contained frayed linen rags soaked in olive oil along with a piece of flint and an iron stone. Everything was in order.

He glanced at the trail below. Sudden movement in the distance made him dive behind a rock for cover. Probably a fellow spy from Aijalon, but maybe not.

Keshub peered around his rock, keeping low. *Not* from Aijalon! Four men traveling together on foot—coming this way along the Wadi-el-Gayeh trail.

He slithered to the best vantage point above where the men would come to the fork in the trail. Who were they?

Were they Hebrews? In Jericho he had briefly glimpsed two Hebrew spies dressed like Moabite tradesmen. What did a Hebrew look like?

The four men continued along the el-Gayeh, not the route to Gibeon. Keshub sighed but waited a few moments at the ridge.

He sighted fellow spy from Kiriath Jearim following the Hebrews, peering from around a boulder to check the trail ahead of him. Without a sound Keshub climbed down to intercept him.

"Hello." Keshub emerged from shadow.

The neighbor from Kiriath Jearim jumped, then hunched his shoulders and whispered. "Did you see the four Hebrew spies go by here?"

"Yes. So they are Hebrews?"

"Surely, they are. Which way did they go?"

"They followed the el-Gayeh toward Ai and Bethel."

"Good. I left the perch after they went by. With them exploring our neck of the woods, it seems wise for you to stay here by the signal fire in case we need to light the warning. Our friends from Beeroth and Kephira are at the perch. I could stay here, but I need to give a report of what is left of Jericho and what is happening now."

"I can keep watch here." Keshub nodded. "I will be all right."

"You are sure?"

"Yes. I have everything I need. Baba will be anxious to hear your first-hand report. By the way, what is left of Jericho?"

The spy's face went slack. "Nothing. Only a smoldering pile of rubble."

Keshub clamped his lips between his teeth. No other words needed.

With a shrug, the other spy headed up the trail toward home.

Keshub shook himself and squashed down the fear of what would happen tomorrow—in the *hereafter*. Baba said we can never know what will happen tomorrow. Baba reasoned there was a Star Namer beyond the star who named it *Toliman, the heretofore and the hereafter*. Baba hoped the Star Namer watches over us.

For today, excitement bubbled up inside him to be entrusted with an important new assignment. He climbed above the signal fire and settled down under an oak tree. He could see parts of both trails at once.

At twilight, he ate his victuals and drank from his water bag. He unfurled his bedroll and leaned back against the oak.

As darkness deepened, he was more alone than he had ever been. He wrapped his arms around his shins and propped his chin on his knees. Night sounds of unseen critters caused prickles of fear between his shoulders like heat lightning on the horizon in summer.

A rim of moon showed on the eastern horizon. A sharp sound, definitely not a critter, sounded to his left.

Keshub unsheathed his flint knife and turned in the direction of the sound.

Out of the darkness from the other direction came a quiet voice. "Are you a Gibeonite?"

Keshub jerked his head. How could someone get so close to him before he was aware of danger? Still clasping his knife. "Yes, I am."

"So, you have a new lookout point."

"Who are you?"

"Jebus. From Jerusalem. When watching in the dark, always check in the opposite direction if the sound could have been made by the toss of a pebble."

"I will remember that next time. Thanks. So, you know my brother Eskie."

"Eskie is your brother? Then the potter is your father. What does your father say, now that Jericho has been destroyed by the Hebrews?" Jebus' tone changed, respect for Keshub's father evident.

"He quoted my gran-baba this morning. 'We will prepare for what we can prepare for, and endure with integrity what we cannot prepare for.'"

"Hmm. Integrity, huh?"

"Yes. Doing what is right and good no matter what the circumstance."

"Hmm. There is a very short supply of that in Jerusalem." Jebus combed his hand through his hair.

"Eskie told you we were spying. How long have you known where we were?" Keshub had to ask.

"I have known you were at the crest of the ridge above us for a fortnight."

"Did you see us or hear us?"

"Neither. I spotted your broom lying by the trail in a different place each time I came, or it was missing altogether. I think I am the only one of Zedek's men who knows. I have not said anything to the others."

"Thank you." Keshub stood.

"You are very young for spying, are you not?" Jebus tilted his head.

Keshub smirked at being measured again. "I am, but I have been to Jericho to market day with my Uncle Yaakoub. I was the logical choice to replace our spy who wrenched his ankle and could not continue spying."

"I see. Well, I will return to my station near your other signal fire—"

"You know about that, too?"

"Yes. I watch more than just the foot trail. A good hunter always does. Keep alert, lad." Jebus turned and faded into shadow.

How did he do that?

At dawn the four Hebrews returned the way they came.

At mid-morning Keshub struggled to stay awake when Eskie slithered up beside him and whispered. "Our man from Kiriath Jearim reported you saw Hebrews go by yesterday. Have they returned?"

"Yes. They went by at first light. And I had a visit from your friend Jebus last night."

"Is everything all right?"

"Yes. Like a visit from a friendly neighbor. He has known of our position at the perch for a while now. Our broom was in a different place each time he came by, or missing altogether."

"Smart man, our friend Jebus." Eskie plopped his knapsack and gear beside Keshub.

"You must go on to the perch now, Kesh, to join the Beerothite so Kephira can return to give his report of the Hebrew scouting party. Baba agrees we should keep a watch here, too. Sir Ghaleb thinks the Hebrews will surely send out their army soon."

Keshub picked up a roundish pebble, measuring the width from fingertip to first thumb knuckle. Rasping it against a larger stone, he looked up. "To attack Ai?"

"Probably. If they come up the Qelt while you are at the perch, Baba says help your partner light signal fire one, then come here."

Eskie pointed north, across the east-west trail that led to home. "If they go toward Ai, I will follow them on a wide parallel track to observe and report what I see. There is a faint ibex trail through a stand of sumac below that large rock jutting up there."

Keshub pushed down the mixture of fear and excitement rising within his chest. He stood and swung his knapsack across his shoulders. "Be careful, big brother."

"You, too, little brother."

Keshub bagged his new sling stone and slipped down to the trail to the perch.

Early the next morning, he lay prone at the perch overlooking the Jordan Valley and gulped. He clunked a small rock down to the nest to wake Du'bo, still in his bedroll.

The Beerothite scooted into place beside him as a large number of heavily armed men marched out of the Hebrew camp at Gilgal. Their column veered clear of still-smoldering Jericho and headed to the trail beside the Wadi Qelt.

Eyebrow arched high, Du'bo rose on his elbows. "Get your gear,

Keshub. Let's get out of here. We have to light the signal fire."

"What about Zedek's men? They are coming up the trail—fast. Should we wait until they go by, then follow behind them? The Hebrews are marching at the same slow pace as when they circled Jericho for seven days. We have a while before they reach this point."

Beeroth rubbed his eyebrow. "You are right. Zedek's men are coming fast." Du'bo slid down to his gear.

Keshub gazed at the column of Hebrew men and called softly over his shoulder. "Du'bo, something is strange about those fighting men. They are not sending scouts to run ahead. How do they know we are not waiting to ambush them around this bend in the trail?"

Du'bo flattened against the crest ready to leave.

Keshub slithered down to the nest and shouldered his own gear and half-full water bag. He crept to the crest and lay flat beside Du'bo listening.

Zedek's men pounded the trail below.

Keshub waited for silence again before grabbing the rosemary broom. He crept down the other side, broom swishing away his footprints.

On the steep trail, Keshub shifted his gear, but stopped short. Du'bo's eyes flared wide, and he breathed in quick short breaths. The farmer's helper had not run yet, but already showed extreme strain.

"Take a deep breath, Du'bo. You can do this. We must do this."

Du'bo took a deep gulp and his chest rose.

"One more and let's go." Keshub turned and pumped his arms rhythmically, determined to keep in pace with Zedek's experienced soldiers. In and out on the bends of the trail, Keshub spied the three soldiers ahead. The Hebrew enemy breathing down their necks had many more.

Du'bo huffed and puffed behind Keshub and lagged a little.

Keshub slowed, heart pounding, but pushed himself. He had to set signal fire one. Would the Hebrews go where their recent spies went? Bethel and Ai. Or would he and Du'bo have to light signal fire two, also?

At signal fire one, Keshub raised the flat rock concealing a pouch of tender and took a portion. He lay on his belly and wriggled under the wood stack, reaching in with both arms extended. Using his own flint stone and iron, he struck the two together. The sparks arced onto the linen threads and the dried grasses. Soon a small flame appeared. He puffed up his cheeks and blew gently.

The flame jumped to the dried pine twigs with needles, and he back-crawled away.

CRSO

"Uh oh." Eskie sighted smoke rising from signal fire one. He lay flat at the oak tree above signal fire two, watching, waiting. Would the Hebrews follow their recent scouts up the el-Gayeh?

After a while Keshub came into view, jogging doggedly. *You can do it, little brother.* Beeroth lagged behind, struggling up the steep incline.

Keshub and Beeroth joined him behind the oak, panting. "How many are there, Kesh?"

"A small army ... Not nearly all. Only a small part of those who circled Jericho."

"Anything else?"

Keshub tilted his head. "They marched slowly. It seemed strange the Hebrews did not send out a scout team ahead of their army. They could be ambushed in these twisting canyons."

"Good observation, little brother. Beeroth, go now to take the report to my father. Keshub, you can rest a bit while I watch. We expect the Hebrews to follow their spies, but it will be a while before they come into sight here."

CRSO

"Ping."

Keshub blinked, instantly alert. He turned and scrambled to join Eskie lying flat beside the oak.

"Here they come, little brother. I will go to the signal fire yonder, ready to light it. Give me a nod, if they turn our way. Then you start home as fast as you can."

Keshub extended his hand, thumb up.

Eskie pointed north across the trail to Gibeon. "If they continue to Ai, I will leave this watch to you and follow them on the ibex trail."

At midday, Keshub tensed and flattened himself against the ground. The invading enemy snaked into view coming around a bend on the trail far below. He let out a long-held sigh when the head of the double column of Hebrews passed by the turn-off to Gibeon. He nodded to Eskie and pointed to Ai.

Eskie grabbed his gear and crouched low. He disappeared through the stand of sumac.

All alone, high above the el-Gayeh and near the unlit signal fire, Keshub fidgeted by smoothing his newest sling stone. How long until he would know something?

Late afternoon, Keshub shook out three almonds and returned the rest to his victuals bag. He munched leaning against the oak, eyes trained on the trail to Ai.

Shouting reached his ears first. Runners fled by his post. No orderly column marched home in victory.

Keshub flattened himself against the ground. But none of the flee-ers looked his way. The Hebrews limped back the way they came, staggering down the trail. Some helped another more badly injured than himself.

This was a retreat. The last stragglers stumbled by pell-mell as Eskie eased in beside him beneath the oak tree.

Keshub shook his head. "They conquered Jericho with a shout. What happened today?"

Eskie swigged water from his bag. "At mid-afternoon the Hebrews stormed the fortress at Ai. There was no circling and no earth trembling. But when the Hebrews got within range, the defenders of Ai let forth a mighty volley of sling stones and arrows. The men of Ai were prepared with weapons and ammunition."

Eskie wiped his forearm across his brow. "As soon as a handful of Hebrews fell, the others lost heart and turned back. Ai's men poured out the shut-up-tight gate on the north side. The rest of the battle was like striking a hornet's nest with a hoe. The men of Ai chased the Hebrews away."

Eskie arched his eyebrows. "I counted thirty or more Hebrews lying dead."

Keshub pushed his hair off his brow. "The Hebrews marched out from Gilgal confident and straggled home defeated."

Eskie nodded. "The Hebrews are not invincible."

The last of the stragglers rounded the bend of the descending trail across the canyon.

Keshub squared his shoulders. "You must report this to Baba. I will wait a while and follow behind the Hebrews to go back to the perch. If it gets dark before I reach the perch, I will wait until the half moon rises."

Eskie placed a hand on Keshub's shoulder. "By yourself, little brother?"

"Eskie, we cannot leave the perch unattended. Who, if not me?"

...“His Month Was Harvesting & Feasting”...
“Harvesting & Feasting”...

Chapter 39:
Not Like Men

Keshub reached the spies' nest when the half moon neared its highest point. Lying on boulders still warm from the sun, he pulled his woolen blanket to his ears and slept.

Late morning, Keshub's heart leapt up to hear *Squee-eeh-yew.*

He answered with his own bulbul's call, *wheet.ru-Tweet!* When Eskie joined him in the groove at the perch, he smiled and nodded. "I was hoping you were coming."

"I rebuilt signal fire one, or I would have been here sooner."

"Something strange is going on at Gilgal. There has been a procession since early morning. Now they have one man singled out and standing apart from all the others." Keshub shook his head and shrugged.

The man stood alone until a woman and several children joined him. Next his sheep and oxen were herded beside him and his family. Perhaps his whole family and possessions were assembled.

The man's fellow Hebrews led him and those with him to a

nearby ravine. A long line emerged from the crowd and curled by the lip of the ravine where each person threw a stone onto the man, his family, and possessions.

Keshub gasped. "What is this?" He turned to Eskie, disbelieving what he saw. His stomach threatened to empty. He gulped.

"An execution." Eskie ran a hand across his mouth.

After a long line of rock-throwers, the Hebrews built a huge fire on top of the heap in the ravine.

Keshub repositioned his elbows and hunched his shoulders. "Ra-gar' got off easy compared to this. What crime has brought such harsh judgment to one of the Hebrews' own?"

Early the next morning, Keshub waved good-bye to Eskie and Kephira, who arrived yesterday in late afternoon. Keshub performed the up-and-over maneuver as always.

On the trail he shook out his shoulders and stretched his back. Hiking home at first light, and at a normal pace—not a jog interspersed with sprints urged on by near panic—lightened his heart. Maybe toting wood to the summit all afternoon would take his mind off the two fires of judgment in Canaan in the last few days. One for Jericho, and one among the Hebrews.

That night on the roof, Keshub awoke. His whole body alert.

Baba called his name. "Keshub, bring your bedroll to the summit. We may need you."

He arrived at the summit to find his father, neighbor Agh-taan, and Sir Ghaleb gazing toward the east.

His stomach clenched as he followed their gaze. Signal fire one was ablaze—again. The Hebrews invaded at night this time?

"Keshub, sleep if you can. We may need you as a runner before the night is over." Baba clapped a hand on his shoulder.

In spite of the tension, Keshub crawled into his bedroll and sank into deep sleep.

CR&O

Ishtaba paced between the ancient olive tree and a young pomegranate with his fifth son sleeping nearby. Signal fire one burned.

The Hebrews advanced into Canaan. Where this time?

He stopped, head bowed, and shook his head. Heretofore, the flooded river had *piled up*, and Jericho fell with a shout. How would Gibeon resist such an enemy? The Hebrews did not fight like mere men. Their god fought their battles for them.

And then two days ago, the Hebrews were defeated at Ai.

Ishtaba jammed his fists on his hips. What was different? Why such amazing victories, followed by defeat? Ai was small compared to Jericho.

Pacing again. And yesterday, what was that about? A whole family and its possessions led out of the Hebrew camp. And stoned? Executed by their own people? Was it something like our dealings with Ra-gar'?

Ishtaba stopped and raised his head. "They are people, just like us."

"What did you say, Ishtaba?" Neighbor Agh-taan came to his side.

"I said the Hebrews are people just like us. But their god is real and mighty, not made by hands. Their god rules the forces of nature, and he fights for them."

Ishtaba's two best friends nodded.

"But their god did not fight for them at Ai two days ago. Why? He could have given them victory as before. He chose not to. Again, why? According to Keshub, they went out confident and limped home defeated and dejected. Then yesterday. What was the execution by stoning about?"

Ishtaba raked his open hand across his mouth and down his short beard. "Did their god refuse to fight for them because of that man or his family? We do not know what the man did, but this tells us something about the Hebrew God. Their god required a penalty for something. Their god is not like men. He is above men."

Agh-taan scratched his ear.

Ghaleb looked at the ground.

Hands limp at his side, Ishtaba turned to the south.

His friends stole away with barely a sound.

The half moon arced its silent course toward the western horizon.

Keshub snored softly and turned to his side in his cocoon of woolen blankets.

Ishtaba found the star *Heretofore and Hereafter* near the southern cross. *Star Namer, are you the God above us all? Show us what to do.*

Signal fire one burned again, so the Hebrews were advancing into Canaan. Would the enemy return to Ai for another attack after their humiliating defeat? Or would they take the left fork and reach Gibeon next?

 begin03 end

Keshub chopped wood for his mother, chips flying. He glanced often to the far side of the wheat field beginning to ripen with the tell-tale sign of lighter green. A wisp of smoke still rose from signal fire one. Nothing from fire two. Big brother should return today, but with the Hebrews in Canaan, who knew what would happen next?

He spotted an approaching runner and leaned the axe against the guest quarters wall. Taking the short stairs to the Ra-eef' courtyard gate by twos, he stuck his head in. "Baba! Mamaa! A runner!"

His parents appeared at the gate and rushed down the steps after him.

Keshub only half expected Eskie. In his brother's place, the spy from Kiriath Jearim topped the last rise of the trail.

Mamaa wound and unwound her apron in shaking hands.

Keshub strode beside Baba to meet the runner at the small spring nearest their homestead. Keshub reached for the young man's flat water bag and grabbed the gourd dipper to refill the goatskin bag part way.

"Sir, we lit the signal fire when the Hebrews marched a much larger army up the Qelt last night. Not the usual trail above the Qelt, but in the wadi itself. In the moonlight, their column advanced across the valley toward us but was swallowed up by the darkness of the wadi far below us. At signal two we watched all night and saw nothing on the upper trail. Eskie climbed down to the trail and found a steep overlook to confirm the Hebrews progressed up the dry wadi toward Ai."

Keshub extended the spy's water bag.

The spy up-ended the partially refilled bag and took a long draught. "Eskie insisted he stay in my place and sent me home. He said he knows the ibex trails and can follow the invaders undetected better than anyone else. I gave him what victuals I had left, but it was not much."

Hands on his hips, Baba shook his head. "Thank you. Signal fire one has been lit twice now. Tell your baba, Gibeon is fully prepared to take refuge on the summit. And the council at the threshing floor must make a decision tonight."

Baba waved the spy from Kiriath Jearim on home.

Keshub searched Baba's face. He had deeper creases around his mouth and above his eyes than Keshub had noticed before. What decision? Had Baba made a plan? What possible action could prevent an invasion of Aijalon Valley now?

"Keshub."

"Yes, sir?"

"Get your bedroll."

"Yes, sir!"

Moments later, Keshub grabbed his bedroll and skittered down the stairs to the courtyard. He stopped short of the half wall.

"Ishtaba, he is too young for this! It is too dangerous."

Baba spoke softly. "I know he is too young, but we have no one else available. He is too young, but he has the experience and skills he needs, and he *is* following orders. An older person could do no better."

Baba, with Keshub's bulging knapsack, rounded the half wall and nodded over his shoulder toward Mamaa. "Keshub, go hug your mother and meet me at the spring."

At the spring Baba filled two water bags and pointed to the

knapsack.

Keshub knelt on one knee to tie his bedroll above the knapsack. Rising, he swung the knapsack across his back and shouldered the two water bags.

"Keshub, the sun sags half way to the Great Sea already. Perhaps you can reach signal fire two before dark. Do not take any chances. The extra water and victuals are for Eskie. Use yours sparingly. Since signal fire two is only a half day away, one of you should come home in the morning and one in the afternoon. We will speed up the rotation accordingly."

"Yes, sir." Keshub shifted the heavier-than-usual pack and hiked through the wheat field.

Near twilight, he crossed the ridgeline trail and veered right, through the thinning trees, leaving the Gibeonites' footpath. Keeping low he came to the large oak not far from signal fire two.

Du'bo, with one eyebrow, startled and turned. "Get down."

Keshub flattened against the ground. Chin resting on his hand, he counted Hebrews by tens. For every ten he picked up a pebble and added it to his mound of pebbles.

Du'bo whispered, eyebrow lifted. "They are heading to Ai, all right. More of them this time, but advancing, like you said before, confident, with no caution. Like they were on a holiday stroll."

Keshub added a last pebble to his count and whispered. "Did Eskie say how to find the ibex trail from here?" Keshub raked up his mound of pebbles and deposited them in his sling stone bag. He sat up and scrunched his shoulders.

"Yes." Du'bo pointed. "He took off through that patch of sumac shrubs early this morning and disappeared around the base of that cliff. He wanted to be in position to hide and watch the other army coming up from the depths of the wadi to attack. He knows by now, perhaps, that the Hebrews have two separate armies heading to Ai."

Keshub took a swig from his water bag. "I hope he is safely hidden when those men arrive. Did you see their weapons?"

"Hah. Clubs, shepherd's crooks, and cattle goads. This daylight force is no better than ours. Too far away to tell about their night force."

"Eskie's supplies are low. I brought him more food and water, but it is too late to follow him. I will take first watch tonight."

⟪⟫

The sun high overhead, Eskie up-ended his water bag and wet his lips. Only a little water left. What were the Hebrews waiting for? They marched out from Gilgal at twilight yesterday and kept to the stream bed of the wadi. Now at dry season, there would not have been any water in it.

Why were they still in the wadi behind Ai, on the sunset side. Waiting to make a surprise attack?

What were they waiting for?

Eskie squirmed in place to stretch his body all over, clenching every muscle, and yawned. A crow flew over cawing a warning. Of what?

Footsteps sounded, approaching from the east—many feet.

Eskie crouched behind a boulder, peering through a stand of sumac in bloom. Another Hebrew army appeared from the el-Gayeh trail, the upper trail. The other army lay hidden on the lower trail, in the stream bed.

Eskie glanced at the sun gliding toward the Great Sea. This unit must have left Gilgal early in the morning.

He sucked on his last dried fig.

The Hebrews marched within sight of Ai, but kept their distance. "You learned your lesson last time, right?" Eskie muttered.

They skirted around Ai and crossed the el-Gayeh on the Mt. Hermon side—and set up camp.

Eskie groaned. "You Hebrews are a patient lot. More patient than I. You are in position, and you have another army hidden in the wadi. You could do this right now. But you are going to wait? Really?"

Eskie's stomach growled. He examined a cloudless sky and an

increasing moon. With the Hebrews making camp, Eskie rose from his hiding place, crouching low, and jogged back down the ibex trail.

Baba would know he was low on water and victuals. There would surely be new supplies at signal fire two. What would his supper be?

Later, with a full stomach—well, what passed for a full stomach in the spy business—Eskie crept back into the stand of sumac. He flipped open his bedroll and wrapped himself up, leaning against a boulder. Surely, the Hebrews would make their move at dawn.

Sun slanting in his eyes, Eskie bolted awake. He was right. The Hebrews advanced at dawn. Ai did not have a chance against such a superior force.

***

Back home at Gibeon the next afternoon, Eskie made a mark for Ai on the Ra-eef' limestone floor at the fire circle with a blackened stick. He looked his mentor in the eye.

"Sir Ghaleb, the Hebrews set an ambush and drew the men of Ai out. The first unit stayed hidden in the wadi. The second unit, camped in full sight over night with only minimal weaponry, advanced toward the north gate at dawn. They came close, then retreated as they did the first time when they lost over thirty men. But it was a trick—a brilliant battle plan!"

Eskie remembered he was talking about the enemy, and toned down his admiration. "Brilliant, and deadly. Ai's soldiers emptied out the north gate and pursued the fleeing Hebrews. The wadi belched a horde of Hebrews armed with real weapons to attack the unprotected walled city. And they set it afire."

Eskie pointed with his stick to the arrow indicating the fleeing unit of Hebrews. "The flee-ers stopped and turned toward Ai again. That is when the men of Ai looked behind them and realized they had been tricked. They were surrounded. No one was spared. Ai is no more." Eskie drew a large black X on top of his mark for Ai.

CRLED

Keshub stayed low at signal fire two while Eskie took his eye-witness report of Ai's defeat to Gibeon. Before the day ended, Hebrews drove flocks of sheep and herds of cattle down the trail. One group sauntered by, talking loudly, each man carrying a goose.

The next morning Keshub munched on raisins and almonds and counted by tens. Pack animals loaded with plunder plodded by just like he and Uncle Yaakoub had done countless times at the end of market day. By mid-day, the mule train had passed. Now men with large burdens of loot on their shoulders traipsed by. Heavily armed soldiers accompanied them—must be the ambush unit Eskie told about.

Keshub counted his pebbles by tens—one pebble representing ten tens. The mid-day sun filtered down on the back of his neck through the leafy oak. How many Hebrews?

Keshub shook his head—many, plus many more!

Eskie glided in at Keshub's elbow.

Keshub jumped. "How do you come in so silently, big brother?"

Eskie forced a grin. "Talent, little brother."

Keshub pointed to the north where smoke from the burning of Ai had increased ten-fold. At the same time the number of looters trekking back to Gilgal trickled to nothing.

Eskie pointed to the Beerothite. "Baba says as soon as the Hebrews are back at Gilgal, we spies must rebuild signal fire one and go to the perch again. We will wait for the Hebrew's next move."

Eskie hooked a thumb in his girdle. "I am going back to the perch, little brother, but Baba has something else in mind for you."

"What?" Keshub squenched his face, afraid his mother had finally persuaded his father he was too young.

"I do not know. All I do know is when I described what happened at Ai to Baba, he said quietly, 'First Jericho, now Ai. Nothing can stop them when their god fights for them.' Then after a short pause, Baba said, 'Tell Keshub to come home as quickly as possible.'"

Keshub arrived at the Ra-eef' courtyard late in the day. He neared the half wall and stopped in his tracks.

"Is it the only way, Mother?" Baba's voice held a strange tremble.

Gran-mamaa's voice rasped. "Ishtaba, only you could have come up with a plan to offer yourself as a servant. You have been negotiating peace amongst your brothers since you were a lad. Perhaps it was the Star Namer who cursed the Hivites, sons of Canaan, to be slaves for just such a time as this."

Keshub sucked in a breath. Hivites? We are cursed to be slaves?

..."His Month Was Harvesting and Feasting"...
"Harvesting and Feasting"...

Chapter 40:
The Delegation

Head down, Keshub attacked the log before him with Uncle Samir's favorite bronze axe. He gritted his teeth while anger boiled inside. He swung the axe as if the log were his enemy. Why? Why had Baba sent him here to chop wood—with Ra-gar' the thief? For two whole days already.

The thief who groaned and moaned about everything. Not enough food, his water bag lying in the sun near him got too hot, the shackles chafed his ankles.

Being near Ra-gar' felt like punishment, but why would he be punished?

His father did not explain.

He could not ask.

Eskie had said Baba had a new assignment in mind. What new assignment?

Baba had hardly spoken to Keshub since he returned from spying. From a lofty perch to back-breaking work at the wood pile, this was his new assignment?

Keshub shook his head, lowered his axe, and scowled. So unfair.

Baba hardly worked in the pottery yard. He had visitors all day. From the woodpile yesterday, Keshub had waved at Jebus, his friend among the Jerusalem soldiers.

Jebus ran beside a donkey-riding emissary from Zedek. On duty, Jebus had only nodded to Keshub—and winked.

Baba went to the Aijalon Valley council meeting every night at the threshing floor. No more fire circles in the Ra-eef' courtyard.

From the rooftop sleeping quarters, Keshub had heard his father returning late at night. Hoisting the heavy axe aloft, he sighed. Why had Baba cut him off from what was happening?

Another gash to the log at his feet. Why not sheep shearing? Lehab and Micah camped across the valley, having fun helping Uncle Yaakoub and Raheeb', the new farmer in the family.

Why wood chopping, when Ra-gar' was supposed to chop for them all? *Why me?*

He leaned the bronze axe on a log and retrieved his water bag from the shade of a pomegranate bush. Cool water coursed down his throat.

He squenched his eyes tight to block out the mid-day sun. Another gulp. Tears attacked his eyelids. What new assignment did Baba have for him?

Flexing his stiff shoulders, he swallowed the anger he felt, along with the cooling water. Perhaps, Baba was not ready to reveal his plan.

Keshub rolled his head side to side. One more cooling gulp, swallowing slowly. *Trust Baba.*

Ra-gar' was right. Cool water tasted better. Warm water from a goatskin bag lying in the sun must be galling.

Keshub grimaced and muttered. *Oh, well. Why not?*

He shouldered his water bag and approached Ra-gar' who swung his axe and sank the sharp head in a fresh log. "Would you like me to pour cooler water for you?"

Ra-gar' looked up, his dark eyes squinting in the sunshine, and scowled.

Keshub remembered the day Ra-gar' struck him for accidentally dousing the man with water as they worked to dig the cistern. He reconsidered. "Lay your axe aside, and I will bring you fresh water."

Ra-gar' licked his cracked lips, hand resting loosely on the butt of his axe and let the handle flop to the ground.

Keshub climbed on the log and lifted the bag high. "Do you want cool water in your mouth or down the front of you?" He grinned.

Ra-gar's face softened, but he gave a sidewise look.

Keshub let pour a perfect stream of water cooled by the shade. He tilted the bag to stop the flow and smiled again. "Not bad for a Hivite." Keshub turned and replaced his water bag in the shade.

His axe felt lighter and cut deeper. After the dousing so long ago, Ra-gar' had called him a "worthless Hivite." What was it Gran-baba used to say? "A kindness is good medicine, for the giver and the receiver."

That night he sat cross-legged at the dinner mat with only his father. His father, deep in his own thoughts, not speaking.

The rest of the Ra-eefs, prepared for attack, would camp on the summit tonight—except Gran-mamaa. Not able to travel there, she said she would not go if she *were* able. Only Gran-mamaa, Baba, Mamaa and he remained. *Trust Baba.*

"Keshub, to your mat now." Baba stared into the fire, eyes blinking rapidly.

"Yes, sir." *Trust Baba.*

Alone on the rooftop for the first time in his life, the low murmur of voices drifted up to him from the fire circle. Baba's closest confidantes had arrived. Sir Ghaleb's clipped cadence mixed with neighbor Agh-taan's higher nasal sound. Baba's deep tone never wavered. *Trust Baba.*

Will the new assignment begin tomorrow? Bone tired from chopping, the faint hum of voices below lulled Keshub to sleep.

Keshub dreamed he led his flock toward green meadows but turned back when he heard his father calling him.

"Keshub."

He awakened to pre-dawn darkness. His father was calling his name.

"Yes, sir?"

Baba set one of Ranine's clay lamps on the parapet and tossed a bundle to land beside him. "Put these clothes on and come to the livestock pen immediately."

"Yes, sir."

Rolling out of his blanket, he stowed it in its place. He untied a large knot in the sleeves of a tunic and found soiled clothing, smelling of someone else's sweat. Sandals, too. Repaired several times. The girdle, grimy.

He grimaced. The refugees. These were ragged clothes the refugees from Moab left when they stole his new ones many moons ago. He had to be fitted twice for itchy and stiff new clothes for Ranine's wedding because of those refugees. Because of the Hebrews, really.

Why wear these? Surely, Mamaa would never approve. *Trust Baba.*

In the courtyard he headed to the outside gate.

"Keshub." Mamaa's tone demanded attention. "Eat."

"Baba said come immediately to the livestock pen, Mamaa."

"Eat first." Mamaa's left eyebrow arched ominously high.

Not wanting to disobey either parent, he stuffed his mouth with the flatbread and honey his mother thrust upon him. He turned toward the courtyard gate with his mouth stuffed. "Shank-zu, mamba."

"You are welcome, Fifth Son. Come home safely."

Keshub stole a curious look over his shoulder as he pulled the courtyard gate open.

Mamaa's never-idle hands hung limp at her sides. Her eyes overflowed with tears.

Rushing down the steps outside, he shook his head. What? No objection to the filthy rags?

He licked the last bit of honey from his fingers and wiped them on the already grubby garment.

In gray light at the livestock pen, Baba stood among three other men—all dressed in near rags.

Uncle Yaakoub and Uncle Samir checked the cinches of five Ra-eef' donkeys loaded with old packs.

Keshub approached his favorite, Raja, and patted her neck. "Long time, friend."

He fingered Raja's pack, tied down with old ropes. Uncle Samir had fashioned new ropes and packs in the cold season. Old clothes, old packs, old ropes. Why?

Sir Ghaleb and neighbor Agh-taan appeared from the gloom. They each kissed the other three men, then Baba, on either cheek.

Baba handed Keshub a knapsack and bedroll and an old goat-skin water bag, so old and patched, it had a missing leg.

Keshub dared not ask any questions. *Trust Baba.* He stood beside Raja, slipping his hand along the frayed lead rope, waiting for orders.

Uncle Yaakoub hugged Baba with unusual force before stepping back with glistening eyes.

Uncle Yaakoub's big arms surrounded Keshub, too, until Baba whistled.

Keshub backed away, turned, and plodded through the plump green heads of grain sparkling with dew—one raggedy boy following after a raggedy band of four men. Why?

Keshub, facing the brightening horizon, whispered. "Raja, this must be our new assignment. Strange, huh? On another day I would guess we were trekking to market in Jericho, but Jericho is destroyed. And the Hebrews are camped nearby."

"Could it be...?" He stopped—not really wanting to know the answer. *Trust Baba.*

At mid-morning, Baba whistled and called a halt at the ridge-line trail—the ancient north-south trail that traversed Canaan on the line of the watershed.

Keshub swung his knapsack to ground and crouched beside

Raja. He lifted the flap of his knapsack and withdrew his victuals pouch. His jaw dropped. What? Moldy flatbread? Dry and tough.

He glanced up the line of donkeys. Baba flicked something off his flatbread with thumb and index finger.

Keshub shrugged and eyed his greenish dried figs carefully, pinching away mold in several places. Really? *Trust Baba.*

When Baba resumed their trek, Keshub bent to his mule's ear. "Uh-oh, Raja. We *are* going to the Jordan Valley. To see the Hebrews?"

Abreast of the lookout perch in late afternoon, Baba neither halted nor hesitated.

Keshub scanned the incline beside the trail for the spies' broom. Nowhere in sight. No Aijalon Valley spy had left the perch today.

Who had replaced him in the rotation? His neck prickled at the thought of three sets of eyes watching his every move going down the steep incline.

At the half-way campground, Zedek's men gripped their weapons and stood abreast across the trail, blocking the way to the Jordan Valley.

A burly soldier stepped forward. "Where are you going, old man?"

Keshub bristled at the impudence. He clenched his fists.

"Gentlemen," Baba responded mildly, using an accent more like Gran-mamaa's than his own and sounding very much like Keshub remembered Gran-baba Ra-eef. "I am Hivite from the north near Mt. Hermon's slopes."

Keshub's eyebrows drew together. Of course, his father's words were true. Baba had grown up there. But why would Baba not claim Gibeon as home to these men?

The young man growled. "What are you doing here?"

Baba shrugged. "Just passing through."

The man placed a hand on Baba's pack animal. "What are you carrying, old man?"

Zedek's man nearest to Keshub reached out a soiled hand. "I want to know what you have to eat. Let me have that victuals bag, boy." He grabbed Keshub's knapsack and tore it open.

"Yech! Yours looks about the same as mine. Long trip, huh?" The man slapped the small bag back into Keshub's mid-section and snarled. "Short trip for us, but bad food is courtesy of stingy old Zedek himself."

Taking his cue from Baba, Keshub nodded and mumbled. "Aye." He might not be able to sound like a northern Hivite like Baba.

Baba led on down the trail to make camp. He stopped at a narrow place on the slanting trail where a stealthy approach from marauders would be difficult. And out of hearing of Zedek's soldiers.

Keshub and the man from Kephira unloaded Raja. Keshub helped him in turn, then tethered all the donkeys. Baba made a small fire and heated water in a crock made by his own hands.

Keshub wrapped his hands around his bowl of hot water and sipped. Baba had added a small amount of dried mutton to make broth.

Keshub shrugged. Stale flatbread was far more tasty dipped in warm broth.

The sliver of moon came up over the ruins of Jericho and Baba spoke. "Perhaps I have been secluded among the good folks of Aijalon Valley too long. I am prepared to meet the Hebrews. I was not prepared to meet Zedek's men."

Baba stole a glance at the southern horizon and smiled. "We were fortunate to be dismissed so quickly because we did not have food worth stealing."

"You are right." The man next to Baba nodded and took another gulp of broth.

Baba swished his bowl. "I have been considering our exit from the valley after we meet the Hebrews. I am now resolved that we should exit another way. We will go up the Wadi Farah toward Shechem. As soon as we are out of sight, we can pick up the pace and make up some of the time lost by cutting through the hills back toward Gibeon."

"Yes, we do not want to encounter Zedek's men again."

"Also, stay close together as we travel. Keshub, stay right behind our neighbor from Kephirah."

"Yes, sir."

Baba continued, barely above a whisper. "We have heard there are scavengers raking through the ruins. We do not want to give them an easy target. I will put out the fire and take the first watch. Friend from Beeroth, will you take the next one?"

"I will be glad to."

"Good. Sleep next to your packs, men, with your weapon ready at your side. We will start early. We want to be at the spring at sunup."

The others murmured agreement and prepared their bedrolls.

"Keshub?"

"Yes, sir?"

"Come."

Keshub followed his father a little way away to a boulder near where the pack animals were tethered. He sat beside his father, looking up at the moon, and waited for Baba to begin.

"I am sorry, Keshub, I did not explain and prepare you for this trip. There was no chance to do so, but also, we wanted as few as possible to know about it."

Keshub nodded. "So, I was not being punished when I chopped wood beside the thief of Gibeon?"

"No, son. We had to wait until all the villages supplied a representative. Tomorrow we will meet the Hebrews as early as possible. We will ask for a treaty. I believe, and I have convinced the leaders of the other villages, that he who fights against the Hebrews fights against their god."

Baba paused. "Keshub, you are included in this delegation for two reasons. The first, is to demonstrate to the others of Aijalon Valley my whole-hearted commitment to this effort. I have committed myself, my son, and Ra-eef' livestock because I believe this is the only way we can survive. The other reason is more practical. If we are not received well by the Hebrews, if they move to seize us or attack us, I am hoping you can slip away to warn Gibeon."

Baba lifted his eyes to the southern sky. "Every night I look for that star above the Salt Sea. Keshub, I believe the One who knows the heretofore and the hereafter is guiding us. I believe, and am hoping with all my heart, that I am right."

Keshub's heart pulsed in his chest like a bronze gong.

"If I am wrong, and I die tomorrow, I want you to know how proud I am of you. I wish my baba Ra-eef' could see you now. He took great stock in you as a lad. If you return to Gibeon and I do not, tell your mother I love her."

"Yes, sir." Keshub gulped.

"Now get some sleep. I will wake you before long."

"Yes, sir."

Crawling into his bedroll, Keshub wiped a tear from his eye and took a deep breath, forcing himself to relax. Tomorrow, he would meet the dreaded enemy.

Surely, my father is the bravest and wisest man in the whole land. I will not worry. I will sleep because I will trust Baba."

Chapter 41:
A Ruse

At first light, Keshub opened his eyes and rubbed them. On the ground nearby, an odd dirt-colored insect with huge eyes and jointed front legs appeared to plead for mercy.

Keshub muttered. "Like us."

He rested his head on his forearm.

The little giant stood motionless as a wood louse meandered by. With lightning speed the giant caught the roly-poly creature in his front legs.

"No, not like us, after all."

The giant trapped the balled-up morsel in his merciless front legs and gobbled up his prey.

Would the Hebrews do the same to this little delegation?

Baba called.

Keshub scrambled out of his cocoon of a tattered woolen blanket. His big toe had found a hole and stuck out all night.

He poured water in a leather bag and held it to Raja's muzzle.

"Just enough to get us to the spring, old girl. You can drink your fill then."

Together, he and the man from Kephira, one of Baba's cousins, loaded their packs onto their donkeys.

When the sun rimmed a red crescent on the horizon, Keshub stood beneath tall palms, now the tallest landmark of Jordan Valley.

Shaking his head, he eyed the heap of ruins. *The mighty here have fallen. Who are we that Baba thinks we could survive meeting the Hebrews?*

He loosed his hold on Raja's lead rope. She slurped at his side while he refilled his three-legged water bag.

Through the palms, he spied a black tent and a small herd of goats. A young boy and an old man knelt with their backs turned, milking.

The old man handed his milk bag to the boy and hobbled their way, headed toward Baba in the lead. He scanned the rest of their party and stopped—and smiled.

Keshub skirted the edge of the pool of water and approached the toothless crippled man. "Hello, Deyab!"

Deyab enfolded him and kissed either cheek.

Baba approached leading his donkey.

Keshub stepped back and extended a hand toward his friend. "I would like you to meet Deyab. He is a wise man like yourself, Baba. He has tended our animals on market day many times."

"I am glad to meet you, sir." Baba bowed slightly.

"Oh, no, not a sir! Just a simple Bedouin here. You are welcome to the water. We do not have much else!"

Baba turned to his pack animal and produced a small bag. With a slight bow, he offered the cloth bag to Deyab.

The old man hefted the bag and massaged its contents before he lifted it to his nose. His toothless smile spread from ear to ear. "Ooh-wee! We will have flatbread tonight!"

"We must go now." Baba bowed again. "We are going to meet the Hebrews."

"Oh, really?" Deyab jerked his head back. "Well, tell them good morning from me, too." He cackled, and placed a hand over his mouth. "We will watch to see how that turns out."

Keshub waved good-bye and returned to Raja's side.

Baba whistled and led his men around the heap of ruins.

Keshub gazed at the mud bricks strewn wide where mighty walls had fallen outward, as Eskie had described. Keshub had marveled at the steep incline that guarded access to the proud city. Now humbled beneath rubble, the fallen walls became a gradual slope and easy access.

He shuddered and pushed back his hair from his forehead.

Ahead, lay the vast Hebrew camp he had spied on from the perch. Eskie watched from there now.

With every step closer, Keshub's admiration grew. Colorful flags fluttered from every center tent pole. Every doorway faced toward the center of the camp with orderly lanes between rows of tents.

Baba raised a hand to signal stop, and then, "Stay here." He handed his lead rope to the man behind him from Beeroth.

Baba turned aside with hands folded together at his waist. Half way up a small hill, he stopped, hands hanging limp at his side.

Only then, Keshub spied a man bowed to the ground on the hill not far ahead of Baba. The man raised his head and stood, then turned. He stopped short, seeing Baba.

Baba bowed deeply at the waist.

The man spoke, and Baba bowed low again before he responded.

Keshub held his breath. One of the pack animals snorted. Raja swished her tail to ward off gnats.

Keshub exhaled and swatted a gnat buzzing his nose.

Finally, Baba turned and motioned with his hand for the rest of his band to come forward. Baba and the Hebrew turned and walked side by side toward the Hebrew camp.

As they drew near the first outer row of tents, a young boy with a water bag stopped to stare.

The Hebrew man with Baba gestured. "Wait here."

Baba returned to join them.

Keshub itched to hear what had been said.

The man from Kiriath Jearim rubbed his mouth. "What did you tell him, Ishtaba?"

"Just what we agreed upon. I began by saying, 'Sir, I am Ishtaba the Hivite and I am your servant.' I also said, 'I am from a distant country, and we want to make a treaty with you because of the fame of the Lord your God.'"

"I told him my son and these three men have come bearing a few small gifts of barley, raisins, honey and some pottery."

A rooster crowed as the sun lost its red glow and bathed the valley in clear sunshine.

"His name is Joshua. He is summoning the leaders of the twelve tribes to make a treaty with us. We are to wait here."

Baba dipped his chin and pointed. "Keshub, take all five pack animals over there where there is a little grass. Tether them, but stay with them. Have the animals between us and yourself in case we are seized. If that happens, you know what to do. I pray escape will not be necessary."

Keshub obeyed. He waited. A swarm of flies joined the gnats buzzing around the pack animals. Keshub folded himself onto a low rock and peered at his father and the other men through the legs of the Ra-eef' pack animals.

The man Baba called Joshua returned from the sea of tents to Baba's side. Keshub counted ten plus two men following behind. Joshua appeared to be more calm than the ones following him.

Keshub drew in a quick breath. The twelve men surrounded Baba and his three companions.

Keshub strained to hear.

"Who are you?" came from a man with hands on his hips.

Baba intoned a short, calm reply.

"Why have you come?"

Baba's companions also replied with calm, low voices. It was impossible to hear every word from this distance.

One of the Hebrews challenged loud enough Keshub had no trouble hearing him. "But perhaps you live near us. How, then can we make a treaty with you?"

Baba bowed low again, followed by the other three. "We are your servants...."

The man from Beeroth bent low, removed a sandal and straightened. He must have shown his worn out footware to each of the Hebrews.

One Hebrew stepped aside when their friend from Kiriath Jearim left the circle and approached the donkeys. He grabbed a knapsack and returned. He bobbed around the circle, held the bag open, and evidently invited the Hebrews to inspect his victuals.

The threatening Hebrews turned up their noses and backed away from bread hardly fit to eat. They seemed satisfied.

Joshua used a formal tone to the leaders of the tribes. "Do you approve....?"

All raised their hands and responded. "Aye."

Baba waved for Keshub to come forward.

Keshub rose and trotted toward Baba. The circle opened.

"Joshua, friend. This is my son number five. I am, indeed, a blessed man."

Keshub bent at the waist before the leader of the Hebrews.

"Son, help the men unload the packs of the things we are giving to these good people."

"Yes, sir." With another quick bow, Keshub ran to gather the tether ropes and bring the pack animals nearer.

Baba opened a bag for each of the leaders, ten plus two in all, and removed from each a piece of pottery sunk into the grain.

When Baba opened the last bag, Keshub's jaw dropped.

Baba produced Mamaa's favorite bowl, the one he had made for her. With its smoothly burnished interior and incised pattern of curves on the exterior, she treasured it.

Baba placed the favorite bowl directly into the hands of Joshua, who turned the vessel all about. He smiled and nodded.

Two young men appeared from the Hebrews' camp. The older one pushed a hand cart. The younger appeared to be about Keshub's age.

Joshua's eyes lit up when the circle opened to include them.

"Elkanah and Hosiah, perfect timing! Meet our new friends, Ishtaba and his son Keshub."

The boys nodded and looked Keshub over.

Keshub licked his lips. A wonderful fragrance arose from the hand cart.

Joshua turned back a spotless linen cloth and presented rounded, freshly baked barley loaves. "Please take them and replace the bread you have."

Joshua tore one apart and handed a piece to each of their delegation.

Keshub sunk his teeth into the soft, warm goodness and closed his eyes. The taste was like spring sunshine and a warm hug.

Baba bowed deeply to his new friend. "Please excuse us. Your servants have a long way to go before nightfall."

"Of course. God be with you in your journey, friend."

Baba's eyes glistened in the mid-day sunlight. Baba bowed low again, and spoke with a catch in his voice. "It is your God's favor and presence that I value more than life itself."

Joshua's eyes, too, moistened. He embraced Baba, and they gave each other the traditional kiss on either cheek.

Up the trail beside the Wadi Farah, Keshub shook his head and took in a full, deep breath—the first since he suspected the purpose of their mission yesterday.

Out of sight of Gilgal over the ridgeline trail, Baba stopped a moment—his eyes red and overflowing. "Let's head cross-country, men. Kephira, give your lead rope to Keshub and scout ahead of us for the best route."

They skirted barren escarpments of steep limestone and hacked their way through brambles in the low places.

Mid-afternoon, Keshub sighted a short-horned female ibex and her kid.

Late afternoon, his heart leapt to his throat at the sight of Gibeon's hill—the pitch of its plateau like the sway of a donkey's bare back.

At twilight a cheer erupted at ein-el-Beled. Lehab and Micah outran their fathers to greet the returning delegation.

"Kesh! We thought we might never see you again." Micah draped an arm on Keshub's shoulder.

Lehab gave a playful jab. "I thought I might never hear you complain again how boring spying was."

Keshub gulped. "Baba says the Star Namer guided us. He believes the One who knows the *heretofore and the hereafter* is the God of the Hebrews. We are in His hands."

Chapter 42:
The Ruse Discovered

"Uh-oh."

"What?" Eskie scrambled to rejoin Keshub on the perch.

"Look!"

"Where?"

"At the spring." Keshub sucked in a breath and held it, fist at his mouth.

Eskie shook his head. "What? A Hebrew brought his herd to water, and he is talking to an old crippled man."

"I know him, the cripple, from market days in Jericho. He is Deyab the Bedouin. Baba and I talked to him on the way to Gilgal three days ago."

"Looks like the old man is pointing our way."

Keshub nodded. "That is what I was afraid of."

"Uh-oh." Eskie pursed his lips.

Keshub dropped his head in his hands. "The Hebrew does not look happy."

"And now he is in a hurry to get back to Gilgal."

Keshub's head in his hands, his voice muffled. "Deyab has surely told the Hebrew we are neighbors, and we live not so far away as they thought."

"Little brother, we must prepare to act at any moment."

"What should we do?"

"Go to the first signal fire and be ready. When you see me rounding the bend below you, you will know the Hebrews are coming. That is when you should begin striking the flint to start the fire. We will give Baba the earliest possible signal of attack.

"If you get the fire burning well before I arrive, head up the trail and start fire two, but rest and wait for me there. When I arrive, I will give you the number and speed of the advancing Hebrews."

Eskie ran his hand over his mouth. "If it seems I am delayed, do not wait for me. Baba needs to know our secret is out as soon as possible."

"All right." Keshub slid down from the perch in a groove worn smooth from more than three moons of observation by the spies of Aijalon Valley. He grabbed his pack and water bag, clawed his way over the ridge to the trail below, and jogged up the trail.

In his head, Keshub could hear how Deyab's conversation with the Hebrew went, probably about the same as with Baba three days ago.

"Good morning! Welcome to our spring! There is plenty of water for all .... So what did you think of your new neighbors? Real nice folks, huh? ... They just live up that-a-way a little piece ... Distant land? ... Maybe a day's walk ... You passed their trail when you went to Ai .... Take the first trail on the left off the Wadi-el-Gayeh."

The Hebrews were sure to find out they were tricked sometime. Keshub waited beside re-built signal fire one. What would the Hebrews do next? Would they honor the treaty?

The sun neared its highest point when Eskie came into sight far down the trail, running with all his might.

Keshub sprang into action, fumbling for his flint and iron inside his sling shot bag. He lifted the flat rock nearby and grabbed the pouch with extra tender inside.

He wriggled flat on his stomach with arms extended to reach under the great stack of firewood. Sparks flew as he furiously scraped his flint and iron together. Some landed on kindling and flickered out, unable to ignite.

Soon the tender of dry grasses and dry pine needles smoked. Thin wavering wisps, followed by a faint glow before a weak flame burst forth.

Keshub blew softly and fed the flickering flame with more tender from the leather pouch. When the flame grew stronger, he backed up slightly and added kindling piece by piece, being careful not to smother the young flame.

In a whoosh, the long, finger size, upright pine branches burst into flame over his head.

Quick as a wink Keshub scampered backward.

An acrid smell reached his nostrils, and he pushed his forelock off his forehead. The hair felt coarse. Brittle bits rubbed off on his hand. The hair on the back of his hand was blackened. A little too close to the fire, but he clamped his lips together in a grim smile. Flames licked the bark on the four-square stack of logs taller than himself.

He tilted his head back. Already, black smoke curled upward through the branches of the four sapling pines leaning together as if they had a secret. Soon the lookout on Gibeon's summit would be sounding the bronze gong.

Down the trail, Eskie pumped his arms, drawing closer.

Hah! If I do not leave now, Eskie might reach signal fire two before me.

At the site of fire two, high above the el-Gayeh trail, Keshub had another roaring fire started. He lounged against the thick oak trunk a safe distance away, taking deep gulps of air. Sweat dripped from his brow as he checked the fire and the position of the sun. *Eskie said go on to Gibeon if he is delayed. I will wait until the sun passes that branch.*

What seemed like only a moment later, He checked the sun's position. *Behind the branch!* He grabbed his knapsack and scrambled to his feet just as Eskie came into view below, doggedly taking each step up the Gibeon cut-off.

Beneath the oak, with his hands on his knees, Eskie managed to blurt out, "Good job, Kesh. Looks like the Hebrews are bringing out all their troops. If they do not honor their word in the treaty, we have no hope. We are tremendously outnumbered."

"How fast are they coming?" Keshub shouldered his pack.

"They came to the foot of the trail marching double time—in a great hurry, but as they reached the wadi trail, they showed more caution. They sent several ahead to check on either side of the trail as though they suspected an ambush. If they continue that strategy, it may take three days for them to reach Gibeon."

"We can only hope we have three more days to prepare. We have prepared for many moons." Keshub swiped his forelock aside.

"Kesh, I am spent. I will spend the night here and check on the Hebrews' progress in the morning. If the enemy has picked up the pace, I will come home tomorrow. If they are still being extra cautious and I do not return tomorrow, I will shoot a flaming arrow after nightfall. A second flaming arrow will mean they are coming fast and will arrive during the night."

Keshub swung his knapsack back to the ground and removed his victuals bag. "I will leave this with you and take only my water."

"Thanks."

Keshub hesitated, wanting to say more, but biting his lip, not knowing what to say. He aimed a soft jab to his brother's shoulder. "Come home whole, brother."

"I will." Eskie smiled and jerked his head toward home. "Go, little brother. Time is short."

Keshub sprinted toward the ridgeline, then an easy jog downhill to home. The Hebrews would be angry they were deceived. What would they do about being tricked into a treaty? Would Eskie be all right?

***

On the third day, Keshub pushed down his fear as he sat on a log and whittled with his flint knife, glancing often toward the ridgeline. The delegation waited—Keshub, his father, and the other three men who went to Gilgal with them.

Baba had insisted the delegation should be the same, though there was no need to wear the refugees' rags this time. A logical decision, since the brambles of the short cut had shredded Keshub's garment. The remnant could hardly be used for anything but wicks in a dish of olive oil. He rubbed his arm, the last of the scratches almost healed.

Yesterday Keshub strode beside his father as he chose this open area on the east slope descending into Aijalon Valley from the ridgeline trail. From there the Hebrews would view the whole of their valley for the first time.

Baba forbade anyone going into the olive grove nearby where the Hebrews would suspect an ambush. "We will honor the treaty with the Hebrews even if they do not. We will meet them completely without guile. The Hebrews who expect an ambush will meet only four men and a young boy who begged for their favor and friendship at Gilgal six days ago."

Keshub glanced across the valley where the women and children of Aijalon Valley camped at the summit. Men of Gibeon worked at a feverish pace in the wheat fields of ripened grain. Almost as much as an attack by a superior force, Baba and the men feared seeing their wheat crop trampled underfoot or set afire. Even if they survived, they would face starvation in the coming year.

Eskie had come home briefly yesterday. Now in position in the oak forest, he would strike a flint to light an arrow when the Hebrews crossed the ridgeline trail. He would aim it at a rocky outcropping in view of the delegation's meeting place.

Waiting for the sun to go down, Baba occupied his hands by making a pair of sandals. Always, someone in the Ra-eef' clan needed new sandals.

Keshub sat cross-legged beside his father, forelock falling in his eyes, tongue clamped between his lips. He bore down on the leather outline of a foot, twisting the flint awl back and forth to make a hole.

He tried to think only of the tool in his hand and making holes around the edge of the leather. He would not think about the Hebrews. He willed his hands not to tremble.

The sun sank into the Great Sea on the horizon. In the twilight, Keshub put away their work and tools, dreading the night. Tonight, the moon would be in the new moon phase—no moon at all.

Would Eskie hear the Hebrews coming? If the Hebrews arrived at night, the delegation might have no notice.

Baba stirred up the cook fire and checked the hot water in a pottery vessel sitting in the embers. He moved about serving a bowl of hot water with herbs and dried mutton and fresh flatbread baked by Mamaa that morning.

With the bright fire in their midst, Keshub saw almost nothing outside the reaches of the firelight. He constantly darted his eyes toward that rock formation.

"How can you be so calm, Ishtaba?" Their friend from Beeroth drained his bowl of broth.

"I do have some anxiety, friend. I fear that perhaps I am wrong about the character of the man called Joshua who pledged a treaty with us. I fear that some of the other Hebrews will somehow over-rule Joshua, and nullify his word and the treaty."

"I fear their God. There is no other explanation for the things we have seen. Crossing a flooded river on dry ground and bringing down the ancient and mighty stronghold of Jericho with a shout. Those events could not be the work of men. Only the ruler of all creation could do those things."

Baba paused and looked into his bowl. "I have fears, but I have done all that I can do, except keep my head. I have placed all that I have in the hands of the One who named the stars and knows the *heretofore and the hereafter*. Now I must wait."

Shortly before morning light, Keshub roused and turned in his blanket near the fire Baba had tended all through the night.

"Keshub. Get up. They are here." Baba's even tone showed no panic. "Eskie shot a flaming arrow."

Keshub rolled out of his blanket and scrambled to his feet. As the sun's first faint golden glow shoved back the darkness of night, he made up his bedroll and stowed it with their gear nearby.

Baba stirred up the fire and added wood. "If we are to be killed for our deception, I will make an easy first target. The rest of you keep low beside the gear until they get closer."

Keshub saw them first.

A double column of stout, bearded men, their faces framed, lion-like, entered Aijalon Valley and fanned out right and left. With spears and bows and arrows at the ready, the right column inspected the olive grove, and the left checked for an ambush behind the small hill to Keshub's left.

Baba spoke barely above a whisper. "Join me now, men."

Obeying, Keshub stood with empty hands held loosely at his sides. Baba insisted they show as clearly as possible the delegation had no weapons.

The Hebrews kept coming. Keshub lost count. He resisted the urge to fidget. Soon the Hebrews surrounded the campsite, with triple the number of Hebrews on the west side watching the hill of Gibeon across the wheat field.

Farmers had fled the fields and stood at the base of Gibeon's hill, armed with farm tools.

Joshua, leader of the Hebrews, emerged from the oak forest, striding briskly toward them.

More Hebrews followed behind him on the trail, as far as Keshub could see.

When Joshua drew near, Baba fell to his knees and bent at the waist with his face on his knees.

Keshub tried to keep his head and followed his father's example. The rest of the delegation did the same.

Joshua halted a stone's throw away. "Bring me the leader and his son."

Bent double, Keshub watched Baba from the corner of his eye. Baba did not move.

A big foot with a patch of dark hair on the big toe appeared at Keshub's elbow. Rough hands grabbed him at his armpit and raised him to his feet. A spear pressed into his back between his shoulder blades, forcing him to step forward.

Beside him Baba folded his hands at his waist as he approached Joshua. Keshub followed Baba's lead.

Father and son reached Joshua and bowed deeply at the waist.

Joshua's dark eyes pierced. "Why did you deceive us by saying, 'We live a long way from you,' while actually you live near us?"

Baba bowed again. "Your servants were clearly told how the Lord your God had commanded his servant Moses to give you the whole land and to wipe out all its inhabitants from before you."

Grumbling from among the Hebrews sounded behind Joshua. One voice stood out. "Yes, destroy them, is what I say!"

Joshua raised his hand to quiet the grumblers. "We have given them our oath by the Lord, the God of Israel, and we cannot touch them now."

Baba extended his hands, palm up. "We have heard of the fame of your God. All that He did in Egypt, all that He did to the two kings of the Amorites east of the Jordan. We ourselves saw you cross the flooded Jordan on dry ground. We also saw your people bring down Jericho with a shout."

Baba bowed his head. "So we feared for our lives, and that is why we did this."

Joshua's piercing look softened. "We will let you live, so that wrath will not fall on us for breaking the oath we swore to you."

Baba lifted his head. "We are now in your hands. Do to us whatever seems right and good."

Joshua spoke softly, but firmly. "You are now under a curse. You will never cease to serve as woodcutters and water carriers for the house of my God."

Baba nodded. "We are your servants. We will begin immediately to provide wood and water as you instruct. We can make our first delivery of wood on the morrow."

Joshua cleared his throat and raised his voice. "There is one other thing, Ishtaba."

Baba looked up quickly, his face clouded with concern at Joshua's tone, but he lowered his eyes and repeated. "We are in your hands."

Joshua turned to Keshub.

Keshub took in a quick breath and held it. What did the leader of the Hebrews have in mind? How would he be involved?

"I will take your son as guarantee and as my personal servant. You will keep your word, and I will treat him kindly. It must be so to satisfy the grumblers among my people."

Keshub ran Joshua's words back through his head. " ... your son as guarantee ... my personal servant." Finally, he exhaled.

Joshua turned back to Baba.

Tears coursed down Baba's weathered cheeks. "Friend, I wish you would take me instead of my son, but I believe you will keep your word and treat him well. You will find he is a fine lad. There is none finer in all the land. I know he will serve you well."

Joshua nodded, blinking rapidly. "We will return to Gilgal now. I will give you a few moments with your son."

Baba grasped Keshub by the upper arms. "My own heart is breaking. I do not know how I will console your mother."

For a moment Keshub was folded into his father's arms. "Keshub, collect your gear."

Released, Keshub retrieved his bedroll, knapsack, and water bag and stood before his father.

"Keshub, I am committing you into the hands of Joshua whom, I believe, is an honorable man, and into the care of the Hebrew God. In my heart I have placed you in His hands."

"Yes, sir."

"Go now, son."

"Yes, Baba." Head held high, Keshub turned, willing his limbs to move though they felt frozen and stiff.

When he reached Joshua, he followed his father's example and bowed at the waist, repeating his father's words. "Sir, I am your servant."

At Joshua's command, the double column of Hebrews still on the trail behind Joshua did an about face and led the way.

Keshub fell into step behind Joshua, aware of the heavily armed Hebrew soldiers at his heels.

To the pounding of many footsteps, Keshub tried to grasp what had happened. His family would not be attacked by the Hebrews. Baba had found a way for the people of Aijalon Valley to survive— being servants, woodcutters and water-carriers.

He had overheard Gran-mamaa agreeing with Baba a few days ago. "Offer yourself as a servant. Perhaps it was the Star Namer who cursed the Hivites to be slaves for just such a time as this."

Keshub gulped. But ... what would life in the Hebrew camp be like?

Chapter 43:
The Education of Keshub

Plod. Plod. Servant. Slave. Keshub's thoughts bounced with the rhythm of the march to Gilgal, down the familiar path. Slave to Joshua, leader of the Hebrews. Alone with the enemy. Guarantee of Gibeon's compliance. What would captivity mean? He could not know. Trust the Star Namer. He knows the heretofore and the hereafter.

Keshub had trusted Baba, and Baba found a way. His family was saved from sure destruction. But with every step farther from home, his heart beat louder in his chest. What would happen to him, Fifth Son of Ishtaba the potter? When would he see home again?

Ahead, the Hebrew camp ranged over a wide expanse of the flatland at Gilgal beside the Jordan River. In the long twilight, Hebrew soldiers drew up at the foot of the small hill where Baba first met Joshua.

Joshua glanced Keshub's way and nodded for him to stay. Joshua

SHEPHERD, POTTER, SPY—AND THE STAR NAMER

mounted the hill and turned. With a loud voice he addressed his
soldiers. "Men of Israel, when God's servant Moses died, God said
to me 'I will never leave you nor forsake you.'"
"The Lord our God was with us today. He is with us now. Go to
your homes, and as you lie down and as you get up encourage your
families with the words of the Lord our God...Dismissed."
Keshub stood alone, an alien.
The horde of soldiers parted as they neared him to give a wide
berth. Some trudged by with barely a glance. One snarled from the
side of his mouth. "A three-day march and we brought home one
measly kid and no loot."
Joshua saluted the last of his men and came to Keshub's side.
"What is your name, lad?"
"Keshub, sir."
"All right, Keshub. Come with me."
Keshub followed behind as before, but Joshua side-stepped to
bring him nearer to side-by-side. Before they arrived at the orderly
arrangement of tents, they passed a small separate camp. The people there prepared their evening meal.
A small boy came out of the make-shift tent and looked toward
Keshub. His eyes lit up, and he waved.
Keshub smiled to see someone familiar—the child from Jericho
who ate his dried fig and begged for more. Jho-ee tugged at the
skirt tail of the young woman who tended the fire.
A question jolted through him. How did the boy and his aunt
survive the destruction of Jericho? Keshub waved but kept his
hand low at his side, attempting not to be seen by Joshua.
The woman turned, and eyed the new captive with silent ques-
tions.
After they passed, Joshua asked. "Do you know that family?"
"Yes, sir. I met them in Jericho when we took our pottery to
market. I gave the child a dried fig. I found out later his mother
had died about that time."
"I see. So your father is a potter?"
"Yes, sir. We are the Ra-eef' ... potters of Gibeon." Keshub

349

changed his tone reminding himself he was a slave now. Perhaps a slave should not be too proud.

Joshua stopped in front of a tent. "This is where you will be staying, Keshub. Stow your bedroll here outside the tent near the door and hang your water bag on a peg on the awning pole, here."

"Yes, sir." Keshub plunked his bedroll and knapsack in place and hung his water bag. He eyed a very small fire circle that seemed mostly unused.

Joshua pointed to a small stand with a basin, water jar, and cook pot beside it. "Wash up quickly. I want to introduce you to the rest of my family."

With only one bedroll inside the tent, where would Joshua's *family* be? Not here. "Yes, sir."

As Keshub poured water into the basin, the pottery vessel seemed familiar. In a flash he saw the same basin in his mother's hands being lovingly presented at the dinner meal on important occasions.

Anger clawed at his chest and made his neck and face hot with the injustice. His mother had to give up her favorite dish for the treaty with the Hebrews. He splashed his face with cool water. Without the treaty, his family would have been destroyed and the dish would have been loot to the conquerors.

When would he see his family again? Every time he washed his face at this bowl, he would see his father's hands and his mother's heart. Did the One who knew the heretofore and the hereafter know he would need this comfort in this strange place?

Keshub stayed in step with Joshua through the Hebrew camp.

Joshua pointed out the layout of the camp. "We have twelve tribes from the twelve sons of Jacob who went down to Egypt over four hundred years ago. The sacred tabernacle is always in the center of our camp. Even though a tent or a building can never contain the one true God who is creator of all, the tabernacle is the representation of His presence with us.

"The camp of the tribe of Judah is always on the east toward the rising sun. We are going to the camp of Ephraim, always on the west.

"My sister-in-law lives there. She is a godly woman who is also a very good cook, as you will see. She has two sons and a servant girl who has a small niece."

Nightfall neared by the time they arrived. Keshub recognized the two young men who came out to meet Joshua. The same boys who brought the wonderful bread to the Gibeonite delegation.

When they saw Keshub, Joshua's nephews stopped and gaped.

"Elkanah, Hosiah, this is Keshub, who is son of a potter, who is leader of the Gibeonites."

"Hello." The brothers responded in near unison.

A woman, with kind eyes and mouth, about Keshub's mother's age, brushed aside a curtain and emerged from the tent. "Joshua. You are back. Did all go well?" She dried her hands on her apron.

"Yes. I believe it did, but now I have another mouth to feed."

"Oh?" One hand went to her hip. "That should be no bother. We like to feed people here."

"Meet my personal servant, Keshub from Gibeon." With an open hand Joshua bade Keshub step forward.

"Welcome, young man. I am Mrs. Elah." Joshua's sister-in-law smiled warmly while looking Keshub over from head to foot. "Please sit down. Co-zi' and I will have something for you very soon. We were waiting for you."

Quickly, the two women rolled a dining mat out on the rug at the entrance to their tent.

Joshua settled and pointed Keshub to sit at his left.

Though smaller, the meal set-up felt much like Keshub's mother's in the Ra-eef' courtyard.

"Gentlemen, we must teach Keshub about God. Before our dinner, let us recite the Shema: *"Hear, O Israel. The Lord our God, the Lord is one. Love the Lord your God with all your heart and with all your soul..."*

A raised hand signaled for Joshua's nephews to stop their recitation.

Zu-zu, sitting nearby at the entrance to the tent, played with her rag doll and continued softly, " ... *and with all your strength.*"

Joshua smiled, as broad as his sun-bronzed face. "Very good, Zu-zu!"

After dinner, Joshua asked his nephews to alternate reciting the Ten Commandments given to Moses at Mt. Sinai.

When they finished, Hosiah leaned in, eyes bright. "Uncle Joshua?"

"Yes?"

"Could you tell us about crossing the Red Sea? I am sure Keshub would like to hear."

Joshua began mildly. But his face lit up as he related the vivid details of the story Keshub had heard already. Nabi, the old one, had told the tale almost one year ago.

Joshua's nephew Hosiah, the one closest to Keshub's age, eyed him closely. "Do you find it hard to believe Uncle's story?"

Keshub swiped at his forelock and lifted his head. "I doubted my own brother's tale of how the Jordan River stopped flowing and how Jericho fell—until I saw the ruins of Jericho for myself. Seeing Master Joshua's face when he tells the story, how could I doubt?"

Hosiah's mother spoke from the doorway to their tent. "Boys, it has been a very long day for your uncle. We must let him go to his rest. And you have work to do tomorrow. Keshub, welcome to our home. I am sure we will be seeing you often."

She placed a small pack in Keshub's hands. "I am glad you will be with Joshua. He gets up very early in the morning, but he says he is too busy to heat water and make tea. One of the boys will bring a meal at mid-morning. This is just a bite to settle a growling stomach ... You do know how to make a fire, do you not?"

"Oh, yes, ma'am." Keshub flashed back to the signal fires he had set only days ago. How would he make a fire so small as Joshua's fire circle? He bowed. "Thank you, ma'am. The dinner was delicious."

Joshua stood and stretched. "Magdalyn, I have been sitting here looking at your ox cart and thinking perhaps the boys could use the cart and your oxen tomorrow to increase the amount of wood the Gibeonites can deliver."

Joshua turned to his nephews. "If the boys take the cart to the spring and meet the wood delivery as it comes down the trail, the woodcutters can go back for another load more quickly. For the use of your cart, you will get a portion of the wood. The rest of it will go to the Tabernacle."

"Joshua, that is wonderful. The boys have been going farther and farther to find wood. We will be glad to help."

Joshua waved and nodded. "Tomorrow."

Keshub fell into step beside Joshua who led by the light of the sliver of moon through the tent encampment. Most cook fires were already extinguished. Deep snores rasped the warm night air.

Joshua rubbed his chin. "Keshub, I noticed you were listening closely tonight. Do you have any questions?"

"Yes, sir. You said 'the Lord is one.'"

"That is right. There is only one true God and creator of all we see. Do you believe that?"

"My baba calls him the Star Namer and points to a star near the southern horizon called *the Heretofore and the Hereafter*. Could the One Lord and the Star Namer be the same, sir?"

"Keshub, the Lord our God created the stars and knows them by name. I suppose you could call him the Star Namer. Any other questions?"

"Yes, sir. What does 'covet' mean?"

"To want something very badly without any concern for the person who owns it. Coveting is expressed with ill will or envy when others own something you would like to have. Do you understand?"

"Yes, sir, I think so. So God not only said, 'You shall not steal,' but then He said you should not want what your neighbor has or be jealous of what your neighbor has. Stealing is something I have seen in Gibeon. The second, I think, cannot always be seen. Sir, does God see what is in my heart?"

"Yes, Keshub. He does. You ask very good questions."

Early the next morning Keshub heard a rooster crowing nearby.

Disoriented, he checked off the possibilities. Not on the roof and not on the perch. Ah, in the Hebrew camp. Joshua's servant. Suddenly, he knew he had work to do.

Careful not to make a sound, he rolled out of his blanket and made up his bedroll. Beside the tent he found a meager stack of wood, kindling, and a pouch of tender. He assembled the pieces and clicked out a few sparks. As soon as a sturdy flame appeared, he nestled the cook pot with water into the edge of the fire.

Keshub inspected the pottery closely. Its color was different from Ra-eef' pottery, and the clay had visible black and gray grains as well as small holes in the rim. Keshub mumbled to himself. "Basalt grit, wadi gravel, and grass or whatever, too? Somebody did not work the clay long enough. This vessel will not last long."

Joshua emerged from the tent soundlessly. "Did you say something, Keshub?"

Keshub jumped. "I am sorry, sir. I hope I did not wake you."

"No, no. The rooster does that every morning. Sometimes I wish he would forget to crow, but I need to get up before people start arriving with their problems, so I am glad he crows."

Joshua warmed his hands over the small fire. "What were you saying to yourself so early in the morning?"

"Sir, I was looking at this cook pot and thinking my father would say, 'Work the clay again, boys. This clay is not good enough for Ra-eef' pottery.'"

"Uh-huh. So Ra-eef' pottery is good pottery?"

"The best around here, sir."

"This one was found in Gilgal. Perhaps we need to see some Ra-eef' pottery. What do you say to that?"

"You would be pleased, sir. My father made your wash basin."

"Ah, he did, did he? It is a fine piece of pottery. Perhaps we can see some more soon?"

"I do not know, sir. We have not gathered new clay nor had a firing day in months because we were preparing for an attack from the..."

For a moment, Keshub had forgotten that Joshua represented

all the fear and frenzy of the past few months. Keshub dropped his chin. "Sir, when the water is hot, would you like herbs or dried mutton? Mrs. Elah sent some flatbread, too."

"The herbs, please. Bring it to me at that little hill over there where I like to watch the sun come up while I talk to God. Before I go, I will teach you a daily recitation. *"O Israel, what does the Lord your God ask of You but to fear the Lord your God, to walk in his ways, to love Him, to serve the Lord your God with all your heart and with all your soul, and to observe the Lord's commands and decrees that I am giving you today for your own good?"*

"Keshub, I want you to know that God Himself gave us these words, not as a punishment or a burden, but because He wants the best for us. His word is for our good. Understand?"

"There is a lot I do not understand, sir."

"Me, too, Keshub. Me, too." Joshua nodded toward the hill near the river. "I will be there."

Alone, Keshub scanned Joshua's possessions. What should he do as a servant? For his mamaa he would get wood and water. He would do that later, after delivering the tea.

At a tent nearby a Hebrew woman shook out the rugs at the entrance to her tent.

Keshub rolled up a henna red woolen rug and carried it away from the cook fire, flipped it open and shook it. He replaced it, tugging on one side to make it square with the tent entrance. Inside Joshua's tent he found a stack of kitchen ware draped with a linen napkin, a couple of pottery bowls, a wooden stirring spoon, and a gourd ladle.

He checked the cook pot and dipped steaming water for two bowls, adding some of the herbs Hosiah's mother gave him. Folding a half round of flatbread inside the linen napkin, he carried it, along with the tea, to Joshua on the hill.

Keshub approached quietly, trying not to disturb. "Would you like your tea, sir?"

"Tea? Oh, Keshub. Thank you. What a treat! You will spoil me." Joshua drank from the bowl and looked up. "When one of my nephews comes by with our morning meal, I want you to return with him. You will go with the ox cart when they take it to the spring to meet the wood delivery."

"Yes, sir." Keshub compressed his lips to hide his smile. The prospect of his day got suddenly brighter. Would he see Eskie and get news from home?

Chapter 44:

The God Most High

At mid-day, Keshub drank from the cool, gushing water at the spring surrounded by palms near the ruins of Jericho. He spotted Eskie in the distance and his heart leapt to his throat. His brother descended the Wadi Qelt trail with five donkeys loaded with wood.

As his brother neared, he swallowed and blinked rapidly, preparing to speak.

Instead, his big brother's arms surrounded him. "How goes it for you, little brother?" Eskie gulped, too.

"I am well, brother. Joshua and his family are kind people. I am not afraid, and already I have learned much." Stepping back, "Let me introduce you to his nephews."

Keshub worked beside his brother as Eskie removed a length of rough wood from a donkey's pack frame and transferred to Keshub's arms. He shifted the hewn branch to his left and placed it in Hosiah's arms, then turned back for another from Eskie.

Hosiah shifted to his brother Elkanah who loaded the wood

onto the ox cart.

While Keshub and Eskie relayed wood side by side, Eskie relayed the news of Gibeon in short bursts. "All the Aijalon spies are now woodcutters .... We have a camp in the oak forest near the second signal fire .... Ra-math, the refugee from Moab and Ja-bal's relative,..arrived last night. He will be our cook .... Uncle Yaakoub will bring us supplies."

"Joshua said he would like to see some Ra-eef' pottery when Baba has some available."

"Baba will be pleased, little brother .... He is back at his wheel .... Uncle Samir and Lehab dug clay at the wadi."

That evening at dinner at Mrs. Elah's tent, Joshua clapped a hand on Keshub's shoulder. "Magdalyn, what did you think about your load of wood this afternoon?"

Mrs. Elah smiled and held her hands together at her chin. "I have thanked God all afternoon for my abundant supply. We now have enough wood to bake extra bread tomorrow for the Sabbath."

"Yes, the Sabbath. Keshub, on the morrow you must tell the woodcutters, 'Do not deliver wood tomorrow. It is the Hebrew Sabbath Day. We are commanded to do no work on that day in obedience to the Fourth Commandment.'"

"Sabbath day, sir?"

"Uncle Joshua, you must tell Keshub how God created the Heavens and the earth tonight."

Hosiah rested his hands on his knees and shook his head at Keshub, smiling broadly. "If you have never heard the account, you must. This is where everything began."

The next day Keshub worked elbow to elbow with his brother. "Eskie, Joshua said you must not bring wood tomorrow. It is the Sabbath."

Eskie broke rhythm, holding a heavy split trunk of wood. "Sabbath?"

Keshub took the splintery wood, quoting Joshua. "God commanded us to rest just as He rested in the beginning on the seventh day after creating the heavens and the earth. Joshua said, 'Instead,

go home to your families and rest. Resume deliveries the next day.'"
Keshub deposited the wood in Hosiah's arms and turned back.
Eskie gaped with hands on his hips. "Go home and rest? How
will Baba react to that? He is always saying, 'We have work to do.'"
Keshub shrugged. "Joshua explained it to me that when we rest
on the Sabbath, we show our faith in God who provides everything
we need. We depend on Him, not ourselves. Mrs. Elah makes extra
food on the day before a Sabbath so everyone can rest."
"Huh. Baba and Mamaa sitting around all day with no work in
their hands?"

CRSO

Eskie neared home and picked up the pace just like the donkeys
would do if they were with him. "Men, we should meet at ein-el-
Beled tomorrow when the sun is half past mid-day to sundown.
Agreed?"
"Yes, we will be here." Kephira and Kiriath Jearim nodded and
took the fork of the trail that would lead them home.
Baba hurried to meet him, his brow drawn with lines of worry.
"Eskie, what is wrong? Why have you come home?"
"Baba, everyone is well. There is nothing wrong. Keshub is
treated well, and he said to tell you he is learning much about the
Hebrew God."
"But why have you come home?" Ishtaba dipped his chin.
Eschol shrugged. "Because Joshua said 'Do not bring wood
tomorrow.' It is the Sabbath, a day of rest for them."
"A day of rest?" Baba tilted his head as if he did not hear right.
"Kesh said God rested on the seventh day after he created every-
thing. And he commanded the Hebrews to rest. He said when they
obey and rest, they depend on God to provide what they need."
Eskie blared his eyes and turned his hands palm up.
Baba eyed him, shaking his head.
Eskie nodded. "Joshua said for us to go home to our families.
We left Beeroth and Ramath there with the donkeys. The donkeys

need the rest. We resume wood deliveries the next day."

"Rest?"

"Are you all right, Baba?" Eskie had never seen his baba look so uncertain, so subdued.

"Yes. I am well. I need to think a while on this, but your granmamaa is very ill."

The next afternoon at the courtyard gate, Eskie prepared to return to the woodcutters' camp. He shouldered a water bag on either side with his knapsack already at his back.

Mamaa tied one of the ducks he shot with his arrow that morning to his knapsack. "Thank you, son, for the other duck. I hope Mother Amara will be able to take more nourishment when I make soup from it."

"Where is Baba?"

Mamaa smiled and shook her head. "He sat by his mother's side all morning. At mid-day, he rested under the old olive tree at the top of the stairs. He is waiting for you at the spring now. Tell Keshub, thank you."

Eskie nodded and slipped out the gate, his burdens preventing him from descending the steps by twos.

Baba stood at the spring, his brow smooth, looking—rested. "Eschol. Tell Keshub I think I understand about the Sabbath. Ask him, what is the name of the Hebrew God?"

CRSO

Keshub settled into his bedroll, leaving his feet exposed. Nights were warmer in the Jordan Valley than in the highlands of Canaan.

He gazed at Baba's star over the Salt Sea and decided Sabbaths would be his favorite days. Not because there was no work, but because Joshua spent long hours reading aloud the words God gave to Moses. After a cold mid-afternoon dinner, Hosiah had asked for one story after another from the history of their people.

The next morning, Keshub looked up as he shook out the rugs. Joshua prayed on his hill nearby with head raised as if he saw the God to whom he spoke.

Yesterday, Joshua told a story about Eleazar, servant to the Hebrews' father Abraham. The servant had asked God to help him serve his master.

Looking toward Joshua again, this time Joshua bowed low. Abraham's servant prayed in his heart, and standing.

Was this potter's son too small in God's sight or would he be too bold if he prayed to the God of creation?

At mid-day, Eskie led the Ra-eef' donkeys to the spring.

Between his brother and Hosiah, Keshub passed wood to the ox cart. "How are Baba and Mamaa?"

"Good. Better after a day of rest, I think."

"How did Baba take the news of the Sabbath?"

Eskie chuckled. "Stunned at first. But after time spent with Gran-mamaa and sitting under the olive tree at the top of the stairs yesterday, he said to tell you he thinks he understands."

Thank you, God, that Baba rested.

"He said to ask you what name Joshua calls God?"

Keshub grabbed the wood Eskie swung his way. "Yesterday, Joshua read a song Moses gave the Hebrews a short while before he died. Moses called him Most High. Joshua says He created the stars and calls them by name."

Eskie hesitated a moment and slung a sidewise glance at Keshub. "Whoa. I will tell Baba—next Sabbath."

Thank you, God, that you revealed yourself to the Hebrews. Thank you I am a slave, learning about You.

After several days of easy routine, Keshub and his Hebrew friends waited again at the spring surrounded by palms.

While the brothers worked together unloading and loading wood, Eskie spoke in a low tone. "Kesh, I had a visit from Jebus of Jerusalem last night."

"Oh? What did he say?" Keshub remembered his encounter with the man who appeared out of darkness at his elbow.

"He said Zedek is getting ready for an attack."

Suddenly alarmed, Keshub blurted. "Attack?"

"Jebus said Zedek has been sitting by a fire and chewing his nails since the Hebrews crossed the Jordan—even more so after he got the reports of the destruction of Jericho and Ai. But he was furious when he heard we made a treaty with them and now have a wood camp serving the Hebrews. He had been keeping in close contact with his allies looking for a strategy for a fight. So, Zedek is now gathering his allies and planning an attack soon...on Gibeon!"

"On Gibeon?"

"Yes, everyone in Aijalon Valley is going back to the summit today. If you see signal fire two, you will know Aijalon is under attack. Keshub, you must speak to Joshua and ask him to honor our treaty. He must come to rescue us from the Amorite kings or Gibeon will be overrun. Also, tell him this is the last delivery of wood unless he helps us. The woodcutters are needed at home."

"I will, brother. And I will pray for God's help in this." Keshub raised his head and squared his shoulders.

Eskie glanced sidewise at Keshub.

Keshub nodded. "We are in God's hands, and we have seen what He can do."

"Well, if prayer works, pray for Gran-mamaa, too. She is getting weaker .... She asked Baba to get a place ready for her beside Gran-baba Ra-eef' on the west slope."

Creator God Most High, help us! Watch over my family in Gibeon.

Chapter 45:

The Curse

Early in the morning Keshub dipped his water pot into a small spring." *Creator God, watch over Gibeon. Help Baba.* He lifted the water pot and glanced toward Joshua's prayer hill.

Two Hebrew men escorted a young man at spear point to Joshua.

Lord, help us! That is Eskie. Keshub left his water jar at the spring and sprinted to join his brother.

At the base of the hill, Keshub slowed and advanced with hands folded, fitting for a slave approaching his master.

Eskie blurted. "Keshub, tell them who I am."

Keshub bowed. "Sir, this is my brother who is Third Son of Ishtaba of the Ra-eef' potters of Gibeon, the ones who asked for a treaty with your people." Keshub ended with eyes cast down. *God, help our people.*

"All right, men. Release him," Joshua commanded. He lowered his chin and eyed Eskie. "You have a message from your father in

Gibeon?"

"Yes, sir." Eskie bowed. "Yesterday we saw from the hilltops that surround Aijalon Valley five armies are advancing toward us from the south and west. We already had a warning that the king of Jerusalem was calling in help to attack Gibeon. It is because we made peace by making a treaty with you."

"Yes." Joshua nodded. "Keshub told me of the warning."

"It is no longer a warning, sir. It is a fact that if you abandon your servants, we will all die. I implore you. Come up to us quickly and save us! Help us because all the Amorite kings from the hill country have joined forces against us. They will be upon us by this day's end."

Joshua clamped his hand on Eskie's shoulder and looked squarely into Eskie's eyes. "Son, I have just now received word from the Lord our God before you arrived. *'Do not be afraid of them. I have given them into your hand. Not one of them will be able to withstand you.'*"

Joshua raised his head. "You will stay with us and rest at my tent for a few hours. Keshub?"

"Yes, sir?"

"Go now to assure your father we will arrive by dawn tomorrow. Take with you the food Mrs. Elah gave us last night. You will need your strength. Your brother will come with us tonight."

"Yes, sir. I will." Immediately, Keshub turned and ran toward Joshua's tent. *Thank you, God Most High! You already knew we needed you!*

He collected his pack, his almost empty water bag and the flatbread Mrs. Elah sent. *Thank you, God, for Mrs. Elah! It is You who have provided the rolled bread filled with honey and chopped dates, just as I needed it!*

He tucked the package into his familiar load and jogged toward Jericho's spring.

Keshub filled his water bag half full while he devoured the first rolled flatbread. He licked the honey from his fingers and washed his hands before waving to old Deyab the Bedouin, in the distance.

Shouldering his pack and bag again, Keshub rounded the life-less mound that was Jericho and headed to the trail beside the Wadi Qelt.

Late morning he forced himself to save his strength for the last leg of this journey that took most of a whole day when walking. *Help me to be wise, Lord. Give me strength to do this.*

At midday Keshub wiped his brow. Perspiration saturated his garment keeping him air-cooled on this hot afternoon at the beginning of the dry season. His steps slowed as he followed the trail above the Wadi-el-Gayeh. Keshub breathed deeply and looked up the trail. *Oh no, Lord! The enemy is in Aijalon Valley! Help us!*

Signal fire two burned on top of the ridge ahead. He whistled the bulbul's cry as he drew near but kept jogging.

When he whistled again, Du'bo peered over the ridge and waved. Du'bo called down. "The Amorites are camped on the ridges, and Kiriath Jearim has been attacked. What word do you bring?"

Without stopping, Keshub replied. "Joshua's men will arrive by dawn!" *Delay the Amorites until Joshua arrives, God! Please!*

Late afternoon Keshub flung his load to the ground at the small spring and sprinted to the Ra-eef' courtyard, knowing his father would not be far away.

He opened the gate to the courtyard and gasped.

Several pallets with injured Gibeonites lay about. Mother Danya, and Aunts Raga and Sabah' tended to the injured.

Keshub gulped. Uncle Yaakoub lay amongst them, groaning. *Lord, help us!*

"Keshub!" His mother called from across the courtyard, "Your father is up..."

Baba himself called from the stairs above the courtyard, "Keshub, is that you? Come up, son!"

Keshub forced his burning legs up the steps that seemed steeper than usual.

Clasping Keshub's arm, Baba assisted his son up the last step to join Sir Ghaleb, neighbor Agh-taan, and himself under the old olive tree at the summit.

"What did Joshua say, son?"

"The Hebrews will be here at dawn. Do not fear, Baba. The Lord God said to Joshua this morning, 'Do not be afraid of them. I have given the Amorites into your hand.'

"Baba, we can trust Joshua, and we can trust His God. He is the Star Namer."

"Yes, son. I believe that, too."

That night Keshub stretched out on his family's roof after being absent for so many days.

Keshub's old familiar place now seemed strange. *Lord, what a lot has changed in the last year and in the last few days!*

Clouds scudded by in front of the full moon. *Thank you, Lord, for your timing! Help Joshua get here in time.*

Micah arrived, flipped open his bedroll, plopped down on his side, and propped his head on his hand. "It is too crowded on the summit. I would rather be with you. When you went away as a slave, I thought I might never see you again. How has it been for you?"

Grateful to have company, Keshub sat up. "Hah! Being a slave has not been so different than being a boy in the Ra-eef' courtyard, fetching water, fetching wood, or whatever else."

"Tell me, Micah, what happened to your baba. Uncle Yaakoub said he would probably never go to market again." *Help Uncle Yaakoub heal, Lord.*

Micah grimaced. "His knee was busted by the kick of a donkey when he turned all our livestock loose to fend for themselves. Yah-ya and I had to leave him behind to get the womenfolk and the supplies to the summit before the Amorites arrived."

"When we came back for Baba, Amorites had arrived at the top of the hill behind our homestead. Raja was there, and we had no other option to get him out of there in a hurry. So we draped Baba onto her back."

"I grabbed a hand, and Yah-ya grabbed the good leg to keep Baba from bouncing off Raja's back. We ran across the wheat field.

I do not know who yelled louder, the Amorites pursuing us, or Baba with his knee paining him fiercely."

Keshub chuckled. "Sorry. I know it is not funny, but I can already hear Uncle Yaakoub retelling the story many times about how roughly he was mistreated. In the future when he is healed, we will laugh at his helpless, bouncing predicament."

Micah sat up and crossed his legs, hanging his head. "You seem sure we will survive. How can we? We were almost killed today."

Keshub raked his hair out of his eyes. "Micah, I am glad I am a slave to Joshua."

Micah blurted. "How can that be?"

"Aside from missing my family in Aijalon Valley, being a slave to Joshua, leader of the Hebrews, has opened my eyes."

Micah raised his head and pointed. "Well, open your eyes now and see those campfires on the ridge across the valley. The Amorites will surely attack at dawn. There are some murmurs on the summit that we should surrender before they attack. Not everyone is as sure the Hebrews will keep their treaty as Uncle Ishtaba."

"Cousin, I am glad I am a slave to Joshua because the Creator God Most High is revealing himself to us through the Hebrews. He fights for the Hebrews. He spoke to Joshua this morning, in fact. The God Most High will defeat the Amorites in Aijalon Valley tomorrow. The Hebrews will arrive in time. Have faith, cousin."

Keshub reached out a hand to his cousin's knee. "Micah, I know our situation seems hopeless, but I am trusting in the God Most High to save us from the Amorites."

"Keshub!" A hoarse whisper came from Ranine on the steps to the roof.

Keshub rolled over, ready to spring up. "What?"

"Baba says come. Gran-mamaa wants to speak to you."

"Gran-mamaa? Me?"

"Yes, she is very ill, but very determined, too. Come quickly." Before Ranine's head disappeared from the parapet, Keshub was on his feet. In an instant he darted down the stairs but slowed to pick his way through the pallets of the injured.

He rounded the half wall to the kitchen and entered the house where he was born. Hewn out of solid limestone, on the slope of Gibeon's hill, the walls felt cool to his touch.

One of Ranine's lamps lit the entrance to Gran-mamaa Amara's small chamber. Baba and Ranine already knelt beside her when Keshub arrived.

Baba moved to make space for Keshub, too.

"Ke-shub. Come clos-er." Gran-mamaa waved a blue-veined hand and rasped weakly.

Keshub crawled closer and took her cold fragile hand in his own. *Lord, she is so weak. Help her.* "Hello, Gran-mamaa. You wanted to see me?"

"Yes, Kesh-ub. I want ... you to hear ... " Deep racking coughs interrupted her words.

She began again. "What ... I must say ... before I ... go to my ... husband's side."

"No, no, Gran-mamaa."

"Shush." More coughing followed before she resumed her ragged breathing.

"Your ... gran-baba ... held ... a secret ... for many years. A secret ... given him ... by his gran-baba ... and ... many gran-babas ... before that. There was ... a flood ... and a curse.

The whole story ... is unclear, but the warning ... of a curse ... on our family ... has been ... passed down."

Keshub glanced at his father to see his reaction. Calm and steady as always, but Ranine's forehead furrowed with worry.

"The curse ... was ... our people ... the Hivites ... would become ... slaves. And now ... Kesh-ub ... the curse ... has come true. All my life ... I thought ... the curse ... would be ... our doom. I now ... see it ... as our hope ... and our salvation. Because ... of the curse ... your baba ... found a way ... for our family ... and our neighbors ... to survive."

Baba spoke for the first time. "Hush, now, Mamaa. Save your strength. I will finish for you."

He took his mother's thin, frail hand into his own. "Now that we are slaves to the Hebrews, it is our privilege to come to know the Star Namer in a way that was not possible when we were free to do our own will."

"Your gran-mamaa and I want to pass the confidence we have about our situation on to you, so that we all may serve well. We are in the hands of the One who has been gracious to us all our lives—even when we only wondered about Him and had no way to know Him except the ancient stories in the stars."

After only a few hours sleep, the full moon had set. Alone on the rooftop again, Keshub waited for dawn in gray light. *Help our people, Lord.*

Micah had left to take a position on one of the natural limestone terraces on the west and south slopes with the other men of Gibeon.

Across the valley on the ridges, many campfires flickered their ominous threat of attack at dawn—by an overwhelming force.

Keshub shook his head in wonder. For months Gibeon had expected and prepared for an attack from the other direction, from the Hebrews. Now the Amorites threatened. A rumor circulated that the five kings had bolstered their courage to attack Gibeon with unspeakable sacrifices to their terrible god Molech. *Lord God, you are the One Lord Most High.*

Keshub, alone on the roof, watched with pack and bedroll at the ready to join Joshua when he arrived. *Help Joshua get here in time, Lord.*

Chapter 46:
When the Sun Stood Still

From his place above the Ra-eef' courtyard where he watched for the Hebrews' arrival from the east, Keshub hunched in gloomy darkness.

A year ago he wondered what he would become. He never thought about, nor would he have chosen, becoming a slave. If it was a curse, he was grateful he was learning so much from Joshua. *Thank you, God.*

Keshub held his breath. Campfires on the ridges surrounding Gibeon, winked out. The Amorites surely were gearing up for attack.

In the semi-darkness a rooster crowed, and a dog barked. Even the sheep in their sheepfold nearby bleated restlessly. Keshub imagined movement behind every bush, tree, and rock that only the sun would confirm or deny. *Help us, Lord!*

Finally, the sun's first glow started in the east. Lines of Amorites, with a torch here and there, advanced from the rims of the hills, dark smudges smeared down hillsides. At dawn they would be in place to launch a full attack.

Keshub tilted his head upward. *Help us, Lord. They are upon us!*

Keshub leaned forward at the parapet, straining to see. At the moment the sun peeped over the hills to scare away the shadows, Keshub saw movement. More than that, he heard the Hebrew multitude shout as they stormed across neighbor Agh-taan's wheat field, "Strong and courageous!"

Thank you, God! They are here!

Even more startling, behind every bush, tree, and rock in Aijalon Valley was one of the Hebrews' best fighting men, the ones with the lion-like beards.

The Amorites, ready to attack, were not ready *to be* attacked. Every nearby shadow produced more Hebrews than they could count. In panic, the Amorites turned, throwing down gear that slowed them, and ran for the hills.

Soon Joshua came into sight following his men with Eskie at his side and accompanied by an eight-man guard.

Keshub scampered down the steps and into the courtyard where he grabbed the water bags and victuals packs prepared by his mother hours ago. Out the gate and onto the well-worn trail in front of their house, Keshub approached Joshua and extended a water bag high.

Joshua, then Eskie drank from the stream.

"Thank you, Keshub." Joshua wiped his mouth but did not take his eyes off his men chasing Amorites over a pass in the distance. "What is that road, Keshub?"

"It is the caravan trail that goes through the pass to Beth Horon, sir. Will you come into our home, sir?"

"No, Keshub. I must stay with my men. I will go up to the Beth-Horon pass now. You and your brother may return to your family."

Eskie turned to go.

Keshub shouldered the water bag and knapsack. "Sir, I would go with you to carry your water and make your campfire when you need one."

For a moment, Joshua took his eyes off his pursuing army and looked at Keshub. "All right, lad. Let's move out."

At mid-morning the searing sun had burned away morning clouds. Keshub plodded behind Joshua as they neared the pass of Beth-Horon where even the limestone had been worn away to reveal the path taken by thousands of feet of men, camels, and armies over hundreds of years.

To his right Keshub spied a fallen Amorite soldier near the trail. The soldier's face had frozen in his last gasp of fright, anger, and agony. The tip of a bronze blade protruded from beneath him, flat on the ground.

"Sir?" Keshub got Joshua's attention.

When Joshua turned, Keshub pointed at the fallen Amorite and asked. "May I, sir?"

"Yes, but quickly."

In a moment Keshub lifted the left shoulder of the dead man and tugged on the recently sharpened bronze blade. Keshub clamped his bottom lip with his teeth, hoping for a dagger. He pulled from beneath the dead man a short sword, taken from its scabbard but never used that morning.

Avoiding looking at the man's unseeing eyes, Keshub untied the leather scabbard from his waist and rejoined Joshua.

Joshua made no comment but turned with his guards back to the rocky trail up to the pass.

With no instruction of what to do with the spoils, Keshub kept in step while inserting the sword into its scabbard and tying the belt around himself.

Late morning, Keshub stopped beside Joshua at the pass of Beth-Horon. Behind them and below in the distance, Aijalon Valley lay strewn with bodies of Amorites. Looking ahead and down to the Great Sea, Joshua's men pursued fleeing Amorites. Hand-to-hand combat raged all around.

Joshua looked back again at Aijalon and then toward the Great Sea. He shaded his eyes from the sun overhead and muttered. "There is not enough time to complete the rout God promised.

Wait here."

Keshub scratched the back of his head. Not enough time? The leader of the Hebrews climbed a nearby outcropping of limestone and lifted his arms skyward in supplication to God.

"O sun, stand still over Gibeon,
O moon, over the Valley of Aijalon."

What did Joshua mean by that? Keshub rested his left hand on the hilt of the unfamiliar sword.

Joshua climbed down, his bearded jaw set firm, his eyes locked on the battle ahead of them.

Descending from the pass, Keshub stayed close to Joshua. More and more bodies of Amorites lay beside the trail.

Finally, his stomach growled, and thirst grasped him by the throat. He addressed Joshua. "Sir, do you need to drink some water?"

Joshua halted. "Keshub, a good idea. Thank you. I see some of our own men approaching from below. We will wait for them here. This will be a good place to make camp for a bit and be refreshed since the sun is not going down today."

Startled by Joshua's words, Keshub shaded his eyes to look up. His jaw dropped. The sun had not moved since Joshua's proclamation at the height of the pass of Beth Horon.

Lord God, another unbelievable story to tell of the Hebrews. This time he saw the unbelievable happen with his own eyes.

Keshub unloaded his pack and started a small fire in a level place, a little way from a large boulder. "Please, sir, sit for a moment and rest. I will gather more wood."

Going farther, Keshub found a wrist-size stick he could break up into fuel for his fire. When he rounded the boulder, a wounded Amorite soldier with a sword in his left hand crept toward Joshua from behind. *Lord, help! Where are his guards?*

Keshub gripped the length of wood about the size of his shepherd's staff in his left hand. His right hand flew to the hilt of his unfamiliar weapon.

"Halt!" Keshub commanded in his most commanding young voice. He advanced with the oaken branch extended in a defensive position—still trying to unsheathe his sword.

Joshua and the Amorite turned at the same time.

The Amorite snarled with gritted, brown-stained teeth and fire in his eyes. In spite of a head wound caked with blood, the enemy gathered his strength to slash downward from Keshub's right.

Keshub met the blow with the oaken staff. Stinging vibrations transferred to his left hand through the wrist-size piece of wood. Keshub dropped the stick as it broke at the point of contact. He clasped the hilt of his newly-acquired, and now unsheathed, sword in both hands.

With all his strength and some he did not know he had, Keshub extended his arms to full-length. He wielded the sword high from left to right, arcing downward with all his might.

The sword came in contact with the soldier's extended left forearm in its follow-through. A wicked gash spurted blood.

The Amorite dropped his sword and grasped his arm as three of Joshua's guards reappeared and ran the man through from three different directions.

Joshua rushed to Keshub's side. "Are you hurt, Keshub?" Seeing that Keshub was unharmed, Joshua's smile lit up his face. "Keshub, you are a brave lad, indeed."

Keshub took great gulps of air, chest heaving. "Sir, God Most High told you 'Do not be afraid of them.' He gave this man into my hand."

Joshua smiled. "Yes, He did."

The Hebrew soldiers arrived from down the trail and reported to Joshua, "Five kings are hiding in a cave down there. What do you want us to do?"

Joshua stood with feet apart, fists jammed at his hips. "Roll large rocks up to the mouth of the cave, and post some men there to guard it. But do not stop! Pursue your enemies, attack them from the rear and do not let them reach their cities. The Lord your

God has given them into your hand!"

"Yes, sir." His men turned and clattered down the rocky hillside to carry out their orders.

Joshua gazed toward the Great Sea where a roiling dark cloud approached. "Keshub, take a message to your father. Tell him there is no more fear of the Amorites. My men will pursue them relentlessly. It may be several days before we return this way."

"Meanwhile, our women and children at Gilgal need wood deliveries to begin again as soon as possible and more often, if possible, since all the men are away. Then Keshub, I want you to take word back to Gilgal and wait for me there."

"Yes, sir. I will."

"And Keshub?"

"Yes, sir?"

"Thank you."

"You are welcome, sir."

Taking up his pack and water bag, Keshub turned and scrambled back up the trail. When he reached Beth Horon pass, he surveyed Canaan all around him. The time of day should have been near sunset.

In the distance below him, a dark, green-tinted cloud loomed, coming from the Great Sea. Lightning flashed, and thunder roared. Turning back to the east, all of Aijalon Valley below him shimmered in mid-day-bright sunshine. *Thank you, God! You gave the victory! Protect Master Joshua!*

Ra-gar's words flashed to mind. The thief of Gibeon declared he would believe the stories about the Hebrews 'when the sun stood still.'

Keshub leaped into the air thrusting his sword high above his head. "What do you think now, Ra-gar'?"

LETTER TO READERS

Dear Reader,

Are you wondering "Did this story really happen?"

The answer? Much of this story is historical record in the Bible, in museums of the world, in archeological records.

I challenge you to dig deeper and read the biblical account for yourself. Scripture passages pertinent to this story appear from Genesis 10 to Psalm 114, but particularly from Numbers 20 through Joshua 12.

Some of the story is from my imagination—of how it happened. Some of the first people I want to see in Heaven are the un-named Gibeonites of Joshua 9 and 10. I will ask them, "So, how did it really happen for you?"

I have prepared a companion Study Guide, available on Amazon. The ...Spy and the Star Namer Study Guide will help you dig deeper into the mysteries of the ancient worlds and into the amazing Bible, miraculously written and miraculously preserved through the ages to make it available to you. This life-changing book is a personal letter to you from a holy God who loves you.

Genuinely seek Truth, as Keshub and his baba did, and you will always find the God of all Truth and His Son Jesus Christ, who died for you that you may truly live.

And may the One who named the stars, who knows your here-tofore and your hereafter, guide you in all that you do.

To His Glory and in His Service,
Peggy Miracle Consolver
Shepherd, Potter, Spy—and the Star Namer

*For TEACHERS and STUDENTS: Please see
Author's website at peggyconsolver.com for your free,
downloadable twelve-unit Study Guide.*

DISCUSSION QUESTIONS FOR SMALL GROUPS:

1. As a child, what did you want to be when you grew up? What influences caused you to make the career choices you made?

2. The caravanner *Haydak*, his brother Eskie, and Sir Ghaleb were Keshub's first heroes. Who were your heroes?

3. In the story, Keshub had four brothers and two sisters. How has sibling rivalry impacted your life?

4. Keshub's family had a system of shared work for survival. How did your family work together?

5. Have you ever been the target of a bully? How did you react? Was the situation resolved? How?

6. How has sarcasm or name-calling impacted your life?

7. Keshub offered friendship to his bully nemesis when he began to understand Da-gan's neediness. When have you found a friend in a former adversary?

8. Have you ever been the recipient of an unexpected act of love or friendship?

9. What events in your own family history proved to be life-changing?

10. Even though this story portrays a male-dominated culture, in what ways do Keshub's mother and grand-mother hold influence over the family?